TIME IS ON
HER SIDE....

PRAISE FOR THE NOVELS
OF KATIE MacALISTER

Sparks Fly
A Novel of the Light Dragons

"Once again I was drawn into the wondrous world of this author's dragons and hated leaving once their story was told. I loved this visit and cannot wait for the next book to see just what new adventures lie in wait for these dragons."

—Love Romances & More

"Fast-paced . . . an entertaining read and a fine addition to MacAlister's dragon series." —Bookshelf Bombshells

"Balanced by a well-organized plot and MacAlister's trademark humor." —*Publishers Weekly*

It's All Greek to Me

"This author delivers again with yet another steamy, sexy read with humorous situations, dialogue, and characters. . . . The plot is fast-paced and fun, typical of MacAlister's novels. The characters are impossible not to like. The hiccups in their relationship only serve to make the reader root harder for them. The events range from amusing to steamy to serious. The reader can't be bored with MacAlister's novel."

—Fresh Fiction

"A fun and sexy read." —The Season for Romance

"A wonderful lighthearted romantic romp as a kick-butt American Amazon and a hunky Greek find love. Filled with humor, fans will laugh with the zaniness of Harry meets Yacky." —*Midwest Book Review*

continued . . .

"Katie MacAlister sizzles with this upbeat and funny summer romance. . . . MacAlister's dialogue is fast-paced and entertaining. . . . Her characters are interesting and her heroes are always attractive/intriguing . . . a good, fun, fast summer read."   —BooksWithBenefits

"Fabulous banter between the main characters. . . . Katie MacAlister's got a breezy, fun writing style that keeps me reading."   —Book Binge

A Tale of Two Vampires
A Dark Ones Novel

"A roller coaster of giggles, chortles, and even some guffaws. In other words, it is a lighthearted and fun read."
                                                        —The Reading Cafe

Much Ado About Vampires
A Dark Ones Novel

"A humorous take on the dark and demonic." —*USA Today*

"Once again this author has done a wonderful job. I was sucked into the world of Dark Ones right from the start and was taken on a fantastic ride. This book is full of witty dialogue and great romance, making it one that should not be missed."   —Fresh Fiction

"An extremely appealing hero. If you enjoy a fast-paced paranormal romance laced with witty prose and dialogue, you might like to give *Much Ado About Vampires* a try."

—azcentral.com

"I cannot get enough of the warmth of Ms. MacAlister's books. They're the paranormal romance equivalent of soul food." —Errant Dreams Reviews

The Unbearable Lightness of Dragons
A Novel of the Light Dragons

"Had me laughing out loud. . . . This book is full of humor and romance, keeping the reader entertained all the way through . . . a wondrous story full of magic. . . . I cannot wait to see what happens next in the lives of the dragons."

—Fresh Fiction

"Katie MacAlister has always been a favorite of mine and her latest series again shows me why. . . . If you are a lover of dragons, MacAlister's new series will definitely keep you entertained!" —The Romance Readers Connection

"Magic, mystery, and humor abound in this novel, making it a must read . . . another stellar book."—Night Owl Romance

"Entertaining." —*Midwest Book Review*

THE ART OF STEALING TIME

A TIME THIEF NOVEL

Katie MacAlister

A SIGNET BOOK

SIGNET
Published by the Penguin Group
Penguin Group (USA), 375 Hudson Street,
New York, New York 10014, USA

USA | Canada | UK | Ireland | Australia | New Zealand | India | South Africa | China

Penguin Books Ltd., Registered Offices: 80 Strand, London WC2R 0RL, England
For more information about the Penguin Group visit penguin.com.

First published by Signet, an imprint of New American Library,
a division of Penguin Group (USA)

First Printing, September 2013

REGISTERED TRADEMARK—MARCA REGISTRADA

ISBN 978-0-451-41743-5

Printed in the United States of America
10 9 8 7 6 5 4 3 2 1

PUBLISHER'S NOTE
This is a work of fiction. Names, characters, places, and incidents either are the product
of the author's imagination or are used fictitiously, and any resemblance to actual persons, living or dead, business establishments, events, or locales is entirely coincidental.

The publisher does not have any control over and does not assume any responsibility
for author or third-party Web sites or their content.

ALWAYS LEARNING   PEARSON

Writers take inspiration from all sorts of things, and in this case, my heroine's two mothers have their origins with Shannon Perry, who works tirelessly to keep me organized, tidy, and happy. This book is dedicated to Shannon and her two moms, with hopes their lives are as happy as their literary inspirations.

Gentle Reader:

At the front of this book you will find a bonus short story, "Time Crossed," that explains how and why the hero, Gregory, and heroine, Gwen, met. The folks at New American Library were originally going to publish it online and call it good, but after much thought, decided that you, the dedicated print reader, deserved to read it as well. It's our hope that you will enjoy this bonus, which is exclusive to the print version of the book.

And while the short story will get you up to speed with the action at the beginning of the story, likewise we've provided a little aid at the end of the book: a handy glossary of words and phrases that might give some folks a bit of confusion. So if you're wondering why someone whose name is Arawn is being referred to as Aaron, you can visit the glossary for more details.

I hope you enjoy this second book in the Time Thief series. I had a blast playing around with traditional Welsh mythology, and look forward to hearing what you all think of Gregory, Gwen, and all the other folks in Anwyn.

Best regards,
Katie MacAlister

1 August 12.14 pm

Malwod-Upon-Ooze, Wales (Whale's Elbow Pub)

Subject: Gwenhwyfar Byron Owens

Seawright Pendleton, junior scribe (third class)

Begin Transcription

Subject Owens, heretofore referred to as "Gwen" per the rules governing those shadowing paroled offenders (not to mention the subject herself, who got a bit snippy when she was referred to in public as Offending Parolee Owens, to the point where she made pointed comments about S. Pendleton, the junior scribe tasked with doing the aforementioned shadowing, specifically with reference to improbable, if not downright impossible physical acts involving junior scribe Pendleton and a large anchor seen at a nearby dock), was located at the establishment listed above at the date and time also listed above.

Gwen appeared to be chatting up a local mortal barman, which is potentially a violation of her terms of parole. For that reason, I felt it prudent to overhear her conversation.

"—curious if there's a back way out, not because I'm some sort of a desperate criminal on the run from the law, but there's this woman who follows me everywhere, kind of a stalker, really, and she's driving me insane. I swear to you, *insane*! You know, let's make that half pint of lager and lime a whole pint. My mother—one of my mothers, I have two, but this is my actual biological mother—she says it's not ladylike to drink a whole pint by oneself, but this stalker woman is enough to drive me to drink. Everywhere I go, whammo! She's there. I managed to ditch her this morning when I was out shopping, but I just know she's going to track me down sooner or later, and really, I think that a whole pint of lager is going to be required in order to cope with having a perpetual shadow who takes down everything you say and do."

The barman, engaged in wiping down the bar in the time-honored manner of barmen throughout Wales, and indeed, the whole of the British Isles, murmured something inaudible and poured the beverage described by Gwen into a larger glass, added more of the requested liquids, and returned it to her.

"Thanks." Gwen slid a few coins to the barman and took a large swig. The bar was empty of all but an old, crusty individual in a corner, and his equally old, crusty dog. "Ah, that's so much better. That should help mellow me out should Seawright show up again. That's my scribe . . . er . . . stalker's name. It's just so unfair that she's been sent to spy on me. It's not like I've done anything wrong. Certainly nothing to deserve a stalker. Okay, I'll admit that the circumstantial evidence might make it look like I've been less than discreet with some things, but I haven't. Not really. My moms have, but that's in the past, and they have learned their lessons. Oh, lord, I hope they've learned their lessons. No, they have, they promised me. And when a Wiccan makes a promise, she keeps it. There's that whole do unto others as they do unto you thing going on that keeps them in line. Most of the time. Wow, lager really makes you babble, huh? You must be tired of hearing me yammer on about the stalker who will not leave me alone. Day and night, night and day, everywhere I go, there she is, taking notes on what I do and what I say, and who I talk to. And she's so fussy! She's always referring to me by the most obnoxious titles, and she's got this 'You're a criminal and I'm sent to monitor your behavior' attitude that just makes me want to punch something. I hate people like that, don't you?"

The barman looked over her shoulder to me. I made careful note of Gwen's words, should the evidence be needed in an assault situation.

Gwen stiffened, and said slowly, "She's behind me right now, isn't she?"

The barman nodded, and moved off to wipe the other end of the bar.

Gwen swore under her breath, the words not quite audible, and since accurate reporting is one of my tasks, I shall not speculate as to the actual words she muttered, and instead say simply that she swore under her breath in a manner that would not have been out of place on a rough sailing vessel filled with swarthy, unkempt men who spat and scratched themselves in public.

"Dammit, Seawright!" Gwen said, turning around to face me, her pint of lager clutched in both hands. "Can't you leave me alone for even a day?"

I glanced down the bar, judged the barman and crusty old man to be out of earshot, and shook my head. "That would be in violation of the terms of my employment. I am a scribe. It is my job to transcribe any and all actions conducted by you, excepting those of a personal and intimate nature, for the review of the L'au-delà Committee, for verification that you are not violating the terms of your recent parole."

"Gah!" Gwen brushed past me and sat down at a settle, taking another long drink before she set the glass down in front of her. Due to lack of other customers in the bar, I deemed it prudent to sit with her, rather than nearby in an observation position. "This is intolerable, Seawright! I shouldn't even have been paroled!"

"If you weren't paroled, then you would still be jailed," I pointed out.

"Wrongly! I was wrongly jailed! I don't sell magic to mortals; everyone knows this. I can't even really do a lot of magic, despite my moms trying their damnedest to teach me. I'm an alchemist, just a simple little alchemist. I make potions and elixirs and sometimes, when I can get the materials, rarer items. That's it. And I don't sell any of that to mortals."

"It seems odd, then, that the L'au-dela should believe you did sell magic to inappropriate persons, and thus jail you for such acts."

Gwen's shoulders slumped. "It's a long story. The bottom line is that I didn't do anything wrong. And I thought the fact that they paroled me meant that they realized they didn't have any proof, but then they insisted on having a whole herd of scribes come down on me. You're the fifth one in as many weeks, you know. The others all had to leave. I don't know why. Maybe they just got tired of it all." Moodily, she took another sip of her beverage. "It's only been a couple of days for you, but five long weeks of surveillance for me. If you could just give me a little space, I'd be super appreciative. I feel like an animal at the zoo, I really do. No matter where I go, there you are, watching me with your beady little eyes."

I squared my shoulders, my eyes on my transcription tablet as I wrote down her statement. I had to remain impartial, and not allow her to see that she could hurt me with words.

She swore under her breath again, then reached across the table and patted my hand. "I'm sorry. That was mean of me, and untrue. You don't have beady little eyes. You have lovely blue eyes, and I'm just being cranky because of this whole scribe situation."

"If you find me personally offensive," I said carefully, willing to forgive the slight, but hesitant to do so if it was just an attempt to sweet-talk me, "you may lodge a request with the Committee to replace me with another scribe."

She gave me a watery smile. "I don't have a problem with you per se. I do take issue with having a permanent tail watching every move I make."

I allowed myself a small, professional smile. "I forgive your insult, then. We shall continue on as harmoniously as before."

Two men entered the pub and moved immediately to the bar. Gwen glanced idly at them, her fingers tracing what looked to be alchemical equations on the scarred wooden table top. "Mmhmm. Let me make it up to you by getting you a beer or something. Glass of wine?"

"I'm not allowed to drink while on duty," I informed her.

"Yeah, but you're not supposed to stand out. I distinctly remember someone at the parole hearing saying that you were to be as unobtrusive as possible, and in no way alert any mortals to your position, or otherwise cramp my style. Since we're in a pub, it will look odd if you don't have some sort of a drink."

"Very well. Since you insist on treating me, I will have a lemonade."

I watched carefully as she smiled and rose, going to the end of the bar nearest our table, but the two men at the far end paid her no heed. She gave her order to the barman, and returned a minute later with my beverage.

"So, you might want to know what I'm doing in Malwod-Upon-Ooze. At least, I assume you're supposed to keep track of what I'm doing. I'm here to make a purchase of some materials I need to craft a quintessence. You've heard of that, haven't you?"

"I'm afraid I'm not conversant with items of an alchemical nature."

"Ah. Well, quintessences are priceless. I mean, literally priceless. If you can make one—and very few alchemists can—you basically can name your price for it. It takes years to make, and has one thousand, two hundred and twelve steps, so it's not something you just whip up on the spur of the moment. The quintessence I have under way is the one I started when I was eighteen, and it's nearing maturity. I just need a few rare materials, and I should be able to finish it off. I heard through the alchemy grapevine that one of the three things I need is near my family's home in Wales, so I'm here to try to buy it from the owner."

"Interesting," I said.

"Alchemy is fascinating, really," she agreed, then stood up and made a wry face. "Tiny bladders run in my family. I'm going to visit the ladies' room. I'll be right back."

I eyed her hesitantly, scanning the pub for potential mortals with whom she might interact. Of the two men who had come in, one was at the bar, hunched over his beverage. The second had left. Another man entered, but he approached the man at the bar and clearly had no interest in Gwen. The barman was on his cell phone, speaking to someone named Cyril about an order of crisps that hadn't come in as promised. The crusty old man–and–dog ensemble were slumped next to a small gas fireplace, the old man's gnarled hand occasionally lifting his glass to his lips.

"Very well, but I will trust that you will not attempt to escape through the bathroom window as you did this morning at the supermarket."

"I didn't go out the bathroom window," she said with a light laugh. "The door to the loading dock was open, so I just left that way. I won't be but a minute."

I sat composedly, checking over my transcription of the day's work, secure in the knowledge that my examination of the pub building prior to entering it had ensured that the bathroom window was too small for an adult to climb through.

End Transcription

Your Text Messages

Me: *Mom! Help! Scribe is here and I can't shake her. What's spell for opening portal?*

Magdalena Owens: *Merciful goddess, you don't want to mess with a portal. They can be dangerous.*

Me: *You are not helping. Need spell in the next ten seconds. Am trapped in bathroom.*

Magdalena Owens: *Is the door stuck? Can you yell for assistance?*

Me: *Not that kind of stuck. Need spell to get out of here!*

Alice Hill: *Mags says you are trapped in bathroom. Is building on fire? Should I call 999? Where exactly are you?*

Me: *Malwod-Upon-Ooze, and no fire. Need spell to get out. Lawyer is here.*

Magdalena Owens: *Alice is calling the rescue people. Stay low on the floor. Don't breathe smoke.*

Me: *For the love of all that's shiny! THERE IS NO FIRE!*

Magdalena Owens: *Caps, dear.*

Me: *ARGH!*

Alice Hill: *So you're not in a fire?*

Me: *NO!*

Alice Hill: *What are you doing in Malwod? Do you know that word means snails in Welsh?*

Magdalena Owens: *Alice says you're being attacked by oozing snails?*

Me: *headdesk*

Me: *Mom Two, give me escape spell. Please. Lawyer you promised incantation is here.*

Alice Hill: *Oh. Is that what you wanted? Why did you frighten your mother by telling her that there was a fire and rabid snails?*

Magdalena Owens: *Use salt, Gwenny. Snails hate salt.*

Me: *I'm taking away your mobile phone, Mom.*

Alice Hill: *PDF of escape spell attached. Love from us. Will see you tonight?*

Me: *Yes, assuming I can escape my tail. Thanks for spell. Hugs.*

Personal Logbook of Gregory Faa

Probationary member of the L'au-dela Watch. Not for Official Review.

On Thursday, August first, the mortal subject Edwin Kleibschiemer was seen entering a pub in Malwod-Upon-Slime, a minuscule coastal town in Wales.

"Think it will go down inside?" I asked Peter, who, as an experienced member of the Watch (not to mention my cousin and professional mentor), had a better feel for this sort of thing.

"I doubt it." We got out of the car we'd rented in order to tail Kleibschiemer. "But just in case it is, you go inside and scope out the place. See if our suspect is inside."

"We could go in together."

He shook his head. "I've been with the Watch too long. She might know who I am. It's better if you do it. Besides," he said, flashing me a grin, "you could charm the spots off a leopard. If she suspects you're trouble, you can simply show her your dimples and she'll swoon into your arms."

"I don't have dimples," I pointed out, punching him in the arm just to let him know I appreciated the quasi-compliment. "And how will I know if it's the right woman? You said there's no picture of Owens."

"That's because the last time she was caught the L'au-dela was just starting to experiment with cameras. For the last century and a half, the best we have is a description, and that varies from a middle-aged woman to a young one, from blonde to brunette. She clearly can manipulate her appearance."

"Great. I just hope I don't end up in mortal jail for following the wrong woman."

"If you can't tell a mortal from a Wiccan after five minutes' acquaintance, then you shouldn't be in the Watch." Peter gave me a friendly shove, and moved off to stand in front of a news agent's shop.

I sauntered into the pub, greeting the barkeep with a friendly word, and ordered a beer. I stood at the bar while I waited for it, casually glancing around the room. Immediately to my left was Kleibschiemer. Another man was with him, a man I didn't recognize from the Watch files, but he left just as soon as I stopped at the bar. I pulled out my phone as if I'd wanted to text someone, and covertly took a picture of the second man as he walked out the door.

As I did so, a movement beyond him caught my eye. Seated in one of the high-backed wooden settles that ringed the pub were two women. One had a halo of fluffy, pinkish red hair, while the other . . . my fingers tightened on my phone for a few seconds as I drank in the sight of the second woman. Raven-haired, she was what popular magazines would call statuesque, with ample curves, shoulder-length hair that seemed to flow around her like inky water, and a bright pair of gray eyes framed with thick black lashes. I could see the lashes even across the room, so dense were they. She was speaking to the fluffy-haired woman, who appeared to be taking down everything the raven beauty was saying, the latter's hands gesturing with little birdlike jabs in the air to emphasize her points. And judging by the gestures, she appeared to have a lot to say.

"Yer beer, mate."

"Thanks." I gave the barman a few coins without taking my eyes off the woman. She got to her feet and turned my way. I picked up my beer and pretended to drink it, spinning around to watch her over the rim of the glass as she headed for the ladies' room.

She wasn't mortal. That I knew the second she passed me, leaving behind a trail of scent that seemed to go straight into my blood. She smelled like the sea air, tangy and wild, and slightly salty. I had a sudden, overwhelming desire to lick that warm, tanned skin to see if she tasted salty, too, but reminded myself that members of the Watch, especially probationary members, were not encouraged to lick suspects, no matter how delectable they appeared.

Found her, I texted to Peter. *Kleibscheimer's here, but just paid tab. Now he's leaving.*

Great. You stick with her. I'll follow him, he texted back.

I waited for a few minutes, then decided it would be less suspicious if I was outside when I began to follow Magdalena Owens. Accordingly, I finished my beer and strolled outside, taking up a position at the end of the street, which handily had a thick cement wall the right height for sitting.

Ten minutes went by, and there was no sign of my prey. I sauntered past the pub, casually glancing in, froze for a second, then yanked the door open and stumbled inside.

It was empty except for an old man and his dog in a far corner.

"You didn't happen to see—" I started to ask the barkeep, but the words stopped when the pinky red–haired woman burst out of the ladies' room, muttering under her breath about the abuse of trust.

"Gents' loo?" I asked the barman.

He jerked his head toward the small hallway down which the dark-haired Owens had gone. I glanced over my shoulder at the door to the ladies and plunged in, prepared to offer apologies should it be occupied.

There were two stalls, both of which were empty. A small

window sat close to the ceiling, too small for the well-curved woman who'd sashayed past me. Dammit, she must have used one of her spells to get out of the pub unseen.

I hurried out of the pub, quickly scanning the street for either woman.

"There's a little problem," I said into my phone a few minutes later as I jogged down the line of shops fronting the tiny harbor that was Malwod-Upon-Moistness.

"What sort of problem?"

"I lost Owens. She went into the ladies' toilet, and evidently disappeared."

"Disappeared how? Never mind, it doesn't matter. We're on the beach to the northeast of town. Go past the harbor and swimming area, and there's a ribbon of rocky beach you follow. If your prey is on the move, she's likely coming this way."

I slowed down from my trot, careful not to draw attention while I scanned the women who were busily shopping, strolling, or marching along the small rocky beach in obvious search for a spot to lie out and sunbathe.

None of them were the beauty I'd seen. Mentally, I reviewed the information—such as it was—we had on her. Other than her name and profession (practicing Wiccan), we knew little other than what an informant had told Peter: the mortal Kleibschiemer made it known that he was in the market for the magic effects known by the popular brand names Romulan Cloaking Spell and Houdini's Famous Escape-o-Matic Incantation. And since one woman had been recently charged with the selling of those magics (and subsequently paroled for some reason that Peter and I hadn't been able to ascertain), it seemed likely that she was back in business.

"Where are you?" I murmured as I continued to walk along the cement wall that kept the tide back from the street above. Women of all shapes, sizes, and ages were arranged on the beach, but none of them gave off a whiff of anything but sunscreen and sun-warmed flesh. I continued to walk along the beach until it petered out, the cliffs that lined either side of the small town suddenly looming up and consuming almost all the shore. A thin, narrow strip of land, littered with tree stumps washed ashore, caught up on jagged boulders that despite the restless waves were sharp enough to cut the soles of most shoes to shreds. I picked my way carefully down the narrow lip of land, avoiding both the tide (which was going out), slimy debris that lay in rotting, salty clumps, and the razorlike rocks. Ahead of me, the base of the cliff had been washed out, leaving the upper portion overhanging like a medieval house. Bare roots dangled in midair, testifying to the power of the incessant surf as it slowly, inevitably washed away the dirt.

I looked upward, trying to judge just how dangerous that overhang was. It didn't look like it was going to come crashing down on me at any moment, but I wasn't willing to take the chance that it would. I edged my way into the wet rocks, and focused my attention on the two figures ahead of me, neither of which were female.

Peter was keeping well to the cliff face itself, moving slowly and cautiously after Kleibschiemer. The latter approached a rickety wooden staircase that zigzagged its way up to the top of the cliff. Despite the distance from him, I threw myself down next to a large piece of driftwood tree trunk as the man approached the base of the stairs. He glanced up and down the beach in a furtive manner, then not seeing Peter (who was pressed against the cliff) or me, he began climbing, and in a few minutes, had reached the top of the cliff. He disappeared from view.

I stood up. Peter waved an arm at me, and took off at a sprint toward the stairs. I followed, but a minute later my phone rang.

"Stay there," was the whispered order. "Stay down on the beach."

I had just about reached the wooden staircase, but stopped, glancing back over my shoulder. "Why? Owens isn't here."

"There's no way for anyone to get up here but the stairs. There's a second cliff above this. Where I'm hiding is a little hollow with a few trees and that's it. I've got Kleibschiemer in view, but he doesn't see me. Owens has to come up from below."

"Right. Taking cover now." I clicked off my cell phone and moved over to the shadow of the cliff, searching for a likely boulder behind which I could hide, when suddenly there was a strange call on the wind, kind of a squawking of a large seabird, that horribly resolved itself into a human voice.

The voice stopped with a loud, wet noise even more unappealing. I stared for a moment at the gruesome sight before me, that of a dark-haired woman lying broken and bloodied on the rocks. I squatted next to her and felt for a pulse, knowing that I wouldn't find one.

I didn't.

My mind reeled with the impossibility of the event. Someone had killed my suspect. Someone had killed the lovely, salty woman. I glanced upward, but no one was visible on the cliff. Toward me, however, a woman picked her way through the rocks. She wore a cherry red skirt and jacket, had short, dark brown hair, and a pair of thick black glasses.

"Good afternoon," she called, heading for us. "I see you have my client. I'm with Reclamations, Incorporated. Would you mind standing aside, Mr. . . ." Her pale blue eyes narrowed on me. "A Traveller? We don't see many of your sort. Step aside, please, Mr. Traveller, and unhand my client."

"Reclamations . . ." The word chimed a warning bell in my head. "You're Death."

"Please!" she bridled, and tugged her suit jacket down. "We prefer the title Reclamation Agent."

"Yes, but you are Death. You're the one who collects dead immortals."

"We collect their souls or prescient essences, such as they may be, yes. And I'm not the head of the corporation, just one of his many busy workers. Now, if you would please stand aside, I need space to take this woman's soul."

I don't know what happened to me at that moment. Call it fate, call it a frisson of something intangible that claimed me when Owens had walked past me in the pub, call it a man's interest in a lovely woman, but for whatever reason, I did the one thing I knew I absolutely should not do.

I stole time.

Roberta Gently, Director

Patient Number: 2144

Date: 2 August

Patient Gwen O. was brought to see me by her mother Magdalena O. and Magdalena's life partner, Alice H. Gwen appeared somewhat distraught by being in the office, and while in reception, declared several times that she had no need of a "shrink" and wasn't in the least bit crazy, despite what anyone thought.

She entered my personal office with another woman.

"I believe this appointment is scheduled to be private," I said, glancing at Gwen's chart.

"Sorry, I'm a scribe," the second woman said, and introduced herself as Seawright P. "Wherever Gwen goes, so goeth I. Or so says the L'au-dela Committee."

"I notice you didn't go to hell with me," Gwen muttered under her breath.

"That's because you escaped me earlier. Again! Just like you have every other scribe for the last five weeks!" Seawright said, her frizzy pinkish hair trembling with strong emotion.

"If you'd give me a little space, I wouldn't have to keep ditching you guys," Gwen countered, her hands on her hips as she loomed over the smaller woman.

"It's my job! I have to record what you do for the Akashic Record, in order to make sure you don't go back to your naughty ways."

"I don't *have* any naughty ways!" Gwen thundered.

I felt it important to stop the budding argument before it continued. "Ladies, please! This office is a haven of calm and reflection. I will not have your personal altercation disturb all the other souls who seek refuge here."

Seawright pointed a pencil at Gwen. "She started it."

I allowed myself a brief glare at the scribe before saying, "We do not judge here. No one is at fault. And since I'm not aware of the Committee having jurisdiction over mental health facilities, unless Gwen would be more comfortable with you being present transcribing all that she says, then I must ask you to wait in the reception area."

Seawright looked pointedly at my windows. "She'll just jump out the window."

"No, she won't."

"Yes, she will."

I tapped my pencil on the file folder in an attempt to keep my emotions in their usual state of serenity. "Gwen, will you give your word that you will not escape my office via the windows?"

"Or any other method," Seawright said with a pugnacious toss of her head.

"Or any other method?"

"If it'll get her off my back for a few minutes, sure," Gwen said.

"Very well. Since Gwen would obviously prefer to continue without your immediate presence, and has given her word that she will not leave via any nontraditional means, you may wait in the reception area until our session is concluded."

"Fine. But it's on your head if she does another runner," the scribe said, giving a hard look to Gwen before she exited.

Gwen noticeably relaxed at the scribe's exit. She spoke with coherence and apparent intelligence, although I noticed her speech pattern was American rather than Welsh or British. She appeared to be in her early thirties, with shoulder-length black hair, gray eyes, no visible tattoos or piercings, and wore a somewhat disheveled linen shirt and pair of black jeans.

"Good morning, Gwen," I said, giving her some time to pick a chair in which she'd be comfortable. She chose the one out of the direct sunlight. "I understand from your mother and her partner that you've recently had a traumatic experience of some sort. Would you like to tell me about it?"

"Not really," she answered pleasantly, then made a face. "But I don't have much of a choice since Mom Two took my passport, wallet, and keys, and won't let me have them back until I talk to you. So here I am."

"Mom Two?" I asked, making a note that she was not coming into the therapy session of her own accord.

"That's what I call Alice. Mom is my mother. Mom Two is my other mother, my mother's partner."

"I see. And how long have you had two mothers?"

She shrugged, and brushed a bit of dried mud off the knee of her jeans. "As long as I can remember."

"Does your mother's relationship disturb you at all?"

She sat up straight in her chair and shot me a glare. "What are you trying to say?"

"I'm not saying anything," I said calmly. "I'm simply asking you how you feel about your mother's relationship with another woman."

"I love my mothers," she said abruptly. "Both of them."

"I'm glad to hear that. A loving home environment cannot be underrated, is that not so? I presume that there must also be a father somewhere in the picture?"

"You'd assume wrong." She crossed both her legs, and her arms over her chest, a sure sign she was locking down both her flow of information, and her emotions.

"Indeed."

"There's nothing wrong with my moms," she continued rather hotly. "And you can't make me say there is. My mothers are great. Well, most of the time. Every now and again they get into trouble, and I have to come to the rescue, but they've been pretty good for the last few years. Kind of. Recently, though . . . well, that's neither here nor there."

I consulted the application form that had been included in her file. "I see your mothers are Wiccans and run a school?"

"Why do you make everything a question?" she asked, her eyes narrowing as she sat forward.

"Do I?" I smiled reassuringly. "It is my job to help people, Gwen. And I can't do that unless I understand what is bothering you, now, can I?"

"What's bothering me is the implication that there is something wrong with my relationship with my moms." She sat back again, her body language once again making it quite clear she wasn't willing to discuss the matter any further.

"What happened yesterday?" I asked, changing the subject.

She looked startled for a few seconds, then her chin lifted in a slightly belligerent manner, as if she expected censure or disbelief. "I died and went to hell."

I raised my eyebrows in a signal for her to go on.

"Well, not so much hell as the afterlife. Anwyn, to be exact. You know what Anwyn is, don't you?"

"It is one of the many afterlives that various beings utilize as way stations before rebirth or transportation to another realm of consciousness. Many mortals think of them as heaven. I thought, however . . ." I typed in a phrase on my laptop, read the result, and nodded. "Yes, I was correct. I thought that the Wiccan afterlife is Summerland?"

"It is. But I'm not Wiccan. I'm an alchemist."

"So when you decide to move on from this plane of existence—"

"Or I'm killed, like I was yesterday."

"Or, as you say, you are killed, not that I believe such a task is easily accomplished with regard to one who is immortal like you, then you will retire to Anwyn, while your mothers will go to Summerland?"

"Basically, yes. And you might not think it's easy to kill me, but I can assure you it's entirely possible. Anwyn isn't quite like Summerland, though. That's all happy Wiccans and picnics and stuff. My moms took me there a few years ago to see my grandmother. Anwyn looks similar, but it's different. Or at least so I've heard."

"I see. Perhaps you would be so kind as to go over the sequence of events for me, so that I might have it straight in my mind?"

"Sure thing. But you have to promise to tell my moms I'm not crazy, because they think I'm making this shi . . . er . . . stuff up."

"We don't use the word 'crazy' at the Gently Does It Centers," I said with another reassuring smile. "Go ahead and tell me what happened. In your own time."

"Well, yesterday I was happily getting ready to go home—I live in a small town in Colorado, in the States, even though I was born here in Wales. I come back to Wales to visit my moms every couple of months, mostly to see them, but also because I'm an alchemist, and the best alchemical auctions happen in London. Anyway, I was just wrapping up a monthlong visit when it happened."

"Forgive me for interrupting," I said, lifting an apologetic hand. "Do you wish to tell me how and why the scribe Seawright became your shadow?"

A dark look came over her face. "No."

"Very well." I made note of the rapidity of her response, and her general body language, and then urged her to continue.

"So I'm packing up my things to go back home, and a call comes in on the phone from some guy named Tesserman. Or Bandersnatch. Something odd like that. And he says that he's got a mortal client for 'the stuff' and that I need to get 'the stuff' down to Malwod-Upon-Ooze pronto. Obviously, I had no idea what he was talking about, but just as obviously, my moms were doing something they shouldn't be doing—and no, I don't want to go into that, because it has nothing to do with me dying and going to hell. Well, okay, it does, but I'm still not going to talk about it. Suffice it to say that I knew that my moms would be in seriously hot water if they did what the guy wanted them to do, so I told the guy that there was no way in hell I was going to let my moms break the law by selling magic to mortals. And he went all ballistic on me, and threatened them with all sorts of crazy stuff. You can imagine how that made me feel, so I told him no again, and he said that if someone wasn't in Malwod to hand over the goods he'd already paid for, then he would take his payment out on my moms. There was no way I was going to let him threaten them, so I went down to Malwod to have it out with him."

"You are a very caring daughter, but do you not feel that you were stepping into a dangerous situation? Would it not have been wiser to call in the Watch?"

She shook her head. "My moms and I are already persona non grata with them. They wouldn't lift a finger to help us. Besides, it appeared that my mothers had already taken this asshat's money for the spells." She took a deep breath, and picked off another flake of dried mud from her jeans. "I managed to ditch Seawright at a shop just outside of the train station and went to Malwod. But Seawright is getting better at finding me, and caught up with me while I was waiting for the buyer in a pub. As soon as he showed up, I managed to get out of the pub without her seeing me, and headed to the rendezvous point, which was halfway up an impossibly hard-to-climb cliff. I ended up going to the wrong place, and had to climb down the scariest drop I'd ever seen just to get to this little area at the top of another cliff. Anyway, I was hiding behind a clump of trees when some guy dashed into the bushes in front of me and crouched down like he's hiding from someone. I thought he must be the guy who set up my moms to meet with a mortal, and was about to crawl over to him and give him a really solid piece of my mind, when whammo! Someone grabbed me from behind and jerked me off balance. Next thing I knew, I was plummeting over the side of the second cliff to the rocks below."

"That must have been horribly frightening," I murmured.

Gwen visibly shuddered. "You have no idea. I mean, it was a long drop, but not long enough that I could speak a protection spell." She paused and rubbed her arms, her expression pensive. "I wish I'd seen who threw me over the edge."

"And you found yourself in Anwyn?"

"Yes. Woke up to find myself lying on a green, grassy hill. The sun beamed down in the bluest sky I've ever seen. Birds sang. Trees, arranged in graceful clumps, swayed gently in the breeze. Daisies that dotted the hill bowed their pale heads and seemed to dance to some distant music that only they could hear. Butterflies landed on me and fanned me with their sparkly wings. Bunnies pattered to and fro on lupine business. A family of deer strolled past. It was the most idyllic thing in the world, and I was just thinking about taking a nice little nap with the butterflies and the bunnies, when suddenly I was yanked out of Anwyn and back onto the road that led to the cliff where I got tossed over the edge."

I made a few notes. "That seems like a very curious thing to have happened. How did it make you feel?"

She gave me what could only be termed a scathing look. "How do you think you'd feel if you were yanked from an idyllic, Disney-esque paradise and were set down on a wind-battered cliff several thousand feet above the place where you died?"

"That would be a remarkably tall cliff indeed," I murmured, making another note. "Perhaps that height is a slight exaggeration?"

Gwen suddenly leaped to her feet and slapped her hands on her thighs. "Well, of course it's an exaggeration. It's supposed to tell you just how I feel about that cliff. One minute I was lying in an exquisite moment of summer bliss, and the next I found myself returned to the spot where I had been a few minutes before some unknown person flung me to my death."

"Mmm."

"Well, of course, what was I to think but that I'd gone crazy and hallucinated the whole thing? I mean, I'm not in the least bit psychic or anything, so that whole dying thing couldn't have been an elaborate premonition of my death." She paced across the room, turned, and paced back. "I figured I was losing it, or that Seawright had slipped me some sort of wacky juice when I wasn't looking, or something like that. And I thought long and hard for about ten minutes about going back to the pub to have it out with Seawright, but that wouldn't really answer the question of what really happened. I *had* to know, you know?"

She waited for me to validate her curiosity.

"You had to know who, if anyone, was waiting for you on that lower cliff top?"

"Exactly. So after arguing with myself for a bit over that, and making sure I wasn't hallucinating anything else, I went over to the edge of the cliff and started climbing down. Just as I arrived at the top of the lower-level cliff, a man shot up over the lip of it—there was a wooden staircase that led down to the beach—and looked around wildly."

"Wildly?" I asked, glancing up from my tablet of paper.

"Yeah, you know." Her hands gestured vaguely in the air. "Wildly. He looked one way, then the other, and his hair was standing on end, and his eyes were as big as saucers."

"Did that make you feel threatened?"

Gwen slapped her hands on her thighs again as she resumed pacing. "Of course I felt threatened! Here was a man right on the same spot where I had been thrown down to my death, and he looked like a madman, all wind-ruffled hair and crazy eyes."

"What did you do?"

"He started asking me about the magic, and I told him I wasn't going to give him anything, and was about to tell him just what I'd do if he continued to harass my moms, when a second guy popped up. Only he came out of the shrubs, so he must have been hiding there."

"You must have been greatly concerned about that situation: one man alone is dangerous. Two against one can be quite daunting."

"Well . . ." Her nose scrunched in thought. "Yes and no. The second guy didn't give off a bad vibe. Not then, anyway. He was blond and had these really nice blue eyes, and a little cleft in his chin that just made me want to bite it."

"Do you think that was an appropriate reaction to have given those circumstances?"

She gave me a look out of the corner of her eye as she strolled to the window. "Look, you deal with potentially murderous, handsome madmen the way you want to deal with them. I'm going to notice sexy chins. Where was I? Oh, so there was the crazy first guy, yammering on about all sorts of threatening stuff, and all of a sudden he grabs me, and the second guy pops up and punches him in the face. I mean, really nails him. Down goes the lawyer—did I mention that this guy who threatened my moms is a lawyer? How ironic is that? Down he goes, and I'm left standing on a windy cliff with this blond stranger. I'm no idiot, so I certainly wasn't going to stand there and let this man kill me again—assuming I was actually killed the first time, and not premonitioning the whole thing. And also assuming that blondie was the one to kill me, not that I think he is now, because it seems to me the lawyer pretty much proved he was the bad guy, but I couldn't know for sure, could I?"

I tried to untangle everything in that statement, and clung to the one thing that made any sort of sense. "I don't believe 'premonitioning' is an actual word."

"And then," she said with a dramatic gesture, "the blond guy said the worst thing he could possibly say, which was—"

The door to my office burst open, causing Gwen to spin around. A middle-aged woman entered, short of stature, and somewhat plump, her dark hair streaked with silver in a short pageboy cut. "Gwen!" she said in an excited manner, rushing over to take the younger woman by the arm. "We have to leave, dear."

"What? Right now? You said I had to talk to this woman before Mom Two would give me back—"

A second woman entered, slamming the door behind her, and turning the knob that operated a bolt. "Quick!" she said, hurrying over to my window, which without even so much as a glance my way, she flung open. "We have to leave now!"

"This is a private session," I said sternly, noting that the second woman was taller, with a close-cropped, masculine hairstyle that nonetheless highlighted excellent bone structure, and a wide, mobile mouth. "Do I take it that you are Gwen's mothers?"

"Yes, I'm Magdalena Owens," the plump woman said, pausing in the act of dragging her daughter over to the open window to smile in a friendly manner. "That's Alice, Gwen's other mother, over there at the window. It's a pleasure to meet you. I do hope you've been able to help our Gwenny. She has been most distraught over some incident that happened yesterday, and since you came highly recommended by a very dear friend of mine—Amor Tantrize, the palm reader—I knew that you would be just the person to help with Gwen's—"

"Mags!"

The interruption from the woman who was now in the process of climbing through the window stopped Magdalena in her verbal tracks. The latter turned to the window, with a mild, "What, dear? Oh! Come, Gwenny, we must leave right this second. Alice is most insistent on that point."

"What is going on?" Gwen asked as her mother resumed dragging her over to the window. For a small woman, Magdalena appeared to have prodigious strength. "Why are you running away? Is there someone out in the other room you don't want me to see?"

Someone pounded at the door, the sound of outraged, raised voices barely audible through its thick panels. I considered the door for a moment, then pressed a button on my desk phone. "Ludwig, would you please inform whoever is pounding so vigorously at my door that it is locked, and that I will not hesitate to present a bill for damages should it suffer from such an onslaught? Thank you."

Alice stuck her head back through the window, and grabbed Gwen's free arm. "It's more that you don't want to see her, ducky. Hurry up. That door won't hold her for long."

"Her who? Wait a second." Gwen reared back and dug in her heels, refusing to allow her mothers to pull her through the window. "What exactly is going on? Who is that banging on the door? Seawright? It doesn't sound like her. And Mom, stop trying to shove me through the blasted window! I made a promise to Seawright that I wasn't going to escape by going through the window, and you know I always keep my promises."

The pounding continued at the door, upraised voices now more audible.

"We're just thinking of what's best for you, ducks," Alice said, and reaching in with both hands, physically lifted Gwen and began pulling her through the window.

Gwen squawked and grabbed wildly at the edges of the windowsill, but she was unable to resist the combined forces of her mothers.

"Tell Seawright I didn't go through the window willingly," was the last thing I heard before Magdalena, with another bright smile, crawled through the window and disappeared with the others.

The pounding stopped for a moment, followed almost immediately by a splintering noise. The door was blown inwards with enough force to send the loose papers on my desk flying in a swirl around me.

A small brunette woman in a bright red woolen suit stood in the doorway, her hands on her hips, and the light glinting off a thick pair of black-rimmed glasses. Behind her hovered the woman Seawright.

"How dare she! I can't believe she . . . argh! Well,

this is the last straw, the very last straw. No one cheats Death, *no one*! Not while I'm responsible, anyway. Where'd that tricky little alchemist go?" the red-suited woman asked without any form of apology for destroying a perfectly nice door, let alone a polite greeting.

I flipped over the page on my tablet of paper, and made a new heading. "My name is Roberta Gently. I am the president of this company. How long have you had these uncontrollable outbursts of anger?"

Akashi Record #2712

2 August 8.55 am

Malwod-Upon-Ooze, Wales (Outside some therapy place)

Subject: Gwenhwyfar Byron Owens

Seawright Pendleton, junior scribe (third class)

Begin Transcription

She escaped. *Again!*

 That's it! I've had it. I quit! Consider this my notice that I hereby abandon this case!

End Transcription

Personal Logbook of Gregory Faa

Probationary member of the L'au-dela Watch. Not for Official Review.

 I knew a meeting with Peter was inevitable. Hell, anyone would have known something was up when I stole time from that pushy reclamation officer (aka Death's perky little minion), but Peter is a Traveller. Even if he wasn't directly affected by the time theft (and thus, aware of the changes made by the theft), he was still prescient enough to know something was up.

 Especially when the second we arrived (again, although he didn't realize we'd been there before) outside the pub, and he got out of the car, I leaped back into it and yelled at him to meet me down the beach at the cliff's head.

 "What? Where are you going?" he asked as I started up the car we'd just exited. Confusion was written all over his face, but I didn't have time to explain what had happened. To be honest, I prayed I'd never have to, since it would mean the immediate end of what I had hoped would be a promising career.

"Can't explain. Have to go save someone. Just head east out of town and follow the beach until you get to the staircase. I'm going around the other way. I think that's how she came."

"Who came where? What are you talking about? Gregory—"

I put my foot on the pedal and shot out into the road, narrowly missing mowing down both my cousin Peter and some elderly old man. By my best reckoning, I had twenty minutes to get to the top of that upper cliff and prevent whoever it was who flung my suspect over the edge.

The five-minute drive out to a rocky, barren field that edged the cliff face was spent mostly in trying to concoct a reasonable story that Peter would buy, thus keeping from him the truth. I had a horrible suspicion that he was going to know something illegal had gone down, however. He was smart enough, and savvy enough, to figure out that some funny business regarding the last half hour we'd just lived had taken place. I fervently hoped that he'd be willing to look the other way in the name of family.

I parked, and headed off across the field at a lope, scanning the area for the raven-haired woman. She wasn't there, but that didn't surprise me. She had been in the pub while Peter and I were outside it, but I knew that it had only been a minute or so after our arrival that she had somehow escaped from the bathroom. Given that its window wasn't a means for that exit, she had to have used some other method of escaping.

Like magic. Not surprising in one who was illegally selling magic to mortals.

I half-slid, half-fell down the slope of the first terraced cliff, onto the top of the second. A small stand of trees and shrubs clung to the wedge-shaped edge. The rest of the area was empty of all persons.

"I just hope nothing happens to you on the way here, because my ass is in enough hot water without having to risk a second theft," I muttered out loud as I headed for the densest bit of shrub and tree, kneeling to keep others from seeing me.

I had prepared for a wait of about fifteen minutes, but only five had passed when the sound of harsh breathing caught my attention. I peered out from my hiding place to see a man emerge over the top of the lower cliff, obviously having just climbed the staircase. He doubled over for a minute, his hands on his legs as he caught his breath; then he stood up, straightened his jacket, and headed straight for me.

A small rock the size of a half dollar cascaded down the upper cliff face behind me, followed by a couple of smaller brethren. We both looked up. The woman Magdalena Owens had a rope, and was rappelling her way down the cliff. I admired the sight for a moment, then recalled that I was an officer of the Watch, and we were not supposed to ogle suspects. I was fairly certain that was one of the rules to which I'd sworn a scant two months before when I joined the Watch.

When I turned back to see what the mysterious stairclimber was doing, he had moved over to the wooden ladder, peering over the top in an obvious attempt to remain out of sight of the woman Owens.

I frowned at the part of him visible to me. He looked vaguely familiar, but he was not the mortal Kleibschiemer, the man Peter had trailed from the pub. At least, he had in the previous version of time.

This man was smaller and slighter, but I didn't care for the way he was avidly watching my suspect. Just as she landed on even ground, he climbed up the last of the stairs, saying, "So you really had the balls to show up, did you?"

She whirled around, her hair flying out like a curtain of raven's wings. "So to speak. You're the lawyer?"

"That's right." He took a step toward her, menace all but

rolling off him. "I hope you've come to your senses. My client should be here any minute, and I don't want him disappointed. That wouldn't be healthy for your family."

With calm deliberation, she brushed the dirt off her black jeans, not even glancing his way as she answered, "I don't take well to threatening, you know. I find bullying of any sort repugnant, and especially so when the person doing the bullying threatens people weaker than him."

"You think I'm afraid of you?" he asked with a laugh.

She finished brushing off her knees and gave him a long look. "I think you should be. I'm no lightweight, and I don't intend to let you harm anyone, let alone my mothers."

"Give me the goods, and no one will get hurt."

"No," she said, taking me by surprise. What was this? She was refusing to sell the magic? Why?

The man shrugged. "I hate to have to do this the hard way, but perhaps a lesson is in order. People will think twice about double-crossing me if they have proof of what will happen if they do."

He lunged forward just at the moment I remembered where I'd seen him—he'd been inside the pub when I arrived at it the first time. He had been standing near Kleibschiemer, but had left immediately thereafter.

All of that raced through my head at the same time that Magdalena Owens gave a high shriek, and turned to run. He caught her around the waist and started to drag her over to the cliff's edge, clearly intent on throwing her down to her death. Again.

"Over my dead body," I snarled, and leaped out, flinging myself on the man in a tackle that sent all three of us rolling on the ground.

"Who the hell—" he started to say.

"I'm with the Watch," I snarled, and somehow, my fist connected with his jaw, and he was out. I flipped him over onto his belly, pulled out a pair of zip ties that I keep for temporarily subduing culprits, and jerked his wrists together, binding them tight enough that the ties dug into his flesh. Served the murdering bastard right.

"Are you hurt?" I asked the woman as I got to my feet. She crouched a few yards away, breathing heavily, her eyes huge and filled with the aftereffects of adrenaline and fear.

"Who . . . no. Who did you say you were?"

"Gregory Faa. I'm with the Watch. I take it you know this man?"

Slowly, she shook her head, her eyes never leaving mine. "Never met him. Um . . . did he do something wrong? Are you here to arrest him?"

"That's a bit of a complicated answer. He did originally kill y—er—someone, but this time I stopped him."

She looked puzzled. I didn't feel inclined to enlighten her.

"That does sound complicated. Well, thank you for stopping him from attacking me. He took me by surprise, so I wasn't ready with a spell or anything."

"I noticed. You should take some mortal self-defense classes."

"I should." For the first time since I'd seen her, she smiled. It was a nice smile, wrinkling up the corners of her eyes. "Well, since you're going to take him away somewhere, I guess I'll get out of your way and let you do your thing."

I stopped her before she could turn away and leave. "I'm afraid the complicated part includes you, Miss Owens."

She froze, her gaze now wary. "What did you call me?"

"Owens. I was sent out here to find you."

Her shoulders slumped, her eyes closing briefly. "I knew it. They did something other than . . . never mind. Go ahead. Tell me the worst. I can take it."

"I'm unsure of who 'they' are, but I'm afraid I've been given the power to arrest you on charges of illegally selling magic to mortals. We were tipped off to the fact that you were meeting with a mortal to do so today, but even though that was . . . let's just say, part of the complicated situation . . . we still have a warrant for your arrest based on past sales. Magdalena Owens, as a duly authorized member of the Watch—"

She started shaking her head before I could finish the last sentence, holding up a hand to stop me. "That's not my name."

I paused in the act of pulling out a second zip tie. I really did not want to have to use it on her. "Your name isn't Magdalena Owens?"

"No. It's Gwenhwyfar Byron O—" Her lips clamped closed abruptly.

"Guinevere?"

"Gwenhwyfar." She pronounced the name GWEN-hiff-arr. "It's the Welsh version. You can call me Gwen."

"Oh?"

"Yes, really. Everyone calls me Gwen."

"No, I meant your last name is Oh?" She didn't look Asian, but one never knew these days.

"Why would you think that?"

"Because you said your name was Gwenhwyfar Byron Oh."

"I did? Ah. Yes." She blinked three times. "That was . . . my name is actually Gwenhwyfar Byron."

"But you said Oh." For some reason, I felt it was important to get to the bottom of that Oh.

"Um." She stared at me for a moment. "That was kind of a leftover oh, from, 'Oh! You think I'm someone else.'"

I couldn't help but smile. "I'm very glad to know you're not the woman I was sent to arrest, Miss Byron. It is Miss Byron?"

"Yes," she said slowly, her gaze dropping to the man who still lay unconscious at our feet. "I should be running along. I have . . . uh . . . some things to do. People to talk to."

The last sentence was spoken through her teeth. She suddenly looked angry as hell.

"If there's anything I can help you with—"

"No," she said quickly, then flashed me another smile. "Just some family issues."

"I hope they are resolved quickly. Er . . ." I touched her arm as she was about to leave. "Look, I realize that this is not at all the way things should be done—women are frequently wary about men they meet on the tops of cliffs, and given the events of the recent past, rightfully so."

"Given the events of the recent past?"

I waved that away. "It's . . ."

"Complicated?"

"Very much so. Regardless, I was hoping that perhaps you'd overlook this odd meeting, and have coffee with me. In a public place, naturally. One where you would feel safe and not at all threatened, or be worried that I might be the strange sort of man who picks up women on the tops of cliffs, and later turns out to be some sort of deranged stalker."

She gave a long sigh. "I have a deranged stalker already, thank you."

I frowned, unsure of whether her non-answer was a yes or no to my invitation. I decided to go with thinking positively. "There's bound to be a tea shop or Starbucks in the town Snail-on-a-Stick. We could meet there in, say, an hour? I should have this processed by then." I nudged the man with the toe of my shoe. He groaned into the ground.

She giggled for a few seconds before her expression turned sober. "It's Malwod-Upon-Ooze, actually. And I'm sorry, but coffee is out."

"If you'd prefer something stronger, there's a pub—"

"No," she interrupted, giving me an odd look before shaking her head. "I'm sorry, I can't."

"If it was because I mentioned deranged stalkers, I can assure you that as a member of the Watch, I take my oath to protect both mortals and immortals alike very seriously."

She wrapped the rope around herself in a manner that indicated she was familiar with the skill of climbing, and began to hoist herself upwards. "I don't think you're a stalker, deranged or otherwise, if that's what you're worried about."

"You're involved with someone? I didn't think meeting

for coffee was tantamount to a marriage proposal, but if you're worried that I was planning on hitting on you—"

"No, it's not that either," she called down, pausing to look over her shoulder at me. "You seem nice. Gentlemanly, even. Kind of old-world."

"I was born in Romania. I'm afraid that air of Old World clings to me somewhat."

"It's nice. You should play on that."

"If I told you that I saved your life, would that make you more inclined to have that coffee?"

She stopped her ascent and glanced down again. "I would have gotten away from him. I was ready for him this time."

"You can't know that you wouldn't have ended up over the edge of the cliff again."

"Again?" Her face was filled with doubt. "Why do you say again? What exactly were you doing up here?"

"Eh . . ." I hesitated. "That's going to be part and parcel of the complicated business I mentioned earlier."

"Uh-huh." She continued to climb.

It would take a stronger man than me not to have spent the time of her climb admiring her legs and ass, but I strove to keep my mind where it needed to be. Which was finding out just what it was that she didn't like about me. I might not be an overly modest man, but I've never had trouble before picking up a woman, and for this one now to be so unenthusiastic about simply meeting me for coffee wounded what my cousin's wife Kiya would call my manly pride.

"If it's not my manners, and you're not worried about me being unhinged and homicidal, then may I ask what it is about me that fails to interest you?"

She grunted a ladylike grunt as she reached the top of the upper cliff, hauling herself up and over the ledge. A few rocks and the small root system of a tiny clump of flowers fluttered to the ground, directly on top of the head of my prisoner. He groaned again, and started to move his legs. No doubt he'd be awake in another minute.

I thought she was just going to walk away without answer, but faintly, almost whipped away by the wind coming off the water, her voice drifted down to me.

"I can't have coffee, or anything else, with you because you're with the Watch. Even if you didn't kill me before, it's just too dangerous."

Now what the hell did that mean?

THE ART OF
STEALING TIME

ONE

"Ticket, yes. Passport, right here. Boarding pass . . . dammit. Where did I put that? I know I printed it out." I did a little dance peculiar to people arriving at an airport, the one where you slap various pockets and juggle luggage, magazines, and purses in order to peer into every easily reached receptacle. Finally, I found the sheet of paper I'd printed before leaving my mothers' flat. "Gotcha! All right, I think I'm set. I just hope the security line isn't too long."

People streamed past me out of the tiled corridor that led to the airport tube station, hauling luggage, children, and parcels of every size as they traveled the moving sidewalks, escalators, and plain old stairs into the airport proper.

A woman next to me, pausing to wait for two bickering teenagers behind her, yelled in a flat American accent that she would happily leave them behind in Wales if they didn't get their asses in gear. She caught my eye as I was rearranging my travel documents to be readily available, giving me a grimacing smile. "I swear, I'm never traveling with kids again. Everyone said I was crazy to bring them along with me, but I thought they'd be old enough to appreciate seeing another culture."

I glanced back to where the teen girl and boy were arguing over what appeared to be a carrier bag filled with magazines. "Didn't work out as you planned, eh?"

"Lord, no! And we still have Amsterdam and Germany to do. How I'm going to survive another week is beyond me."

She gave me an appraising look as I finished tucking away my magazine, stuffed my purse (denuded of travel documents) into my carry-on bag, and pulled out the handle of the monstrous wheeled suitcase that housed the bulk of my possessions. "You're American, too?"

"Actually, I was born here in Wales, but I've lived so long in Denver that I pass for American."

"Ah. Here on business?" the woman asked. If she had been British, I'd have wondered what was up, but many decades of living in the U.S. had made even the most personal of questions seem totally natural when asked by a relative stranger.

"You could say that. My mothers live in a small town near the coast. I visit them every six months or so."

"Mothers? Plural?" Her forehead wrinkled for a moment, then smoothed out quickly with an "Oh! You mean your mother is . . . How . . . interesting."

My mouth tightened. If she was going to be one of those people who hated on my mothers, I would have a thing or two to tell her.

She shrugged, turned back to warn the still-arguing teens that they had exactly three seconds before she would abandon them to the airport staff, and said simply, "It takes all kinds."

"It certainly does. Good luck with your trip," I said politely, and gathering up my things, I moved off before she could say anything more. The experience had left me feeling a bit prickly, which in turn made the inevitable delays at the security lines all that much more annoying. But a memory of my mothers' teaching about tolerance got me through it without once wishing I could remember the spell to give people ingrown toenails.

I had just settled down in the waiting area with all the other people who would be on the flight to Orlando (my connecting flights to Chicago, and then Denver would extend the trip by another seven hours) and pulled out my tablet computer to see if there was any news in the alchemists' forum, which I frequent, when my cell phone buzzed in my jacket pocket.

The number displayed on the phone didn't ring a bell. I ignored the call, figuring it was just another solicitation to try some service or buy something that I didn't want, so when the phone buzzed a second time, I started to turn it off.

Mom Two, the text said above the photo of a face almost as familiar as my own. I frowned. I'd had somewhat hurried good-byes earlier with both my moms, hurried because of some bizarre notion they had that I was in danger and the sooner I got out of Wales, the safer I'd be.

"Hi. What's up?" I asked, answering the call. "You can't be missing me already, Mom Two. I left you guys less than . . . what . . . four hours ago?"

"Of course we miss you, Gwen. We always miss you when you leave. But that's not what I wanted to say, although I do, in fact, miss you despite having seen you earlier this afternoon before you went to the airport. Your mother misses you as well, although just at the moment she's a bit busy with Mrs. Vanilla. I just wanted to warn you to keep your eyes peeled for that besom in a cherry red dress."

"Besom?" I tried to dredge through my mental dictionary. Mom Two, aka Alice Hill, my mother's partner for longer than I'd been alive, had once been a headmistress at some posh girls' school and frequently used words that most people didn't recognize. "A woman? Wait, you're not still talking about that woman who you claimed was chasing me at the shrink's office yesterday, are you? Because I thought we worked it out."

"We didn't work it out. We simply decided that since we lost the besom in the mad dash from the psychologist's office—which, really, was a complete waste of time since Dr. Gently couldn't cure you of that wild notion you have that you died and went to heaven and came back to earth—we decided that we'd just stop talking about it, which would placate you. Your mother felt strongly that your last day with us should be a happy one. It was a happy one, wasn't it?"

"Very happy," I said, my brain a bit of a whirl with the conversation. Mom Two, when she really got going on a subject, could talk circles around you to the point where you didn't know which of the many conversational tidbits to follow. I decided to go with the most obvious one. "And I'm not crazy. I did die. I did wake up to find myself in Anwyn, which incidentally isn't heaven. It's just an afterlife, like the ones you Wiccans go to when you die."

"Nothing is like Summerland," Mom Two said complacently, then evidently clapped a hand over the bottom of her phone for a few seconds, if the muffled voice was anything to go by. "Not even the Welsh version of the afterlife. Especially since your mother tells me that there are all sorts of legends tied up with Anwyn. But we will discuss that another day. I must dash, Gwen. Your mother sends her love. Mrs. Vanilla would most likely send her regards as well, but she doesn't speak. We just wished to remind you to be on guard. Do not talk to any women with short dark hair and red wool suits! Shun them, Gwen. Shun them with all the power of your shunningness!"

Mom Two was also prone to making up words where they didn't exist. "Who's Mrs. Vanilla?" I asked, a faint sense of unease tingeing my amusement with the conversation. I adored both of my mothers, even though they were sometimes scatty when it came to focusing on the here and now, but as a rule, Mom Two was the more reliable when it came to making sense out of confusion.

"She's our student."

"Wait . . . I thought you guys were taking the entire summer off from classes so that you could focus on renewing your bond to the craft." Wiccans varied widely in their beliefs, but most found it necessary periodically to recharge their spiritual batteries through some communing with nature, study, and bonding with fellow Wiccans.

"The Lambfreckle School for Womyn's Magyck is closed until the Autumnal Equinox," Mom Two said primly.

I winced at the name of their school, just as I did every time I heard it. "One of these days J. K. Rowling is going to hear about you—"

"There is nothing wrong with the name of our school!" Mom Two protested, then put her hand over the phone again. "I must go, Gwen. Have a safe journey, and blessings go with you. Stay away from red-suited women!"

The phone clicked and slowly I lowered it from my ear, wondering why I had a growing sense of unease. Why did they have a student with them if they had closed the school for the summer? Why didn't my mother get on the phone to say good-bye one last time? It wasn't like her to at least not yell something while Mom Two was talking to me. And was some woman really following me, as they said? If so, why? The moms had never given me an answer to that question. I had a faint idea that perhaps this mysterious woman might be an attempt by them to distract me from something that they didn't want me to know.

I started to put my phone away, shook my head at my fancies, and despite that, typed out a message for my mother. *Who is Mrs. Vanilla?*

Who, dear? came the answering text.

Mrs. Vanilla. Mom Two says you have a student with you named Mrs. Vanilla.

Yes. She is our student. Don't worry. She wanted to come with us.

"Oh, like that's not going to make me worried as hell," I muttered as soon as the text appeared on my phone's screen. I thought briefly of calling my mother, but I had a nasty suspicion she would not answer the phone. She tended to shy away from confrontation if she could help it, leaving Mom Two to do the dirty work.

Where are you? Why would I worry about you having a student? What is going on?

There may be a bit of a fuss, but don't pay it any mind, my mother texted back. Fear started to grow in the pit of my stomach. What the hell were they up to now? *Disregard any mention of kidnapping. She wanted us to save her. It was the only thing we could do.*

And that pushed me over the edge. I dialed my mother's cell number, sure that she wasn't going to answer, and was more than a little surprised when her breathless voice said almost immediately, "Gwenny, I just told you not to worry, didn't I? And now here you are worrying. Don't deny it. I can tell you are. Turn right, dear. No, the other right!"

I looked wildly to my right (and left, because long acquaintance with my mother had taught me that she had difficulty telling directions). "What? Why should I turn right?"

"Not you, dear. That was for Alice. Oh, my. No, no, dear, don't get onto the main roads. Don't you remember that show on the telly we saw last month?" Her voice dropped to a whisper. "They have those spiked things they lay in the road."

Spiked things? What spiked things? What was she—? With a horrible presentiment, I suddenly knew. They were on the run from the police.

"What the hell is going on?" I asked, my voice rising loudly at the end of the sentence, enough that everyone around me stared. I turned in my plastic seat so that I half faced the wall behind me, dipping my head down so I could speak sternly, but more quietly, into my phone. "Mother, are you, at this moment, running from the police?"

"Alice, dear, not so fast around corners," my mother said in a near shriek. "Poor Mrs. Vanilla is on the floor."

"MOTHER!"

"Oh, hello, Gwenny. How was your flight home?"

I took a deep breath, but it didn't go any way toward calming what were quickly becoming frazzled nerves, so I took five or six additional breaths.

"Are you hyperventilating?" the man nearest me asked,

lowering his newspaper to look at me in obvious concern. "Do you want a paper bag?"

"No, thank you, it's just my mother driving me crazy as usual," I said through gritted teeth, and swiveled around even farther in my chair until I was almost off it entirely.

"Mother," I said in a low, mean tone of voice that under normal circumstances I would never think of using to her. "What. Is. Happening?"

"Lost 'em!" a triumphant Mom Two said in the background. I slumped sideways in despair, and promptly fell off the chair. By the time I reassured the newspaper man that I was fine, and not in danger of passing out, my mother had hung up her phone.

I moved over to the corner of the waiting area, found a relatively empty spot, and facing away from the room, called her back. "Tell me you didn't kidnap some old woman and are not at this very moment running from the mortal police."

"We did not kidnap some old woman and are not at this very moment running from the mortal police," she said promptly.

I waited for the count of three. "Is that true?"

"No, of course it isn't. But you asked me to say it, so I did."

Gently, so as not to brain myself, I thumped my forehead against the wall. "Mom, you do remember that it was only six months ago that I was arrested by the Watch because they thought I was you, don't you?"

"Yes, but they let you out because you aren't me."

"They let me out because I had an alibi. They still think I'm you, or at least that blond Watch guy does." The memory of him had haunted me at odd moments during the last two days.

"What blond Watch man?"

"The one who stopped the lawyer from killing me." Anticipating her next question, I added, "The one you agreed to sell magic to, remember?"

"Of course I remember the lawyer," she said in a scolding voice. Faintly, oh so faintly, I heard the sound of a police siren coming from my phone. I slumped against the cool wall, closing my eyes for a moment. "He wasn't a very nice man, but we needed the money, and it's been decades since anyone from the Watch was interested in us."

"Centuries," Mom Two said loudly. "Eighteen-something. Seventies, was it, Mags?"

I was so close to going home. Even now, I could see the plane being serviced by various technical people. In just an hour or two, it would be in the sky, heading toward the States. I could be on that plane.

"No, it had to be longer than that," Mom argued. "Because they tried to make me sit for one of those sepia-toned photographs, but I kept moving just enough that it turned out blurry. It had to be the 1820s."

I had the ticket right there. I could be on that plane, leaving my troubles behind me.

"They didn't have cameras in the 1820s," Mom Two told her, and behind their voices, the sirens grew louder.

Life would be sane again. No more would I find myself being killed, in the afterlife, or suddenly (and inexplicably) resurrected.

"Daguerreotype! I think that's the name for it. Gwen, do you remember if that's what they did?"

I eyed my phone. Just the touch of one finger on its screen, and I could hang up. My mother probably wouldn't even notice I'd done so for at least several minutes. Then, carefree, I could blithely go on with my life, leaving my mothers to cope with whatever they'd done with theirs.

I turned around so the wall was to my back and slid down it until I was sitting on the floor, my forehead resting on my knees. I couldn't leave them. Not if they had gotten into yet another tight place. There wasn't even any pretense I could make about having a choice. They were my mothers, and I loved them. They had a knack for getting into trouble and a disregard for pretty much all forms of common sense, but I loved them, and I couldn't leave them. Not this way. Not when the Watch so clearly had us in their sights.

"Sooner or later they're going to follow me to you, and put two and two together," I told my mother.

"I don't think daguerreotypes came out around until the 1840s— What was that, Gwenny?"

"The Watch. They may be confused about our identities now, but they're not stupid. At least the blond guy isn't. I told him I wasn't you, and he believed me. They're going to find you, and then they'll put you in jail."

"But, dear, we haven't done anything wrong!"

"You were selling magic to a mortal! That's *so* incredibly illegal!"

"But we didn't actually sell anything to that man. Or to the lawyer. We just said we would."

"And took the money to do so." I made sure to mention that. It was one of the points that rankled so greatly with me.

"Well, of course we took the money. We needed it."

"The fact remains that you were poised to engage in illegal activities, but I stopped you from actually doing so. And got killed in the process."

"She's going on again about being killed. I do wish she could have had more time with the counselor," she said to Mom Two before addressing me again. "Gwen, dearest, I am your mother. I think I'd know if my only child was killed."

I thought seriously about rolling my eyes at both the statement and the chiding note in her voice. "The point is that you were about to do something very illegal, and the Watch knew that. They sent someone to catch you in the act. The only reason they didn't is because I went down to tell the lawyer who arranged for the sale to stop threatening you with all sorts of horrible things if you didn't honor your contract with him. A wholly illegal contract, I'd like to point out."

"He's a lawyer, Gwen. I'm sure it was illegal."

"Where are you?" I changed the subject, knowing the argument was going to go nowhere. We'd had it several times during the last few days, and it always ended up the same way: my mothers refused to admit that they'd done anything wrong. "The siren sounds louder. Can you pull over and cast a spell to escape the mortal police?"

"Of course we can cast an escape spell. Any third-year pupil of Lambfreckle can cast a basic escape spell, and your other mother and I are more than two hundred years old, so we certainly know—"

"Mom," I interrupted. "You know what I mean."

"I do, and much as I love you, Gwenny, I'm insulted that you think we can't take care of ourselves and get away from mortals. Oh, dear, Alice, Mrs. Vanilla is on the floor again. Perhaps if you pulled over I could right her—"

I stood up, and without even one poignant glance at the plane that was being fueled so that it could fly me back home, collected my luggage and started the long journey back to the train station that connected to the airport. "Where are you?" I asked as I wove my way through the people who milled around the shops and the airline kiosks.

"Outside of Emylwn," she answered, naming the small coastal town where they had lived since before I was born.

I thought for a few minutes while I continued to forge my way against the stream of people arriving for evening flights to the Continent, then said, "They are going to know you're in that area."

"Pah. I told you that we can escape the police."

"No, not them. I'm not worried about the mortals. The Watch found me in Malwod-Upon-Ooze, and that's only, what, ten miles away from Emylwn?" I shook my head. "That's too close for comfort."

I glanced up at the sign at the entrance to the airport, and made a swift decision while my mother was protesting that the Watch didn't even have an inkling of what was going on.

"The mortal police don't know that the Otherworld Watch

even exists, Gwenny. There's no reason to worry that they'll call them. Besides, they—the mortal police, that is—have no idea who we are. Or rather, what we are."

Evidently, Mom had put me on speakerphone, because I could hear Mom Two say, "That's right. Mrs. Vanilla was in a mortal retirement home when we snatched her."

"Snatched?" I said, freezing in the act of going through a door to the escalator that led down to the trains.

"Rescued," my mother amended. "We rescued her. We didn't kidnap her at all."

"Then why are the police chasing you?" I hefted my massive bag and bumped my way down the escalator, apologizing to the people it smacked. One or two people looked askance at me as I descended, but I sent up a silent blessing for stoic Brits who wouldn't be caught dead blatantly listening to someone's phone conversation.

"There was a little issue with the rescue," Mom Two admitted in her usual brusque voice. "We had to change one or two attendants into frogs."

"MOMS!"

"Just temporarily," my mother hurriedly added. "Just for the time it took to rescue Mrs. Vanilla from her captors."

I shoved some coins into a machine and accepted the ticket it spat out at me, hauling my luggage down another level to the train I wanted. "Do you have any idea of how bad this is? Not only have you kidnapped a mortal woman—yes, I said 'kidnapped'!" I ignored the sputtered protests from both mothers. "Not only did you do something as completely heinous as to take an old lady from her caregivers, but you also magicked up mortals. You know how dangerous that is! What were you thinking? That no one would notice that people had suddenly been turned into frogs?"

"No one did notice that," Mom Two said in a disapproving tone. "Your mother told you it was a temporary spell. Only lasted two or three minutes."

"Then why"—I parked my luggage at a grimy bench and took a deep, acidic-scented breath—"why are the police chasing you? Why didn't you just go home?"

"We might have forgotten that mortals have those spy cameras everywhere," my mother admitted.

"Big Brother!" Mom Two added righteously. "He's everywhere, watching us all!"

I rubbed my hand over my face, wondering how on earth I was going to pull my mothers out of the hole into which they'd managed to dig themselves. It was possible, just barely possible, that they could magic their way out of trouble with the mortal police, if the thing was planned properly. But once the Watch got wind of it . . . I groaned aloud. "We are so doomed. They're already in the area. The blond guy is looking for you. They'll hear that you stole a mortal and used magic in front of other mortals, and that'll be all she wrote."

"Who wrote what?" Mom asked with benign interest.

"We have to meet up," I said quickly, glancing down the platform and noting at least three security cameras. Even now I was being filmed. I had to get somewhere out of sight of those cameras, had to get my mothers tucked away someplace where we could talk. I needed all the details of their latest shenanigans before I could put things right. But where could we meet? Where could we find the anonymity we needed?

A dirt-encrusted woman shuffled past me to the nearest trash can, digging through it and muttering to herself under her breath. Her coat was matted and filthy, having long ago given up any pretense at color. She extracted several pieces of trash and shoved them deep into a plastic carrier bag clutched in one of her grubby hands. A piece of paper fluttered out of her bag as she moved off.

I stared at the leaflet advertising a tourist event, then sat up straighter. "Mom, go to Bute."

"Go where, dear?"

"Bute Park."

"But it's nighttime. One should never go to the park at

night. I've warned you about the bad people who can be found there after dark."

"They're doing illuminations of the castle this week. All week, while they celebrate the history of Cardiff. There will be fireworks, and music, and hordes of people. It's the perfect place to hide in plain sight. I'll meet you at the Animal Wall in"—I glanced at my watch and did some quick mental calculations—"forty minutes. OK?"

"I don't think we—"

"Meet me there," I said in a growl that should have scared the pants off her. A whoosh of air from the arched tunnel at the end of the platform warned of the near arrival of a train. "Or else."

"Or else what?" she asked, clearly curious.

"Or else I'll invoke some very bad magic!"

"Oh, Gwenny," she said with a dismissive laugh, "you couldn't do bad magic if you had a spell book in front of you."

"Try me," I snarled, and hung up my phone.

I had a lot of things to do, and little time to do them.

TWO

"Hello, my old friend."

The stone Animal Wall is one of my favorite places in Cardiff city proper. I was just a child when it was first carved, and I have vague memories of being taken to see the original painted animals. Sometime in the early 1920s, about thirty years after it was placed outside of Cardiff Castle, it was moved to the edge of Bute Park, where it still resides.

"You're looking as placid as usual," I told my favorite animal where he sat atop the wall, the stone images illuminated by the floodlights planted along the base of the wall. Directly in front of me, a stone seal gazed serenely into the distance, his flippers poised as if he were about to leap off the wall. "You know, Mr. Seal, I used to think that a spell would turn you to flesh and blood, and I'd beg my moms to give it to me so that you could slip out into the bay and swim away. They never did."

The statue said nothing, for which I was extremely thankful—the last thing I needed was an animated statue, or a nervous breakdown. Although at times, I was ready to swear that the latter had some good points to it . . .

Around me, music sounded from a stage across the park, where a local Welsh band was entertaining folks who were out enjoying the history festival.

The air was filled with scents as well as sounds: the cooling of the sun-warmed lawn had a pleasant earthy note that mingled nicely with the salty tang wafting in from the bay. A more artificial, but no less pleasing, aroma came from the food stalls that had been set up for the festival, selling everything from Indian food to fish cakes to Welsh beef burgers. I salivated, my stomach rumbling uncomfortably while I contemplated enduring the crowds to feed my soon-to-be-uncontrollable hunger.

Common sense prevailed. I would never find my mothers in the throngs of people who queued up in front of the food area. Blue and red and gold lights lit Cardiff Castle beyond the Animal Wall, but I turned my gaze from its familiar ramparts to the crowd that moved like so many fireflies in a random pattern around the park. Fake torches lined pathways, while vendors in small pushcarts sold the inevitable glow sticks, bracelets, and necklaces. Soft neon glows of green, blue, and orange lit up faces old and young, but I ignored them to try to pick out the familiar shapes of my mothers: Mom, short and somewhat round (unfortunately, I inherited her propensity to abundance, although not her lack of height), and Mom Two, as tall and angular as Mom was the opposite.

I glanced at my watch, tilting it to catch illumination from a nearby faux torch. The fireworks would start in about fifteen minutes. "I swear, if I have to come and find you—" I started to grumble under my breath, pulling out my phone to call one of my mothers, but at that moment my peripheral vision caught the flicker of a familiar form.

"Mom!" I raised my hand and moved toward the three shapes. "It's about time. I've been waiting for almost fifteen minutes. Hello."

The last was spoken to the tiny old lady that both moms held in a firm grip.

"Gwenny, dear, we're late, aren't we? We had to stop for a wee. You know how your mother is."

Mom Two made a grimace. "Pessary, you know. Makes me have to go sometimes. Must have shifted. Will have to have it checked out again."

I wrinkled my nose. "Yeah, we don't really need to talk

about your bladder-holder-upper device right out here in the park. Is this Mrs. Vanilla?"

"Yes, it is. Oooh, is that Chicken Korma I smell?"

I grabbed my mother's nearest arm and held on, as she was about to head straight for the food booths. "Yes, it is, and if I have to starve myself, so do you. It's not on our diets."

She sighed, and her shoulders slumped. "I know. But it smells so very delicious, and we've had a very stressful day, what with you returning to the States, and then the rescue of Mrs. Vanilla. Oh, I haven't introduced you. Dear, this is my daughter, Gwenhwyfar. Mrs. Vanilla is our student, as I think I told you."

I eyed the old lady between my mothers, trying to assess how likely she was to lodge a charge against them. If she was as confused as my mother made her sound, perhaps she wouldn't remember anything that happened once she was returned to her nursing home. She was a tiny little thing, smaller even than my five-foot-three mother, but as delicate as a bird. She had narrow little hands that flitted about with graceful darting gestures that reminded me for some reason of shorebirds as they ran up and down the beach looking for food. Her hair was mostly white, cropped short, but there was an unusual black stripe right down the middle. A cowlick in the back made the tip of the stripe stand up on end, giving her a somewhat comical appearance. Her eyes were dark, but clouded with cataracts, and her hands had the faintest tremor to them. A thick greenish-black dressing gown covered her from neck to ankles, embroidered with what looked to be fanciful creatures from mythology. All in all, she looked like a perfectly nice little old lady.

I sighed, shaking my head at my moms, noting that a short distance away a family that was in possession of a bench had gathered up the remains of their dinner and moved off to a trash can. I steered my mothers' captive over to the bench and turned to give both mothers the eye. "You two know you've gone way over the line this time, yes?"

Mom startled to bristle, while Mom Two looked haughtily down her long nose at me. "We have a duty to our students, Gwen," the latter told me. "Not to mention a duty to save those who are under the protection of the god and goddess. We couldn't hold up our heads if we were to let Mrs. Vanilla languish away in the mortal old-person prison."

"OK, first, it's a nursing home, not a prison. And second, you are not supposed to steal mortals. Third, and most important of all, you have no right taking this nice old lady from the people who care for her. What if she needs special medicines? Or stuff like adult diapers?" I gave the little old woman a twisted smile. "Sorry. Don't mean to imply you need them. For all I know, your bladder is stronger than my mothers' is."

"It's not," Mom said with a wry look. "We thought of that, naturally, Gwenny. We're not monsters, you know. We brought all of her medicines, and bought her a jumbo pack of bladder pants, as well as a pair of really warm wool socks in case her feet get cold at night like Alice's do."

"Always had poor circulation," Mom Two said with a nod. "Got that from my father. He was a mage. Mages are notorious for their cold feet."

"Regardless," I said, attempting to keep the conversation from wandering, which I knew full well it would do if I didn't keep the strictest control over it. "The fact remains that you stole a mortal woman. You can't keep her, Moms. You have to take her back."

"We will naturally take the very best care of her—" Mom Two started to say, but I cut her off with a sharp gesture. Mrs. Vanilla made little eeping noises of distress, her hands fluttering like the wings of tiny doves.

"She is not a pet! She's a person, a mortal, an innocent woman who needs the care of the people who are paid to take care of her."

"Pah," Mom Two said, while my mother added, "*We* don't want money to take care of her. We will do it because she is our student, and is in need of help, and the god and goddess have charged us to take care of others whenever possible."

I took a deep breath. "I know full well what the Wiccan creed is, so don't try to blow smoke up my ass."

"Gwen!" my mother said, waving a hand at the old woman. "Not in front of Mrs. Vanilla!"

I glanced at her. She had stopped squeaking, but her hands were still flittering a few inches off her lap, almost as if she was trying to use sign language. "Sorry, ma'am. Mother, might I have a word with you?"

"What do you need?" Mom Two asked the old lady, bending over her to bellow. "Do you need to use the toilet again? No? Paper? You want paper?"

"Gwenny, I think you're being very close-minded about this whole thing—" my mother started to say when I pulled her a few yards away.

Mom Two was digging through the messenger bag she always had strapped across her torso, pulling out a tattered notebook with pen attached by means of a grubby bit of string. She gave that to Mrs. Vanilla.

"I am through explaining why you can't kidnap a mortal and keep her. What I need from you and Mom Two is your plan on how to return her. She doesn't look like the sort of woman who remembers much, so we'll have to trust that once you get her back to where she belongs, she won't file a charge with the police. But the fact remains that she has to go back."

"We can't take her back," Mom Two said, moving over to stand with us. The old lady was busily drawing on the notebook, which I gathered was her thing to do in spare moments.

"If you're worried about that video of you and Mom taking Mrs. Vanilla, then you could throw a glamour or something on yourselves so the mortals wouldn't recognize it was you bringing her back."

She raised one eyebrow. "I'm surprised to hear you suggest that we should do something so illegal as to use magic to fool a mortal being, Gwen."

"Balanced against abduction? Yeah, not such a big worry, especially when it's done in order to return the old biddy."

My mother whapped me on the arm. "It's not nice to refer to the elderly by that term."

"Kidnapping isn't nice, either." I took a deep breath, wondering if I'd be able to change my ticket for one the following day, and said, "OK, here's the deal: you guys clearly don't want to take her back. Yes, I know, you rescued her. That's not the point. She has to go back to her home, and since you won't take her, I will. Keys." I held out my hand.

Mom Two looked mulish for a moment, but dug into her pocket and pulled out a set of car keys. "I do this under protest, Gwen."

"Duly recorded. Where'd you leave the car?"

She described the parking lot where she had taken the car after dropping off Mom and Mrs. Vanilla at the entrance to the park.

"All righty. I'll bring the car around to the disabled people's entrance and will meet you there to pick her up. Once I have her back at her place, I'll come back here for you two. We'll have to stop by the train station for the luggage I left there, but that shouldn't take long."

"And then?" Mom asked, sniffing like I'd said something mean to her.

"And then we'll find somewhere safe to park both of you while the dust settles."

"Where, exactly, would that be? We can't go home, not with the mortal police seeing us. And don't say that we should wear a glamour for however many months or years it will take the police to forget about us." Mom Two gestured toward my mother. "Mags dislikes glamours. She couldn't tolerate one for longer than a few hours."

I slapped my hands on my legs, frustrated but aware that I owed them some sort of an answer. "Well . . . maybe you could go away. Go to the U.S. with me?"

"We don't have passports. The authorities want passports

nowadays. You remember the trouble we had getting you one?"

"Yes, well, the people at the passport office just don't expect to see people born in 1888 needing a passport. Besides, we ended up getting me a fake one. We could just do the same for you two."

"And where are we to stay until that is ready? It took you four months to get one made that would pass scrutiny by mortal security personages," Mom Two said.

She had me there. I racked my brain for somewhere that they could lie low, somewhere they would be safe from all contact with the mortal world. "Well . . . I don't know exactly." I bit my lip and tried to think of all the places I'd ever been. I said, with an ironic little laugh that was to come back and haunt me later, "What we need is a place like Anwyn. You could stay there and the mortals couldn't touch you. I don't think that even the Watch has jurisdiction there. It would be ideal, except, of course, that you'd have to be dead to go there."

"Don't be ridiculous," Mom snorted, giving Mrs. Vanilla's arm a reassuring pat when the old lady started squeaking and drawing sharp little lines on her tablet of paper. "We wouldn't go to Anwyn. It's a Welsh afterlife."

"Mom, you *are* Welsh, just like me."

"I'm also a Wiccan, and since your other mother wouldn't be eligible to rest in Anwyn, not being Welsh by birth, I certainly wouldn't go there without her. When our time comes to depart for the next stage of our lives, we shall go to Summerland."

I eyed her, thinking hard. "Can you . . . this is crazy, I know, but needs must and all that . . . can you get into Summerland without being dead?"

"Of course," she said, murmuring softly to Mrs. Vanilla. "So long as you know where the entrance is, you can enter its domain. Mind, you can't stay without permission of the lord and lady, but assuming you have that, it's an easy thing to do."

"Then that's our answer!" I said, feeling as if a great weight had been torn from my shoulders. "You and Mom Two can go to Summerland. You'll like it there, I'm sure, and I can't imagine why the lord and lady wouldn't let you stay there. You're both super Wiccans."

"They might grant us permission, but we could never do that," Mom Two said, and my mother nodded her agreement.

"Why not?"

"Have you not listened to any of our teachings? Summerland is a place of great importance, Gwen. It is a holy place, if you will, one sacred to us. We do not tread on its green fields and fertile pastures unless we have been sent there."

"But—"

"No," Mom Two said firmly, giving me a sharp nod that let me know she was done discussing the subject. "We will not go."

"Well, hell!" I said, doing some more of that hand-thigh-slapping thing that no doubt looked juvenile but did so much to release unpleasant emotions. "You can't go to Anwyn, you won't go to Summerland. . . . Where else can you go that would put you out of reach of both the mortal and immortal worlds?"

"We could go to Anwyn if we wanted," Mom said complacently, glancing in surprise at Mrs. Vanilla when she began to squeak again, shoving the notebook toward me. "What is it you want Gwenny to see, dear? Your lovely drawing?"

"Mom, you just got done saying you couldn't go to Anwyn because Mom Two isn't Welsh—"

"That has nothing to do with it," Mom Two interrupted, leaning forward to see the paper. "We could get in if we wanted."

"But you were born in Scotland."

"Location of birth has nothing to do with whether or not Arwyn will allow you to stay in Anwyn."

"Who's Arwyn?"

"The king of Anwyn, of course. That's very interesting, Mrs. Vanilla."

My mind was a whirl of frustration and worry. "So, you're

saying that if we found the entrance to Anwyn, you would go there?"

Mom Two looked thoughtful for a moment or two, then raised her eyebrows at my mother. "I would have no objection to visiting there, assuming we would be left to our own devices. Mags?"

"Well, I wouldn't want to spend much time there, but I suppose it wouldn't hurt us to drop in and see it. I have one or two friends who might still be there, and it's always pleasant to renew old friendships."

I got all hopeful for about five seconds, then remembered the snag. "We don't know where the entrance to Anwyn is. Unless one of you knows how to find it?"

"No, but—"

I mused aloud, worrying the problem like a terrier with a chew toy. "I didn't see a door or anything when I was there and, of course, I died to get there, so it's not like I just walked through an entrance. Damn. It was such a good idea, too."

"Gwenny, you did not die—" my mother started to say at the same time Mom Two said, "I think you should look at Mrs. Vanilla's drawing."

The first of the fireworks went off, dragging my attention from the offered bit of paper to the sky, then down to my watch. We were fast running out of time. The longer it took me to get the old lady back to her home, the harder it would be for me to explain how I'd found her.

"Later. I've got to get moving right now. Stay here, and don't get into trouble," I said, grabbing my purse in preparation for heading off to the car park. "I'll meet you in about ten minutes at the entrance."

Mom Two straightened up to her full height (about an inch taller than me) and said with injured dignity, "We are not children, Gwenhwyfar. You do not need to speak to us as if we are. Mags, I believe that in view of the evening's events, we deserve to treat ourselves to an ice cream. You stay here with Mrs. Vanilla, and I'll fetch us all a cone."

I bit back the urge to tell them that I would treat them like adults when they stopped indulging in the harebrained (and illegal) plans that threatened to get them banished to the Akasha, or worse, but as I turned around and took a step, I bumped into a large body that had his back to me.

"Whoops. Sorry." I started to apologize to the man, but stopped when he turned to face me. "Oh, it's . . . uh . . ."

"You!" he said, a smile spreading over his face, going so far as to touch his eyes. Which, as I remembered, were a remarkably clear shade of topaz blue. "Gwen Byron, right? What a surprise meeting you here. A pleasant surprise."

I stared at him for a few seconds. He was the man I'd met two days before, the one who had wrestled to the ground— and later arrested—the lawyer who had threatened my mother and, incidentally, tried to throw me over the edge of a cliff to certain death. My mind, annoyingly, went blank at the partial use of my name, but luckily, before I corrected him, I remembered that in my attempt to hide my relationship with my mom, I had given him only my first and middle names.

"Uh . . ." I felt utterly and completely stupid standing there staring at him. I didn't know his name, but the one thing I knew for certain now filled me with a spike of pure, adrenaline-fueled fear: he was with the Watch, and my mother was not ten feet behind me, chatting pleasantly to her kidnap victim.

Without thinking of the wisdom of my act, I grabbed his arm and walked past him, forcing him to turn so that his back was to Mom. "Hi!" I tried to think of something to say that wasn't a shriek of fear, but my brain didn't appear to be up to the task of witty banter in the face of danger. "I . . . I don't think I ever got your name."

"Gregory Faa." He made a bow, an old-fashioned move that was simply elegant on him. But that was no surprise; everything about him was elegant, from the dark blond hair that swept back off his forehead to his mobile, sensitive mouth and firm chin, right down to the sapphire blue raw-silk shirt and what had to be Italian shoes. He had said something at our only previous meeting about being born in Romania, which went a long way to explain the polished manners. "I had no idea you were still in the area. But then, I had no idea why you ran away from me so quickly the other day."

I gave him what I hoped was a placid smile, but which I fear turned out to be more of a grimace, and endeavored not to look over his shoulder at the bench where my mother and Mrs. Vanilla sat. Watch members were notoriously sharp and intelligent, and I was certain that he would notice if I kept looking over his shoulder at the bench.

"I was . . . um . . ."

I focused instead on his chin, but that just filled my mind with wholly inappropriate thoughts about biting it, so instead I stared at his left earlobe. An earlobe would be safe to look at. "I was . . . er . . ."

He wore a sapphire stud earring. It glittered darkly in the torchlight, contrasting pleasantly with the hair that curled around the back of his ear. I had the worst urge to run my fingers through his hair, wondering if it was as silky as it looked. I shifted my gaze to his cheek. The faintest hint of golden stubble was visible in the warm light of the torch. "I was . . . erm . . ."

Dammit! What was wrong with me? I was no stranger to the attraction of a handsome man, but neither was I a giddy young thing who couldn't talk to a good-looking man without wanting to bite his chin and run my hands through his hair and lick his mobile lips.

"Were you, now?" he asked with a little laugh that made the lines around his eyes crinkle up in a way that made my stomach go warm and happy.

"Sorry. I'm an idiot," I finally said, my brain evidently deciding that I'd had enough time to make a fool out of myself. "Nice to meet you, Gregory. Or do you prefer Greg? Or . . . Rory? That sounds kind of like a long shot, nickname-wise, but sometimes people go that way."

I was babbling, pure and simple, and for that I blamed him. If he didn't look so very . . . golden . . . in the torchlight, I could have concentrated and behaved in the manner of a normal human being. In desperation, I dragged my gaze away from the stubble that made my fingertips tingle with the need to touch it.

"'Gregory' is fine. Only my cousin Peter calls me Greg, and usually then it's to tease me."

A question rose in my mind, and I'll be damned if it didn't just pop out of my mouth even though this man, this golden, crinkly-eyed man, was about the most dangerous person I could ever come up against. "Why would calling you Greg be considered teasing?"

"It's the way he says it," he answered, smiling again. "He's around here somewhere with his wife. Perhaps I might introduce you to them."

Great. Just what I needed—a member of the Watch and his family. A little shudder went through me at the thought of what would happen if Gregory-not-Greg were to turn around and see my mother, the very woman he had been sent out to arrest two days before.

"Sounds lovely," I lied, and taking his arm, I tugged him in the direction opposite Mom.

A look of surprise flitted across his face for a moment, but he walked next to me docilely enough.

"Are you here for the fireworks?"

"Fireworks?" I asked stupidly, my mind busy wondering how far I could drag him away from the bench before I re-leased him and called my mother to warn her of his presence.

He pointed upward. I looked. A burst of red and silver and green exploded overhead.

"Oh, those. Yeah. We always come to the park for the big festival."

"'We'?"

He stopped.

Panic hit me. I moved forward, urging him along with me,

needing to put as much space between him and my mother as was humanly possible. "Me. Not we. I meant to say 'me.'"

"Me always come to the park for the big festival?"

"Ha ha ha ha ha!" The braying laughter was of a quality that was well over the border of merry and smack-dab in the middle of deranged, but honestly, my brain refused to come up with any sort of an explanation, feeling that laughing it off was the way to go. My brain was wrong. "No, of course I meant to say that *I* always come to the park."

The look he gave me was no longer one filled with amusement, and that, for some bizarre reason I didn't even want to examine, made me sad. "I see. Would you think me boorish if I were to inquire where you're taking me?"

"Taking you? I'm not taking you anywhere," I said, pulling on his arm when he tried to stop again. "We're just out for a little stroll to see the fireworks. Oh! Unless you're here with someone. Someone female? Or . . . er . . . male?"

He gave me an odd look. "You're the second attractive woman in two months who's hinted that I'm gay. Do I give off some sort of homosexual vibe of which I'm unaware?"

"No! Far from it! That stubble is really . . ." I coughed and sternly reminded myself that he was the Enemy and I needed to stop thinking of him as a sexy, sexy man. "I don't like to assume. People's sexuality is their own business, and I'd hate to presume."

"I appreciate such thoughtfulness, but in my case it's unnecessary. I assure you that I am as heterosexual as they come. Risqué pun not intended."

We reached the far edge of the open park area, and I judged that we were about as distant from my mothers and Mrs. Vanilla as we could get without actually pushing him off the park grounds altogether. I dropped his arm and gave him a bright smile. "Nice to know that! Well, it's been super fun, but I really have to get moving. I've got a plane to catch."

"A plane?" He looked moderately interested.

"Yes. I'm returning home to Colorado." I didn't want to

have to lie outright to him again—I'd already done so once, and many members of the Watch had very finely tuned mental lie detectors. In addition, my mothers had taught me that every lie was returned threefold, so I didn't say any more than that I was returning home. That, at least, was true enough. "I'll let you get back to your girlfriend. Or wife. Or significant whatever. Thanks for the walk!"

"You're welcome, but I feel obligated to point out that the fireworks display is still going on, and the only people I'm here with are my cousin and his wife. They are newly married and probably are enjoying my absence more than they would my presence, so if you'd care to drag me back toward that wall with the stone animals, I'd be happy to oblige."

"Ha ha ha ha!" I did the hysterical laughter again, looking around quickly for the nearest means of escape. Damn him for noticing where I had bumped into him! One thing was certain: I couldn't let him go back there. I ignored the odd look he was giving me and said quickly, "I *hate* that wall. It gives me the willies every time I'm near it. You couldn't *pay* me to go back there."

"Do you know," he said slowly in a near drawl, "I get the oddest feeling that you don't wish for me to see the Animal Wall. Which is a very odd thing, for which I have very few explanations. And yet, the sensation is there. It leads me inevitably to the question of why you have so carefully hustled me across the width of the park."

I stared at him in abject horror for the count of seven, then spat out, "I have to run!" And I did. I turned on my heel and ran like the hounds of Anwyn were after me, weaving in and out among people, hurdling small children, and dashing past booths and tents to the parking areas beyond the edge of the park. I ran until I had a stitch in my side, whereupon I slowed down to a jog until I spotted my mothers' car. I stopped next to it, gasping for air, searching the lit streets behind me for signs of pursuit. There were none, thank the gods, but that didn't mean anything. Hurriedly, I dialed Mom Two's phone number.

"Where are you?" I gasped in between panting breaths.

"At the entrance. I thought you'd be here by now. Mrs. Vanilla has something to show you."

"The Watch is there." I unlocked the car and got in, starting it up as I continued. "He's blond, about six one, and is wearing a sapphire blue silk shirt and black pants. Fancy shoes. Little cleft in his chin. Golden stubble. Earring. Hair slightly curly in the back and crinkles around his eyes. If you see him, get the hell away and call me. I'll be there in about two minutes, traffic willing."

I pulled out into the traffic, my fingers tight on the steering wheel. How on earth could the man see through me so easily? What if he found the moms? How was I to get them off of a kidnapping charge? The people at the L'au-dela had been very specific when they arrested me, believing I was my mother—they'd said one more crime, one more incident of straying from the path of righteousness, no matter how small, and they'd toss my mother into the Akasha, where she'd stay for all eternity.

"That was an unusually detailed description, Gwen," Mom Two said thoughtfully. "What is this golden man's name?"

I turned onto the road leading to the park drop-off zone. "Gregory Faa. Don't call him Greg."

"Why not?"

"He doesn't like it. I'm almost there. Stay safe."

The three of them were waiting for me when I pulled up a minute later. I was nervous as hell as the moms assisted Mrs. Vanilla into the backseat of the car. I scanned the people around the entrance until everyone was strapped in.

"Right," I said, jerking the wheel and slamming my foot on the accelerator. "Now we take you to Summerland."

"What?" My mother shrieked a little at the way I took the corner and clutched madly at the back of the driver's seat. "Dear, you almost knocked Mrs. Vanilla to the floor, and she's already been down there when your other mother was driving."

"Told you to strap her in," Mom Two, who was riding shotgun, said complacently. "Not my fault if you didn't do that."

"I did strap her in, but she must have unhooked it. No, dear, leave it on." Mom was addressing Mrs. Vanilla, gently patting her hands. "Gwenny is a very . . . intrepid . . . driver, and you'll need to be wearing that for safety's sake. Gwenny, we cannot go to Summerland."

"You don't have a choice now," I said through my teeth, swearing under my breath at the red light. Every ounce of my being urged me to flee the area, to take my mothers and hide them somewhere safe, out of the reach of the handsome Gregory and the organization he worked for. "The Watch is here. They're still looking for you. And that damned man is too smart for my comfort. Why can't you go to Summerland?"

"The man you fancy?" Mom asked.

I shot her a startled look in the rearview mirror. "Huh?"

"Alice said you fancy him. I'm pleased for you, naturally, because you've been alone for a hundred and forty years, and you're not getting any younger."

"I am only a hundred and twenty-four, thank you," I said somewhat acidly. "And I've had boyfriends. Now, about Summerland—"

"Pah." Mom Two said, gesturing away my past. "Emphasis on the 'boy.' Your mother has always said that what you need is a real man, not one of those manosexual flibbertigibbets who walk around with their messenger bags and their manicured hands and such. I believe you can't go wrong with a woman, but that doesn't seem to be something you wish to pursue."

Manosexual? It took me a few seconds to work that one out. "There's nothing wrong with metrosexual men, Mom Two. They tend to like arty movies and visits to Starbucks. And, no, I'm sorry. By now you know I prefer men for romantic relationships."

"Pah," she said again, then returned to the previous subject. "We can't go to Summerland, and that's that."

"You have to go!" I said, pounding the steering wheel when another light turned red. "Dammit, I don't want either or both of you sent to the Akasha! You have to go somewhere to lie low until the Watch gives up trying to find you. I'll take Mrs. Vanilla back right now, and then we're getting you two to safety. They won't keep after you long once she's back. You'll only have to stay there for a few months. Six at the most."

"No," my mother said, and I could see in the mirror that she was shaking her head. Worse, she had that stubborn look on her normally placid face that I knew boded ill for me.

"Then where do you want to go? It has to be somewhere beyond the reach of the Watch."

She gave a little half shrug. "I suppose we could visit Anwyn, as you suggested."

I wanted to bang my head on the steering wheel, but knew that would do no good. Besides, the light had just turned green. "I'd take you there in a heartbeat, but we don't know how to get in."

"Mrs. Vanilla does," Mom Two said.

I shot her a startled look. "She does?"

"Yes. That's what she wanted to show you. Mags, do you have it?"

There was a click as my mother unfastened her seat belt in order to lean forward and wave a piece of paper in front of my nose.

Suddenly blinded, I swore and jerked the car to the side of the road. Luckily, it was empty of parked cars. "Mom!"

"See? Mrs. Vanilla drew a map showing the entrance of Anwyn." Mom sat back and with a smug look snapped her seat belt into place.

I stared at the crumpled piece of paper, willing my heart rate to slow down as I smoothed out the wrinkles. "OK, this is a mistake."

"I doubt if it is, dear."

"No, see, this can't be right. The old biddy—sorry, Mrs. Vanilla, no offense intended—the old lady is a shrimp or two short of a cocktail. She has to be."

Mom Two frowned. "Why would you put a shrimp in a cocktail?"

"That was a reference to a shrimp cocktail. I was trying to be witty. It relieves the feeling that I've gone insane."

"Mags," Mom Two said, her gaze never wavering from my face, "I have changed my mind. A second visit to Dr. Gently may well help our girl."

I shook the paper at her. "I am not the one who needs to see a mental health counselor! I didn't the first time you guys dragged me in to see her, and I sure as shootin' don't now, although all the little gods and goddesses know that I'm entitled to one, given what you're putting me through."

"Gwenhwyfar Byron Owens!"

I looked upward, knowing full well what was coming next.

"You are very well aware how offensive we find it when you say things like that. We raised you to be a proper Wiccan, one who worships the Deity, not a mingle-mangle of assorted gods and demigods." Mom had her sternest face on, the one I had run into quite a bit in my teenage years when I rebelled against their Wiccan beliefs.

I was older and wiser now, however. "I don't think 'mingle-mangle' is technically a word, and don't try to change the subject. We need to be focusing on how to find the entrance to Anwyn, and no"—I held up my hand with the paper in it—"this isn't it. The entrance to heaven isn't in a Krispy Kreme shop."

"Have you ever had their cocoa?" Mom Two asked. "It's pretty close to heaven." With a hurried look over her shoulder at my mother, she added, "If I believed in such a thing, which of course, I don't."

"Anwyn is not in a Krispy Kreme," I said firmly.

"How do you know? Have you been there?" my mother asked.

"No, but—"

"Then I don't think you have the right to say harsh things to Mrs. Vanilla about her lovely map."

"Mom, it just doesn't make sense. She's either kidding, or . . ." I made a circular motion with my finger.

"I don't think she is either. She seems to know where the entrance is. Perhaps she has been there herself."

Mrs. Vanilla made her peculiar squeaking noises and fretted at the seat belt.

I looked up and over to Mom Two, shaking my head as I said, "This is crazy."

Mom Two smiled and patted my hand. "I've always said that crazy is in the mind of the beholder."

"Yes, but we can't indulge in that when so much is at stake."

"Drive," my mother ordered, tapping me on the back of my shoulder. "We'll see when we get there."

"Oh, for the love of all that's shiny and sparkly!" I took a deep breath and pulled out onto the road, mentally plotting the fastest route to Mrs. Vanilla's nursing home. "Fine, we'll go to Krispy Kreme, although the mall is sure to be closed at this time of night. First, however, we're going to take Mrs. Vanilla back where she belongs."

Both mothers opened their respective mouths to protest, but as I stopped at an intersection, waiting to turn onto the road that led to the nursing home, two police cars suddenly zipped across our line of vision.

I swore under my breath and jerked the wheel in the opposite direction, pissing off the car behind me. "Right. Krispy Kreme it is. But when we get there and it's closed and there's no entrance to Anwyn, you guys will owe me a great big apology. And a hot chocolate. With extra whipped cream."

THREE

The fireworks were over, but Gregory Faa felt as if he'd been caught up in some sort of residual whirlwind that left him baffled, intrigued, and with an overwhelming sense that he'd just been duped.

"And I don't like that feeling," he announced after arriving at the spot where his cousin's wife, Kiya, was sitting on a small woolen blanket.

"What feeling?"

"That someone has just pulled the wool over my eyes. A lot of wool. At least three or four sheep's worth. Perhaps a small flock."

Kiya scrunched up her nose, pursed her lips, and looked thoughtful. "That's kind of odd, isn't it? I mean, you're not the easiest person to pull the wool . . . over . . . on. That got mangled. How should I end that sentence?"

"—'on which the wool can be pulled.' At least, that seems a fairly grammatically correct version." Gregory scanned the area, but didn't see his cousin. "Where's Peter?"

"He went to the north gate to watch for the lady you guys are after. I've been stationed here with this"—she showed him the blurry printout from a security camera that showed a short, round woman stuffing a tiny elderly woman into a blue sedan—"and strict instructions that if I see either woman, I'm to call Peter immediately and not attempt to talk to the lady myself."

"I take it you haven't seen anyone?"

"Lots of people, but none who look like this lady." She studied the picture for a moment. "She doesn't look like a kidnapper."

He continued to scan the crowds of people moving to and fro in the night, many of them beginning to drift out of the park now that the fireworks were over. "Finding her would be so much easier if it was daylight. There would be fewer people about, for one."

"Ah, but then your canny kidnappers seldom flee to parks with their victims, since they would be noticeable there. In fact, I think it's downright odd that she came here to begin with. I mean, why? Why would you go to the trouble of kidnapping an old woman out of a nursing home only to take her to the park?" She narrowed her eyes. "Are you sure she really kidnapped the woman?"

"I'm not sure of anything yet. The only thing we know is that a police report came across the radio, and they gave her name as being attached to the car." Static and unintelligible conversation burst out of the small electronic device concealed in his pants pocket. He pulled out the police scanner that all Watch officers used when a case involved someone who wasn't a denizen of the Otherworld, listened for a moment, then shook his head. "The mortal police are still trying to find her car. Thought they had spotted it, but it turned out to be someone else."

"So she's still in the park?"

"To the best of our knowledge, yes." He made another visual sweep of the area, mentally cursing the fact that he and Peter had been there when the call came through that one of "their" cases had suddenly come to the attention of the mortal police.

Why hadn't he left Wales two days ago, after arresting the man who had killed Gwen? The memory of that day rose up in his mind again, just as it had done approximately every hour for the last two days, the sight of the broken, bloodied body on the rocks before him driving him to do the unthinkable—steal time.

His shoulders slumped.

"You're not still brooding over what happened, are you?" Kiya's voice penetrated both the soft night air and the dark, twisted cloud of his thoughts. With a gesture of surrender, he plopped down on the blanket next to her, leaning his arms on his knees while staring glumly into the darkness. Pools of artificial light drove away some of the night, but the park was too big, and it was too late to find someone if she wished to stay hidden. "Gregory?" Kiya gently patted his arm.

"If I am brooding, it's because I have every right to do so. If Peter ever wishes to disguise himself as a fish, he would be absolutely indistinguishable from a piranha. He certainly chewed me up and spat out my shredded remains just as good as any piranha."

"That's because you did something seriously illegal," she said with a calmness that pricked his skin. He liked Kiya, he truly did, but he didn't always appreciate her frankness. Not where his slipup was concerned. "Not that I think stealing a little time here and there is a big deal, especially since you saved a woman's life while doing so, but still, you knew the rules about Travellers joining the Watch when you signed up."

"I did, and I make no excuses now. I'm simply saying that when Peter found out what I'd done, he could have taken down a full-grown bull moose in about ten seconds flat."

She laughed. "Now you're being a drama queen, and that's the last thing I ever pegged you for. Peter's been very good to you, and you know it."

"I do know it. He didn't tell the Watch what I had done. He covered up the incident with Gwen. He read me the lecture of my life and came close to tearing off actual strips of my flesh with his tongue, but I'm still employed, and for that I'm truly grateful."

She gave him a long look out of the corner of her eye. "Peter never told me just exactly why you saved that lady's life. You didn't know her, did you?"

"Not then, no." He thought of how the light from the electric torches had shone in Gwen's black hair. There was something about her that went beyond the appreciation that a mere buxom, pretty woman stirred in him. She was . . . mysterious. There were hidden depths in her, an undercurrent of tension that she tried to belie with light banter and smiling eyes, but he was no stranger to female wiles, and she was up to something. Just what that was, he had no idea, but he was a bit surprised to realize how determined he was to unveil her secrets one by one.

"So why did you?"

"Hmm?" He stopped worrying over whether or not his interest in learning more about Gwen bordered on unhealthy (the last thing he wanted was for her to consider him a stalker of sorts) and focused on what Kiya had asked. "Oh, Gwen? I didn't really stop to think about it, to be honest. I simply reacted. And that's why Peter was so furious with me: I stole the time as a gut reaction."

"It'll be all right," she said, patting him again. "You've been a Traveller all your life, and you only just started having to rein back unauthorized time stealing. You'll get used to reacting without automatically going into rewind mode. And to be honest, Peter isn't a saint when it comes to stealing time. Sunil is proof of that."

Gregory stopped brooding over the hell that was his life and looked around again, this time searching not for a short, round woman but for the slim young man who had formerly been a ball of golden light. "Where is Sunil?"

"He saw a carousel and couldn't resist it. I'm so glad he got his body back. Being confined to a ball of light was hard on him when he has such . . . such . . ."

"Joie de vivre?"

She nodded. "That's what comes from being killed when

you're only eighteen, I guess. As long as you're here keeping me company instead of looking for that sweet little woman—"

"Gwen?" How did she know that he fancied her? Did it show? He slid a covert glance down to the fly of his jeans. No, all was well there. Not that he felt he was sporting an erection. Usually he had a warning of such things, and although he was perfectly willing to admit that Gwen could probably cause that result in him with very little effort on her part, all he'd felt while she dragged him across the park was a pleasant tingling that swept up his back and inner thighs.

"No, not the woman you saved. The other one. The kidnapper."

Guilt drove him back onto his feet to resume the visual scan of the area. "What on earth makes you think a woman who sells magic to mortals as well as kidnapping them is sweet?"

"She looks nice. Did you guys ever consider that maybe there was a perfectly good reason for her taking this old lady out of her home? Maybe she was a friend and promised her a night out watching the fireworks. Or maybe she wanted to do a random act of kindness, and getting the woman out and about was that act. Or perhaps—"

"Perhaps she has a history of illegalities where mortals are concerned, and this is simply the latest in a long line of transgressions."

Kiya got to her feet as well, stretching before shaking out the blanket and folding it into a square. "I just think that maybe Peter and you are jumping the gun a bit. All you heard on the police scanner was that she was seen driving off with the woman. Maybe the old lady called her and asked her to take her somewhere?"

"The nursing home would hardly be likely to call the police and say she'd been abducted if that was the case. Ah, there's Peter."

"I think you should take another look at what's going on," Kiya said, turning to smile at her husband. "There may be more there than you think."

That was certainly the case with Gwen, at least. Why had she dragged him across the park? Had she been hiding from someone? Had she been nervous about being alone? Was someone threatening her? He dug through his memory of the cases he'd read up on in the last few months, but came up with nothing regarding Gwen Byron.

"No luck?" Gregory asked when Peter was within hailing distance.

"None. It's an impossible task. I walked half the park, but everywhere I looked, there were a hundred possible hiding spots. If she's here, we'll never find her." He stopped next to his wife, smiling down at her with obvious affection.

"I've come to exactly the same conclusion."

Kiya leaned into Peter, kissed him, giggled when he squeezed her behind, and handed him the blanket while announcing, "I'm going to go see what Sunil is up to, and perhaps ride on the carousel, too. I haven't seen one in donkey's years, and if there's one thing that living with a former-animus-now-turned-lich has taught me, it's to embrace whatever life gives you."

Both men watched as she walked off to the bright section of the park where a couple of carnival rides were running, their garish lights and tinny music enticing many people into nighttime revelry. Gregory smiled at the besotted expression on his cousin's face, giving him a nudge with his elbow. "You're going to be the one who's arrested if the local coppers see you with that leer on your face."

Peter grimaced, then smiled. "You have to admit she's a sight for sore eyes."

"She's very pretty, but I prefer my women dark rather than strawberry blond." That hadn't been the truth until a few days ago, but it was perfectly natural that now and again a man's tastes changed.

Peter shot him a curious look, and slowly the two men followed the path that Kiya had taken. "Since when?"

Gregory shrugged. "Brunettes usually have an air of mystery to them that bodes well for not losing interest after a few weeks. Have you ever heard of Gwen Byron? Full name Gwenhwyfar Byron?"

"Yes."

Gregory stopped, startled.

"She's the woman you saved the other day. At risk of not only your own life but your career, and quite likely mine as well," Peter continued, giving him a dark look.

"Ah." Gregory continued to stroll alongside his cousin. "I thought you meant that you had heard of her in an official capacity. Other than the events of two days ago."

"No, the name doesn't ring a bell, although we can always run it past Dalton." He pulled out his cell phone and typed in a text to his boss. "You're damned lucky, you know."

"That you didn't tell Dalton the full truth of what happened?"

"No. Well, yes, but what I meant is that the shuvani didn't punish you for saving that Welsh girl's life."

"I've always paid my debts," Gregory said somewhat stiffly. "That minion of Death was well rewarded for the time I took from her. Besides, she's immortal. Yes, we have to pay for that which we take, but the shuvani only comes down hard on us when we steal from mortals. She minds less if you take time from someone who has the potential for a life measured in millennia rather than years."

Peter held up his hand. "You don't need to lecture me about the ways and hows of Travellers, cousin. I might not have been raised in the family, but I assure you that I am well versed in how we can be punished for thefts. Ah, here's Dalton's response."

Gregory leaned over to see the text on the small phone.

No records for person with the name Gwen Byron. Are you sure it's not an alias?

"Hmm," Gregory said, mulling that over. "I have a pretty accurate mental lie detector, and it didn't seem to me like she was giving me a false name."

"It's a bit odd that there's no record whatsoever," Peter said, frowning at his phone.

"But not unknown. After all, the Watch doesn't maintain a database of all individuals in the Otherworld. It didn't have me in it."

"No, but you said that the lawyer had killed Gwen. The first time, before you rescued her. That would imply that she had something to do with him."

"She isn't Magdalena Owens. She's not old enough, according to what Dalton told us yesterday."

"That's only because he found some updated records from a few months ago when there was a mix-up in an arrest of someone who was erroneously thought to be Owens. Your Gwen might be Owens wearing a glamour to look different. Younger," Peter suggested.

Gregory shook his head. "No. I'd have known once she touched me."

"She touched you?" Peter looked surprised. "After you saved her?"

"No, tonight. She's here in the park."

Both of Peter's eyebrows rose. "That's a bit of a curious coincidence, don't you think?"

"How so?" Unreasonably, Gregory felt irritated by his cousin's suspicion, and then was irritated at his irritation. He wasn't so new to either women or the Watch that he couldn't separate his own emotions from facts.

"She shows up two days ago when we were supposed to find the Owens woman. And now, after Owens has kidnapped a mortal, she's here in the park at the same time."

"There is a festival going on," Gregory pointed out, gesturing at the people still present. "She probably lives around here. There had to be at least six or seven thousand people here tonight."

"I'm just saying it's a bit of a coincidence."

His temper got the better of him, something that seldom happened. "Yes, all right, it's a coincidence. And it's true that Gwen is hiding something. It was quite clear that she had some motive for dragging me across the width of the park, but just because she didn't inform me of her every concern and worry doesn't mean she was up to something nefarious. She could have been uncomfortable about the nearness of an old lover. Or afraid of the dark. Or hell, maybe she just wanted to put her hand on my arm and that was the only way she could think of to do it! There's any number of reasons she should be in the park on this night, and obviously keeping some secret from me! It doesn't follow that she has anything to do with our case!"

Peter's round, startled eyes gave Gregory pause.

"Did I just rant?" he asked.

"Yes." Peter looked thoughtful. "Interesting. Very interesting. You don't . . . uh . . ."

"Of course I do. She's got a magnificent ass. But that is neither here nor there."

"I don't know," Peter said as they continued forward toward the rides. "I think it's pretty here. But I suppose your interest in the woman whose life you saved—again, I feel obligated to point out at the risk of your own life, your job, and possibly my job—being present at the park at the same time as the Owens female doesn't necessarily mean they're related. She dragged you across the park?"

Gregory laughed at the incredulity expressed in Peter's last sentence. "She did. She was trying to be subtle about it, too, so I didn't want to hurt her feelings by letting on I knew she was doing it. So I simply allowed her to pull me where she wanted me."

Peter gave him an unreadable look, started to say something, stopped, then finally shook his head and spoke. "We haven't known each other for long—obviously, I knew of you and the other members of Lenore Faa's family—"

"Of which you're one," Gregory interrupted. Although Peter and Lenore, their grandmother, had somewhat made their peace, it was clear that Peter still didn't feel that he was truly a member of the family. And given his past, and their uncle's and a cousin's actions of late, Gregory didn't blame him one bit. But since they had started working together, he felt it important to remind Peter that he was, in fact, part of the family.

"Yes, thank you, of which I'm one." Peter grimaced slightly before continuing. "Regardless of the length of time I've known you personally, I feel obliged to discuss something that could have an impact on your career."

"What have I done wrong now?" Gregory asked wearily. Part of him couldn't help but wonder if being a member of the Watch was going to be worth all the sacrifices he was making.

"Don't make that face," Peter said, pointing at him. "I know what you're thinking."

"I doubt that you do."

"Then you're fooling yourself. You're thinking that you're a Traveller, renowned through the centuries for your ability to manipulate time and lightning, and that it goes against your nature to deny access to both powers as you have been asked to do for the last few months."

"I understood the rules of the Watch when I joined," Gregory said carefully. Then he added with a wry smile, "All right, you knew what I was thinking. I only admit it because I know damned well that you think the same way. You just have better control over yourself."

"And that's exactly what I wanted to talk about—control. I don't question your dedication to the job at hand, and yet despite your desires to the contrary, you let a woman you hardly know haul you all over the place. You have to ask yourself why you did that, and whether you're allowing your emotions and desires to rule your mind. I'm sorry to say that if so, it will affect your future as an investigator for the Watch."

Gregory was silent while he struggled with his inner self, hating to admit that his cousin was absolutely right, and yet the truth was that he did feel resentment toward the loss of his natural talents. Why was he expected to deny his true nature, when other members of the Watch were not? Oh, he was used to being persecuted for who and what he was— Travellers had always been outside of society, both mortal and immortal—but the demands placed on him by the Watch had been more onerous than he had imagined.

And yet the reason for his being there with Peter was compelling, and one that he knew was right. Travellers as a whole were an insular group, not mingling with outsiders unless such contact could not be avoided. Over the last few centuries, they had withdrawn even more into their own society as the mortal and immortal worlds had grown more fearful of their powers. The mortals saw them as Gypsies, Romany folk whom they were unable to distinguish from the similar—but quite separate—Travellers. The members of the Otherworld were little better, viewing Gregory and his kind as thieves and worse.

"I don't know what to tell you," he said slowly, knowing in his heart that he couldn't go back to his life of just a few months ago. Too much had happened since then; he had seen himself and his family through his cousin's eyes, and he knew that he had to make a stand against the old way of life. "I can swear to you that I'm devoted to the job. To the Watch. To the idea that Travellers must be held accountable for their actions. But at the same time that I fully agree that our people must cease reveling in their status as outcasts, I recognize that it is our very nature to do so. To go against nature itself seems impossible at times. Perhaps you are able to control your need to use your powers because you are . . ."

"Mahrime?" Peter asked, his eyebrows rising slightly.

Gregory's shoulder twitched at the word. "Mahrime" could mean simply an outsider, one who was not a Traveller, or when applied to one of their own people, someone who was unclean. Tainted. Impure. "I was going to say that you and Kiya have distance, growing up outside of the Traveller society, whereas I do not. To us, acting in accordance to our true selves is as natural as breathing."

"You don't need to lecture me about that. I've had ample proof that Travellers go blithely about their way regardless of who they hurt or how many laws they break."

"And I don't condone either. I'm simply trying to explain that what you see as impulsiveness is my way of coming to grips with this new way of life. It might be easy for you to not steal time as you go throughout your day, but I assure you that I'm aware every time I pass by a mortal of the potential to steal just a few seconds."

To his surprise, his cousin gave him a swift, rough hug. "I know it's hard fighting what is an automatic reaction."

Gregory's expression caused Peter to laugh. "Where did that come from?" he asked when the laughter died down.

Peter made a face and nodded toward the carousel. "Kiya. She says I need to hug more. She thinks it's good for me to be more open with my emotions. She is probably right."

"Possibly, but if she convinces you that you need to kiss me next, I warn you that I have a mean right hook."

"Noted. Now—"

"Well, well, well. What a coincidence finding you here." The voice that drifted through the blare of music was filled with suspicion. Gregory turned to see its source, his fingers tightening when he beheld a slight woman in a smart cherry red wool suit coat and skirt. The light flashed off the lenses of her glasses as she eyed first him, then Peter. "Two Travellers? How very interesting. You wouldn't happen to know the location of my client, would you?"

"Who's this?" Peter asked, sotto voce.

"Reclamation agent," Gregory answered out of the side of his mouth before turning to face the woman, who now stood with her hands on her hips. "Good evening. To whom are you referring?"

"That woman who died on the rocks a couple of days ago. The one you were standing over." Her eyes narrowed. "The one who was stolen from me a few seconds later."

Gregory spread his hands in a show of innocence. Employment with the Watch prohibited him from lying except in the most dire of circumstances, and while he might have been inclined to play a little fast and loose with that rule in private, he couldn't very well disregard it in front of Peter . . . especially coming on the heels of the grand speech he had just made about his dedication to the job. "I have stolen no woman, dead or alive."

"Of course you haven't. But have you seen her? Do you know where she is?"

He chose to answer the second question, since he could do so truthfully. "I have no idea where she is."

"Odd," the woman said, giving them both another once-over. "According to my sources, Owens was seen coming to this park in the company of another woman and a mortal."

He exchanged a startled look with his cousin.

"Owens?" Peter asked. "What is your interest in her?"

"I just told you. She owes me a soul!"

"Are you saying that the woman who died on the rocks a few days ago was Owens? Magdalena Owens?"

"Yes, of course. Although I thought her first name was something else. Oh, it doesn't matter. She's the one, all right." The woman made an impatient gesture. "I don't have time for this nonsense. I have to find that woman and take what she owes me."

"I don't know for certain," Gregory said with a nonchalance he was far from feeling, "but I suspect that she's not going to want to give up her life just so your records will balance. Or whyever it is you are pursuing her."

"Look, I have a job to do, one simple little job: I collect the spirits of those who've passed on. I'm responsible for those spirits, and when someone goes and gets herself resurrected"—here she gave them both a very stern look—

"then I can't go back to my boss and say, 'Oh, well, that one got away.' I mean, he's Death! He's just not going to understand! Plus it does throw the books out of balance, and the accountants get all pissy if you mess with their books. You wouldn't know how to resurrect someone, would you?"

Gregory smiled a grim, grim smile. "I have no knowledge of resurrection at all. I believe that is the purview of necromancers."

"Mmm." She eyed Peter, then made a dismissive noise. "Very well. But I expect to hear from you if you see her. Drat, who's this calling?" She moved away a few steps to answer her phone.

She could expect all she wanted; he had absolutely no intention of turning Gwen over to Death's minion. Not when she was wanted by the Watch.

"She lied to me," he said to Peter in a soft voice. It hurt to say the words, and he couldn't understand why that was. Yes, Gwen—Magdalena—had betrayed his trust, but it wasn't as if he'd invested any time or emotion in her. So why did it feel like he had? "She lied to my face. Looked me straight in the eye and said she wasn't Magdalena Owens."

"It's been known to happen," Peter said, his gaze on the reclamation agent. "I'm sorry to hear it, but on the other hand, it explains a lot. And will make it easier for us to catch her. Now we know exactly what she looks like."

Gregory ignored the sense of foreboding that settled over him with those words. He didn't like to contemplate what the Watch would do to Gwen (as he still thought of her) when they turned her over. Most likely she'd be banished to the Akasha, the place of punishment from which no one escaped. He hardened his heart. He couldn't allow sentiment to taint his duty. Gwen had broken the laws, those governing both mortals and immortals, and she had to pay for her crime. The fact that she was a barefaced liar was just proof that she wasn't to be trusted. "I won't let her fool me again, that's for certain."

"Bah. I must go scour the park before the others get here."

The reclamation woman tucked her phone away and glanced around with distaste.

"Others? What others?"

"The mortals. The ones chasing her. I ran into them outside some psychology place yesterday." She gave a little shrug. "They said something about a debt she owed them, but I didn't pay much attention. The debt she owes my boss is much greater, and naturally takes precedence."

"Naturally," he said, thinking furiously. Someone else was chasing Gwen? A mortal someone? It didn't surprise him—anyone who would kidnap a mortal certainly would have no qualms about double-crossing other mortal beings. But still, the idea that people other than him—and the annoying reclamation agent—were tracking her filled him with unease.

"I wouldn't like to meet them in a dark alley—and I'm immortal," the woman finished, flicking a piece of lint off her sleeve.

That didn't bode well. Not for them, and certainly not for Gwen.

"Do you know the names of these other people—" Peter started to ask, but he stopped when the police scanner squawked to life. The first few words were lost in the noise of the carousel, but a man's voice suddenly spoke with unfortunate clarity. "—Owens seen heading toward the Cardiff Shopping Centre. Units are in pursuit."

Peter didn't hang around to ask his question again. He simply ran for the carousel, gesturing at his wife.

"The game's afoot!" cried the red-suited woman. She spun around, racing off into the night without another word.

Gregory swore at the timing of the police scanner, swore at the unknown people who were so threatening that even Death's minion quailed at meeting them, and swore at his own stupidity for allowing a pretty woman to fool him.

By the gods, things were going to be different from here on out. He'd be damned before he believed a single word that came out of Gwen's delicious mouth.

FOUR

"Left. Go left!"

"If I go left, we'll end up in the bay," I said through gritted teeth, my hands gripping the steering wheel so tight it hurt. I spun the wheel and we took a corner on what felt like only two wheels, a municipal sign pointing out the location of the Cardiff mall.

"Your other left!"

"That would be right, Mom."

"Of course I'm right, I'm looking at Mrs. Vanilla's drawing. She has it all mapped out."

The wail of sirens behind us grew louder as another police car shot out of a side road, fishtailed wildly for about five seconds, then did a three-point turn and fell into place behind us. About five blocks back, two other cars raced toward us. They were closing fast. I figured we had a matter of seconds to make the mall and get into Anwyn before the mortal police got too close to avoid.

"A slowing spell! That's what we need," Mom Two said, and rolled down her window.

"Mom Two!" I yelled as she thrust her torso out the window, facing backward so she could cast her spell. "Get back in the car. The mall's straight ahead!"

The words of her spell were whipped away on the wind, or drowned out by the siren as the nearest police car, with a burst of speed, zoomed up almost to our bumper, but I had no doubt that she was fully intent on buying us a little time. I grabbed her belt with one hand while slamming my foot down on the accelerator, forcing my mothers' car to its limits as it shot across the last intersection, tires squealing when I swerved to avoid traffic, and into the mostly empty parking area outside the mall.

"Get back inside the car!" I bellowed, my eyes scanning the front of the mall. My mother had sworn that the Krispy Kreme—and I had a moment of mentally shaking my head again over the fact that someplace as mythical and renowned as the Welsh afterlife had an entrance in a doughnut shop— was open twenty-four hours.

Sure enough, at the far end of the mall there were a few cars outside a lit storefront.

"Done! I think that should help us," Mom Two said as she pulled herself back into the car. I glanced in the rearview mirror. The police car had stopped, the driver banging his hands on the wheel in frustration.

"You could have been killed," I chastised Mom Two as I spun around a barrier and headed for the lights. We rocketed past a security patrol, who instantly flipped on his lights and started to follow. Luckily, there wasn't much traffic, since most everyone was still at the park or at home, so I blatantly disregarded proper driving lanes as we hurtled toward the entrance of the doughnut shop. "OK, as soon as I stop, I want everyone out and into the store. I'll decoy the police away—"

"No!" Mom shouted, clutching the back of the seat. "You must come with us."

"It'll be safer for you if I lead them away from Anwyn."

"No!" she repeated, and tugged on the headrest in an annoying way. "You have to come to Anwyn, too."

"The police aren't after me. I'm sure they don't know who's driving this car."

"It's not the police you need protecting from, Gwen," Mom Two added. "It's the woman in the red suit."

"That's right! She's looking for you. And you know what that means!" Mom said, tugging on the headrest.

"No, I don't, because neither of you would give me a good explanation of just who this mysterious woman is, or why she is after me."

"It's better if you don't know," Mom Two said with a knowing look.

"You don't know who she is, do you?" I asked with sudden insight.

"I don't know her name, but that doesn't mean I can't sense danger when it's near. There." She pointed, and for a second I was confused as to whether she was pointing out something dangerous. "That's the entrance to the Krispy Kreme."

I glanced behind me. The security car was close, but not so close that the occupant could physically grab us. Two police cars were heading straight for us, however. I didn't have the time to argue, so I simply yelled, "Hold on, everyone!" and slammed on the brakes.

The tires squealed in a satisfyingly dramatic fashion as we slid to a stop right in front of the doors. I flung myself out of the car and yanked open the door behind me, running around the car to help Mom Two get old Mrs. Vanilla out.

The security guard hit his horn and slammed on his brakes, but he was too late. Mom Two and I more or less carried Mrs. Vanilla into the doughnut shop at a full run, my mother holding the door open for us.

"Where is it?" I asked as soon as we were inside, frantically scanning the interior. A couple of people sat in brightly colored booths, while behind a long glass counter an employee stood frozen in surprise, a pot of coffee in his hand.

"I'm not sure exactly," my mother started to say, but Mrs. Vanilla began squeaking loudly and kicking her legs. We set her down and she bolted, moving amazingly fast for an old lady. Around the counter filled with doughnuts she dashed, and into the back area.

We didn't wait. We ran after her, the electronic *ping* of the door chime letting us know that the security guard was hot on our heels.

Mrs. Vanilla scurried past the doughnut-making equipment, heading straight for a door to what must be a storage room. I prayed to every deity I could think of that it was, because if it wasn't, we were going to be in a serious world of hurt.

Mom Two threw open the door and without a look back, dashed inside, followed by Mrs. Vanilla and my mother. I hesitated for a second. The security guard appeared behind me.

"I so hope I don't see you in a few seconds," I told him, then turned on my heel and leaped through the open doorway into the storage room.

Only it wasn't a storage room.

I fell with a loud *thwump* onto soft, daisy-spotted green grass, getting a good mouthful of it before I managed to roll over onto my back.

The stars sparkled overhead, like so many glittering diamonds scattered on an indigo cloth. They looked so close, I wanted to reach up and touch them, to let their cold, brilliant light cleanse me of all impurities.

I sat up and spat out the bit of grass, half a daisy, and a very surprised potato bug. I looked around. Although the moon was high in the sky, a quarter moon that was as bright as a full moon, closer to earth a reddish haze hung over the land, like smoke from an odd sort of fire.

Directly in front of me were the three shapes of my two mothers and Mrs. Vanilla, the last of whom was being supported by the former.

"You guys are OK?" I asked, getting up. "I guess I owe Mrs. Vanilla an apol—"

The words dried up on my tongue as Mom Two shifted, allowing me to see beyond her.

A semicircle of men in plate-and-mail armor stood looking at us, each of them holding a drawn sword.

"Oh, hell," I said on an exhale of breath.

"Anwyn, not hell, I think," Mom Two corrected.

As she spoke, the ranks of men swept aside like a human parting of the Red Sea. Through the opening strode a woman, tall, pale, and slender. She was clad in a black leather bodysuit and had daggers strapped to either hip. Her eyes were a dark shade of green, and she had long black hair with green extensions that matched her eyes.

She looked like she belonged on the set of a martial arts movie. "Who are you?" she demanded as she approached, making an impatient gesture toward us.

I pushed my way in front of my mothers. I wasn't abnormally courageous, but I had no intention of letting someone who looked like she could kick Jackie Chan's ass get pushy with my moms.

"My name is Gwen. These are my mothers. The old woman is Mrs. Vanilla. Who are you?"

"Holly," she snapped, her gaze raking us all over for the count of three. She turned, and with an imperious wave of her hand at the nearest guy in armor, added, "Arrest them. They're spies."

"What?" I shrieked as the men moved in. "Wait, we're not spies! This is Anwyn, right? The afterlife? The happy bunnies and sheep and lovely rolling green hills place?"

Two men grabbed each of my arms and more or less frog-marched me toward an array of sharp black silhouettes. I looked over my shoulder to see my mothers being escorted as well, but they didn't appear to be in distress.

"You all right?" I asked my mother, who was immediately behind me.

"Of course. You were the only one who fell coming through the entrance."

"No talking," the man on my left arm said, his voice gruff, if muffled, behind his steel helmet.

I bit back the words I wanted to say to him, instead focusing my attention on where we were being led. The black shapes resolved themselves into tents, of all things. Small fires dotted what could only be called an encampment, with at least a hundred (and probably more) tents of differing sizes arranged in orderly concentric rings, with larger tents in the center and the smallest on the outer ring. There were a number of dogs roaming around, all of which appeared to be of the same breed: that of a medium-sized hound that looked like a cross between a beagle and a greyhound.

A few men and women were present as we moved through the camp, some of them wearing armor like the guards, others in what I thought of as Renaissance Faire clothing—lots of leather jerkins, cotton tunics, and leggings that were bound by thin leather cords. It had the feel of a medieval military camp, which just confused the dickens out of me.

"What is a military camp, a *medieval* military camp, doing in the middle of Anwyn?" I asked loudly so my mothers could hear.

"Anwyn is the place of legends. Why shouldn't there be a medieval army here?" I heard Mom Two say before she was told to be quiet. My own guards squeezed my arms in warning as we continued to trek through the tents. A small army of dogs fell into place at our heels.

In the center of the camp was a massive tent, at least three times the size of the next-largest one and flying a couple of fancy banners. I couldn't make out what was on the banners when we were marched past the big tent, but it definitely looked like the prime accommodation.

It was not, needless to say, our destination. The guards—they couldn't be anything but soldiers, given the armor and the way they obeyed the woman named Holly—stopped in front of a silver tent.

My hopes of a structure from which we could make an easy escape were dashed when the tent flap was pulled aside to reveal two tall iron-barred cages. They weren't small—the two of them filled the entire tent—but they were very much a prison.

"Right. I am not going in that," I said as one of my guards released my arm in order to open the door to one of the cages.

It was about seven feet tall, and probably a good twenty feet wide, containing what looked like a couple of camping beds, two wooden chairs, and a small table. "I am not a spy, no matter what stabby girl says. I refuse to be caged like an animal."

"Enter," the guard said, flipping up his visor to give me a good glare.

"Like hell I will."

He made like he was going to pull me into the cage, but I didn't go through three years of self-defense classes to put up with being stuffed into a box. I dug my feet in, shifted my weight, and flipped him over my hip, heavy armor and all. He hit the ground with a loud crash and a grinding of metal, the dog nearest him managing to scramble out of the way just in time, but before the other man could so much as shout, I was on my nearest mother's guard, trying to find a point of vulnerability that I could exploit.

Here's the thing about armor—face on, there's not a lot there to exploit. With little choice, I did what I could to disable him before intending to move on to the next mother-guarding man.

"This is intolerable!" I yelled as the door-holding guard ran over to pluck me off Mom's guard, whom I was beating on the head with his own helm. A couple of dogs leaped about excitedly while I was hauled off the man, who now had a cut over one eye that ran in gruesome glory down his face. I tripped over another dog, apologizing as I did so. "Sorry, doggy, but this mean guard jerked me and made me step on you. Look, buster, I don't hold with people abusing animals, so stop dragging me over the top of these dogs. Boy, there are a lot of them, aren't there?"

I didn't have time to continue, since my two guards threw me bodily into one of the cages, slamming the door behind me. I heard a key turn in the lock as I picked myself up and ran to the steel-barred door in an attempt to wrench it open.

Two dogs sat outside the door, panting and clearly hoping I would continue the fun romping game.

"Gwenny, dear, are you hurt?" my mother asked as she, Mom Two, and Mrs. Vanilla were placed in the matching cage. The guards didn't manhandle them, I was relieved to note. Although there was a space of about six feet between our cages, I was comforted by the fact that they were nearby, and as safe as an unjustly incarcerated person finding herself in the Welsh afterlife could be.

"No. Just very, very pissed. Hey, you, plate boy. My mothers are old, and Mrs. Vanilla is really elderly. Give them some food and water and blankets and stuff."

The guard said nothing, just lit a torch inside the entrance, and left, letting the tent flap drop as he went.

"Bastard," I muttered, and began to prowl the cage to look for weakness. The dogs accompanied me. "Sorry, guys. I'm not going to play right now. Maybe later, OK?"

Oddly enough, the dogs seemed to understand, because they both turned and wandered out of the tent, leaving us alone. A few minutes later, another guard appeared, this one minus his helmet but with his arms full of blankets, with two carefully balanced jugs on top. A second guard carried a couple of long flat metal platters bearing bread, cheese, and what looked to be some sort of smoked meat.

I wasn't surprised to find a fresh company of hounds on his heels, evidently very interested in the food.

The guards passed the food through the bars to us, ignoring my pleas to be taken to whoever was in charge so that we could clear up the situation. Thankfully, they shooed the dogs out before them when they left. So it was that a half hour later, fed, hydrated by ice-cold water that was actually very good, and with the warmth of a thick woolen blanket around us, we all settled down to get a little sleep.

"Things will look brighter in the morning," my always optimistic mother said as she curled up with Mom Two on one of the camp beds in her cage, Mrs. Vanilla having been settled on the other. "They always do."

I said nothing, but as I watched the torch sputter and finally die, my thoughts were as dark as the night outside the prison tent.

"See? I told you things would look brighter," my mother said some seven hours later. I shot her a brief glare, and she had the grace to look abashed.

"I wouldn't call a bloodred sky brighter." My attention was momentarily distracted by the fact that the sky was, in fact, deep, dark red and striped with dirty gray wisps of what I assumed were clouds. Smoke, thick and dark, wafted upward in long, lazy curls from some unknown—but nearby— source. Every now and then, a little rumble of thunder sounded in the distance, and twice my peripheral vision caught the sudden flash of lightning.

There were no clouds in the sky.

I took a deep breath, one of several that I had taken during the last ten minutes since we had been released from our prisons. We'd been given more water (which again was fresh and cold and almost sweet, it was so good), thick slabs of bread, a little pottery bowl of butter, and rough-cut slices of the best cheese I'd ever had. Three young-looking dogs who could have been siblings snuck in after breakfast was delivered and waited patiently outside my cell until I couldn't stand their hopeful eyes any longer and handed over bites of bread and cheese. Two apples completed my food allotment, both of which I stuck in my hoodie pockets for later.

Luckily, I'd just finished using what could only be described as a camping toilet, discreetly located in the corner and hidden behind a long blue curtain that was hung from the bars across the ceiling of the cell.

"Say what you will about the accommodations," Mom Two said as they settled in to their breakfast. I noticed somewhat jealously that they had also been given plump, juicy-looking grapes. "The food is delicious. Gwenny, don't give those hounds any more cheese. It will give them wind. Is there more butter, Alice?"

Mrs. Vanilla made happy little noises as she ate grapes.

It was a good thing that we were all hungry, because we were given only a few minutes to eat before a new contingent of guards appeared and herded us out of our prisons.

"Who exactly are we being taken to see?" I asked my guards. I noticed with irritation that I had two of them, while my mothers and Mrs. Vanilla had only one each. The morning sun glinted off the armor they wore, which appeared to be made of pale golden-plated pieces, bound together with mail of the same color. Men and women alike wore the armor, I was somewhat gratified to notice. At least wherever we'd ended up, women weren't treated like inferior beings. "Hey, I asked you guys a question, and I expect an answer!"

"Gwen, I don't believe an antagonistic attitude is going to benefit us," Mom Two cautioned from behind me.

I could have told her that I was fully aware it wasn't the way to make friends and influence people, but that, at the moment at least, wasn't my goal. I wanted information, and if being obnoxious was the only way to get it, then I could be VERY obnoxious.

"Dude," I said, dragging my heels and jerking the guards on each of my arms to a halt. "I am not taking another step until someone tells me what's going on!"

The guards picked me up with a hand under each of my armpits and simply carried me forward.

"Dammit!" I yelled, kicking my legs and trying to be as dead a weight as possible. "Put me down! Why the hell won't you speak?"

"They are not allowed to speak to spies," a man answered. The guards stopped and set me down in front of him, which was at the opening of a purple-and-white-striped tent. The man was also in armor, although his had fancier bits of embossing and little round medallion plates on it. Obviously, he wasn't just an ordinary soldier. Next to him, on the ground, lay an elderly version of the dogs who had hit me up for part of my breakfast. She lifted her head when the man spoke, her tail thumping on a dark purple rug.

"We are not spies," I said, straightening my clothing with exaggerated gestures. "I am an alchemist. My mothers are Wiccans. The old lady is just an old lady. She doesn't talk much. Who are you?"

"Your name?" the man asked, his long, mobile face not at all what I would have pictured as someone in charge of soldiers. He looked goofy, like a young Hugh Laurie pretending to be someone he wasn't.

"Gwen Owens."

"I'm Gwenny's mother, Magdalena," my mom said as she came forward. She gestured to the right. "This is my partner, Alice Hill. Mrs. Vanilla is our client."

The man bowed with a metallic rustle. "Colorado Jones."

I stared at him for a minute. "You mean like 'Indiana Jones' but with 'Colorado' instead?"

He blinked somewhat vacant blue eyes at me. "I'm not acquainted with Sir Indiana, my lady. Is he with Lord Aaron's army?"

"OK," I said after a moment's pause, "I think for sanity's sake we're just going to let that go and move forward. Who do I speak to about this patently ridiculous claim that we're spies? I don't even know who we're supposed to be spying against, or for, and why, but I can tell you that it's all wrong. We just got to Anwyn about ten seconds before we were captured."

"You're not spies?" the man asked (I made an effort to think of him by the name he'd given, but it was difficult). Relief flooded his face. He gestured toward the guards, dismissing them. "It's all been a terrible mistake. I will inform Lady Holly that these damselles are here to help us, not harm us."

I started to protest, but my mother grabbed my arm and

gave me a look that had me biting off the words. It was better to be thought a friend than a foe.

"Witches are most welcome to Lord Ethan," Colorado was telling my moms. "*Most* welcome. As for your compatriot—" He eyed Mrs. Vanilla. She weaved a little, making a creaking noise as she did so. "Yes, I'm sure we'll find something for her to do. Everyone must have a use, that's what the Lady Dawn says. She isn't in Anwyn at the present, but we must still abide by her rules. You ladies may have Mistress Eve's tent. She has returned to her home, and needs it no longer. My squire will take you there, and then to the apothecary so that you might procure whatever you need to weave your magic."

"Oooh, an apothecary," Mom said, looking pleased.

"Now, hold on here a minute," I said, jumping a little when Colorado bellowed, "Branwyn! Front and center! And see that you're suitably garbed—ladies are present."

"We're not going to go anywhere until we find out exactly where we are and what's going on."

He looked surprised. "Why, you are in Lord Ethan's encampment."

"Who's Lord Ethan when he's at home?"

"Gwen!" Mom Two scolded me, then said apologetically to Colorado, "You have to forgive our girl. She spends most of her time in the States."

"Lord Ethan is Lord Ethan," Colorado said, his hands flapping helplessly. "He is our lord and master."

"I got the relationship basics, but who is he, exactly? And why does he have an army in Anwyn? Wait, we *are* in Anwyn, aren't we?"

"Yes, this is Anwyn." He gave me a look filled with pity, as if I was the one who was a sparerib short of a barbecue. "This is the battleground, my lady."

"Why do you keep calling me—no, never mind. I refuse to be distracted by minutiae. Who is Lord Ethan battling?"

"Lord Aaron, of course. Ah, here comes Branwyn."

A stout young man of about sixteen burst out from a nearby tent, bright freckles dotted across a face that was almost as red as his hair. "You bellowed, Sir Colorado?"

"Aye. Take Lady Alice and Lady Magdalena and . . . er . . . Mistress Vanilla to Mistress Eve's former tent, and then hence to the apothecary's. And do not dally. They are powerful witches and will bespell you should you waste their time."

The boy's eyes widened as he looked from me to my moms.

"Hold your horses there, Hopalong Cassidy," I said, putting up a hand to stop him. "We're not going to anyone's tent until I find out exactly what's going on."

"Oh, you are not to go to Mistress Eve's tent," Colorado said with a sunny smile. "You are young and comely and mightily built. Lady Holly would have my head if I didn't bring you to her."

"We've already met Holly." I bristled a little at the "mightily built" comment, tugging down my hoodie so that it covered the expanse of what my mother referred to as "child-birthing hips."

"I'm sure we'll see you shortly, Gwen," Mom Two said, taking Mrs. Vanilla by the arm. "After we see what stores the apothecary has."

"I think we should all stay together," I told both mothers as they urged Branwyn forward.

"Don't be silly, dear. We're safe now, and Mrs. Vanilla clearly needs to rest. We'll get her settled in our new tent so she can replenish her strength."

"But—"

"You know how your mother and I dearly love a visit to a well-stocked apothecary's shop," Mom Two added. "We'll see you later. You go off and meet with that young woman again. Perhaps she'll lead you to the people in charge. Give her our best wishes. Young man, do you know if the apothecary has wortsbane in stock? We've been out for the last two centuries and unable to find a reliable source for more . . ."

"This way," Colorado said, gesturing in the opposite direction. The old dog started to get to her feet. "No, Rosemary, you stay there. I won't be long seeing this lady to her destination."

I bit my lip, watching my mothers wander off, part of me feeling it really was better for us all to stay together, but the other part of me wanting them out of the way in case the situation turned dicey. I didn't like the look of that woman Holly, so all in all, it was best that I confront her on my own.

Colorado chatted about nothing in particular as we wound our way through the camp toward the far edge, most of which I didn't listen to because it was something about trees and plants and how he had an affinity to aspens, or something of that ilk, and I had more important things to chew over. Like whether the Holly woman would throw me back into a cell and how I was going to convince her that we weren't spies.

I kept my eyes peeled as we walked, not only so I could retrace my path if necessary, but because I wanted to get a better idea of why there was a battle going on in Anwyn and why it wasn't being fought with modern weapons.

Men and women moved busily through the camp, some people clearly employed as blue-collar workers, hauling buckets of water, trays of food, armor, bedding, and sundry other items. On the outer edge of the camp, visible down one of the aisles, a parade of horses marched past, on their way to or from a stable. And everywhere there were dogs, dogs, dogs.

"—of course, what was I to do but to answer the call of Lord Gideon?"

Startled, I realized that Colorado had been talking to me about something other than his love of trees, and I'd missed it all in my musings. "Um. Sure, why not?"

I glanced around, noticing something. I expected that with so many dogs around, there would be a lot of dog poop. But there was nary a pile to be seen.

He nodded. "That's what I said. It was my duty to answer

the call. I was honored when Lord Ethan chose me to be one of his knights."

"That's got to be a big honor," I said, hoping that was true.

"It is indeed."

"Who is Lord Gideon again?"

He shot me a startled look. I made a little face. "Sorry. I was thinking of something else and must have missed that bit."

"Lord Gideon is a magician of much power and breadth. He is responsible for all of this," Colorado answered, gesturing toward the camp. "He is also Lord Ethan's younger brother."

"Ah. Gotcha." I had a feeling that "magician," in this case, didn't mean the guys in Vegas who pulled off the kind of illusions that made tigers and elephants disappear. No doubt it was a reference to the Otherworld version, the kind of mage who performed public feats of magic . . . real magic. "You guys must really like dogs. And have them really well trained, because I don't see any obvious signs that so many live here."

"We all must take a rache, yes."

"Rache?"

"Hunting dog. All that you see here are the spawn of Lord Ethan's bitch, Ergo. She is long dead, but as you see, her progeny live on."

"They do indeed." And I had to admit, all the dogs I saw looked happy and healthy. There wasn't a single dog that had that air of skulking around hoping for a bite to eat or a friendly pat; they were all glossy-coated, well fed, and apparently well cared for. "You must have someone pooper-scooping on a full-time basis."

"Naturally, we make prisoners attend to their droppings. It is suitable punishment."

That surprised me. "You have other prisoners? Other than my mothers and me, that is?"

"A few that we've taken over the centuries. Here we are. Lady Holly, I bring to you the lady Gwen."

We stopped in front of two people, one of whom was the pale-skinned bedaggered woman from the night before, the other of whom was a man in armor who sat on a wooden stool, holding out his arm.

"It's an RSI," the man was saying, the words giving my brain a moment of trouble resolving a modern acronym for a repetitive injury with the anachronism of armor. "I can't even grip the hilt of the sword without my entire arm burning in pain. Lo the healer says the MRI shows I need time off so that the herbs and physical therapy can heal the injury."

"Injury, schminjury," Holly said in a disgusted voice. "We don't have a spare soldier, so you're just going to have to get out there and do your job."

"But Master Lo said—"

"Lady Holly!" Colorado said loudly, tapping her on the shoulder.

She spun around, her hair whipping like little blades of black silk. "Do *not* touch me!"

"My apologies, but I did not think you heard me when I said that I was here with Lady Gwen."

Her dark green eyes shifted to me, narrowing as they raked me over. "This is the spy from last night, isn't it?"

"I am not an it, nor am I a spy," I said, meeting her gaze. I'd never been one to let someone intimidate me, and I certainly wasn't going to start with this thin, prickly woman.

"Who are you?"

"Gwen Owens. I'm an alchemist. I came to Anwyn last night in the company—"

"Suit her up," Holly interrupted before striding off. "She can take the place of the injured soldier."

"Suit—whoa now!"

I stared at her back for a second as she marched off, then ran after her, grabbing her arm to stop her.

She whirled around, a dagger in her hand that was at my throat before I could so much as blink. "Are you deaf as well as stupid? I said not to touch me."

"You didn't say that to me, and I'm not deaf, or stupid. Nor do I tolerate being pushed around," I snarled, shoving her hand (and the dagger) away from me. "Not by you, not by anyone. Got that? Good. Now, I don't know what you think I am, but I'm not a spy, I'm not one of your soldiers, and I'm not going to allow you to push me around."

She watched me with glittering green eyes while I spoke, and when I finished, she was silent for a few seconds before saying, "Brave words from a woman who spent the night in a cell."

"I just told you that I'm not stupid. Fighting ten armed men while in the company of my mothers and an elderly mortal isn't a bright idea."

"That is possibly true," she said, sheathing her dagger. "Regardless, you have two choices: you can be executed as a spy or you can replace the injured soldier and take up his banner on the field of battle." She glanced at her watch. "His shift started twelve minutes ago. You have thirty seconds to decide."

"You have got to be out of your mind!" I said, shaking my head. "I'm not going to make that sort of a decision! I'm an alchemist—"

"And now you're either a spy or a fighter. Fifteen seconds."

I stared at her openmouthed for the count of five until I realized I was wasting time. I was between a rock and a hard place, and I knew it. I couldn't fight her, not with all the soldiers around us, and I wasn't willing to risk my mothers' lives by attempting an escape. Not at that moment, at least.

"Fine," I said, glaring at her. "I'll pretend I'm a soldier if it gives you your jollies. But I'm going to suck at it."

She made a dismissive gesture. "That matters not."

She strode off again, leaving me damning my life, damning my decision to bring my mothers here, and most of all, wishing they hadn't abducted Mrs. Vanilla in the first place.

I turned to go back to where the soldier was, and bumped

into Colorado, who was standing right behind me with an anxious look on his face.

"I assume you heard what was said."

His eyes widened. "Yes, but only because I was worried that Lady Holly might . . . er . . ."

"Stab me?"

He made an apologetic little wave of his hand. "She doesn't suffer fools well."

"Uh-huh." I straightened my shoulders and headed back to where the RSI soldier was being assisted in the removal of his armor. "Neither do I, as a matter of fact. I'm not a soldier, Colorado."

"Well, so far as that goes, none of us were before Lord Gideon called us up," he said, lifting the newly discarded breastplate and eyeing it before turning his gaze to my chest. "But you are most sturdily built, and I'm sure you will have no trouble lasting two hours."

"Two hours?" I crossed my arms over my breasts despite the total absence of sexual interest in his eyes as he considered my torso. He discarded the breastplate and went into the tent, coming out with two others.

"That is the length of each shift. It goes quickly, I promise you." He held up a chest piece, squinted at my boobs, then dropped it in favor of the other one. "I believe this will offer the best fit. There's no time to have armor made to your specifications, but once your shift is over, we'll have the armorer get to work on a set so that you're equipped for tomorrow. We have a very good armorer. She makes Lord Ethan's armor and has a wonderful touch with the blacksmith hammer."

"Back up a sec," I said, obediently holding up my arms when another teenager, this time a slight girl with a pixie haircut who held an armful of chain mail, instructed me to do so. "What's this about a shift? You guys fight in shifts?"

"Of course," he said, assisting the page or squire or whatever she was called to slip the chain mail over my head. A few strands of my hair snagged on it, making me wince. Surprisingly, the mail was very light, and although it hung down to mid-thigh, it didn't seem to be overly large. "If we fought longer than that, we'd get tired."

It was hard to dispute that logic. I said nothing more while Colorado and the girl (whose name turned out to be Columbine) slapped a plate chest piece on my front. It was attached to the mail with leather buckles, and although it was significantly heavier than the mail, it wasn't overwhelming.

"You guys do know that I've never lifted a sword in my life," I said conversationally as they strapped on shin guards, plates that resembled wrist braces but that Columbine referred to as gauntlets, and finally, handed me a small oval shield.

"None of us had when we started," Colorado answered with a cheerful smile. "You'll learn quickly. Now, as for a helm . . . I'm not sure what we have to fit you. We'll try a couple, shall we?"

What followed was a painful five minutes as I tried on, and rejected, a number of closed helms. Most of them were simply too small, which just irritated me since I knew that both Columbine and Colorado were thinking what a fat head I had, but one of the helms that wasn't too small was far too massive to be worn. In the end, Colorado said, "I believe that for today we'll do without a helm. Now, what do we have left? I'm not sure what we have in the line of a lady's sword . . . My lord!"

Colorado bowed low.

I turned, ignoring the little spurt of adrenaline. A dark-haired man with a short goatee strolled up, wearing what can only be described as a maroon velvet smoking jacket, a white silk ascot, and a fez. One of his hands was in his jacket pocket, while the other waved as he spoke. Two young women in harem costumes trotted behind him, one bearing a tablet computer, the other holding a spiral notebook and pen. "—That was the last that was ever seen of those brigands. Naturally, I offered to return the jewels and fine silks that had been stolen, but the fair maiden insisted I keep them as a sign of her gratitude. That and her virginity, but we need not speak of that now. End chapter. What have we here? A new recruit?"

"Yes, my lord," Colorado said, bowing low again while gesturing awkwardly at me. "It is my honor to present to you the Lady Gwen."

"Hi," I said, refusing to be awed or give in to my curiosity about the man's bizarre outfit. I held out my hand to shake his.

He looked at it for a moment, then pulled a monocle from his breast pocket and eyed it like it was made up of worms. "Greetings," he said finally, tucking away the monocle. "You are not one of Aaron's souls?"

"If you mean am I alive, yes. My mothers and I sought sanctuary here from some mortal police," I said, hoping my exclusion of mentioning the Watch wouldn't come back to sting me. "We were promptly arrested for spying. We aren't spies. My mothers are Wiccans, and I am an alchemist."

"Wiccans. Are they here?" He looked around.

"They are housed in Mistress Eve's tent, my lord," Colorado said quickly.

"Excellent. I have need of Wiccans. Tell them to start bespelling Aaron's men immediately. Now, as for you . . . can you make fiery orbs that will rain down from the sky and decimate my enemy?"

"No," I said firmly. "I don't make bombs."

"Pity." His left arm, the one with the hand in his pocket, twitched and started to move. He grabbed his elbow and jammed his hand back down into the pocket. "You will be fighting on my behalf, I see. Colorado, make sure she wears my colors. All ladies like to wear my colors. And give her one of my signed head shots. The one used in my last book. It's in profile. Ladies love my profile."

"I will gladly see that she wears your colors, Lord Ethan, but first I must find a sword suitable for a lady's use."

Ethan stroked his chin for a moment, then waved an airy hand. "Give her the Nightingale."

Colorado's eyes opened wide. "Are you sure, my lord? That is Lady Dawn's own sword—"

"She never fights anymore. She's far too busy trying to find husband number seventy-one. My mother has issues," Ethan confided. "She will insist on wedding mortals, and they never last. Still, it's a hobby. Daisy, where were we?"

"End of chapter twenty-eight," the woman with the notebook said promptly.

"Begin new chapter. By midsummer in the year eleven ninety-two, I had taken control of all the kingdoms of Wales, and was one day considering what act of derring-do I should next accomplish, when a Saracen prince arrived at my castle gates demanding entrance . . ."

Ethan and his entourage wandered off, leaving Colorado and me staring after him.

"So that's the head of your team. He's kind of . . . eccentric, isn't he? What book is he writing?"

"He is engaged in taking down into print the many dashing and thrilling adventures of his life."

"That explains the artsy outfit. Is something wrong with his hand?"

A pained expression crossed Colorado's face. "Lord Ethan was smote with a mysterious ailment, no doubt by Lord Aaron."

"Warts?" I guessed.

"Alien Hand Syndrome," Colorado answered with a sigh. "It troubles him greatly, but do not mention it. He dislikes people discussing it."

There was really nothing I could say to that, so I just stood patiently by while Colorado sent Columbine off to fetch the oddly named sword.

"This was Lady Dawn's," he said when she returned with it. It was a smaller sword than that which Colorado bore, with a narrow blade and a delicately scribed hilt that flashed blue and green. "She named it the Nightingale because it would sing when she slew her enemies. It was her favorite sword when she ruled the mortal world."

"It's very pretty. Are those emeralds?" I examined the hilt, seeing a couple of spells woven into the intricate design.

"And sapphires. You will take the utmost care of it, I have no doubt. Lady Dawn would not care to know her Nightingale was being abused."

I tried to remember the history of Wales that I had learned a long time before, but I didn't remember anything about a woman named Dawn.

"Absolutely," I said, making an experimental slash or two in the air. The sunlight flashed and glittered on the sword, the gems adding brief bursts of color. I'd never so much as picked up a sword before, but this one pleased me on a primal level. It felt good in my hand. It felt right. "I'll take very good care of it. So, what exactly do I do when I get to the battlefield? Join up with the other people?"

Colorado took me by the arm and steered me toward the far edges of the camp. "Oh, you won't be fighting with others. Each soldier fights his or her own shift."

"But—this is a battle, isn't it?"

"Yes, of course." We broke free of the encampment and walked up a slight incline to a knoll. Overhead, thick oily black and gray clouds blotted out much of the bloodred sky, periodically streaked with blue-white fingers of lightning. A distant rumble of thunder completed the nightmarish scene.

"But you have just one person fighting at a time?"

"Just one."

"But . . . ," I repeated, shaking my head. "That doesn't seem to be a very efficient way to fight."

"On the contrary, it's quite very efficient. Lord Ethan found very early on that to have all of our troops fighting at the same time meant that many people were killed."

"Isn't that the whole point? I mean, killing your enemy?"

He looked horrified. "I do not know how you do things in

your native land, Lady Gwen, but here in Anwyn, we do not condone slaughter."

I felt like a genocidal fool. "Sorry. Obviously this way makes much more sense."

"It does. We send out one person for a two-hour shift, after which he—or she—is free to rest until the following day's shift. Few people are injured, and even fewer are killed. It is, as Lady Dawn says, a win-win situation."

"Kinda makes you wonder why you bother fighting at all."

"Oh, we don't wonder that. We know why we fight. Lord Aaron attacked my lord. He had to answer. It was the only honorable thing to do."

We crested the top of the knoll as he spoke. He stopped, nodding toward the center of the hilltop, where the grass had been blackened, eventually wearing away to nothing but dirt as red as the sky. Standing with his arms crossed (not as easy to do while wearing armor as you might think), his sword sheathed at his side, was a knight in full armor, including helm, obviously awaiting me. "That is the battlefield."

I looked around. The area surrounding the knight appeared to be about twenty feet in diameter. "That's a battlefield? The whole thing?"

"Indeed it is, although if you wish to get a running start, you are permitted an extra fifteen paces." He clapped me on the shoulder, making me stagger forward a couple of steps. "Good fighting, Lady Gwen! Your replacement will be up in a little less than two hours."

I watched him trot down the hillside, and then I turned back to look at the knight and the so-called battlefield. It could have served as a baseball diamond for guinea pigs. I took a few steps forward until I was at the edge of the scorched grass. "Um. Hi. I'm Gwen. I guess I'm supposed to fight you."

The man inclined his head, a flash of lightning reflecting off the closed metal visor.

"Just so you know, I'm new to all this. I'm an alchemist,

not really a soldier. I was kind of . . . er . . . conscripted into this job. Totally against my will, because as I said, I'm not a fighter, but there are times when you just have to take the lesser of two evil choices, and this was it. The lesser, that is. So, what's your name?"

Yes, I was babbling, but there was a method to my madness. I figured I had at worst an hour and a half to kill before someone else came to fight, and if I could use up some of that time in pleasantries, I was willing to chitchat like I'd never chitchatted before.

The knight didn't answer for a moment, but then he shifted his visor up so he could look at me unimpeded by metal. "I can't tell you."

"Is it against the terms of the fighting or something?" I asked, digging the point of the sword into the ground so I could lean on it.

"Don't do that."

I blinked at him. "Don't do what?"

"Don't bury the tip of your sword in that manner. You'll damage it. Here, see?" He marched over to me and lifted the tip of the sword in his mailed hand, showing me where the metal was dusty with bits of dirt and dead grass. "A sword is a valuable weapon. You must treat her with respect and honor."

"Oh." I blew on the end of the sword, took off my metal gloves, and carefully, so as not to cut myself, brushed off the dust and grass. "It is a pretty sword. It even has a name: Nightingale."

The man's eyes widened. Although I couldn't see a lot of his face, he looked pleasant enough.

"You bear the fabled Nightingale? You must be a very great warrior indeed."

"See, that's just the thing. I'm not, not at all. I'm an alchemist. Did I mention that? My moms—I have two—my moms and I just got here in Anwyn, and all of a sudden I found myself with armor on and this pretty sword in my hand. So if you wanted to forgo fighting, I'd be fine with that . . . er . . . what was your name?"

"I told you that I cannot tell you my name," he said primly, lowering his visor again and pulling out his sword, obviously in preparation for skewering me.

"Why not?" I asked quickly, desperate to distract him from the actual act of fighting.

He lowered his sword and raised his visor again. "I am King Aaron's man."

"Yeah, so?"

I could have sworn he rolled his eyes. "A warrior of King Aaron cannot be vanquished unless his name is known to his enemies."

"Really? So if I guessed your name, I'd win?" I considered him, trying to think of as many male Welsh names as I could.

Up went the sword. Down went the visor. "That is so. Are you ready to begin? We have wasted much time in conversation."

"Hold on just a second," I said, lifting a hand. "I'd like to have a few shots at guessing your name."

"Why?" he asked, his voice muffled behind the visor.

"Because I'm not a fighter. I'm a . . . well, a scholar, I guess. And besides, I can't fight someone whose name I don't know."

"Why?" he asked again, but he lowered his sword once more and lifted the visor so I could see the annoyed look on his face.

"I can't think of you as 'the knight dude' in my mental narrative, now can I? Daffyd?"

This time I saw him clearly roll his eyes. "No, that is not my name."

"Herbert."

"No."

"Owen?" It was my own surname, but there was a chance it was also his first name.

"That is not my name, no. Now, shall we fight?"

"I'm not going to fight you until I have a name that I can think of you by. Darryl?"

His shoulders slumped for a moment before he straightened up and said, "You may pick a name to use for me."

I really didn't want to fight him. He looked strong and immovable, and that sword was much larger than mine. "Fine. But if you hurt me, my moms will come after you. They're very protective."

He lowered his visor for the umpteenth time. "We shall begin. What name do you choose for me?"

I thought of whatever was the least threatening and the least likely to harm me. "When I was a child, I had a soft, fuzzy purple bunny named Douglas. I guess I can call you that."

This time he didn't just lift the visor—he took off the entire helm, pulling with it the soft cotton cap that was worn under it. His hair was close-cropped, and spiky with sweat. "Are you insulting me?" he asked, pointing the helm at me.

"Me? No!"

"You named me after a child's toy! A rabbit toy! I am a warrior of Aaron! I am feared by all! The very ground itself trembles beneath my feet! I am not a soft, fuzzy Douglas!"

"Sorry. I can try to think of something else if you like."

"You do that!"

I considered him, trying to formulate a vision of who he looked like. Maybe a Simon? An Alex? A Cadwallader?

"I'm sorry," I said, slumping just a little. "Now that I've thought of Douglas the bunny, that's what is stuck in my brain."

He looked like he was about to explode, but he simply slapped the cloth hat and helm back onto his head, hefting his sword and waving it in a menacing manner. "It matters not what you call me, servant of Ethan. Commence the battle."

"You know, I think I need a little coffee break. How about I go get us a little light refreshment?"

"You're not going anywhere. Not again."

The voice that spoke didn't come from Douglas. He pulled up his visor, his frown being sent over my shoulder. I turned to see who it was that had joined us in our battle.

It was Gregory. And he looked angry as hell.

FIVE

The gentle glow of the Krispy Kreme sign lit Gregory Faa's face. He was not happy, and he didn't have one iota of trouble letting the man who stood with him know that fact. "I am not happy."

"It's hard luck that your girlfriend duped you again, but we need to focus on what's important," Peter said, without the slightest shred of sympathy.

"That just makes me want to punch you, you know," Gregory answered, tired and cranky and utterly unable to keep from telling his cousin what was on his mind. Another day he might have been more circumspect, but tonight, as the two of them stood outside the Krispy Kreme shop in the Cardiff Shopping Centre, he lacked the verbal check needed to keep his emotions to himself.

Peter looked up from his notebook, wherein he was recording information on the chase that they had just undertaken across Cardiff to the shopping center. The fruitless chase. Gregory ground his teeth again at the thought of how Gwen had fooled him. Wantonly and brazenly.

"Why, because you don't like me pointing out that she misled you?"

"Because you aren't the least bit sympathetic with my plight. And she's not my girlfriend."

"You're interested in her," Peter insisted.

"I've never once said that," he protested, wondering how

Peter could tell that he was, in fact, quite interested in the delicious—if wicked—Gwen.

"You don't have to. You saved her life. Twice, according to the account you gave of what happened after you stole time."

Gregory looked into the distance, ignoring the flashing lights of the police cars as the officers continued to mill in and around the shop, interviewing workers and customers alike about the events of twenty minutes before. "I thought we weren't going to speak of that again."

Peter laughed. "We aren't. Why do you need sympathy if she's not someone you'd like to have a personal relationship with?"

He found it difficult to answer that question, and decided instead to answer another one, despite the fact that it hadn't actually been asked. "I don't think she escaped by means of a spell."

Peter returned to making notes. "You interviewed the security guard. Didn't he say that Gwen and her abductees ran into the doughnut place?"

"Yes. And I'm not so sure they were abductees."

"Look, I know your pride is still stinging over this betrayal," Peter said, giving him a sympathetic look that he found he didn't like or want after all. "But you've got to face the facts that this woman is not someone you should be lusting after."

"I never said—"

"You didn't have to. Anyone who uses the terms 'lush' and 'delicious' when describing a woman lusts after her. She's a bad egg, Gregory. She's rotten to the core, and she's not above using you to get what she wants."

Gregory fought back the urge to argue with his cousin about Gwen's character. He didn't, but not because he realized that arguing at that moment would be futile—surrounded as they were with the mortal police, who, by means of some false identification cards, they believed were members of

Scotland Yard—but because he had better things to do with his time and energy. "The guard said that Gwen helped the women out of the car. He said that the women, in turn, helped the kidnap victim very carefully and that Gwen and one of the others more or less carried the woman into the shop. Would you do that if you had the cops right on your heels?"

"I might," Peter said, thinking about it. "If I didn't have a weapon, and needed to use the victim as a hostage to secure my own safety. As for the other two women—they're clearly her accomplices. The nursing home said that there were two of them who abducted the old lady."

It didn't make sense to Gregory. Despite what Peter claimed, he didn't think Gwen was a cold, callous woman who cared nothing about the people around her. Yes, the facts were irrefutable in that she had kidnapped an elderly woman, but according to the security man, she'd been very careful to make sure the victim wasn't harmed in the act of escape.

"I'm going to talk to the police again," he said, coming to a decision. "I want a look at that storeroom they went into."

"The police scoured it already. It's empty," Peter said without looking up from his notebook. "The only way she could have gotten out is by using an escape spell of some sort."

"If that was so, then why didn't she use one earlier, when the police were chasing her? Or even earlier still, when she abducted the victim?"

Peter looked up at that, but clearly didn't have an answer. Gregory, his false identification badge pinned to the outside of his jacket, went into the shop to have another look around.

"They didn't look like criminals," one of the customers was saying to a policewoman who was interviewing her. "They just looked like a bunch of old ladies and one young one. They ran around the counter and into the back, and then a bloke dashed in shouting at them to stop, and went in after them. That's all we saw."

Gregory passed the investigation team, moving around the

counter to the doorway of the supply room. The room was filled with metal shelving units on either side, with the usual accoutrements scattered about—wheeled bucket and mop, cans of industrial cleaner, boxes of napkins, straws, and cup lids, which he assumed had been stacked tidily but were now splayed out in disarray. The back wall held a sink with a notice about washing hands, a small desk stacked high with take-out boxes waiting to be assembled, and huge drums of cooking oil. There was no exit door, no window, no possible way out of the room except by means of magic.

Gregory stepped into the room, intending to test whether he could sense any sort of residual magic, and came face-to-face with an anomaly: smack-dab in the center of the room was a portal. He glanced at the policeman who was at the rear of the room, tapping the walls in order to find who knew what, then back at the portal. He approached it. He'd never seen a portal in person, Travellers not having much of a need to visit places like Abaddon or the Court of Divine Blood (what most mortal people thought of as hell and heaven, but which were in reality quite a bit different), but he knew that what he was looking at had to be a portal. He circled it, examining it from the back. It appeared the same as the front.

He glanced again at the mortal, who didn't seem to notice the oddity at all, and then returned to Peter's side.

"I figured out how they got out of the shop," he said in a conversational tone.

"Magic," Peter said, in the middle of sending a text message, no doubt to his wife.

"Not really. There's a portal in the room."

"A what?" Peter stopped texting to look askance. "I looked in the room. There was nothing there but what you'd expect to see in a storage room."

"Smack-dab in the center of the room is a long oval that runs from ceiling to floor. The air in it is thicker, and twisted in long ropes that seem to spiral down in a never-ending pattern. If that's not a portal, I don't know what is."

Peter looked thoughtful. "It does sound like one. But I swear to you that it wasn't there when I looked in the room earlier."

"I didn't see anything, either, until I got within a yard of it. How far into the room did you go?"

"Not very far—just enough to see there was no exit and no place to hide. Damn. We're going to have to find out where the portal leads to."

"The cop in there didn't seem to see it."

"He wouldn't." Peter finished up his text message and punched in a phone number. "Portals are generally warded and protected so mortals can't see or access them. If this one didn't appear to you until you were right on top of it, it's probably heavily protected. Dalton? It's me. Gregory and I have found a portal in Cardiff. In a doughnut shop. Can you find out where it leads to?"

A small car pulled up. Gregory watched a familiar woman get out of the car and march over to the nearest police officer. She flashed some sort of a badge.

"Probably has identification set up through her boss like we do," he said softly, his eyes narrowing as she entered the shop.

"Uh-huh. Got it. You're sure? Damn. Thanks. Yes, we'll wait until you get permission. So long as there's no other exit for her to leave there, we should be OK until we are allowed in." Peter stopped Gregory as he was about to follow the red-suited minion of Death into the shop. He didn't like the woman at all, and worried that she might see the portal if she went far enough into the room. "Dalton says the records say the portal is to Anwyn."

"What's that?"

"Some sort of Welsh afterlife."

"Great. So we'll have to fight our way through dead people to get Gwen." He started forward again, only to be stopped once more.

"It's not that easy. We can't go in."

"We can't? Do you have to be dead? Gwen wasn't dead, nor was her victim and the other women."

"No, you don't need to be dead to go to the afterlife, but some agreement with the Akashic League and the L'au-dela prohibits the Watch from marching in there and arresting people."

"What's the Akashic League got to do with it? I thought they headed up ghosts and ghouls and the like . . . oh. After-life. Dead people."

Peter nodded. "We can't legally enter Anwyn without per-mission of the person who runs it."

"Who's that?"

"According to Dalton, there are legends about Anwyn. Ah, here's the file Dalton said he was sending." Peter looked at his phone, reading aloud. "Arawn is the king of Anwyn, the Welsh underworld where tradition says he has ruled in peace for several centuries. Let's see . . . there's a bit about him switching places with a mortal for a while. . . . Ah, here's something interesting. It's written that a powerful lord named Amaethon ab Don and his brother, Gwydion, started a war with Arawn when Amaethon stole a dog, a lapwing, and a roebuck from Arawn. There's something about trees, and the length of the battle, and a guessing game held to find the name of a warrior—your usual folklore stuff."

"How long is it going to take us to get permission to go after Gwen?" Gregory asked, feeling antsy. He didn't like the fact that the red-suited reclaimer had been in the shop so long. Had she seen the portal? Had she entered it? Did she have permission to do so?

"Don't know." Peter gave him a grim smile. "But it looks like we'll be on stakeout here for a bit to make sure that Owens doesn't pop back through the portal and make a run for it. I'll give Kiya a call and let her know we won't be back tonight."

He moved off to do so. Gregory frowned at the entrance of the doughnut shop, every muscle in his body urging him to follow Gwen. But he was already on shaky ground with Peter over the time theft episode, and to blatantly disregard the laws of the Watch would finish his budding career for good.

Hours passed. Each one seemed like an entire week to Gregory, and each subsequent hour seemed to bring more and more anguish. Death's servant hadn't reappeared, which meant she'd gone through the portal after Gwen. And there he was, stuck playing a waiting game, unable to do his job. It was pure torment, a veritable storm cloud of frustration.

"Stop it," Peter said at one point as the sun was about to rise. The two of them were in their car, waiting for the official permission and to make sure that Gwen didn't try to escape from Anwyn.

"Stop what?"

Peter nodded toward the front of the car. Gregory glanced out, pursing his lips a little at the flash of lightning across the pale bluey-pink sky.

"Sorry. I'm just frustrated."

"We both are, but making freak lightning storms isn't going to help."

"I didn't mean to. It just happens sometimes when I'm distraught. You keep a good control over your emotions. I've never seen you make it storm."

"I can't." Peter gave a little shrug and a half smile. "I think it's because I'm mahrime."

Gregory was silent for a moment. Until he'd met his cousin, he'd never had trouble with the Traveller belief that those of impure blood—those with only one Traveller parent—were unclean, but now he felt the full injustice of the attitude. It reflected just one of the ways he felt the Traveller society as a whole needed enlightenment. "You can't control lightning at all? But you have the mark."

Peter touched his chest where the long, feathery pattern had been branded into his skin by a lightning strike. Kiya had a name for it—"lightning flower." Gregory himself had a similar mark spreading across his back at the shoulders, but he never bothered much about how or why he had it. "Not in the way you can. I can't manifest lightning except when Kiya and I . . ." He gave an embarrassed cough and stopped.

Gregory decided that was a subject he had no business pursuing, and so he merely returned to his sense of frustration and irritation over the delay. An hour later, a car pulled up at the front of the shop, this one carrying two men. Both were built like bulls, with thick, almost nonexistent necks that rolled down to shoulders rounded with muscle. Their jackets hid most of the outlines on their upper halves, but the way the fabric stretched across their wide backs signified that they were men who had a serious interest in a steroids company. The men didn't look to the right or left; they simply entered the shop, not pausing when one of the remaining policeman called out for them to stop.

Gregory had a very bad feeling about those two men. He hadn't forgotten what the reclamation agent had said about two thugs being on Gwen's heels.

"I'm just going to check inside again," he said, getting out of the car. "I need to be doing something."

He didn't wait for Peter's response. There was no way in hell—the Welsh version of it or any other—that he was going to allow thugs or Death's agent to claim Gwen. She was his.

In a professional sense, of course. Nothing more, despite the fact that he wouldn't at all mind getting to know her better. Much, much better.

He shoved the erotic pictures that immediately popped into his mind out of it, and reminded himself that he had a job to do and that he'd be damned if he let someone else put that job in jeopardy.

The outer shop was empty of either a woman in a red suit or two thuglike bulls in human form. He smiled at the policewoman who was staring with a worried look at the supply room, and then he entered it.

It was empty.

He stepped farther into the room. The portal shimmered away in an annoying business-as-usual manner. He ground his teeth. He couldn't go in. Not without permission. Peter had made that absolutely clear.

But those two men and Death's agent had gone through it. They would get to Gwen first. And they might hurt her.

He couldn't go. He couldn't break the rules. Not again, not when he was so close to achieving what he most wanted out of life. Not when it would mean destroying not only his own professional future but his blossoming relationship with Peter, and more importantly, their plans for dragging fellow Travellers into society, where they could use their abilities for good.

He couldn't throw away all of that just to capture one woman.

One delectably enticing woman.

"Damn everything to perdition and back," he snarled, and pushed his way through the portal.

It was the noise that he noticed first. Or rather, the lack of it. It was quiet in Anwyn, the sort of rural, pastoral quiet that comes with birds going cheerfully about their business, sheep and cattle lazily grazing away with nary a tail swipe at irritating flies, and the soft wafting of gentle breezes about one's temples. It was, in short, as idyllic a spot as any place he had ever seen. More so, given the lack of the irritations that had plagued his life ever since he had joined the Watch.

He stood next to a low stone wall, the kind made by farmers for hundreds of years out of rocks turned over from plowing. On the far side of the wall lay a faint dirt track. Behind him rose a large rock, about twelve feet high. He took that to be the portal out to the mortal world, since the way out was frequently separate from the way in.

"Hello, cow," he greeted a brown and white cow that was grazing near him. She was a clean cow, her whites very white, her browns a rich milk chocolate, her hooves shiny. He wasn't overly familiar with the world of cows as a whole, but brief glances he'd had out of car windows when passing through farmland had led him to believe that cows were frequently splattered with mud and feces. Particularly their hindquarters. And yet here was this cow, all shiny and clean and looking as if she would give already pasteurized milk. "I had no idea they had cows in the afterlife, but I guess you too need somewhere to go when you die. You look plump and clean and happy, so this is good. Have you seen a woman named Gwen?"

The cow stretched out her neck and snuffled his front.

"A smallish woman in a red suit?"

A large pink tongue emerged from the cow's mouth. With a delicacy that surprised him, she tasted the buttons on his jacket.

"How about two large men with no necks? You couldn't miss them; they're roughly the same size as you."

She returned to snuffling his chest. Her ears wiggled happily.

"I'll take that as a no. Or as a statement that I smell good to cows. Good day, madam." He patted the cow on the head, stepped over the low wall, and strode off down the dirt track, wondering just how he would find Gwen. And whether or not the others had already found her.

"I'm not going to worry about what I've done," he said aloud to a large green, white, and black bird as it flew in front of him across the track, a few twigs in its beak. The bird fluttered in a circle around him, then alighted on the stone wall, spitting out the twigs.

For one startled moment, he expected it to speak. It didn't. It just cocked its head as it looked at him, picked up a twig, and flew over to drop it at his feet. It then flew a few feet at right angles to the path.

He looked at the twig. "A present? How thoughtful of you." He retrieved the stick and examined it. It did not, alas, have Gwen's current whereabouts engraved on it. "I would reciprocate, but I have no idea what to get a bird."

The bird fluttered a few feet, then landed on the grass, clearly watching him.

"I'm not the smartest man in the world, you know," he told the bird, "but I'm also not the most obtuse. Do you want me to follow you?"

The bird just sat there, waiting for him.

He pointed down the track. "There's no cow or sheep shit if I go that way. There's bound to be some if I cross the fields."

The bird spat up a beetle, twisted its head around to look at the carcass, then consumed it again.

Gregory grimaced. "What the hell. It's not like I'm not up to my elbows in it already."

He left the path and headed toward the bird, which immediately took wing and flew about a hundred feet ahead, then paused and waited for him. "Your name wouldn't be Lassie, would it?"

Gregory followed the bird for some time, the bemused feeling of being led by an animal eventually fading, allowing regret to darken his mood. "I'll get fired for sure. Peter will be angry as hell, but with time he might forgive me. My grandmother will be sure to hold my failure over my head for the rest of my life. But nothing I can do now will change any of that, will it?"

The bird said nothing, but continued to lead him through trees, and up and down the rolling hills. Despite his brave words, he did, in fact, fret over the situation that his impatience had cast upon him, but all the chiding words he hurled at himself faded away when he passed through a small copse of trees and crested a slight hill. Before him lay a panorama of . . . well, he was hard put to name exactly what it was. More gently rolling green hills. Periodic clumps of trees. A stream, silvery bright, cut a serpentine path through the hills and wound its way past him on the right. Fluffy white blobs that were no doubt spotlessly clean sheep dotted the grassy undulations, the latter of which were sprinkled with the yellow, red, and blue of wildflowers. Large blobs indicated more cows. But it was the man-made structures that held his attention.

"I take it this is what you wanted me to see?" he asked the bird, who was now perching on a tree branch and consuming yet another insect. The bird looked at him with its bright, intelligent eyes, two sets of beetle legs kicking and thrashing out the side of its beak. "I thank you for your assistance. Assuming, that is, you're not leading me to something heinous."

He looked closer at the scene before him. To the left of a stream, a large camp of tents was splayed along the slight rise of one of the hillocks, like a large bull's-eye made from tents of every hue. To the right of the stream sat another tented encampment, this one made up wholly of black tents that glittered with touches of gold in the morning sun. Those tents weren't laid out in any order, and if he squinted, he could make out tiny figures moving to and fro.

"That's interesting." He started walking toward the camps. "And not at all in keeping with the pastoral setting. It almost looks like two camps about ready to battle."

The bird flew in front of him, then disappeared into the distance, obviously finished with him. He wondered idly if all the animals in the afterlife had agendas.

The sense of martial strife, which grew stronger as he approached the center area, was aided not a little by the fact that the sky darkened from its clear topaz blue first to a dusky purple and then to reddish gray. Little snakes of lightning streaked across the red and gray sky, causing reciprocal tingles along his skin. He paused, waiting, and as one of the flashes spread out above him, he raised his hand and called it down. The lightning obeyed, encasing him in long, delicate tendrils of static that jumped and snapped with a familiar tingle. He embraced it for a moment, then released it into the earth.

What was this place? He narrowed his eyes on a mound just this side of the stream that had been blackened and scorched until it was nothing more than bare earth. Two figures stood there, one of whom was clearly a man in armor. The other was almost as tall, but held himself with less grace. It wasn't until he caught sight of the hand moving as the latter talked that he realized the figure was a woman.

As he moved closer, he recognized the black hair of the woman as it fluttered behind her, lifted by a breeze. She, too, was in armor, but seemed much less comfortable with it, holding herself very still.

Relief swamped him that the thugs and Death hadn't found her before he did, and he sent a mental thank-you to the bird for pulling him off the path and setting his feet in this direction. That emotion was quickly replaced by anger, determination, and no little amount of admiration for how gracefully Gwen gestured while being encased in armor.

As he strode up behind her, he overheard her say to the man she was facing, "How about I go get us a little light refreshment?"

"You're not going anywhere," he said with grim finality, stopping immediately behind her. "Not again. Not on my watch. And yes, I mean that literally, although this little stunt of yours is likely to cost me my job."

Gwen whirled around and stared at him with wide, startled eyes. He could have sworn that they were as innocent as a newborn babe's, but he wasn't going to allow himself to be fooled again. He placed a proprietary (and prohibitive) hand on her arm.

"Gregory? Goddess above, what are you doing here? And what do you mean, I'm going to cost you your job?"

"I'm here to arrest you, Magdalena Owens," he said firmly, fighting back the need to take her in his arms and kiss the startled look right off her face.

"You can't arrest me!" she protested.

"On the contrary, I can. I may be a probationary member, but I am fully able to arrest denizens of the Otherworld."

"I'm not Magdalena Owens!"

He turned a deaf ear to her claim. He wouldn't be fooled again. "I arrest you in the name of the Watch for the abduction of a human woman, and for the sale of magic to non-immortal individuals."

"Look, you annoying man, I just told you: I'm not Magdalena Owens!"

"Pardon me," said the man in knight's armor. He had a slight Welsh accent and raised the visor of his helmet as he spoke. "You are interfering with our battle. This warrior and I are engaged for the next . . ." He consulted his wrist, swore, then cast a look at the red and gray sky. "Another hour. Kindly step off the battlefield so that we might commence our battle."

"And I just told *you* that I'm not a warrior," Gwen told the man.

"Who is this?" Gregory asked Gwen, nodding at the knight.

"His name is Douglas."

"It is not!" the man declared.

"Well, that's what I call him," she amended, giving Gregory a conspiratorial smile that he felt down to his toes.

"She named me after a rabbit. A toy rabbit!" Douglas said, clearly outraged by this fact.

"It was one of my favorite toys. My mother says I used to suck on his soft, velvety ears while I was teething."

The man made a disgusted noise of protest.

"If you don't like the name, surely you don't have to use it." Gregory couldn't help but be distracted by the odd situation. "I wouldn't care to be named after a rabbit, either, although I wouldn't mind if you sucked on my ears."

Silence fell following that statement. Gregory felt all shades of awkward, an emotion he hadn't experienced in a very long time. If ever.

Both Gwen and Douglas were looking at him with doubt.

"Dammit," he told Gwen, "I am a very erudite man! I am known for my smooth personality, my very polite manners, and my blond good looks. My cousin's wife insists that I'm really a cover model! Erudite and smooth potential cover models do not say things that make people look at them the way you two are looking at me."

"Sir Cover Model," the knight said, gesturing with his sword. "You just told the warrior that you'd like her to suck on your ears. I take it you two are a couple?"

"No," Gwen said quickly. Too quickly for his taste.

"We have a complicated relationship," Gregory told Douglas.

"No, we don't. We don't have any relationship short of a casual acquaintance. We just met a few days ago." She gave him a look that spoke in no uncertain terms. "And I have no intention of sucking on his ears."

The knight pursed his lips. Gregory looked over her shoulder into the distance and fought to keep from smiling.

"Shall I say it?" Douglas asked. "I will. Ahem." He looked at Gwen and said in a tone that implied he was finishing her sentence, "Or anything else?"

Gwen's expression darkened. She walloped Gregory on the arm. "Stupid men and their penises!"

"I said nothing," Gregory pointed out, rubbing his arm. "I mentioned no penis. He did!"

"No, but you were thinking about it. And probably snickering to yourself. It's just a very telling point when you can't even mention sucking someone's ears without grown men turning into ten-year-old boys giggling about their penises."

"My apologies, Gwen," he said, his abused hand on his chest as he made her a bow.

"Stop being erudite and smooth at me," she snapped. "I don't like it at all. Why did you say I was ruining your job?"

"Alas, the discussion the two of you are having— fascinating as it is—will have to wait for another time. We must battle now, or you will forfeit the fight."

"What fight?" Gregory asked at the same time that Gwen said, "What happens if I do that?"

"Forfeiting a fight means that you have failed to do your lord's duty and are released from his service."

"Well, hell, I'm totally on board with that," Gwen said, handing Gregory her sword to hold while she pulled off the metal gauntlets. "I only did this to keep from being put back in prison."

The word "prison" brought Gregory's mind back to his reason for being there. "Magdalena Owens—"

"Will you stop calling me that? I'm not my mother!" Gwen shouted, smacking him in the chest with one of the gauntlets.

He stared at her. Could it be true? Or was she lying to him again? "Your mother?"

Her gaze skittered to the side. "Yes. That's my mom. I'm Gwen Owens."

"You said that your name was Gwenhwyfar Byron." She sounded like she was telling the truth. Did he dare believe her?

"It is. It's Gwen Byron Owens."

"You lied to me." He gave her his sternest look. It was necessary in order to keep from grabbing her and kissing her as she deserved. The very fact that she was ashamed of herself lent truth to her statement. She wasn't the Owens they were looking for! She wasn't a criminal!

"Kind of. Not really." At last her gaze met his. "All right, I did, but it was more a lie of omission than anything else."

"Again, I must point out that this conversation is not appropriate at this time," Douglas said, gesturing toward the tents behind them. "The battle must commence now, or you will forfeit the fight."

"I forfeit," Gwen said, spreading her hands in a gesture of apology. "Sorry about gabbing away at you for so long, but I really am not trained for this sort of thing."

"A pity," Douglas said, then turned and put his fingers to his mouth, blowing a loud, piercing whistle. "But perhaps we can change that. You are under arrest. Both of you. Please come with me of your respective free wills, because otherwise I will have to bind your arms and legs, and I understand that being trussed up in that fashion is not at all comfortable."

"Arrest?" Gregory said, moving to stand protectively in front of Gwen. He held the sword that she had handed to him, and although he was unused to wielding such a weapon, he felt that given the need, he could find it in him to do so. "I am a member of the Watch—"

"Which has no authority here," Douglas interrupted. "You are clearly in cahoots with this lady, and since she has forfeited the fight and shamed herself before her lord—"

"Hey!" Gwen protested.

"—thereby making her my prisoner, you also are in my charge."

A thin man in a long black and gold tunic and black leggings arrived in response to Douglas's whistle. "Ah, Tallyrand. I believe the king would like to meet these two. Can you arrange transport for Lady Gwen and Sir Cover Model?"

"My name is Gregory Faa, not Cover Model," Gregory snapped. "And if you think I'm going to let you take me prisoner, let alone Gwen-who-isn't-her-mother, then you're madder than Gwen's mother."

"Oh, you did not just say that," Gwen said, jerking him around so he faced her. That she was furious was clearly evident in both the dangerous glint in her eyes and the stubborn set to her jaw.

"You have a very nice nose," he told her. "I even like it when you're incensed and your nostrils flare, as they are doing now."

"My mothers are not mad! You take that back."

"Mothers?"

"Yes. I have two. My mom and her partner, who is my second mom. And I don't tolerate anyone saying anything bad about either of them."

"Your mother, or mothers, have kidnapped a mortal woman."

"Yes, well—"

"They have also attempted to sell magic to another mortal via the lawyer who we met on the cliff outside of Snails-on-the-Half-Shell."

Her nostrils flared again. It was utterly adorable. "The name of that town was Malwod-Upon-Ooze. I don't know why you have such a hard time remembering it!"

"You cannot deny that to do such acts, especially given the history of Magdalena Owens, indicates a lack of mental stability."

She hit him. Right on the chest, the same place she'd smacked him with the gauntlet. "Look, I never said what they've done is right. Lord knows I've had to spend much of my adult life cleaning up after them and keeping them on the straight and narrow—but they are not insane! They're simply . . . forgetful."

He looked at her.

She looked away, a flush darkening her cheeks.

"Even you don't believe that," he pointed out.

"I know." She sighed and met his gaze again. He was pleased to see that her expression had lost its hard, angry edge. "One of the problems with being raised Wiccan is that it's very hard to lie to anyone, but especially to yourself."

"You had no problem lying to me."

"Oh, I had a problem with it. I just figured it was more important to protect my mothers than to shield myself from karmic repercussions. If you had arrested me, I wouldn't have been able to extricate them from the situation. Which, I'll have you know, I was doing just fine."

"My definition of doing fine doesn't include dying in the act."

She stared at him with stark amazement. "How do you know I died?"

He hesitated, glancing to the side, a bit startled to find that except for the thin young man in the tunic, they were now alone. Evidently Douglas had gone off to his camp, leaving a guard set to watch them. He smiled to himself. He would have no trouble taking care of the young man when it came time for Gwen and him to leave. But first he had to dance around the delicate subject of the events on the cliff a few days past. "I was there."

"I know you were there. I saw you. You stopped that lawyer from throwing me over the edge. But how did you know he'd done it before?"

"I was there when you were killed the first time."

"You were?" She clutched his wrist, her eyes searching his. "So it was the lawyer who did it? Did you see who resurrected me? How come you weren't there when I came back to life?"

"Yes, in a way, and I was. Just not where you expected me."

She stared at him in incomprehension.

"I'm a Traveller, Gwen. Do you know what that is?"

"No. At least . . . no. The word seems like it is familiar, but I guess not. Wait . . . yes, I know it. There's a family who visits the town my moms live in. They're Travellers. Mom says they used to have a horse and one of those wooden trailers all painted up, but now they just bring camping equipment and hang out on the edges of the town."

"I suspect they are Romany, not actual Travellers. The Rom frequently use the same word to describe themselves, but I assure you that despite superficial appearances, we are very different from them."

She eyed his hair. "I suppose you don't see many blond-haired, blue-eyed Gypsies. So what is the Otherworld version of Travellers?"

"Most of the people in the Otherworld think of us as time thieves."

Her lips pursed for a moment before relaxing. He had the worst urge to taste those lips. "How do you steal time?"

"Travellers see time as a physical possession. You have so much time. I can take it if I so desire. But we always pay for it."

"That's not really stealing, then, if you pay for it."

He shrugged. "It's a matter of perception."

"What does this have to do with me dying? If you stole my time, then I'd have less of it, not more in terms of being reborn."

He glanced again at the young man next to them, but he appeared occupied with drawing something in the dirt at their feet. "I didn't take your time. I took someone else's, and . . ."

"And?"

He didn't want to tell her, but he'd turned over a new leaf when he joined the Watch, and that meant taking responsibility for his actions. It would be so much easier to lie to Gwen, or rather, to hide the truth from her, but he knew instinctively that she would much prefer the harsh truth than comfortable lies.

And suddenly, her wants had become quite important to him.

"When a Traveller takes time, the people in the immediate vicinity are affected by the loss just as if their time was taken as well. You have to be very close for that to happen. The woman whose time I took was standing right next to you. So when I took her time, it set her back about half an hour . . . and you, as well."

"You resurrected me by resetting time?" Gwen asked, incredulity in her voice.

"I did."

"I don't know whether to kiss you or smite you on the head with that sword," she said, her face a delightful mixture of emotions.

"I would suggest the kiss. Smiting is never as satisfactory as you imagine it will be."

"I don't know," she said with a dangerous edge to her voice. "I think there might be times when—"

Her words fell to the earth at the same moment that a yawning abyss opened at their feet and they plummeted into it.

SIX

"That was totally uncalled for!"

The voice that rumbled above and through me was pissed. Very pissed.

"You could have hurt Gwen!"

"Yeah," another voice said, and it took a few seconds before I realized that it came from my mouth. I put a hand up to my face to verify that fact, realized my eyes were closed, and opened them.

I was sitting on the floor, propped up against something hard and warm, wrapped in a delicious scent that reminded me of a campfire in the mountains. I turned to look, and my nose brushed Gregory's chin. "Hello," I told his chin.

"Are you all right? Do you hurt anywhere? You hit the floor hard."

"I don't feel hurt." Slowly my gaze moved upward until it reached his eyes. They were filled with concern now, the little laugh-line crinkles around the outsides making my stomach feel all warm and happy. "What happened?"

"Evidently that twit in the tunic was a mage. He threw open a portal at our feet."

I stopped looking at his nice eyes and nicer laugh lines to look around us, allowing him to help me to my feet. We were in a long rectangular room paneled in dark wood and bedecked with various antique weapons arranged in decorative fans and crosses. The floor was black-and-white-diamond marble tile. At one end of the room stood a tremendous fireplace, the kind that they used to have in medieval castles in order to roast whole oxen. The other end had two double doors, while overhead, dusty banners wafted gently in a ghostly breeze. A couple of long benches sat along one wall between suits of armor, while the other wall held a large curved desk with a sign that stated in three languages that tours would be conducted only in the company of an official guide.

No one else was in the room except a white cat that sat on the desk. As I watched, it jumped down and strolled over to us, tail held high.

"Where are we?" I asked, squinting at the sign in hopes it would tell us. It didn't.

"I have no idea. I wanted to make sure you weren't hurt before I went exploring. Shoo, cat."

I looked at him, guilt welling up inside me. "I'm sorry," I said before I could chicken out.

His eyebrows rose. "For?"

"Not telling you who my mother was. I just—you were with the Watch, and my moms have had so much trouble lately, and the last thing ended up with me being arrested, and then the Watch people released me, but they had this annoying scribe follow me around until I drove her mad and she quit, and the Watch couldn't find anyone else who would do the job, and then my moms didn't really believe me when I said that if they screwed up again, they'd get sent to the Akasha, and I died trying to get that lawyer off their backs after I told him that they weren't going to give him the magic after all, and my moms didn't believe that, either, and I had to see a therapist who thought I was loopy."

Gregory frowned. "That was quite the run-on sentence."

"It was, wasn't it?"

"It had a lot of meat to it, a lot of things to discuss and think about, and perhaps ask for more explanation about, but right now I believe the more pressing matter is to find out where we are, and why the scrawny mage sent us here. Cat, move." He nudged the cat, which had decided to plop its butt down on his shoe.

"Aw, don't be mean to the poor kitty. It clearly likes you."

"It can like me all it wants so long as it stays out of my way."

"Not a cat lover, eh? I am." I bent down to pick it up. The cat gave me a long look, unsure of whether or not it approved of this action, and finally, after some deliberation, sank its teeth into my hand. "Ow! You little monster! Fine, I won't pet you, then."

The cat jumped out of my arms, gave me a scornful look, ignored Gregory, and marched over to the nearest bench, where it attended to some grooming of a highly personal nature.

Gregory took my hand and examined the bite.

"Little beast has sharp teeth." I shot a glare at the cat. It paid us no attention.

"You'll live," was all Gregory said before he herded me to a door on our right. I had to admit, I didn't mind his hand holding mine. His thumb stroked over the bite a couple of times until it stopped stinging. What that simple touch did to my stomach was another matter. "Come. We will find out who is in charge here."

He flung open the door. It was a bathroom. A man sat on the toilet, holding a computer gamer magazine. He looked up in surprise. Two cats emerged from the room and twined around Gregory's legs.

"Whoops!" I said, turning around quickly.

"Our apologies," Gregory said, and closed the door.

"Well, that was embarrassing. How about I get to pick the next door?"

"More cats!" His tone was disgusted. "No, I do not want to pet you. Go away. What did you say, Gwen?"

"I offered to pick the door we open next. Those cats sure do like you. Here, kitty, I'll pet you if you're not bitey like Snowball over there."

The white cat, now sitting with its front feet tucked under it (what Mom Two always called "meat loaf mode"), glared at me.

"I wouldn't, if I were you," Gregory said, shooting the cat a dubious look.

This cat, which was mostly white with some orange splotches on it, didn't seem to mind being picked up. He purred amiably as I rubbed his ears and neck. His buddy went over to fling himself down in a pool of sunlight that glowed on the marble floor. "I told you that I like cats. Dogs, too. Actually, all animals, and they like me as well. I think it's because my moms are Wiccan. They know that we're animal-friendly."

Gregory made a noncommittal noise. We crossed the hall to open the door opposite. It was locked.

"Guess we try the big ones," I said, tucking the cat beneath my arm so I could gesture to the far end of the room, but before we could reach it, the sound of flushing and water running reached our ears.

"Who the hell are you?" asked the man who emerged. He was in the process of wiping his hands on a towel, which he flung to one side as he stalked forward. He was a little taller than Gregory, had curly black hair, dark eyes, and one of those dashing narrow mustaches that make me think of Errol Flynn and swashbucklers.

"We were about to ask you the same question," Gregory said in a haughty tone that I had a feeling wasn't going to go over well with Mr. Mustache.

"I live here. I get to ask questions first. Are you tourists?" He narrowed his eyes at us, answering himself before we could. "No, you're not mortal. You're also not deceased, and therefore you have no right to be in Anwyn. You can have that cat, though. Make you a present of it. Be glad to get rid of the beastly thing."

"We don't want a cat—"

"Speak for yourself," I said, chucking the cat under his

chin. He purred louder and kneaded my arm. "My moms love cats, and they just lost one to liver disease."

"—and before I explain myself to anyone, I desire to know to whom I'm speaking."

The man, who had been making a face at the cat, snapped to attention. "I am Aaron, lord of Anwyn, king of the Underworld, and ruler of these lands. Now, non-mortal, *who* are you?"

"Aaron?" Gregory asked.

"It's actually Arawn, but no one but pesky people call me that anymore. I've gotten with the times," the king answered with an air of being well-pleased with himself.

"Oh, dear," I said, unsure of how to greet a real, honest-to-Pete king, no matter how hip he was. Did people still curtsy? I wondered if I even knew how, or if he'd be offended by a bow?

"Gregory Faa." He bowed, making me swear at myself because I wasn't quicker off the mark. Now if I tried to bow, it would look like I was copying Gregory, plus I didn't think I could pull off the move with quite as much panache. Especially not with a cat tucked under my arm. "This is—"

"Gwenhwyfar Owens, Your Majesty," I said, making a little bob that I hoped would pass for a courtly curtsy. "We were evidently sent here by a mage."

"Ah?" The king crossed his arms and gave us a considering look. "You can drop the 'Your Majesty' business. I'm a man of my people. Why did a mage send you here?"

"That is a very good question," Gregory said.

I peeked at him out of the corner of my eye. He hadn't mentioned being with the Watch . . . that was odd. If I were a policeman, I would mention it, whether or not I had authority in that place. And he certainly hadn't had a problem telling Douglas that. Hmm.

"I'm sure I'll get a message about it," the king said, dismissing the subject with a wave of his hand. "You wouldn't happen to know anything about machines, would you?"

"Machines?"

"What kind of machines?" I asked, tucking the cat more firmly in place as Aaron strode to the door, obviously expecting us to follow him. "I know a little about computers."

"Such things are unreliable. They are always breaking down." He must have noticed Gregory pulling out his cell phone, because he added, "I believe you'll find that your mobile device will not work here. It's something to do with the static in the air. Now, about your experience with machinery . . ."

"I'm a Traveller, Your Maj—er—"

"Aaron."

"I'm a Traveller, Aaron," Gregory said as we left the hall and blinked at the bright sunlight flooding the grass bailey before us.

"Ah? Oh, I see what you mean. Your kind does not do well with machinery. Just so," Aaron said, nodding, then cocked an eyebrow at me. "Are you a Traveller, too?"

"No, I'm an alchemist."

"Hmm. Alchemist. Hmm. No, my newest weapon, the Piranha, has no use for that. Now, if you had some way to smooth out a balky gearshift, I could put you to work. But as it is—oh, lord. This is all I need."

Irritation flitted across his face as a woman strolled out of a small outbuilding. She was dressed in a Victorian artist's idea of medieval wear, a long silken white gown known as a kirtle, touched with gold shimmering in the slight breeze. Her hair, the same color as the gold trim, hung down to her waist in waves that would have made a shampoo-commercial producer fall over in a swoon. Two orderly lines of mostly white cats followed her, tails standing tall like so many furry staves.

"What do you want? Can't you see I'm busy?" Aaron snapped before the woman and her feline escort stopped before us.

"No, I do not see that you're busy. You're never busy. You

simply amuse yourself with a variety of toys and pretend it's work."

Aaron bristled. "I am the king of the Underworld! The king of the Underworld does not have toys! He has vitally important machinery of war."

The woman pursed her lips and tapped her chin. "So that thing you're always hunched over on that computing device wherein you construct villages and towns isn't a game?"

"SimCity is a highly intelligent computer simulation. It is a tool, woman, not a game. With it, I can plan out the next stages of development of Anwyn to ascertain the best allocation of funds and labor without having any negative impact on the indigenous population, souls in transit, or the wildlife native herein."

She smirked. "Which explains why you have statues of yourself dotted about the simulated town and cackle loudly when you send a giant lizard monster to destroy the townspeople?"

"They are virtual townspeople. They aren't real."

"But you enjoy destroying them with monsters and tornadoes and virulent venereal diseases."

Aaron made a disgusted noise. "There are no venereal diseases in SimAnwyn, virtual or otherwise. That's another program."

"The fact remains that you enjoy destroying the people of your town."

"Your facts are erroneous. I reject them. Begone. I am busy talking with these fine people."

The woman turned lovely, if cold, greenish-gray eyes upon us. "Who are they?"

"I have no idea. Someone that one of the mages at the front sent out. It matters not."

"It matters to us," I said, smiling politely when the woman glanced at me. "I'm Gwen. This is Gregory."

"You are not dead," she said, as if making a profound judgment.

"No. Although I did die earlier in the week if that makes you feel any better."

"Hmm," she said, then turned to consider Gregory. She seemed to like him better than me, a thought that made me narrow my eyes. Did she have to ogle him so obviously? We weren't a couple, but she didn't know that. What if we had been?

I glared at Gregory when he smiled in a friendly fashion at her. He caught the edge of my glare and raised his eyebrows. I resisted the urge to kick him in the shins.

"Introduce us, Arawn," she said, pronouncing his name with a heavy Welsh flourish.

"This is my ex-wife, Constance," he said with a martyred sigh. He gestured toward the double line of cats behind her. "And her hell-spawn creatures."

"My cats are beguiling furry little beasts of wonder and delight, although technically they are hell-spawned, but only because this is what many mortals think of as hell. And I am *not* your ex-wife. I do not recognize your divorce proceedings; thus we are still very much married." She bit off the last few words in a manner that reminded me of the piranha that Aaron had mentioned earlier.

"Only because you live in your own little fantasy world that in no way resembles any form of reality. No, no," he said, raising a hand to stop her even though she hadn't responded to his comment. "Far be it from me to interrupt you on your daily torment of the poor, hapless souls who reside here. Stay and talk to the strangers all you like. I have important things to do. The Piranha calls." And with a curl of his lip (and the slightest hint of an obscene gesture to the feline honor guard), he left.

"You really do have piranha here?" I asked, glancing at the cats. "Isn't that kind of dangerous for them?"

"It isn't a real piranha," she answered with another assessing ogle at Gregory. "It's what Arawn calls his Velociphant."

"Do we want to know what a Velociphant is?" Gregory asked.

"No," she said, then pinned me back with a look that had me straightening my shoulders. "Why did the mage send you to us?"

I slid a look to Gregory. He slid it right back to me, leaving me to stammer, "Uh . . . well . . . you see . . . that is . . ."

She turned to Gregory. I could see that he was struggling with an answer that wasn't an outright lie, and yet shielded the truth a bit.

"I see," she said after a few seconds of silence. She waved imperiously at a couple of men who were hauling in giant bags of what appeared to be kitty litter. "You there. Take these two to the captain of the guard and ask that they imprison them in the deepest, darkest part of the dungeon."

"What?" I shrieked.

"I should inform you that I am a member of the Watch—" Gregory started to say, but the woman said nothing as the two men dropped the bag of kitty litter and approached us. She simply lifted the hem of her gorgeous dress and delicately moved away, the double line of cats following her.

"No," I told Gregory. "I'm not doing this again. I'm simply not doing this."

The fight that followed wasn't pretty, nor was it even fair. Just about the time Gregory declared, "Touch one hair on her head, and I'll pound you into the ground, Watch or no Watch," a handful of other men appeared from the depths of the nearest outbuilding and joined the fray, the bulk of which was centered on Gregory.

And when I say "on Gregory," I mean just that. He started swinging the second that one of the men grabbed my arm in the same familiar, "imprisoning innocent women is my middle name" sort of manner that I had experienced the day before, and it only took a couple of heartbeats before Gregory went down under the onslaught of several pissed-off cat-litter toters, or whatever their respective job titles were.

Naturally, I did what I could. I screamed, I bit, I kicked, and I punched. I tried to flip several men over my hip this time, too, but in the end I was ignominiously hauled off yet again to forced imprisonment.

The men had a harder time with Gregory. Once the bulk of them peeled off the pig pile, he came up fighting again. I winced in sympathy when, as I glanced over my shoulder to where he was being carried by six men, I caught sight of not only an eye that was quickly swelling and turning a deep crimson purple but also a fine spray of blood across his dark blue shirt.

We were hauled down smooth-cut stone steps into what I assumed was going to be a dark, dank, rat-infested dungeon.

"I have to say that this is the cleanest, most pleasant dungeon I've ever been forced to visit," I told the man who was attached to my left side. "It's well lit, it smells good, there's no garbage or people's bones lying around, and I don't hear so much as even one little scream of torment."

"Lord Aaron believes that a healthful dungeon is a productive dungeon," the guard said.

"That's quite forward-thinking of him."

"Aye, but to be honest, he had them cleaned up when the tourists started coming through," the man on my right commented.

"Tourists?" Gregory asked from behind me. His voice sounded hoarse and muffled. "Did he just say 'tourists'?"

"He did. That's probably what that sign upstairs was all about."

"What sign?"

"The one that mentioned tours."

"Why," I heard Gregory ask one of his attendants, "does Aaron run tourists through the afterlife?"

"Why not?" the man said.

"I have to admit," Gregory called up to me, "that he has me there. Literally as well as figuratively."

"We wouldn't be havin' to carry ye iff'n ye didn't fight us," one of his guards answered. "Ye fair on crippled poor 'Erbert."

"Aye, he did. I may never walk again," said the man on my left.

I looked at him. He immediately started to limp.

"Poor Herbert, indeed. He tried to kidney punch me," Gregory pointed out.

"Then there's what you did to Maltravers," my right guard said.

"Who's Maltravers, and what did Gregory do to him?" I asked.

"'E's the 'ead litter cleaner, and yer boyfriend 'ere broke his thumb. The one 'e uses to scoop!"

"Christos, not the scooping thumb!" Gregory muttered. "Was Maltravers the one who broke my nose?"

"Nay, that'd be Jones, there on yer left calf."

"Pleasure to meet you," said Jones. I assumed it was him, but I couldn't actually see behind me.

I giggled, but felt obligated to say, "Gregory isn't my boyfriend."

"And then there's Wenceslaus," another man behind me said.

"OK, now you're just getting silly," I protested. "This is Anwyn. We're in Wales. I'm willing to let 'Herbert' and 'Maltravers' pass, but 'Wenceslaus' isn't even remotely Welsh."

"Nay, 'e isn't, and now 'e can't talk what with the beating your boyfriend 'ere gave him about the throat. Got a clean left in the Adam's apple, 'e did."

"He got me in the bollocks." A thin, reedy voice drifted up from the back. "With his elbow! I may never have children again!"

"You ain't had them to begin with," called my chatty guard. "So don't you be going on about something what isn't likely to happen to begin with, Ned Bundy. Not that I'm saying getting a man in the bollocks is right," he added to me. "A man's bollocks ought not to be touched excepting by him. And possibly his missus, if she has a light hand to her."

"In general, I agree, with the firm exception of self-defense. What did Ned do to Gregory?"

"Nothing," Gregory answered. "He just got in my way when I was trying to keep from having any more of my teeth knocked out."

"There, you see? Self-defense."

"Aye," the guard said, sucking on his teeth as he thought. "That's as might be."

"What's your name?" I asked him.

"Me mum named me Aloysius, but the lads 'ere call me Al. I'm by way of bein' the 'ead of his lordship's guards. When 'e has need of 'em. Othertimes, I does a bit of light tanning."

"I don't suppose we could convince you to let us go?" I asked without much hope.

The look he gave me was pitying. "Now, then, what sort of a 'ead guard would I be if I was to be lettin' you and 'im go?"

"A nice one?"

Al scratched his neck. "That's as might be, but I can't see my way clear to it without word from my lord or 'is lady."

"This really sucks," I said somewhat pettishly. "I don't want to sit in a cell by myself, twitching at every sound, and with no one to talk to."

"Well, as to that, I'm afraid accommodations are what you would call a wee bit tight at the moment." Al stopped before a solid-looking wooden door. One that I couldn't help notice was fitted with a small cat door. "What with the tourists and all."

"You *imprison* tourists, too?"

"Only those that pay for it," Herbert the guard said, leaning in to add, "It costs extra."

"Wow," was all I could think of to say, and say it I did. A few seconds later, that pithy exclamation was joined by "Holy carp!" and "Oh, you poor thing. Is your nose broken?" when the guards summarily dropped Gregory on the floor and closed the door firmly behind them.

I knelt next to him as he rolled over and sat up. His eye was swelling even as I watched it, and a trickle of blood from a split lip dripped sluggishly down his chin.

"You look," I said, pulling out the end of my shirt and using it to dab at the blood, "like a man who's gone five rounds with a Velociphant."

"What on earth do you suppose that is?"

"Love child of a velociraptor and an elephant? That or some sort of elephant on wheels? I don't know the answer to that, but I do know that I'm getting sick and tired of being imprisoned. First it was the Watch, then it was that Holly woman, and now it's the queen of the Underworld."

"We imprisoned you? For what crime?"

"Nothing that I did. They thought I was my mom, and later released me because they couldn't prove I was her."

"Ah, I recall hearing something about that."

"Now you know why I'm so tired of this shtick. Does this hurt?"

I grabbed his nose and gave it a sharp snap, causing him to jerk back and howl. "Bloody hell! What are you doing? Oh." He took a stuffy-sounding breath. "I guess it was broken."

"You're welcome." I stood up and looked around, wondering what we were doing there, and more to the point, how we were to get out. "This really is the nicest dungeon. Those cots have memory foam mattresses. And look, I think that walled-off area is a bathroom." I went behind a closeted section of the dungeon, noting with approval the clean toilet and sink. "Yup, that's what it is. No shower, though."

Gregory was gingerly feeling his mouth when I emerged from the toilet area, pulling away his fingers to glare at them. "How bad is it?" he asked, and grimaced.

"Not bad at all. The toilet is clean, and the sink means they must have running water—"

"No, not how bad is the privy. How bad is my mouth?"

I tried very hard not to notice how enticing his lips were.

The man had just fought off at least ten attackers and had the battle scars to show for it. I would not embarrass myself by staring with blatant lust at his mouth. "Not bad at all," I said nonchalantly. "It's very nice and all, especially when you smile, but I wouldn't give up ice cream for it. Not unless, you know, I had to."

He stared at me as if the ice cream in question was coming out of my ears. "What are you talking about?"

"You asked me if I liked your mouth. I said I do. What's the big deal?"

He showed me the tips of his fingers, then bared his lips at me. Just to the right of his upper two front teeth, a dark gap showed. "I meant how bad was the damage? Does the missing tooth make me look dashing and dangerous, like a pirate, or creepy and disturbing, like a crack addict who lives under a bridge?"

"Dashing," I reassured him. "Definitely dashing."

He eyed me. "You're lying."

"Just a little. You're not quite a sexy pirate, but also not a bridge-dwelling crack addict. More . . ."

"A swashbuckler?"

I wrinkled my nose. "More someone who was in a bar fight and lost a tooth."

"Lovely." He made a face that turned to a frown when I wandered over to bounce on one of the three cots in the cell. "What are you doing?"

"Testing out the mattress to see if it's soft or hard memory foam. Seems pretty decent." I stretched out on it, feeling myself sink into it. "Ahhh. Nice."

"What about me?"

I gestured toward the other two beds. "Take your pick."

"You're not going to tend me anymore? That dab at my lip and the vicious jerk on my nose was the sum total of you nursing the wounded?"

There was outrage in his voice, righteous outrage. I sat up, unable to hold back a little giggle. "You don't need tending, do you? I mean, you're immortal. The bleeding has already stopped on your mouth, the swelling around your eye will go down in probably less than an hour, and I'm willing to bet you that the bones in your nose are already knitting back together."

"That doesn't mean I don't appreciate a little sympathetic care," he said sulkily.

That just made me giggle more.

"I would remind you that I suffered these grievous wounds when a full score of men descended upon me as I attempted to protect you from them!"

"A full score? Ha! It was a dozen at most." I didn't let on that I was impressed he had handled himself so well with all those guards. I suspected he'd just get a fat head if I did. It would be far better to turn his attention. "I didn't need protecting, anyway. I just objected to being imprisoned a second time in so many days."

He maintained an injured silence for about a minute, then rose and stumbled over to one of the comfy cots, saying, "No doubt you were imprisoned for some illegal act your mother performed."

I glared at him. "No cracks about my moms, either of them. And for your information, Mr. 'I'm the Watch and I Know Everything,' neither my moms, Mrs. Vanilla, nor I did anything deserving of imprisonment. We were just in the wrong place at the wrong time."

"Mrs. Vanilla?" He lay back on the cot, groaning in relief as he did so.

I sat up to assess whether or not he really was hurt to the point where he needed healing. Most people of the immortal persuasion had self-healing abilities, some more powerful than others. Perhaps Travellers had a harder time healing up their wounds? "She's a mortal, one of my mothers' clients evidently."

"Ah, the old woman they kidnapped."

I made a face, but he didn't see it since his eyes were

closed. Quietly, I moved over to stand next to him. Blood from the broken nose was giving him two black eyes, although the swelling around the one abused eye had gone back to normal. The split on his lip had also healed, and I assumed the empty socket for the missing tooth had sealed up as well. "You look like a raccoon," I told him, bending over to brush a bit of dried blood off his chin.

"Thank you," he said without opening his eyes. As I stood up, he grabbed my wrist and gently pulled me down so that I was half sitting and half draped across his torso. His eyes opened. My stomach went a bit wobbly at the clear blue depths of them, made especially noticeable by the dark purple and black mask resulting from the broken nose. "Why do you have two mothers?"

I had to drag my attention off his mouth and chin and the warm, solid chest beneath my breasts. My skin tingled where it was pressed against him. "Because they fell in love. Why do you have a mother and a father?"

"What makes you think I have a mother and a father?"

"Most people do."

"True. I did, as a matter of fact, but they weren't together because they were in love. Theirs was an arranged match. They didn't much like each other, and they parted ways soon after I was born."

"How sad for them. And you. I much prefer being raised by two mothers who love each other and me."

"I would prefer that as well. Why did your mothers kidnap a mortal woman?"

"You're just full of questions, aren't you?"

"Yes. Here's another: would you object if I kissed you?"

I thought about that for a minute. Although every instinct in me told me to keep him at a distance, both emotionally and physically, I couldn't help but admit that there was some sort of magnetism between us. I didn't want to get up off his cot, even though I knew I should. I wanted to touch that golden hair, and stroke my fingers down his jawline, now bearing blond stubble that made my legs feel shaky. But most of all, I wanted to kiss him ever so gently on those tempting lips, not hard enough to hurt his mouth if it was still tender, but enough to let him know that he'd been kissed.

"No. You cannot kiss me," I said firmly.

His eyes grew grave.

I leaned down and gently, oh so gently, nipped his lower lip. "I, however, will kiss you."

"I'm not normally aroused by bossy women," he warned as I feathered little kisses along the edges of his mouth. His hands slid down so that they rested warmly on my waist.

"Who says I'm trying to arouse you?" I asked as I licked the tip of his nose.

His eyes crossed. "You're doing a damned good job of it if you're not. Are you going to stop teasing me and kiss me properly?"

"Now who's being bossy?" I didn't let him reply. I just leaned in and let my lips do what they'd wanted to do ever since the moment I'd seen him on the cliff. His mouth was warm and soft and infinitely pleasing, but when his lips parted in a happy sigh, my pleasure in the kiss went into overdrive. I touched the tip of his tongue with mine, then retreated. It was such an intimate gesture, it shook me for a moment or two, and I felt the need to give him time to adjust himself to the invasion.

Gregory obviously did not share such thoughts, because before I could tell him that he was an extremely good kisser, his tongue was there in my mouth, being just as bossy as he had claimed I was. I didn't have long to think about that because not only was his tongue laying siege to my mouth—in a way that made me feel as if my toenails were steaming—but both hands had moved up along my sides until they were cupping the undersides of my breasts. That was pleasant, very pleasant indeed, but when Gregory sent his thumbs into action in the form of soft little sweeps across my nipples, I pretty much stopped thinking and just wallowed in a delicious world made up of Gregory and his magic mouth and hands. And chest. And I had a feeling that the rest of him would be pretty damned fine as well.

"All righty, 'ere we go with dinner, and a few visitors to—oy!"

It took a couple of seconds for Al's voice to penetrate the thick fog of desire that had rolled over me, but Gregory's stiffening beneath me did a lot to bring me back to my senses.

I sat up, my mouth feeling strangely bereft, my breasts very much protesting the removal of his hands from their premises.

"Oh," I said, staring at the two guards who held trays bearing food. Behind them stood three people, one of whom held a camera. "Um. This isn't what it looks like."

"Yes, it is," Gregory said, and crossed his ankles as he put his hands behind his head.

The guards—Herbert and another man—looked at each other.

"I can't see!" a voice squeaked from behind them. Al opened the door wider, gesturing for Herbert and his buddy to set down the trays of food. The others behind them spilled into the cell. "What does it look like?"

"It looks like a man and a woman having sex," a thin, rat-faced woman said and took a picture of us. "Henry, I'm shocked and appalled by this. It isn't at all what I thought we'd see in a dungeon."

"This is hell, dear," a short, round man said softly. "I expect that's the sort of thing they get up to, here."

"We are *not* having sex," I said a bit desperately.

"Not yet, anyway," Gregory added.

I glared at him. He winked.

"I still can't see!"

"You're too young to see, kid," the rat woman said, taking another picture of us. I stopped glaring at Gregory and stood up, trying to think of something to excuse our actions that didn't sound inane.

"See what?" A spotty teenage boy pushed his way around the guard. He looked disappointed to find that we weren't engaged in a full-fledged orgy. "Oh. It's just some chick and a dude. I thought there would be more skin."

I narrowed my eyes at him. "Excuse me, but just who are you people?"

"This is the After-Hours Tour." Al smiled cheerfully. "We don't be normally sendin' tours down 'ere, what with the payin' customers enjoying their bit o' privacy, but since you and Sir Bollocks Puncher over there ain't payin', 'is lordship figured folks might want to see actual prisoners in their native environ, so to be speakin'. We weren't to know that you and 'is nibs would 'ave preferred to be alone."

"I believe," Gregory said as he sat up and swung his feet to the ground, "that of the two, I prefer the name Sir Cover Model."

We all ignored him.

"I thought there would be more torture. Shouldn't there be torture, Henry? There should be torture. Blood, and hot irons, and torture—that's the proper sort of thing to have in a dungeon."

"This tour has got to be against some sort of rules," I protested to the guard and tourists alike. "You're invading our privacy, and we don't like it."

"I'll pass along your complaints to 'is lordship," Al said, jerking his head toward the door. His two henchmen shuffled out, but only after giving us wide, amused grins.

"I will be sure to say something on the comment cards about the lack of blood and tormented people, of that you may be certain!" the woman snorted.

Her husband smiled a watery smile, and shared it with Gregory and me. "Mariah does love a good torture scene."

"Bully for her!" I gave her a look that I normally reserve for people who spit in public.

She sniffed and took a few desultory shots of the cell. "Not even a proper set of shackles here. What sort of hell is this where there's no torture and no shackles?"

"Look, lady—"

"Nothing but a strumpet and her love toy."

I gaped at her for a second, then took a step forward, intending on giving her a piece of my mind, but Gregory was suddenly in front of me, one arm blocking me.

"Madame," he said, and his voice was one of commanding dominance. The rude tourist woman shrank before him. "You will kindly refrain from referring to Miss Owens by that word. It is untrue, and upsets her. Furthermore, you will remove yourself, your husband, and that adenoidal teen from our presence."

"Well, now, well, now," Al the guard said while the two others backed away from Gregory. I have to admit, I smirked a little behind his back. I wasn't normally one for expecting someone else to save me, especially a man, but Gregory seemed to slip into the protector role easily, so who was I to complain? "There's no need for anyone to be gettin' angry-like, is there? We'll just be on our way and leave you two to the kissin' that you were up to."

"We weren't kissing!" I objected, then swore to myself. "We might have been, but that was all we were doing. Gregory was wounded, if you recall. I was merely seeing if he had healed up properly. I was . . . *tending* him."

The last couple of words fell from my lips with a pretense made limp with disbelief. Even I couldn't say it with any conviction.

"Have a very . . . fulfilling . . . evening tending 'im." Al's parting shot was delivered with a knowing smile. He closed the door, leaving us standing in the middle of the room.

The food wafted a heavenly smell toward us. Gregory moved over to examine the meal, making approving noises at a bucket of ice containing a bottle of champagne. "Ah. Very good year. How pleasant. And now, my dear—"

"Don't say it," I warned, pointing a finger at him. "Don't you dare say it."

"I don't know what you're talking about," he answered, then sat back down on his cot. "Even if I did, I'm too weak to actually speak. Feed me?"

"You big ham. You need a sharp smack to the head."

"No, what I need is some of that tending you spoke of." He patted the cot. "I'm in considerable pain. Don't you want to come back over here and give me the benefit of your healing powers?"

"No." I went to my cot, grabbed my pillow, and hugged it to myself to keep from doing as he asked. Damn the man for his tempting mouth and eyes and oh, dear goddess, the sight of him splayed out on that cot all hard and masculine and bulgy with muscles and did I mention hard? He looked very aroused indeed if the largest bulge of all was anything to go by.

I reminded myself that those bulges were attached to a man who was by definition if not my mortal enemy then *not* someone I should be having illicit thoughts about, let alone indulging in related touches with.

He was with the Watch. They were dangerous, even here in Anwyn where they had no jurisdiction. If I fell victim to the lure of his sensual ways, he'd be able to play me like a violin, and before I knew it, my mothers would be out of Anwyn and into the custody of the Watch.

I hardened my heart, mentally girded my loins, and told my libido to take a cold shower.

"No?" he asked, giving me a come-hither look to end all come-hither looks.

I almost went thither.

"It's out of the question. I'm tired. I'm going to sleep."

"It's about four in the afternoon."

"Very tired. I didn't get much sleep last night. You eat the food and drink the champagne, and if you so much as come within two feet of me, I'll scream bloody murder." I grabbed a blanket and wrapped it around me like a cocoon, rolling over on the cot so that my face was to the wall. I prayed that the buzz of excitement that had filled me at our recent activity would die down enough so that I could at least rest.

Sleep, I knew, was out of the question. Not while Gregory was near. Not while everything in me wanted to ignore common sense.

I sighed. It was going to be a long, long night.

SEVEN

The night was long. Hellishly long. That was a better description, Gregory decided somewhere around two in the morning. Not only did he have a sleepless night in which to consider his sins, mostly focused on the fact that he had charged into Anwyn without official permission, but he didn't even have the deliciously ripe form of Gwen to distract him.

"Blast it all," he said into the close, dark night.

"You can say that again," came the soft reply.

He stopped staring at the stone ceiling—which he couldn't see once the guards turned off the lights for the night—and squinted across the cell. Was it his imagination, or could he make out a dark shape that was Gwen's cot? "Are you awake, too?"

"No. Go back to sleep."

"I haven't been to sleep, so I can't go back to it." He hoped she would reply. If she would at least talk to him, then he stood a fair chance of wooing his way onto her cot. Or having her come and "tend" him again. That had been most pleasant, and not a little bit surprising.

"I like your mouth," he said conversationally, putting his hands behind his head as he once again looked up into the darkness. "It is sweet, and hot, and very enjoyable."

"We are not having this conversation."

He smiled to himself. She had refused to speak to him for hours, her breath evening out until he thought she had dozed off. But he had been wrong.

What he hadn't been wrong about was her interest in him. No woman could kiss him like she had if she wasn't the littlest bit attracted to him.

"I liked how your tongue touched mine. But it seemed to lose interest."

He cocked his head, but there was no reply.

"I did enjoy how it twined around mine after that, though. It was very erotic."

There was a small noise in the darkness, like that of a frustrated woman stifling a sigh into a pillow, followed by the determined rustle of blankets.

"I also very much liked touching your breasts."

An exhalation of breath. Good. She was listening to him, at least.

"I like that they are . . ." He let the silence build for a minute and a half before there was a sharp sound of blankets being pushed back, and the squeak of a bed frame.

"What?" Gwen demanded to know. "They are what? Horrible? Repulsive? Off-putting?"

"Abundant. And warm. And so very sensitive to my touch."

"They are not sensitive to your touch," Gwen said in a huffy tone and from the sound of it, lay back down on the cot.

"No? So the thought of me touching them right now isn't making your nipples tighten in anticipation?"

"Certainly not!"

"The idea of me nuzzling them, licking them, taking the tips of them into my mouth doesn't stimulate you in the least?"

"Not at all."

He smiled. Her voice sounded strangled, and he could swear her breath was coming faster.

"Odd. I freely admit that the thought of your breasts, of touching them, of rubbing my cheeks on them, of tasting them and pressing them against my bare chest makes me hard." Sadly, that was very much the truth. He shifted on the cot, trying to ease his now strained fly.

She didn't answer, but he heard the sound of her legs moving restlessly. That thought led to another. "I bet your belly is sublime."

"You'd so lose that bet."

"Really? What is it, if not sublime?"

"A stomach. A poochy stomach. If you haven't noticed, I'm a big girl."

"Statuesque."

"Large."

"An Amazon goddess."

"Mom Two says plump is in these days. I hope so, because I can't seem to lose this last twenty pounds no matter how many Zumba classes I go to."

"I don't care for women who have no padding on their bones. I prefer my woman with curves, and ample flesh for me to caress."

She snorted. "You're worth your weight in gold, then, because most men like skinny women."

"That is their loss. Would you like me to go over there and show you just how much I appreciate your lushness?"

"No!" There was a *whump* as she obviously turned over, no doubt giving him her back again. He wondered if she knew that he simply had admired her delectable bottom when she'd done so earlier. Probably it was best not to mention it.

Then again . . . "You have a nice ass, too."

"Bloody hell, Gregory!" she snapped as the cot squeaked again, followed by the slap of two bare feet hitting the stone floor. He could just imagine her shaking a finger at him. "Stop cataloging my body! I'm trying to sleep over here."

"You are not. You are trying very hard to not imagine me naked."

The startled inhalation of breath confirmed that wild shot (literally in the dark). "You are deranged." She curled up again.

"It's all right. I'm doing the same. Imagining you naked, that is. I already know what I look like."

She muttered something under her breath, but refused to rise to his bait.

A thought struck him. "You appear to be shy about things of a sexual nature."

"I am not shy!"

"You were shy when you kissed me. You touched the tip of my tongue with your own, and then seemed to be overwhelmed with the sensation."

"That is not shy. That is just . . . circumspect."

"Since you are shy, would you like me to describe myself?"

"No!" Their silence was pregnant with unspoken thought that quickly became spoken. "I am not interested in what you look like naked. You are the Watch. You want to arrest my moms. You could look like Adonis, and I couldn't care less."

Ah, so that was what bothered her. He had had a suspicion that she was feeling threatened by his employment. Unfortunately, he couldn't reassure her that he meant her family no harm, when the truth was that he fully intended to arrest her mothers. Bringing in criminals who posed such a threat to the well-being of the Otherworld was likely going to be the only way he could salvage his career after he'd disobeyed orders.

He decided to set aside that problem for the moment. It wouldn't be resolved then and there, and he wanted to have Gwen fully on his side before he had to make the arrest.

Thoughts of how he could present his case to her filled his head, and he didn't realize how long he'd been quiet thinking that over until she interrupted his thoughts.

"Well?"

"Hmm?"

Her voice was disgruntled. "Aren't you going to tell me anyway?"

He chuckled to himself. She truly was a joyful contradiction. He was certainly no stranger to women, and knew full well what effect his appearance had on them, but Gwen's refusal to be lumped in with those women amused him. And entertained him. And most dangerous of all, intrigued him.

"I'm six foot one, blond, and have blue eyes."

"I can see that for myself, thank you. Oh, forget it. It's not like I want to know."

"My tailor would tell you that my waist size is thirty-four and my inseam is thirty-two. My shirt size—"

"I am not going to be knitting you a sweater!" she burst out, interrupting him. "I don't need to know your shirt size."

Silence fell. It lasted thirty seconds.

She sighed. "Fine. What is your shirt size?"

He told her. She muttered under her breath again.

"If I came over to your cot, would you strike me in any way?"

"Yes. Possibly. Almost certainly."

"I've been wounded already tonight."

She chewed that over. "I wouldn't punch you in the face, but I don't want to kiss you again." The words choked to a stop, and she quickly corrected herself. "I don't want you to kiss . . . dammit!"

He wiggled his toes in delight. She wanted so badly to lie to him, to deny the attraction, and yet her own moral code wouldn't allow it. He began to think that perhaps a few weeks in her company might not be enough.

"Just . . . stay over there! I'm going to sleep now. And no, I don't want to hear you describe your body anymore. I've had enough."

He let her be, partly because he had believed her when she said earlier that she hadn't had much sleep, but mostly because he wanted to study the problem of how to overcome her objections to his position with the Watch.

The lights came on sometime around six a.m., and an hour later breakfast was served.

The guard raised his eyes at the two of them lying on their respective cots, but said nothing, just delivered a five-starhotel-quality breakfast of fruit, omelet, and the best bacon he'd ever eaten and then left them.

They ate, but conversation was desultory. He tried a couple of times to get her chatting about her work as an alchemist, but she curled up on the cot and pretended to read one of the magazines that had been delivered with the breakfast.

Gregory thought some more, found no solution, and instead paced the perimeter of the cell looking for possible means of escape. He found none other than the very solid door.

"I don't suppose you would care to cast the spell you used in order to get out of the bathroom in Slugs-Upon-Snails?" he inquired politely at one point.

"I've told you," she answered without looking up from the magazine. "The name of that little town is Malwod-Upon-Ooze, and no, I can't. I don't have the spell with me."

"You don't remember it?" He was momentarily surprised by that thought. He'd assumed she was well versed in the art of magic, given her mothers' backgrounds.

She shot him a quick look. "No. I'm really bad at magic, so my mothers gave up trying to teach me. I can cast simple spells, but only if I have them written out in front of me."

"Blast," he said.

She did not reply. He continued to pace, very aware of her warm presence, while the scent of her made him think of all sorts of ways he'd give her pleasure when she finally admitted their mutual attraction.

It was about two hours later that the captain of the guard opened the door again. "Come on—'is lordship wants to see you both."

"The king?" Gregory asked, holding out a hand for Gwen.

She spurned his hand and strode past him through the door, her head held high.

"Aye. There's been a letter about you two, there 'as."

"What did the letter say?" he asked politely as they climbed the stairs to the ground floor. Immediately, three cats that had been curled up together on a bench stood, stretched, and jumped down to follow them.

"No clue. I'm not privy to messages from the front."

Gwen stumbled. He grabbed her, but he needn't have worried that she would fall—judging by the look of concern that suddenly appeared in her eyes, she had something on her mind.

"What is it?" he asked softly as they followed after the guard as he led the way out the great hall to the courtyard.

Gwen slid a glance at him, looking away quickly, but he could tell by the way she bit her lower lip that she was distressed.

He wanted to bite her lower lip. That thought wafted through his mind and refused to be ousted. He reminded himself that he was an honorable man, a man who cherished women and did not view them as mere playthings. Gwen especially deserved to be treated with respect and care, and if she was worried about something, now was not the time to be thinking about just how wonderful it would be to bite that lush little pink lip. Or to taste her mouth again. And certainly not what the feel of her tongue touching his did to his various and sundry lower parts.

He *really* wanted to bite that lip.

"You know that if I can help you in any way, I will," he said, pulling her back so they were out of Al's hearing.

"It's . . . it's just that the letter is probably from Douglas."

"I have no doubt that it is. Why are you so concerned? The worst he can tell the king is that we were sent here because we are prisoners, and we've already acquired that status."

"You don't know these people," she said with a little jerk of her hand in his. He wondered briefly how her hand had come to be there, and then decided that he liked it. His fingers tightened in support.

"You don't either."

"I've been here longer than you."

"By about twelve hours."

She made a disgusted noise. "That's long enough to know that they aren't normal."

"Well, this *is* the afterlife."

She waved that away with her free hand. "This goes beyond that. I'd expect some quirky characters to be hanging around, but these guys are just downright strange. Take that Ethan guy. He had dogs everywhere at his camp. And this place is overrun with cats. Not to mention the fact that the king has a Velociphant, whatever that turns out to be. Who do you know who has a million cats and a Velociphant?"

"You have a point."

Her thumb stroked absently over the back of his hand. Inexplicably, the touch made his groin tighten.

"I'm telling you, this isn't going to be good news."

He released her hand, sliding his arm around her to pull her up to his side. She shot him a startled look, but didn't object when he said, "Then we'll face it together. I won't let anyone harm you, Gwen. Have no fear of that."

He felt brave, and strong, and very much like a warrior of old, protecting his woman from a herd of marauding Vikings. Or Goths. Or whoever it was who stormed castles and caused men like him to defend women like Gwen. History had never been his strong point.

Al led them through various outbuildings to a lower section that was surrounded by thick walls. Gregory glanced back and was only moderately surprised to note that the main structure was, indeed, a castle. One with tall pointy bits, and parapets, and other castle-ish details that he couldn't remember the names of, assuming there had been a time when he knew them. As they emerged from between two small sheds, Gregory stopped, Gwen at his side, both of them stupefied by the vision that lay before them.

"I take it *that* is a Velociphant," Gwen said.

"I would assume so. It looks mechanical, and Aaron said he needed someone with engineering experience."

"Come along, come along. 'is lordship doesn't 'ave much patience when things are going awry with 'is contraption."

They moved forward again at the guard's urging, Gregory examining the large structure that squatted like a mechanical behemoth. Scaffolding surrounded it on one side, with a half dozen men crawling all over it. Three wooden tables had been set up nearby it, both littered with papers that appeared to be held down by a couple of cats curled up with paws tucked under their fronts. At one table, the king of the Underworld stood with another man, both of them consulting what appeared to be plans for the machine. Beyond them, about twenty feet away, a woman clad in an orange blazer and white walking shorts stood talking to a group of about ten people.

"—famed Velociphant," the woman was saying as they passed her. "The king intends on using it to mow down an uprising of trees and shrubs. You will notice that in lieu of teeth, it has a set of spinning blades reminiscent of a large lawn mower. Oh, goodness, we are in luck today. Just arriving on the scene to plead for their lives are two prisoners. A little bird told me that they were getting up to some pretty racy hijinks last night as seen by our After-Hours Tour (five pounds per person, old-age pensioners two pounds fifty). Now, if you'll come this way, we'll have a quick peek in at the foundry to see where the Velociphant's parts are created, and then be on our way to the gift shop, where you can buy not only a miniature reproduction of the Velociphant but also a life-sized stand-up of Lord Aaron in traditional Underworld garb. Follow me!"

"This is really the strangest place I've ever been in," Gwen said in a whisper.

"It's definitely not what one thinks of as an afterlife."

The tour moved off with only a few people snapping photos of Gwen and Gregory. Aaron and his buddy both ignored them. A cat was draped along the former's shoulders, its tail flicking gently as the king raised an arm and gestured toward the machine.

"M'lord, I've brought the prisoners what you requested." Al made a bow, with a little flourish toward Gregory and Gwen.

"Eh? Oh, it's you two again." Aaron turned his head, found himself staring up the nose of the cat, and with an annoyed *tch* removed the animal. It jumped up to the nearest table, and with careful deliberation, stepped into an upturned top hat that was resting next to a cane. "The thief and the other one."

"I would object to being referred to as 'the other one,' but given my options, I'll settle for it," Gwen said, moving a few steps away from Gregory.

Al murmured something about some tanning to be done and left them.

Gregory did not like the sense of loss he felt at the removal of Gwen's warmth pressed to his side. He frowned at her, but she was too busy staring with wonder at the machine that loomed over them. "I, however, have no compunction in denying the term 'thief' as applied to me. I am a Traveller."

"A thief, yes, that's what I said. It's a fine beast, isn't it?" Aaron turned to Gwen to ask the question of her. Pride was evident in both the satisfied expression on his face and the fat note of congratulation in his voice. "It's been seven years in the making, but at last it's about ready to be unleashed. Behold, thief and the other one: the Piranha Mark Five."

Gregory dragged his gaze away from Gwen and studied the machine for a few minutes. Its shape bore a vague resemblance to a giant elephant, with a thick, bulbous head, a rounded back, and four girders for legs, but unlike the actual animal, this was made up of metal struts, cogwheels, pistons, and valves. A little hiss of steam emerged from the nearest valve. The man next to Aaron shouted and pointed at it, sending a worker to scurry over and give the round control a twist.

"It's very large," Gregory said, since obviously the king

was expecting some sort of comment. "Why do you call it a piranha when it resembles an elephant?"

"It's bitey," Aaron said. "Also, once it has my enemies in its dread maw, it will consume them with much gnashing of its internal shredding blades."

"Ew," Gwen said, giving the king a disgusted look. "That's just mean, even for the Underworld."

"I have been sorely grieved," Aaron said, turning when his man said something. "Yes, yes, go attend to the lubrication of the pistons. We must have it working no later than tomorrow. Oh, no, not now."

The man made an abbreviated move to collect his hat, now serving as a cat container, grabbing his cane instead as he trotted off to yell and gesture and assumedly order the workers about. Gregory turned to see what Aaron was frowning at. The blonde from the day before tripped lightly down the hill. She was escorted by a semicircle of cats, each of which wore a golden collar equipped with bells that tinkled gently.

"Arawn! I want to talk to you!"

"Ignore her," Aaron said, turning his back to the approaching woman. "If you don't speak to her, she'll get angry and go away. That gentleman was my chief engineer," he added, waving at the man who was now yelling at some workmen.

"Arawn!"

Aaron strolled to the second table, where he pulled out a blueprint from under two cats, both of which got up and leaped off the table to join the approaching feline guard. "A solid man, but not brilliant, if you know what I mean. We're having a bit of a problem with one of the legs. It wants to move out of rhythm from the others." He looked up at them. "You're *sure* you don't have any mechanical engineering experience?"

"None," Gregory told him. "Nor, I believe, does Gwen."

"My Google Fu is very strong, though," she added. "I'm a whiz at looking up information."

"Will you stop behaving like an infant!" Constance reached them with a swirl of cats. She glared first at Gwen, then Gregory, and finally settled on Aaron. "What are the prisoners doing out of the dungeon?"

"Hmm? Oh, it's you." Aaron shook his blueprints and pretended to be absorbed. "I'm busy. Go away."

"The prisoners!" Constance snatched the blueprints from him. His resulting scowl was fierce enough that Gwen took a step closer to Gregory.

He smiled at her.

"You could have told me you were having them executed! You know how I always enjoy a good morning execution! It's just like you to be so completely selfish as to keep it to yourself." She glanced around, her lips a thin line. "Where's the executioner?"

"We don't have one," Aaron said, and tried to reclaim his blueprints. "Release my plans, woman!"

"What did you do with him? We had one a little while ago. I remember distinctly that we had one. There was that pesky demon who infiltrated his way into Anwyn, and you gave me a grand execution of it as a birthday present."

"That was centuries ago. Jabez, the executioner, turned out to be a first-rate blacksmith. He's at work in the foundry now," Aaron said through clenched teeth, still trying to wrestle the plans from Constance. "Release your hold, besom! This paper is worth more than your life!"

"Don't be a bigger fool than you already are," she snapped back. "If there's no executioner, then you'll just have to kill them yourself."

Aaron looked horrified at the idea. "I am not a killer!"

"You're the head of the Underworld," she answered, releasing her hold on the blueprint. Aaron staggered back a couple of steps at the unexpected move. "Of course you're a killer. You've murdered countless people over the centuries."

"Those were during wars. Everyone kills other people in wars. It doesn't mean you're going to volunteer the next time a couple of prisoners need their heads lopped off." Aaron glared at the nearest cat, which had plumped down on half of the plans that were draped across the table. "Move it or lose it, furball."

"Fine!" Constance drew herself up and looked down her nose at Aaron. "Be that way! Ruin all my fun, just as you always do. Get an ice pick and I'll do the job myself."

"Whoa now!" Gwen protested. "We are not going to allow you or anyone else to execute us! We haven't done anything wrong!" She paused a moment, slid Gregory a look from the corner of her eye, and amended that statement. "Not lately, anyway."

"No one is going to harm us," Gregory told her with much calmness and serenity. He didn't like to see Gwen with that hint of fear in her eyes. He much preferred her trying to deny her attraction to him. "This woman is all bluster."

Constance gave him an almond-eyed look. "Give me an ice pick and you'll find out for yourself."

Gwen gasped.

"Go!" Aaron ordered, jerking the blueprint from under the cat so that he could wave it at his ex-wife. "Leave. Begone. You are not wanted here."

"But I want to see the ex—"

"Leave before I feed those beasts to my Piranha!" he roared.

Constance opened and closed her mouth a couple of times before leveling him with a look that Gregory felt could well have brought down an entire skyscraper. "Fine! Take all my fun, you selfish, irritating man! Come, my children. We will seek out Daddy's shoes and piddle in them!"

"I do hope she's talking only about the cats and not herself," Gwen said sotto voce as Constance spun on her heel and marched off accompanied by most of the cats.

"There are days when I have my suspicions," Aaron said darkly, then frowned at them, seeming to recollect why they were there. "Since my executioner is at present busy making a new knee strut, and also since you can't make yourself useful to me by working on the Piranha, then you shall have to do so by other means."

"What other means?" Gregory asked, suspicion gripping him in its sticky embrace.

"You're a thief," Aaron said, frowning slightly at the plans as he read them over. "You will steal for me."

"I've told you: I'm not a thief. I'm a Traveller."

"And Travellers steal time," Aaron said without looking up. "So it should be no problem for you to take a few things that I want. After all, they were mine to begin with."

"What things?" Gwen asked, leaning against the table, one hand stroking the nearest cat.

"My dog, my deer, and most of all, my bird."

"Your what now?" Gwen's nose wrinkled in a delightful manner that wholly enchanted Gregory. He wanted to kiss her nose. And her lip. And, if he was honest with himself, the rest of her.

Aaron looked up and gave her a dissatisfied look. "My bitch, my white roebuck, and my lapwing. They were stolen from me by that fiend Ethan and his trickster brother."

A memory smote Gregory alongside his head. "Ethan? Would that be Amaethon ab Don?"

"That's the fellow, the devil blast his hide." Aaron's expression turned highly incensed. He shook the blueprint at Gregory. "He stole them and then when I tried to get them back, he declared war against me. *Me!* Have you ever heard of anything so devious?"

"Yes, but I admit that I've also heard about this. My partner was reading me something about Anwyn before I came here, but I could have sworn he said it was mythology."

"Bah. Where do you think the myths come from?" Aaron snorted, tossing aside the plans. "I want my things back, and you can just steal them for me."

"I'm not a thief."

"If you don't get them back"—Aaron's voice turned sly—

"you'll spend the rest of your not inconsiderable days in my dungeon. As for you—"

He turned to Gwen. She looked startled. "You said you didn't need an alchemist."

"I don't, but my soldiers at the front inform me that you're one of Ethan's warriors who wanted out of his service. I will grant you a place with my contingent."

Gwen looked like she was going to protest, but evidently she thought better of it, because she just looked thoughtful for a few seconds before saying something that took Gregory by surprise. "All right."

"You can't be serious," Gregory said.

"Why can't I? I'd rather be a warrior than be stuck in a dungeon."

She had a point, damn it. He considered stealing enough time to keep them from being captured in the first place, but knew that down that path lay only grief and sorrow.

"Very well. Since Gwen doesn't mind being forced into a role that isn't by nature hers—"

"Hey! I could be a warrior if I wanted to!"

"—then I will do likewise. I accept your offer of an exchange for our freedom if I return to you the three items stolen."

Aaron made a notation in a leather journal. "I don't believe I made any mention about granting you freedom."

"Then mention it now. Those are our terms," Gregory said firmly. He put his arm around Gwen again in order to give her support, but mostly because he just liked the feel of her tucked up next to him. "They are not negotiable."

Her frown was potent, but she didn't object to the fact that he spoke for her.

Aaron's face was stormy for a few seconds, then cleared up as he shrugged. "Very well. You will have your freedom once you return what was stolen from me and the other one has served the span of a moon in my army."

"Two days," Gwen countered. "I'll be a soldier for two days."

"A fortnight," Aaron countered.

She narrowed her eyes at him. "A week. That's my final offer."

"Done. You may go to the stables and tell the grooms to give you a horse. You may leave immediately."

He returned to making notes in his notebook, clearly dismissing them from his thoughts.

Gregory didn't stay to argue; with a slight pressure on Gwen's waist, he started back up the hill to the castle with her.

"One thing . . ."

They stopped as Aaron's voice, suspiciously silky, reached them. They turned together to look back.

The king's gaze was filled with portent. "The mortals have a saying. Perhaps you've heard it? *Hir yw'r dydd a hir yw'r nos, a hir yw aros Arawn.*"

"I don't speak Welsh," Gregory said.

"I do." Gwen hesitated, then translated, "Long is the day and long is the night, and long is the waiting of Arawn."

"The mortals think that refers to the events of the past, but really, it touches on the fact that I always, no matter how long it takes, have my revenge for a betrayal." Aaron smiled. "Something to remember, yes?"

EIGHT

"Have you ever wanted to take a vacation from your own life?" I asked Gregory as we walked up the hill to the upper bailey.

"I can't say that I have."

"Count yourself lucky." I couldn't help but sigh as another orange-coated tour guide herded a group of what looked like Catholic schoolgirls, complete with matching uniforms and attendant nuns in full traditional garb, past us. Faint echoes of "The brewery is renowned for its popular From Hell Ale, made with honey gleaned from Anwyn's happy little bees. We'll have a sampling right after we visit the armory, where the blood-encrusted weapons of Anwyn's brutal past are on display" followed us.

The schoolgirls cheered. The nuns murmured happily about the ale.

I wanted to alternately sit down and weep and run screaming away from the castle.

"Are you allowing that talk of execution to distress you, *dulcea mea*?"

"Dulcea mea?" I asked, distracted from my general sense of worry, concern, and befuddlement. "What does that mean?"

"It's Romanian for 'my sweet.' And before you say it—and yes, I know you were about to—I used the endearment because your kisses were very, very sweet."

"Kiss," I said, jerking my hand away from his. I didn't

even remember holding his hand! What on earth was going on that I could hold a man's hand without consciously thinking about it? "We had one kiss. Just one."

"And it was a superb one."

It most certainly was. Just the memory of his mouth made me feel restless, like I wanted to run a marathon, or rip his clothing off. With an emphasis on the latter. "That was an error of judgment on my part. I should never have kissed you. I can only guess that I was feeling guilty about you having been beaten up and wanted to make sure that your mouth still worked."

He laughed. "Do you really believe that explanation?"

"No," I said miserably, and was startled to find that I was holding his hand again. His thumb rubbed against mine in a manner that was both reassuring, and arousing. Damn my libido! I firmly turned my thoughts from those concerning a naked, warm Gregory rubbing other parts of himself on me and focused on the fix we were in. "How are you going to steal a dog, a deer, and a bird from Ethan?"

"I have no idea." He looked amused at the change of subject, but didn't challenge me. "I've never had to steal anything before."

"Except time."

His fingers tightened on mine. "I believe I've mentioned already that we don't steal time—we purchase it."

"Without the people's knowledge that you're doing so. How on earth does the Watch let you get away with that?"

"They don't. So far as mortals are concerned, that is. We may barter or outright purchase time from immortal beings, of course, but many people are touchy where the sale of their time is concerned, and few are willing to do so."

"So what do you do in such cases?"

He shrugged. "I'm in the process of trying to find a person who is willing to sell time to me. My cousin has someone to provide time for himself and his wife, so I hope to arrange for the same accommodation."

"Maybe your wife won't want you to buy time for her," I said loftily.

"That is a possibility, although marriage outside of the Traveller society is frowned upon."

"No, I meant that perhaps she wouldn't want you doing the he-man for her. Wait . . ." I stopped and squinted up at him. He had an inscrutable air that I didn't buy for one moment. "Are you saying that you can only hook up with another Traveller?"

" 'Hook up with' as in engage in a sexual relationship?" His thumb swept the back of my knuckles. "No, that is allowed. Marriage, however, is a different matter. To marry one who is mahrime—an outsider—is a grave sin to Traveller families."

I stared at him. "Talk about insulting! You are joking, right? No one could be so ass backward in this day and age. Especially considering the double standard of it's all right to milk the cow, but not to buy it. That alone makes me incensed, but the whole idea that a group of people won't allow family members to marry outside of said family—for one, it's unhealthy. You need diversity in a gene pool. For another, it's . . . well, unhealthy mentally and emotionally as well."

"Alas, I'm not joking." He smiled at me, the warmth from it not only reaching his eyes but kindling something that made me feel as if I had butterflies in my stomach. "That is one reason why I am here."

I wasn't sure at first what he was alluding to, but then it struck me like a bolt of lightning that occasionally flashed in the distance. Dear goddess in all the good, green things! He meant me! He was defying his own people just to be with me. It boggled my mind, but it made sense. The kiss, the way he was flirting with me, the constant hand-holding . . . it was all explained if the reason for him being in Anwyn was that he had followed me here based on an instantaneous attraction.

"Gregory, I . . . I don't know what to say. I'm flattered, naturally. I don't think I've ever met someone who's risked getting in trouble just to be with me, but I have to tell you that even though you have a really nice way of kissing, I'm not looking for a man in my life, especially a husband."

It was his turn to look startled. "I suspect that you are under the impression that I just proposed to you. Is that so?"

I felt a blush crawl up from my neck to my face. "Well . . . yes. Didn't you?"

"No."

The blush deepened before I realized what that meant. I released his hand only to wallop him on the arm. "Oh, I get it! It's just fine for you to kiss me silly, and make me spend far too long imagining just what you look like without your clothes on, and to have what amounts to an unhealthy obsession with your chin and mouth and that little spot behind your ears where your hair curls. That's fine, but to make an honest woman out of me isn't? You, sir, are a bastard! A great, big, hairy pustule of a bastard!"

"All that because I didn't propose to you?" He shook his head as if in wonder.

"No, all that because evidently you believe I'm the sort of woman who goes around kissing men in dungeons, and holding their hands, and indulging in extremely smutty fantasies about them, but am not worthy so far as your family is concerned. Of all the self-righteous, bigoted—"

"Gwen," he said, stopping me with a little laugh that had my hackles bristling. "Stop. I didn't realize that you wanted to marry me."

"I don't!" I was quick to say.

"And yet you are upset that I didn't ask you?" He put a finger under my chin and tipped my face (filled with embarrassment) up so he could better torment me by looking at me with eyes that were the color of expensive blue topazes. "I meant no insult, *dulcea mea*."

"Stop calling me that," I said irritably. "I'm not your sweet."

"Ah, but you are," he said in that complacent manner that

was starting to annoy me. I've always hated it when people remain calm while I'm all riled up. How dare he not be emotional, too! "Or at least, I'd like you to think you are."

I reeled back, sure that he had just insulted me again, but he grabbed my arm and pulled me out of the way of another passing herd of tourists. "Do not say whatever biting thing you are about to say. I did not mean to give insult to you. I simply meant that I would like you to be my sweetheart."

"But not enough to marry me," I snapped and jerked my arm from his grasp, still incensed.

He sighed. "Do you want to marry me?"

"No! Of course not! I don't even know you, and I'm sure that when I do know you, I won't want to because I will have found out that you're the most irritating, frustrating, heinous man alive."

"Heinous?" He looked thoughtful. "I suppose there are worse things to be called. No, do not flare up at me again. As it happens, I agree with you."

I stopped thinking about punching him on his formerly abused nose. "You do?"

"Yes. I prefer having some sort of a relationship established with a woman before I engage in sexual acts. I've lived long enough to know the difference between a casual relationship and one that holds the promise of an eternity spent in bliss. So you see, about that we are of one mind."

"Oh?" I eyed him. "Just how old are you that you have achieved this state of wisdom?"

"Sixty-four."

My eyes widened. "You're what?"

"I was born in 1949. I am the youngest of all my cousins, although not the youngest of the entire family. Several of my cousins have reproduced."

"Great. I'm older than you."

"Really? You look the same age as me, but admittedly that is common amongst members of the Otherworld. Would you smite me if I were to ask how old you are?"

"I was born in 1888. Lovely. Now I can't date you even if I could get past your family's massive prejudice against non-Travellers."

"I see nothing that would prohibit us from having a relationship just because you were born almost fifty years before me. It matters little to our kind, after all." He paused, looked surprised, then continued. "You are serious, are you not?"

"Yes. People would say I was a cradle robber. I'm fifty years older than you, Gregory!"

"You look like you're age thirty at most."

"Thank you, but the fact remains that I'm a hundred and twenty-five, and you're just a baby!"

A roguish twinkle filled his pretty eyes. "If I told you that I liked older women—"

"I'd punch you on your nose and break it again," I said, waving a fist at him.

He laughed and grabbed my hand, then to my utter surprise, pulled me up tight against his chest and said, "You are delightful, do you know that? You always seem to say exactly the opposite of what I'm expecting."

I opened my mouth to tell him to unhand me in front of all the tourists and workpeople who trotted about doing their daily chores when his mouth settled on mine with a possessiveness that simultaneously annoyed me (I wasn't an object to be possessive about!) and thrilled me to my toes (dear god and goddess, the man had to be the world's best kisser).

His mouth teased mine, coerced mine, pleaded with mine to yield to his. And of course, it did, allowing his tongue entrance, where it swanned around the place like it owned it. I wanted to be irritated about that, but I was too busy clutching his shoulders to keep from swooning. And then when he made a little noise in the back of his throat, the softest little exhalation of pure pleasure, I melted, my fingers sliding through his golden hair as I pressed myself against him in a shameless manner that my breasts and thighs and female parts wholly embraced. I touched my tongue to his, and melted even more, uncaring that we were snogging in full view of anyone who glanced our way. The sounds of tittering and electronic beeps and clicks indicated that the tourists had returned, but not even the thought of them brought sanity to me.

"OK," I admitted when I managed to peel my mouth from his. "You win the award for kissing."

"Oddly, I was just thinking the same thing about you." His eyes were soft and somewhat smoky with what I recognized was purest desire.

A rush of feminine knowledge swept over me, making me very aware of all the differences between us. "You're so hard," I couldn't help but say when I swept my hands down his shoulders to his biceps.

"Extremely so, to the point that it's going to be painful to walk."

I couldn't help a little wiggle that had him groaning and clutching at my hips. "And if you do that again, I may very well throw all my much-lauded manners to the wind and haul you onto the nearest bale of hay, where I will ravish you as you deserve."

I would be lying if I said I didn't, for at least two minutes, consider letting him do just that, but at long last, better judgment won out and I managed to get my raging hormones under control.

Gregory had used the time I was doing so to speak to a young boy who was scooping up grain and pouring it into a metal bucket. The lad disappeared into the stable and returned with a blond woman with jagged cropped hair.

"I'm Clarence, the chief groom."

"Clarice?" Gregory asked.

She studied him. "Do I *look* like a Clarice?"

"Well—"

"My name is Clarence. Just Clarence. You are the spy Lord Aaron told me about?"

"Thief. I'm a thief, not a spy."

She made a "same difference" sort of gesture and snapped an order at the bucket boy. "I'm to give you and your woman horses. How well do you ride?"

Gregory hesitated. "I've been on a horse," he said slowly.

"*Tch*. I'll give you Old Mabel. You'd have to be an imbecile to disturb her. And you?"

"When I was growing up, I attended all the local hunt meets," I said with quiet pride.

"You hunted?" Gregory asked, puzzled. "You don't strike me as the type who goes in for blood sports."

I smiled demurely. "I rode on behalf of the foxes, actually. As an alchemist, one of the first things I learned to make was a fox scent that fooled all the hounds. After a few decades of without so much as a single fox appearing, the meet broke up."

"A job well done," Gregory said, approval shining in his eyes.

Clarence entered into the stable, saying over her shoulder, "As you've riding experience, we'll let you have Bottom."

Gregory and I followed her into the dark confines of the stable. The delicious odors of alfalfa, horse, and saddle soap mingled and made me think of days long gone when I'd ridden to and fro over the countryside, sending the mortals and their dogs on all sorts of wild-goose hunts. "Why on earth do you call the horse Bottom?"

A horse's head snapped up at the nearest stall, his eyes wide, and his nostrils flared as he took in our scent. He bared his teeth and let loose with a whinny that just about deafened me.

"I have a nasty suspicion as to the identity of that horse," I told Gregory.

He shuddered. "I can say with all honesty that I am sincerely grateful for Old Mabel."

Clarence strode past us, unlatching the stall. Gregory and I backed up as the horse, black as midnight, charged out, hooves flashing, ears flicking forward and back, and eyes rolling in his head as Clarence caught him by the halter and cuffed him affectionately on the shoulder. "Aye, you old murderer. You're going to have a nice long run, aren't you?"

"Oh, goddess," I said softly.

"To answer your question, he's called Bottom because you'll need a hell of a seat to ride him."

The stableboy led another horse, a solid-looking cob who didn't so much as flick an ear to where the black devil was now tap-dancing in his attempt to get away from Clarence. She threatened to use a twitch on him if he didn't behave himself and thumped him again on the shoulder as she half led him and was half dragged herself out into the sunshine.

I sighed.

"Thinking of that vacation again?" Gregory's voice was as warm on my ear as the breath that touched it. I shivered at the sensation.

The stable seemed to be a small bubble of privacy. Rays of sunlight streamed in through gaps in the boards that made up the walls, motes of dust and hay drifting in lazy patterns like little golden fireflies. The stable itself was quiet, the noises from the yard muffled and distant, as if coming from a very long way. For a moment in time, the world was made up of only Gregory and me.

I turned my head slowly. Our noses brushed first, then our lips.

"We've got to stop doing this," I said against his mouth, suddenly too weary to fight the attraction that seemed to swamp me whenever he was near.

"Why?"

I searched his eyes, but I saw nothing there but honest curiosity. "Because you are who you are, and I'm who I am, and my moms are who they are."

"And never the twain shall meet?"

"Something like that." I licked the corner of his mouth. He moaned softly and would probably have kissed me as I not so secretly wanted him to do, but the world intruded upon us once again, heralded by the cry that we should get our arses in gear because some people had work to do and couldn't stand around lollygagging all day.

The feeling of being suspended in time dissolved.

"Don't be so sure that you have *all* the answers, *dulcea mea*," Gregory said in what I can only describe as a maddeningly cryptic manner. He left me standing in the stable, swearing to myself over the tangled sensations of loss, arousal, and general irritability.

"Did you just call me a know-it-all?" I asked him as Clarence gave us instructions on how to treat Aaron's horses while they were on loan to us.

"I wouldn't dream of doing such a thing."

"Then why did you say—"

"If it wouldn't be too much trouble for you to actually pay attention—" Clarence's voice cracked like a whip around me. Guiltily, I turned toward her and put on my best listening face.

"Sorry. Go on."

The look she gave me wasn't any too friendly, but duty won out over personal satisfaction, and she didn't tell me to go to hell, though she obviously wanted to. "You are to walk next to the horses for one hour out of every four that you ride. This saddlebag"—she patted a canvas bag that had been strapped to Mable's ample back—"contains grain. They are to get that no more than once a day. Hobbles are in the other bag. Use them when you stop to rest, and in the evening. The horses are trained to return here if they are left unattended and unhobbled, so fair warning."

"This is going to sound like an odd question, I'm sure," I said, unable to keep from voicing the question that had been uppermost in my mind ever since I saw Bottom up close. Even now, his ears were flattened, and his back hooves had a tendency to fly out whenever someone drifted into the large circle of what he considered his personal space. "But why aren't there cars here? Or planes, or helicopters, or for that matter, personal jet packs? Why do you still use horsepower when Aaron mentioned having a computer, and he's building some monstrous machine to chew up Ethan's warriors?"

"Lord Aaron distrusts modern machinery on the whole, unless it has something to do with his project. He's always saying that a horse is reliable, whereas a man-made vehicle isn't. Right. Up you go." She gestured to Gregory, who approached his horse with reluctance. She got him into the saddle, showed him how to hold the reins, and gave him a basic ten-minute lesson on riding while she led him around the stableyard.

I preferred to watch Gregory learn how to how to use his legs and hands as cues rather than watch the stableboy dash forward and attempt to strap assorted bundles and a small picnic basket to the treacherous Bottom's saddle.

At least they had remembered to feed us as well as the horses.

It wasn't until another lad staggered up with a bunch of metal in his arms that I had an inkling that things were about to go from bad to worse.

"Your armor, my lady," the young man said as he came to a halt before me, panting with the exertion.

"Oh. I suppose Aaron figures I'll need that. Um. OK. I guess I can take it with me. Go ahead and put it on."

He looked at me like I was a Velociphant. "You want me to put it on?"

"Yes." I waved at the black equine devil, who was standing still by virtue of Clarence's brilliant contrivance of shoving a pail of grain in front of the brute. The horse happily chomped away while the last of the bundles was strapped to his saddle. "I don't know where you're going to find a spot to hook it to, but maybe we could readjust some of those packages."

"The armor ain't for him," the boy squeaked, shoving it at me. "It's for you."

"I understand that, but I won't need it until we reach the

camp. I can't carry it, and I certainly am not going to wear it while riding, so it'll have to be attached."

The boy opened his mouth to say something, but an older boy arrived with a familiar sword. "The Nightingale, Lady Gwen."

"Where did you find that?" I asked, taking the sword. I had to admit it felt good in my hand, almost as if it was made for me.

"'Twas sent from the front."

"She wants me to put her armor on the horse," the armor-bearing kid said. His eyes rolled in a dramatic fashion. *"On her horse."*

"Armor's for you, not the horse," the older boy told me with gravity that made me want to giggle.

"Yes, that was a little misunderstanding. Perhaps you could help this young man to hook the armor that I shall indeed wear later on onto the saddle for now."

"We can't do that."

"Sure you can." I pointed at the saddle, the rear of which was admittedly awfully full what with all the bundles that had been tied onto it, including the small picnic basket. "Just shove some of that stuff around and make room for it."

"We can't do that," the older boy repeated.

"No, they can't," Clarence said as she left Gregory and marched over to us. "You must wear the armor. It would disturb Bottom to have it clanking around his sides. Strap it on and get going. I don't have all day to spend outfitting you."

"I can't ride in all that armor," I protested.

"Why not?"

My hands flailed around a little as I tried to think of an explanation that didn't make me sound like a grade A wuss. "It's . . . cumbersome. I might poke Bottom with my sword."

Gregory, who had been practicing his riding skills by walking the placid Mabel back and forth behind us, said as he passed, "If I had a nickel for every time I heard someone say that . . ."

"You are *not* helping," I shouted after him. He raised his hand to show he heard me.

"Look," I told the three people in front of me, quite prepared to stand there all day and argue if that's what it took. "I'm not going to be able to ride in all that mail and plate. What if I have to pee? How on earth am I supposed to get off the horse, pee, and then get back on? I can hardly walk in the stuff, let alone move around."

"You should have trained better before you volunteered to be one of Lord Aaron's warriors," Clarence said, dumping another cup of grain into the bucket when Bottom started to fret.

"I didn't train at all!"

"There's your problem," said the grave young man. "You ought never to have said you were a warrior if you weren't trained."

The younger boy, perspiring freely now, nodded, and staggered back slightly.

"They have a point, you know," Gregory said as his well-behaved horse strolled past with a snort of equine disgust.

I snatched up the helmet and shook it at him. "You know full well I've been telling everyone who will listen that I'm not a warrior!"

"And yet you are the one with the armor and the sword." He shook his head as he carefully negotiated a turn with Mabel.

I took a step toward him, murder in my eye. "And would you like to meet that sword up close and personal?"

He laughed when he drew abreast, swinging one leg over Mabel and sliding to the ground. "You are exceptionally easy to tease, my dear."

"And you are extremely irritating. You could be helping me, you know! These people don't seem to understand that I can't do anything while wearing that stuff."

"I'm told that well-fitting armor is not cumbersome at all."

"That may be, but I can guarantee you that this stuff isn't well-fitting in the least."

He looked at the armor, lifting first the chest piece, then the shin protectors, glancing at Clarence. "There hasn't been time for armor to be made for Gwen. This won't fit her well, and will, in fact, most likely hinder her as she conducts her appointed duties."

Clarence grabbed Bottom's saddle cinch, and gave it a mighty jerk. The horse's eyes narrowed. A back hoof lifted in warning. "That is not my problem."

"It will be if we have to report back to Aaron that you willingly sent her off unable to do the job he specifically asked her to do."

Gregory's tone was mild, but there was something about him, either a look in his eye or a set to his jaw that carried a lot of weight with it. I couldn't help but be impressed that he could command so much attention without lifting a finger.

Clarence hesitated, then snapped an order to the two boys. "Take away the plate. She can wear the mail. It, at least, doesn't have to be so fitted. But it's on your head if Lord Aaron finds her running around without being properly equipped."

He murmured something noncommittal, and despite my protestations, assisted the older boy in sliding what amounted to a thick cotton tunic over my clothes, followed by at least twenty pounds of finely made mail. The mail was also in tunic form, and hung down to mid-thigh.

We headed out about ten minutes later, Gregory having been given directions of how to find the encampment and me swearing to myself as sweat formed between my breasts.

"If I'm already this hot and uncomfortable," I bitched as we rode out of the lower bailey and into a panorama made up of rolling green hills, "I'm going to be outright miserable by the time we get to the camp. What time do you think we'll roll in there?"

"To the camp?" Gregory squinted up at the sky. "Probably about lunchtime tomorrow."

THE ART OF STEALING TIME   187

"Tomorrow!" Bottom, who appeared to be temporarily sated by his consumption of treats, tossed his head and did a few warning dance steps to the side. I got him under control again, although he saw fit to bare his teeth, attempt to bite my foot, and as a pointed comment on my equestrian abilities, poop in a particularly loud, obnoxious fashion. "What do you mean, tomorrow? Like *tomorrow* tomorrow? The day after today tomorrow?"

"That's generally how the word 'tomorrow' is defined, yes." He slid me a curious glance. "Apparently the battleground location is at the opposite end of Anwyn."

"Great! Just great! Bottom, so help me, if you try to bite my foot again, I won't let you have any of that special traveling food that Clarence packed for you."

"Why are you so upset?" Gregory asked as the horses adopted a comfortable distance-eating walk.

"Because he's got big teeth, and I have no doubt he'd shred my shoe if he actually got hold of it."

"Not why are you upset that the horse is trying to bite your foot; why are you so upset that it will take us a day to reach the camp? Is it your mothers that you are worried about, or something else?"

I didn't look at him. I couldn't. The man had the most uncanny knack of seeming to know what I was thinking. "Of course I'm worried about my mothers. They're prisoners, held by a man who evidently doesn't have a problem stealing someone's deer, dog, and bird. I wonder if that's why there are so many dogs at Ethan's camp? I bet no one spays and neuters their pets here."

"That was an excellent change of subject. It almost sucked me in," Gregory commented.

Damn him.

"All right, let's just get this out into the open, then, shall we?" I took a deep breath, corrected Bottom's course when he decided that a butterfly flitting past us was a deadly threat and attempted to shoot off at a forty-five-degree angle, and said with as much composure as I could muster, "You wish for me to sleep with you."

"Not necessarily."

I looked at him in surprise, embarrassment making my cheeks go bright red.

"I'm willing to sleep with you, instead, if that makes it any better."

"You . . . no, I said . . . Wait a minute. That's the same thing!"

He smiled. "If I told you that I love that you are just a little bit gullible, would you consider that an insult?"

"Yes! It's very insulting." We rode in silence for two minutes. "I am not gullible. I just believe that people are telling the truth."

Gregory pursed his lips, but said nothing.

"Fine, I'm gullible! But that's better than being jaded and weary of life."

"It is indeed. Now, let us discuss the sleeping arrangements. I prefer to sleep on the left side, but if we are unable to find accommodations that give a certain amount of shelter, I am more than happy to take the outside. For protection, you understand. Not, I hasten to add, that you need protection, especially as you are armed, and all I was given was a cloak, but just as a general courtesy. Do you have a preference as to sexual position?"

"We are not having sex."

"I beg to differ."

I gawked. "There is a word for what you're thinking!"

"Yes: seduction."

"Ha! Seduction implies consent on both sides. I do not wish to have sex with you." That lie lasted for about four seconds before it irritated me so much I had to take it back. "Gah! Fine, I may wish to have sex with you, but that doesn't mean I'm going to."

"I enjoy many sexual positions, but in this I'm happy to defer to your tastes." He didn't even look at me as we rode, a somewhat dreamy expression on his face. "You straddling on top of me would be an excellent starting choice, because you would be able to set the pace. Also, your breasts would be free for me to enjoy."

"You are insane. No sex, Gregory. None. Talking about it won't make me change my mind."

"Now, the reversed version of that—with you still on top of me, but facing in the opposite direction, is also enticing. Again, you would have free rein of the tempo, while presenting me with the view of your derriere. I enjoy looking at your derriere clothed, so I can only imagine that the sight of it unclothed will be even more spectacular."

"I do not have a spectacular butt. It's just a butt, a normal butt, a butt that you can find on any woman." A mental vision of me riding Gregory was hard to dislodge from my mind, so I let myself enjoy it for a few minutes. What was the harm in indulging in a little fantasy?

"The traditional position of you beneath me also has its charms," he continued, still not looking at me. I was grateful for that, since my blush seemed to be a permanent part of me now. "You are not a tiny woman, so I won't feel like I am squashing you. That's always off-putting. No, you are built so that we might indulge ourselves in a manner that would allow our movements to achieve maximum extension, if you will."

I imagined just how flexible he could be, and what maximum extension he could achieve once he really got going. My tongue suddenly seemed too big for my mouth.

"Now, for middle-of-the-night action, side by side, with you draping one of those long, long legs over my hip, would be appropriate. By then we will have sated the most immediate of desires and can settle in for long, lazy lovemaking. I find that I have quite a bit of stamina in the side-by-side position."

I shifted in the saddle. It was suddenly very chafing, rubbing me uncomfortably in locations that desperately wanted Gregory's touch. While lying on my side next to him.

"I wonder . . ." He thought for a moment. "I wonder if it would be possible to rig up some sort of a swing. All that would be needed would be a couple of young trees, some rope, and padding for the seat. That would allow me to stand, and you to wrap your legs—long, as I believe I've mentioned—around my hips, bringing a new depth of motion to the experience. Hmm."

My mouth went dry at the thought.

"Right," I said, pressing Bottom's side with my heels. "That's it. You can sit there and think all the smutty thoughts you want about being flexible, and having extension, and touching my breasts, and the long, sensual sweep of your back right where it meets your hips, and how the muscles in your thighs and chest and arms move when you walk, which you do on purpose, I have no doubt, and all the other enticing bits of you, but I'll have no part in it! I'm going to get to Ethan's camp so I can check on my mothers and not have sex with you, no matter how good it will be, because you're the Watch, and sooner or later, my moms will do something that will make you want to arrest them, and then I'll have to do something horrible to you, and I don't want that because other than the whole Watch thing, you're really nice, and I believe that you'd have excellent extension and flexibility."

Bottom leaped forward before I finished the last sentence, so it came out as a bit of a shriek, but I felt better for saying it. For about eight minutes. Then Bottom, in full canter, shied at a family of adorably fluffy bunnies, and I went sailing off the side of him to land in a patch of mossy wildflowers.

I lay there staring up at the blue sky, green willow branches dappling me with shade. Bottom, relieved of my presence, stopped and began cropping the grass. I wondered how long it would take Gregory's slower horse to reach us. I wondered if Mabel could even canter, so broad in the beam was she.

Overhead, a few bits of gauzy clouds gathered and formed into a shape that was vaguely horselike.

"Three minutes and change," I said aloud when Gregory's face blocked out my view of the sky. "I had only reached one hundred and ninety-two Mississippi."

He tickled my nose with a pink flower, and lay down beside me. "You think I'm nice?"

Trust him to focus on that first. "Any other man, a man of honor and consideration, a man who claims to have superb manners, would have asked me if I was hurt before pandering to his ego."

"But you do think I'm nice?" A high breeze made the clouds shift their shape into that of a petaled flower.

"Yes," I said, wanting to laugh and run away at the same time.

"Excellent. I like you a great deal, too. Enough that I looked you over to make sure you weren't hurt before I spoke."

The wispy white clouds overhead drifted lazily into the shape of a heart. "I'm not hurt. Moss is very forgiving. Bottom shied at bunnies."

"He appears to be an extremely high-strung horse. Do you really wish for me to be gone out of your life despite all my niceness?"

The clouds melted into the blue sky. I rolled over onto my side to study Gregory. "That depends. Can you promise me that you won't arrest my mothers?"

His eye crinkles smoothed out. "No, I can't."

I rolled onto my back again. There was nary a wisp of cloud in the sky, and yet I felt as if I was standing in the middle of the biggest, blackest thunderstorm ever. "Thank you for being honest."

"I will always be honest with you, Gwen, even when it is something that I know you do not want to hear."

Despite the words, the sincerity in his voice touched something inside me. I wanted so badly to throw caution to the wind and just give in to the urges my body was making. I wanted to forget there was a world outside of Anwyn. I wanted to remove the fear for my mothers that had been my constant companion for the last half of my life.

I wanted desperately to be in love with Gregory, and to let him cherish me as instinct told me he would.

Tears stung behind my eyes. "It isn't fair," escaped my lips, and the second it did, I was ashamed of how juvenile it sounded.

"No, it isn't," Gregory said, and brushed my cheek with the flower. "I've found that life seldom is. Gwen, if I—"

"No." I rolled over to put my fingers across his mouth. He kissed them. "This isn't your problem, Gregory. You are what you are. You have a job to do, and I am not going to ask you to shirk your duty just so we can be together."

"You make it all so black and white," he said against my fingertips, opening his lips to suck one inside. The swirl of his tongue against the pad of my finger made my entire body tingle. "As if it came down to having you or having my job."

"Doesn't it?" It took a great deal of mental strength to speak, but I managed to get the two words out, and I was proud of that fact.

"No. There are shades in between that you don't seem to see."

I pulled my fingers away, suddenly chilled and tingle-less. "Because I'm not one of your people, you mean?"

"That is a very minor shade of gray, and not one that concerns me."

"But it is still there." I took the flower he held and tucked it behind his ear. "Tell me, what if I changed my mind and wanted to have a relationship with you? What if I wanted the whole nine yards, marriage, kids, eternity spent together. What would your family say to that?"

He smiled, making the eye crinkles return. "A few months ago my grandmother would have had the biggest fit you had ever in your life seen. She would have banned me from the family, named us both mahrime, and forbidden anyone to ever mention either us or our children again. She would have notified all the other Traveller families of this exile and demanded that they honor it. We would have, in effect, ceased to exist for every living Traveller."

"What's changed in the last few months that would alter that?"

"Many things, but mostly me."

I thought about what he said. "And you consider the annihilation of your heritage not of concern?"

"It wouldn't happen. Not only am I my grandmother's favorite out of all my cousins, but Peter has done much to soften her previous view on marriage to outsiders. She might raise a fuss, but she'd soon come about. She did so with Peter, and although things are not overly affectionate between them, she has named him as family before the annual gathering of Travellers."

I bit back the urge to say "Bully for her," and instead contented myself with a simple "It proves my point, however. We aren't meant to be together, Gregory."

He reached out and put a hand on my breast. I stared down at it in shock for a second or two. I couldn't believe he just stuck out his hand and copped a grope! Then the tingling started again, and I watched in amazement as he lifted his hand about half an inch from my breast. Little snakes of blue-white light snapped and twisted like miniature lightning.

"That . . . that's not just static electricity, is it?" I asked, wondering why a shock to my boob wasn't hurting me. On the contrary, the sensation of his hand above my breast just made it feel warm and tingly, and very, very sensitized.

"In a way, yes." His hand slid down my breastbone to my stomach, still not actually touching me but leaving a trail of electricity that sent out tendrils of pleasure all over my body. "Travellers can harness lightning, which is basically just a very large static charge that explodes with a tremendous amount of energy. This is a very personalized version of that."

"So this is something you do often?" I asked, watching with concern as his hand moved lower and hovered over my pubic bone. I was half braced to move away if the mini-lightning touched sensitive parts, but just as it did elsewhere, the electricity that came from his hand triggered only an arousing sensation that buzzed up and down my skin. "Oooh," I said in a long breath as his hand circled my crotch before moving on down one leg.

"No. I've never been able to manufacture *porraimos* with another woman. My cousin and I were speaking of this just the other day. He said he can with his wife, but I've always heard that it's a rare phenomenon." He waggled his fingers over the tip of my shoe, and inside it my toes wiggled in happiness. Then he moved to the other leg and started up it. My crotch was extremely happy at the thought of a return visit.

"*Porraimos?* That's the word for . . . er . . . personal lightning?"

"The word itself means many things. One definition is 'devouring.' Another is 'opening,' and that is what it means to Travellers—it means to open oneself up to another person, and to the elements, and to all that is or will ever be. That it happens at all proves just how wrong you are."

I clutched handfuls of grass as he swirled lightning over my groin, belly, and breasts. The sensation of tingling moved into heat, making me feel as if I was burning from the inside out. "In what way?" I managed to gasp out, my back arching as he held both hands about an inch above my breasts.

"*Porraimos* only happens when the two people share an inalienable bond." He leaned down, his mouth claiming mine at the same time his hands closed on my needy breasts. Even through my shirt and the mail, his touch made the fire inside me roar to an inferno of desire. I pulled his body down onto mine, kissing him for all I was worth, sliding my hands under his shirt in order to stroke the smooth swoops and valleys of muscles that made up his back. Carefully, I twined my tongue around his, careful to avoid the spot where his tooth was missing even though I knew the wound had long since healed.

His words echoed in my head, going around and around until they became a chant. We were meant for each other. We had a rare bond, one that few people experienced. It would be the sheerest folly to discard such a gift, wouldn't it?

It would. I gave myself up to the feelings that his touch had triggered, feelings that whipped through me until I felt like I was caught in an whirlwind of passion, desire, and heat so great I thought it would surely consume me.

"Gwen, tell me now if you really do not want me," he said against my lips, his hand pulling the mail up my body. "Because I won't be able to stop if I kiss you just one more time."

I said nothing, but wrapped one leg around him and kissed him with the power of all my tangled emotions. I knew what I was doing wasn't smart, wasn't the least bit wise, and certainly was going to mean a world of trouble not only for myself and my mothers but for my heart, but at that moment nothing really mattered but Gregory.

And then suddenly he was gone, having leaped up off me with a strangled oath. I sat up, bereft, my body still humming its happy little song of anticipation. Gregory stood twisted to the side, trying to see behind him.

"Your damned horse bit my ass!" His face was filled with outrage as he turned to show me the tear in his pants.

I collapsed laughing when he charged over to where Bottom was standing, an innocent expression on his horsey face while Gregory threatened him with all sorts of dire punishments. I was well aware that I'd just had a very, very narrow escape.

The question was whether I would be so lucky the next time.

NINE

"How's your behind?"

Gregory pulled his thoughts from the dark place they'd gone ever since the scene some hours earlier, and experimentally flexed a butt cheek. "It's better. No thanks to that carnivore you've been riding."

Gwen stifled a giggle, but he heard it nonetheless, and he managed to share a sour look between both her and the horse she led, all the while adopting a martyred air.

"Sorry," she said with contriteness that didn't for one minute fool him. "I know that being on the receiving end of those teeth isn't funny, but if you could have seen the look on your face when he did it . . ."

Her words trailed away again, leaving her throat working as she fought to keep from laughing out loud.

He thinned his lips and looked straight ahead. They were walking the horses in order to let them have a break from constant riding, and he had found the exercise beneficial to his thoughts. If nothing else, marching across the landscape made it hard for one to be aroused. "It's not the bite I object to so much as it is the interruption. I can now attest to the fact that it's impossible to seduce a sweetly ripe maiden when one's ass has been manhandled. Or in this case, horsehandled."

Gwen lost her fight and whooped with laughter.

"Sorry," she said, dabbing at her eyes. " 'Horsehandled' pushed me over the edge."

"Delighted to provide amusement." He tried to preserve his injured mien, but failed. Even if his posterior was the one that had suffered the abuse, it had been a very funny—if wholly frustrating—moment.

"Ugh." Gwen pulled her mail shirt out from her plump, tempting breasts and tried to generate a breeze. "Not to be gross, but I'm just a giant ball of sweat in this mail. I don't suppose there's an afterlife hotel around here where I can take a shower?"

"I doubt that any such facility exists. However . . ." He squinted into the distance. "Yes, the woman at the stables said we should let the horses have a rest at a small lake. We are more than halfway to the camp, assuming that water ahead is the lake she mentioned."

"A lake." She made a face that turned into a shrug. "It's no hot shower, but if there aren't leeches or water moccasins or anything icky like that, it sounds like heaven. Ha. Afterlife. Heaven."

He looked at her.

She gave him a wry smile that made his stomach turn over. "Sorry. My jokes are suffering the effect of the heat, too."

"I find you nothing but delightful."

"Yes, but that's because you want to get into my pants."

"That is highly offensive." He frowned, wondering if he had given her that impression by his actions or if she just held misguided notions about men. Perhaps it was both. "If I have led you to believe that I desire you simply for your ample, lush person, then allow me to disabuse you of that notion right now. I believe I've mentioned the fact that my cousin's wife claims I could be a model. Whether or not that's true, the fact remains that women have always been available to me. Women of all hues, sizes, and shapes, I would add."

Gwen looked furious. For some reason, that pleased him. Could it be she was jealous of the other women who'd been in his life, even though they had little meaning to him now that she occupied his attention? "Oh, really," she said in a drawl that was meant to grate on him, and it succeeded admirably. "No doubt you're going to detail all of your relationships for me, so I can see just how available they've been for you."

She sounded like she was grinding rocks between her teeth.

"No," he said thoughtfully. She was definitely jealous. On the whole, he felt that was a good sign. Too much jealousy could become problematic, though, and would require steps on his part to assure her that he was not a man who believed in multiple partners at any given moment. But a little jealousy, an awareness that he had favored her above all other women, was, on the whole, not a bad thing. "I don't see that such a discussion has any benefit to us."

"Good. Because if we had to go into a mutual dissection of our past relationships, I was going to have a hissy fit. The reason my ex-boyfriends are ex is because I don't want to think about them anymore."

"Just so," he agreed amiably.

He stopped suddenly, a horrible, vile, reprehensible thought striking him with the impact of a meteor on the moon.

Gwen had ex-boyfriends. Men she had been intimate with. Worse, men she had probably loved, men to whom she had given her heart and soul and splendid, incredibly sexy body. Who knew how many of them there were out there, smugly living their lives secure in the knowledge that they had once engaged her in a way that was by right his. The fact that she shared *porraimos* with him proved that they were fated to be together, and yet great big herds of men roamed the earth who had dared to usurp his position.

"Are you growling?" Gwen asked, giving her horse a wide berth in order to come around the front to look at him. "Is something wrong?"

"I am not a vindictive man," Gregory informed her. "I am calm and sensible and with the exception of that which concerns you, always weigh my options before acting. With that in mind, you will furnish me with the names, locations, birth dates, mothers' maiden names, and dates concerning all of these former boyfriends. A spreadsheet with pertinent links to related Google Earth and social media entries is preferable, but if necessary I will take notes while you dictate the information to me."

She stared at him in disbelief for a moment, then began laughing so loudly that her devil horse, laying back his ears, danced an agitated circle around her, the various bundles and baskets attached to the saddle making clanking noises. She held on to his bridle, wiping her eyes once she was able to bring her hilarity into check. "Oh, Gregory, I can't thank you enough for that laugh. It totally distracted me from how miserably hot I am. A spreadsheet with Google Earth links." She chuckled to herself as she led the horse forward.

He hesitated, wondering if he should inform her that he wasn't actually joking, but decided after a moment's introspection that he would hold off that discussion for a later date.

They walked for approximately two hours, sometimes talking about the sights they saw (mostly deer, sheep, and cows) and sometimes enjoying a companionable silence, each deep in his or her own thoughts. Gwen seemed disinclined to discuss any of the weighty issues that occupied his mind, and he wordlessly agreed to the truce, content to simply enjoy being in her company.

He volunteered to water the horses while she went to cool off in the lake. That accomplished, he hobbled the horses as instructed, doled out their supplemental feed, pointed out the ample grass to be had for the savvy horse who knew his way around the concept of grazing, and returned to their little camp to lay out the food contained in the picnic basket before shaking out the two bedrolls that had been attached to the saddles. Once all was arranged to his satisfaction, he went to tell Gwen that their supper was ready.

She was naked. Naked and wet, her dark hair slicked back like a seal while she swam lazily near the shore, a look of abstract pleasure on her face. He imagined the cool water caressing her flesh. He imagined how it would turn her already satiny skin into that which resembled oiled silk. He envisioned the way the water would lap gently at her breasts and woman's parts, and all those wonderful other bits and pieces that made up the enticing whole.

It took him all of three seconds to uncleave his tongue from the roof of his mouth and strip himself before plunging into the lake with much splashing. The noise caught her attention and she stopped swimming to stare at him, her eyes widening as the water closed over his (rampantly erect) penis. Not even the chill of the water could quell his aroused state. Once the water was waist-high, he dove, heading straight for the two long legs that sang such a sweet siren song.

"Glorious heavens," she gasped as he broke the surface of the water. He pulled her to him, reveling in the feel of her body sliding against his. The water reached to about the middle of his chest, allowing him to stand in the soft mud of the lake and hold her tight. The sensation was almost as good as her mouth, which he tasted again and again until they were both out of breath.

"It's not heaven yet," he promised with a knowing look, taking a gulp of air. "But give me a couple of minutes, and it will be."

"Gregory—"

That was all he heard before he dove back into the water, pulling one leg up so he could kiss a watery path upward to her thigh. She squirmed, her hands windmilling in the water to keep her balance. He released that leg, waited for her to put her weight on it, and repeated the process with the second leg.

"What on earth do you think you're doing?" she asked when he surfaced again. He bent to take one plump breast, bobbing on the water and clearly awaiting his attention, into his mouth. Her flesh was cooled by the water, the contrast between it and the heat of his mouth making them both moan. "Do the other one. Do the other one!" she demanded. Her fingers dug into his shoulders, urging him on.

He obliged, swirling his tongue across her nipple, savoring the feel and taste of her, but needing more. Oh, so much more.

"More!" he said, unable to find any of that suavity that he was so known for. His brain had stopped all unnecessary processes, such as language and thoughts of anything but Gwen, focusing the full of its power on one thing: his need for her.

"Hell, yes, more!" she agreed, and slapped her hands on his arms. "Now!"

He grinned and dove again, picking up the serpentine line of kissing at her knees and heading straight for her hidden secrets. He couldn't hear her moans as he probed and touched and swirled his tongue around in a manner that he hoped would please, but he judged by the way she clutched his hair and pulled him closer to her that she was, in fact, enjoying his attentions. He knew he was, although when the dark spots began to form in front of his eyes, he reluctantly admitted that there were limits to what even he could do.

"Nnrng!" Gwen said when his head popped out of the water. Her eyes were glazed, her hands urgent on his chest. "No stop!"

"Be patient, my demanding one," he said as he gasped for air, amused that her brain, too, had ceased its ability to form actual words. "I shall take you to the finish line, have no doubt of that."

"Yes, yes!" she yelled, pulling at his hair. "Finish!"

Filling each hand with one rounded globe of her ass, he pulled her hard against him, lifted her up so that her legs were around his hips, and said, "You must help me, *dulcea mea*."

"Are you insane?" she snarled, pounding at his shoulders. "I can't even think, let alone do anything but teeter on the precipice of the most amazing orgasm ever. If you don't finish it, I will die, and then you'll have to explain to my two moms why I died unfulfilled. And let me tell you, they will have a thing or two to say about that."

He grinned again, kissed her because he just couldn't believe how wonderful she was, and then, for both their sakes, clarified the situation with, "You have to guide me into you, Gwen. All I'm finding is your hip socket. Unless this . . ." He concentrated for a moment. She stiffened, her eyes startled. "No, that doesn't seem to be right, either."

"Most definitely is not right," she said, and reached between them to position him. "Go!"

He went. Straight to heaven, is what he would have told her had it been in his power to speak at that moment of absolute bliss. Her muscles rippled around him, gripping him in a way that he had never imagined possible, and frankly didn't know if he would survive. Slowly he sank into her, her breath caught in his mouth as he kissed her, the sensation of both just about spelling an end to him.

But when she started to move on him, her legs flexing as she found a rhythm that left him feeling as if he was made up of flowing lava in the form of a man, he knew that he hadn't long to last.

"Gwen. My darling. My sweet. My heaven and earth and stars. If you move like that again—no, the other way—yes, that—I'm afraid that I will be doomed to disappoint you."

Her heels dug into his buttocks as she stiffened against him, her nails scratching his back at the same time she yelled into his mouth.

That was all he needed. Her climax caused her muscles to grip him with the force of a velvety hot vise, sending him well past what any mere mortal could endure.

"It is a good thing," he panted some minutes later, when they lay damp and exhausted on the bedrolls, a light linen sheet covering them from view of passing sheep, deer, and the odd occasional rabbit, "that I'm not mortal, because that would definitely have stopped my heart."

Gwen lay draped over him, her limbs tangled with his, her wet hair splayed across his neck and chest.

He'd never felt more wonderful in all his sixty-four years.

She lifted her head. "You can talk."

"Yes. So can you." He trailed his fingers down the silky softness of her ass. "I love your derriere. Have I mentioned that?"

"Actual words. You can say them." She squinted at him. "You're thinking thoughts, aren't you? Don't deny it; I can see you are. I can't do anything more than quiver with little aftershocks of sheer, unadulterated rapture from what was, hands down, the best sex that has ever been performed in the whole history of mankind, and possibly the universe, and you're there indulging in brain processes, and talking, and touching my butt just like nothing happened."

"Oh, something happened, my sweet one," he said with a leer.

"Gah!" she said, and slapped his chest before rolling off him, pillowing her head on his arm in a manner that he knew would leave the latter numb in a few minutes. He didn't care. A few pins and needles would be worth it.

She stared up at the sky, now dusky with both the oncoming evening and the red haze that grew darker and more intense as they neared the battlefield.

He smiled at her. "It was pretty damned good, wasn't it?"

"Oh, yes," she said on a sigh. "There's only one thing that could make me happier . . ."

He sat up and stared down at where she lay. "Woman," he said in his sternest voice, "I have pleasured you as I have pleasured no other woman, almost to the point of my demise. You yourself state that you are even now experiencing aftershocks. You do not aftershock if the experience is in any way less than absolute perfection. Therefore, there is nothing that could make you happier, and I will thank you to retract your complaint about my performance!"

"It wasn't a complaint—" she started to say, but he would brook no objection.

"Slur, then. It was a slur upon my manhood."

She lifted the sheet and looked under it. "Goddess! I didn't realize you were that large. Even all tuckered out you're . . . wow. Gregory, I can say in all honesty that I have no slur to make against your manhood. The only thing that would make me happier is if you'd feed me. I'm exhausted with all the aftershocks, and so hungry I could eat Bottom. Well, not literally, but you know what I mean."

"Please imagine that I am even now making a risqué play on words concerning your bottom," he said, mollified enough that he offered her a plate of food.

"Done. Oooh, is that a crab quiche?"

"Apparently so. And this appears to be some sort of rolls stuffed with various meats. Grapes?"

They dined happily, although Gwen insisted that they put on clothing just in case someone strolled past them.

"How are you going to steal the things that Aaron wants you to steal?" Gwen asked him some time later as they lay snuggled together, watching the stars overhead emerge from the velvety darkness to twinkle down on them.

Gregory had never been one to see the romance of the night sky—so far as he was concerned, it was simply a moon and light reflected from astral bodies too far away for him to easily understand. And yet at that moment, with Gwen warm in his arms, the softness of her body pressed against his, he could have sworn that the arrangement of stars and moon was created just for them.

"Gregory?"

"Hmm?"

"Are you thinking about sex?"

He blinked at the stars, then looked down at the top of her head where it lay on his chest. One of her hands rested on his breastbone, not stroking him, just lying there. It felt right. "I wasn't until you asked that, but now I am."

She laughed, pressing a kiss into his chest. "Then what

were you thinking about that was so consuming you couldn't answer my perfectly reasonable question?"

"I was considering whether or not I should attempt to write a poem to just how beautiful you are lying naked under the stars. Now I shall have to change that to an ode on making love to you."

"I don't think my heart could stand it," she said lightly.

He froze, wondering if she had, unbeknownst to him, abilities to read his thoughts. Did she sense the warm feelings that had been growing with each hour of her acquaintance? He'd been careful to not acknowledge them, even to himself, lest he hurt either or both of them. He hadn't ever been one to give his heart easily, and he knew with the knowledge born of man that in Gwen he'd found a woman who could destroy him should she so desire.

No, it was far better to keep things unemotional. Lust was fine. Sexual appreciation was appropriate. Desire was welcomed. But anything else . . . no. It was better this way.

She lifted her head and grinned at him, at the same time tweaking his nipple. "You're not the only one who almost croaked because the sex was so good. So, how are you going to steal the stuff?"

He relaxed. She wasn't making a declaration of his emotions after all. "I don't know. I've never stolen anything before. I guess I'll check out the camp and locate the items first, then make a plan."

"My moms are there. I'll have a chat with them and see if they can help. I'm sure they would. I think they'll like you." He felt inordinately pleased until she added, "They always cotton to the most inappropriate people. I can't tell you how many times over the years I've had to separate them from bad influences."

He pinched her ass. "That is no way to talk about a master thief, madam. Go to sleep. You're going to need your strength."

She sighed heavily into his chest and snuggled closer.

"Yes, I know. I have that stupid armor to wear, and when we get to the camp Doug will probably make me fight right away."

"I was referring to the method by which I am intending to awaken you," he said, wrapping his arms around her. He'd never felt so happy in all his life. He had Gwen, and that was all he wanted.

On the heels of that thought came another one, much more disquieting. . . . How on earth was he going to keep her?

TEN

"Who the hell are you?"

"Good gravy, it's a naked man!"

"Penny, where's the camera? I must get a picture of him. Here, you take a picture of me standing next to him. It'll make quite the blog post, won't it?"

"Hey, little boy. Daddy wants some of that sugar."

"I don't know who you people are, or why you've intruded upon my privacy, but I do not intend to allow you either to photograph me or to engage in acts of sugar. Go away, all of you, before I take my woman's sword and—"

"Now then, now then, let's be 'avin' none of that."

It was the voices that woke me, and not, unfortunately, Gregory with amorous thoughts on his mind.

"Dammit, there *is* a woman there. She's wadded up in the blankets. Crap."

I sat up, blinking and shoving my hair out of my eyes with one hand while clutching the sheet to my naked breasts with the other. The sight that met me was less than thrilling.

Gregory was also naked, his hands on his hips as he stood facing a semicircle of four people—two women and two men, one of whom bore a familiar face.

"Hello, Al," I said, holding the sheet tighter to myself. "Don't tell me—this is another tour group?"

"Early-mornin' Ramblers Tour," he said with a nod and a grin. "For those mortals what like to keep fit and see the sights normal tourists don't see."

"Go away," Gregory repeated. "We are not a sight."

"I don't know," said one of the women, a slight, mousy-looking girl in a dowdy gray skirt and sweater. She held a camera in her hands and snapped a quick shot of him. "You look pretty good to me."

"Penny!" the woman next to her shrieked and punched her in the arm. She had bright red hair, a sharp little nose, and was dressed all in pink. "I'm the ballsy one! You can't say things like that—it's my shtick. You're the good cop, I'm the bad cop, remember?"

"Sorry," Penny apologized, and took another picture of Gregory. "I won't do it again."

"See that you don't. Now, I'm going to stand next to him, and I want you to get several shots so that I can have some mugs and book bags and things made up. I think my blog readers will love that, don't you?"

"Oh, for the love of . . . Here." I tossed Gregory his pants, which I was gratified to see he pulled on immediately. Penny looked disappointed.

"Hey!" her pink friend said. "Here, you, take those pants off again. No one is going to want to buy my merchandise if you're not full-frontal."

"Yes," the other man in the group said in a low, slow voice. The word came out almost as a hiss. His eyes were avid with enjoyment as his gaze crawled over Gregory. "Such a fine, fine specimen. Daddy likes."

Gregory scowled at him. "Daddy can just shove it up his—"

"I suspect," I interrupted quickly, "that there's no way you can end that sentence that isn't going to be more to someone's taste than an actual insult."

"I saw him first," the pink woman said, rounding on the oily man.

"Yes, we saw him first." Penny took another picture, as if to prove her ownership.

"That doesn't matter," the man said, barely glancing at

them. "You are only women. You cannot give him what I can give him. Daddy is always the best."

"I don't give a damn who was here first," Gregory said in his coldest, most formal voice. "I have one word for all of you: scram."

"Now, now," Al said, sliding a sidelong glance toward me. "We're perfectly within our rights to be where we are. Ain't no one but 'is lordship who owns this 'ere land, and 'e's said that all are welcome to walk on it."

While they were speaking, I had grabbed my own clothing and clumsily donned it under the cover of the sheet. Once decent, I stood up and grabbed my sword that Gregory had alluded to. I wasn't normally one for a show of violence, but I really had had enough of tours.

"You heard him," I said, moving over to stand next to Gregory. I held the sword easily in my hand and tried to look as mean as possible. "Scram."

Al eyed the sword thoughtfully, then turned to his group and made shooing gestures. "All right, now, we've seen the south side of the lake. We'll be goin' round to the north side, where 'is lordship has provided ye all with a pancake break-fast."

"Will there be a naked man serving the pancakes? I'm quite disappointed that this one is so surly and unwilling to cooperate with the simplest of requests. Not to mention the woman and that sword. Is it a real sword? If it is, there could be a serious health and welfare violation in progress. Penny, get a picture of the sword-bearing woman just in case."

"Daddy does not like pancakes," the man said as Al hus-tled them off. "Daddy likes waffles. With a side of nubile young man."

We watched them leave. When Gregory turned to look at me, his expression was as dark as the sky to the north. "I take it that since you are dressed, you are not going to let me make love to you as I intended to do?"

"We kind of lost the moment," I said, with a wry little

twist of my mouth. I gestured toward the retreating tourists with my sword. "I don't think I could really enjoy myself knowing that Daddy and the Pink could happen upon us at any time."

He sighed, pulled me into an embrace, and kissed the dickens out of me. "I will consider myself in debt to you."

"Because I rescued you from their clutches with my spiffy sword?" I asked, giving it a little twirl as he moved over to release the horses from their hobbles.

"Because I owe you ground-shaking, aftershocking love-making at the nearest opportunity. If you will fill up our water supply, I will see to the horses."

We didn't encounter anyone else, tourists or otherwise, until midafternoon, although we did see signs of habitation some distance off to the west. Gregory was all for investigating what looked to be a small village, but I was anxious to check on my mothers' welfare.

"I think we should have a game plan," I said when we were almost within yelling distance of Aaron's camp. People bustled to and fro just as they had the first time I'd been there. In the distance, I could make out the battle mound itself, and two silhouetted figures who danced around, the light glinting off their weapons and armor.

The sky above us was now as disturbing as it had been the first time I'd seen it, the red, roiling clouds blotted out here and there with drifting wisps of gray smoke, and the occasional rumble of thunder. The hairs on my arms stood on end as lightning flashed above. "Did you do that?" I asked Gregory.

"Do what? Oh, no, that wasn't me." He looked upward, examining the sky. "Why is it red?"

"I think it has something to do with the nature of the battle. Maybe it reflects the blood spilled or something?"

"You said that the battle was only single combat. That can hardly qualify for enough blood spilled to be reflected in dramatic environmental effects."

THE ART OF STEALING TIME   211

" 'Stranger things . . . ,' " I half quoted. "About this game plan: I was thinking—"

Gregory held up his hand to stop me and pulled his horse to a stop, quickly dismounting, then standing very still and frowning in concentration.

"What is it?" I asked, reining in Bottom when he took exception to halting (he took exception to everything, but I was getting used to his ways). "Is something wrong?"

"No. Wait for it."

"Wait for what?"

Gregory held up a finger, then grinned and reached up to snatch something out of the air. I'd caught just the glimmer of lightning as it started to stretch out across the sky, but Gregory had caught it before it could go anywhere and redirected it down his body. He was lit up in blue and white light that sparked and snapped off him for a few seconds before dissipating.

"Show-off," I said, impressed nonetheless.

His grin was cheeky in the extreme. "What's the good in having a talent if you can't use it to impress your woman?"

"She'd be more impressed if you could do something useful with it, like zap some sense into these people and make them stop throwing her in cells."

He picked up Mabel's reins and led her forward. At the camp, someone had clearly seen us and had set off to the largest tent at a fast trot. "I suspect using lightning on a person who isn't a Traveller—or one who can participate in *porraimos*—would be a direct violation of the Watch code of behavior."

"I suppose so. OK, quickie game plan time: I'm going to check in and let Doug set me up with whatever it is I need to do, and then I'm going over to Ethan's camp to make sure my moms haven't gotten into any trouble. I'll introduce you to them then, all right? They might be able to help you find the stuff that Ethan stole from Aaron, although I suspect that at least the dog is going to be an issue because there's like a hundred of them there. That's assuming the dog is still alive, and there's no guarantee it's immortal."

"Halt!" called a high, reedy voice. Gregory kept walking toward the two men who were approaching us. One was a tall, thin figure in armor; the other, larger and bulkier, strode up behind the first. "Stand and be recognized."

"Really?" Gregory said as we continued onward.

The larger man passed the first, cuffing him on the back of his head as he walked by. "Ignore him. He spends too much time watching Errol Flynn movies. I see that Lord Aaron has sent you back to me."

"He has." Gregory stopped when Doug, now stylishly garbed in black leggings and a black tunic with a gold outline of a stag, halted. Doug and Gregory considered each other for a minute. I couldn't tell if they were having a silent manly weighing-up of the enemy, or some form of male bonding, but I didn't at that moment care overly much.

"Hi, Doug. Don't get too close—this horse bites." I added the last sentence quickly when Doug, evidently finished having a stare-down with Gregory, moved over to help me off my horse.

"He knows better than to bite me," Doug said with a look at Bottom. To my astonishment, the horse looked the other way, and if he could have whistled innocently, I swear he would have.

"Wow," I said as I swung a leg over Bottom's neck, allowing Doug to help me dismount. "I didn't think it was possible to intimidate him, but you did."

"I could have intimidated him if I'd wanted to," Gregory said loudly, then looked horrified that the comment had come out of his mouth.

Both Doug and I looked at him. Bottom bared his teeth until he saw Doug glance his way.

"Please forget I said that," Gregory said with an embarrassed cough. "And Gwen, cease looking as if you were pleased that I was jealous of a man who is able to frighten that hellish nightmare of a horse. I am not jealous of the fluffy bunny, although I do find it amusing that he insists on holding on to you despite the fact that you are fully capable of standing on your own. Ha ha. I laugh at such a notion."

I stared at Gregory, growing delight welling up inside of me. Not jealous, my shiny pink butt! He was practically green with it. He marched over and plucked my hand from where Doug had been holding it, giving both Doug and me matching glares.

"Ah," Doug said, glancing down at where now Gregory held my hand, then up at me. "It's like that, is it?"

"Yes, it is, and I'll thank you to stop ogling my woman."

"Hey," I said mildly, giving him a mail-clad elbow to the ribs. "I'm standing right here. If I don't want to be ogled, I can speak up. Not that he was ogling me. Were you, Doug?"

"I might have been, just a little bit, but that's only because the sight of a woman in mail is a turn-on." A little frown creased his forehead as he shifted his attention to Gregory. "I assume Lord Aaron sent you both back to fight, although you appear to have lost your armor."

"Unfortunately, it's worse than that," Gregory answered with a grimace.

"Is it? I'd better hear about this in my tent, then." He gestured to the tall, skinny young man, who had remained several paces behind him. "Have their horses seen to. This way."

We followed Doug to the biggest tent and took adjacent canvas stools that sat in front of a long wooden table littered with papers. Doug settled behind the table and nodded at Gregory.

"There isn't a great deal to tell," Gregory said, and proceeded to give a succinct accounting of our last meeting with Aaron.

"A thief," Doug said slowly when he finished. "How very novel. It hadn't occurred to me to engage the services of a thief to end the war, but I can see the value in Lord Aaron's thinking. Very well. Lady Gwen will take the place of one of my warriors who wishes to return to his home for a short period. His wife is due to birth their first child any day. You may have Sir Dedham's tent. Your shift begins at vespers."

"Um . . ."

"About six in the evening," Gregory told me, giving my fingers a supportive squeeze.

"How on earth do you know that? You're only sixty-four years old," I pointed out.

"I read a lot. Where is my tent?" he asked, addressing Doug. "I'll wish to get a few things together before I start my career of crime."

Doug shuffled through his papers, apparently deeply engrossed in them. "Accommodations are only for those members of Lord Aaron's household who are fighting or are present in a support role to ensure the comfort of the warriors. You are neither; therefore I am not obligated to provide you with food or shelter." He looked up and gave Gregory a wicked smile. "Technically, the rules of war forbid me to acknowledge the existence of rogues, thieves, and highwaymen. You can't even be classed as a spy who has obvious uses to the campaign. I'm afraid I must henceforth institute a policy of neither seeing nor hearing you. I'm sure you'll have no trouble finding a place to sleep amongst the other camp followers."

"That seems unnecessarily harsh," I protested. "Gregory is here because Aaron asked him to do a job. And a successful completion of said job will end the battle, so you should be kissing his butt rather than engaging in this medieval-esque pissing contest."

Doug's eyebrows rose. Gregory, who had been looking irritated, gave me a warm look that had his eye crinkles standing out. He lifted my hand and kissed my knuckles. "It warms my heart that you defend me, *dulcea mea.*"

"Well, it's not fair! And I, for one, am not going to—"

"Quibble," Gregory interrupted, and pulled me to my feet while giving Doug a long look. "I assume the audience with your august self is over?"

"It is."

"There's just one more thing." I resisted when Gregory tried to escort me out of the tent. "Have you heard anything about my mothers?" I asked Doug.

"Who?"

"My moms. They were captured by that Holly woman with me a couple of days ago. I guess Ethan needed a couple of witches, because they were given some accommodations and access to an apothecary. I haven't heard from them, since it's impossible to get any sort of cell phone reception here, but I thought there might be a chance that you've heard if they're OK." I told him my mothers' names, and waited, hoping for good news.

My stomach fell as Doug's face grew darker and darker. "Lord Ethan has kidnapped witches to use against us? Why did you not tell me this when I first captured you?"

"They aren't bad witches," I said, but then honesty prompted me to correct that. "Not evil, that is. Sometimes their magic doesn't work like it should. But they would never willingly harm someone. They're very big on the Wiccan Rede, and not doing harm that can be returned to one."

"Lord Ethan is unscrupulous! He'll find a way to use their magic against us! I must communicate this to Lord Aaron immediately. You are dismissed, both of you. Be sure to see the armorer about having some new armor made that fits you."

"I won't be here long enough to need it," I said gaily as we left the tent.

"What? What do you mean—"

Gregory let the tent flap drop, which wouldn't have stopped us from hearing Doug, but it did shut him up. "Shall we make our way into the enemy's camp?"

I glanced up at the sky, making a frustrated noise when it didn't yield any hint as to the time. Behind us, someone screamed, followed almost immediately by the sound of shouting. Bottom thundered past us, eyes glinting with an unholy amusement, nostrils flared, and hooves pounding. His saddle was off, and a halter had been placed on his head, but a dangling short bit of rope hinted that someone had gotten a bit too close to him.

"Godspeed and good riddance," Gregory said as Bottom disappeared into the distance.

I waved.

"As I was saying—"

"Good evening." A soft, gentle voice behind me interrupted Gregory. I turned to see who it was. A small, tonsured woman dressed in a monk's garb bowed to us both. A rosary swung from her waist. She smiled. "I'm Brother Helene. I understand that you are going to replace Sir Dedham at the front. If you will come with me, I will take you to his quarters, and thence to the armorer, who will no doubt wish to take some measurements."

"Brother Helene?" I couldn't help but ask. "Shouldn't that be Sister?"

She looked surprised. "No, I am a monk, not a nun."

"But . . ." I looked at Gregory. He shrugged. "OK, moving on. Thanks for the offer to show me around, but I'm going to take Gregory over to Ethan's side and show him around."

"Oh, you can't do that," she said in her breathy voice. She sounded like Marilyn Monroe about to burst into "Happy Birthday." "They are the enemy."

"I know that, but I was over there a few days ago, and—"

"And I'm afraid that I must ask the thief to leave now. He is not allowed within the confines of our encampment. I understand from the squires that accommodations are to be had in the fornicatresses' camp. That's to the northwest, just beyond the curve of the stream," she said helpfully. "They always appear happy to see men."

My hackles rose. I hadn't, until that moment, known that it was possible for people to have actual hackles, but I swear that I felt a tingling between my shoulder blades that paired nicely with the ire that burned hot and fast. "Gregory is not going to sleep with prostitutes!" I said loudly.

Gregory looked thoughtful until I whapped him on the arm.

"Isn't he?" Brother Helene's eyes opened very wide as she looked him over. "I don't see why he couldn't. Is he diseased? The whores usually don't mind that unless it's leprosy, and then they tend to use . . . specialists."

Gregory rolled his eyes.

"He's not diseased, and he doesn't need a specialist. He doesn't want to be with prostitutes."

"He looks virile enough," she said mildly, then added, "Oh! He is a sodomite? I've heard—this isn't from firsthand knowledge, mind you—that there is a camp for those who favor man-minx entertainment a few miles to the south. Evidently they used to be located with the whores, but there was a falling-out over the decorating of the tents, and the male harlots struck out on their own."

"He does not want man-minxes!" I protested. "And he's totally virile. He's the most virile person I know."

"Thank you, sweet," Gregory said with a smug little smile.

"He's virile from here to the moon, but that doesn't mean he's on the prowl for some nooky, either male- or female-based."

"That's not quite true, but I agree with the sentiment," he said, pinching my behind.

"Sad," Brother Helene said, giving him one last look. "I'm sure the strumpets of both genders will regret that decision, but that does not affect the fact that he cannot stay here. Now, if you will come with me, Lady Gwen, I will show you to your quarters."

She took hold of my arm with surprising strength and tugged me forward. "I really need to go see my mothers—"

"I will take you to your quarters, and you will then see the armorer!" she said in a voice that had shifted from sexy to one that wouldn't be out of place in a demonic demonstration of dark arts.

"You are not at all monklike," I told her as she hauled me off down one of the aisles. "Monks are supposed to be nice."

"We don't like to be crossed," she growled. "I have a job to do, and no one, certainly not you, is going to stop me from completing it in the manner I see fit."

I looked back over my shoulder, waving my free hand at Gregory. "I guess I'm going to see my tent now."

"And the armorer," he added with a little twist of his smile. "I will find you later."

"Not here you won't!" Brother Helene said loudly, grunting slightly when I tried to dig in my heels. She just jerked me forward until I had no choice but to walk or be dragged. "I will see to it that the guards have orders to remove you should you venture into the camp again. If you do not stop struggling, Lady Gwen, you will force me to render you insensible so that I might easily deliver you to your quarters."

"Oh!" I gasped, glaring at her when she gave my arm a hard yank. "You are so mean! I'm going to report you to whoever is in charge of monks around here."

"That would be Brother Anselm, and he's busy right now with a village of insurgents who are fighting Lord Aaron's rule."

"Busy as in tending to their wounds, and helping the innocent people, and providing comfort and all that stuff that one normally thinks of monks doing rather than being a bully, like some people I could name?"

She made a face. "Of course not. Brother Anselm is helping to capture the insurgents, and hunting down those who have taken to the woods in order to avoid justice. He is quite adept at the art of extracting information from unwilling subjects."

"Great. The head monk is an expert torturer. This place is just so weird."

"Here is your tent. You may leave your mail inside. I will find a squire to attend it and you. Be ready to visit the armorer in ten minutes."

She departed before I could voice my intentions to do otherwise, and after a brief consideration of the sort of antics that monks got up to in Anwyn, I decided to get the armor appointment out of the way so I could go find my mothers.

"My arm is bruised in three different spots," I told Brother Helene exactly ten minutes later when she reappeared.

She *tch*ed without any sign of contriteness, and gestured down another pathway. "We will go to Mistress Antoinette now."

"Fine, but you can be sure that I'm going to tell Doug or Aaron if I can't fight because my arm is too sore."

"Doug?"

"Yeah. The head knight dude."

"Ah. Him." She proceeded down the aisle.

I followed, walking a bit easier now that the heavy mail was no longer on me and I'd had a quick wash with an ewer of water that was waiting in the tent. I hadn't any fresh clothing to change into, but figured I'd address that issue once I was done seeing my moms. "What do you call him?"

"I prefer not to say. The king's warriors do not share their names, as you know."

"Because they can be defeated that way, yes, I remember, but everyone knows my name, and I'm now one of his warriors."

"You are an outsider brought in to fight. You are not the same as one of Lord Aaron's trusted guard."

"Pfft." I pretended that I wasn't the teeniest bit hurt at not being one of the elite squad, and focused my attention on the surroundings.

The people in Aaron's camp looked the same as those in Ethan's camp across the stream—they bustled, they talked and laughed and sang little ditties to themselves. Horses were escorted hither and yon, and a plethora of young men and women scampered about, obviously running errands for their elders. There were no dogs to be seen, but I did spy a few cats lounging around in the sunshine. Almost everyone wore black tunics with gold designs on the front, the designs varying from person to person. Most were animals, although some were runic and other devices.

The next hour was spent talking to a very nice middle-aged woman with yellow hair and piercings in a number of visible locations (and I suspected just as many that weren't visible), who deftly took my measurements, then circled me silently for three minutes before she said, "I know what'll do for you."

She disappeared into her tent, which stood alongside a makeshift forge, and emerged with a couple of pieces of plate in her hand and her assistant, Marigold, trotting behind her. "Lady Constance asked me to make this for her a few decades ago, but she's yet to visit the front, so we can modify it to fit you. Here, hold this up and let me see what changes I'll need to make to it."

I did as she asked, admiring the metal chest plate while she fussed around me. It was a gorgeous piece of armor, well crafted and even graceful in its lines. It looked like it was made of sterling silver, although I knew it had to be some kind of steel. The breastplate was curved to fit a woman's form, with breast cups that would please the heart of Grace Jones. The center of the breastplate curved down in an inverted arrow, much like a corset's busk, the sides of which swept out to little hip flares that reminded me of a peplum. It was held on the torso by leather straps, and as Antoinette and Marigold strapped me into it, I was aware that not only did it fit reasonably well (although I overflowed the cups a bit), but it was also surprisingly light.

"Wow, I can bend and stuff," I said, bending down to touch my toes. "This is much nicer than the other armor I was given."

"The mail will be too small for you," Antoinette said, eyeing me as I flexed and stretched to determine my range of motion. "But we can patch on a new section easily enough. The skirt, however . . ."

"There's a skirt?" I looked down at my jeans. "I can't imagine fighting in a dress."

"It's a mail skirt. It hangs down over your hips to your knees."

"Oh. I thought that was part of the shirt thingy."

"Men wear those. We've found that ladies prefer the flexibility that separate pieces provide. Marigold, fetch the skirt. Lady Gwen looks to be bigger in the hips than Lady Constance, which means we'll have to make a few extra links."

"Sorry about my hips." I felt stupid apologizing about something I couldn't control, but at the same time, there I was creating extra work for them. "My mom says I get them from her. She's always been broad in the beam, too."

"Nothing wrong with good birthing hips. Ah, here we go." She held up what I can only describe as a wraparound skirt made up of links of shiny silver metal teardrops that overlapped in a beautiful floral pattern. Antoinette strapped it around my waist. The two edges were supposed to strap together, but a three-inch gap kept it from closing properly.

"Well, now I feel like a great big elephant," I said, glaring at the gap. "That's it. I'm going on a diet."

"Don't be stupid," Antoinette said in what I was coming to realize was her usual gruff tone of voice. "Men like women with a bit of meat on their bones. Marigold, get the fire stirred up. Three rows of links should do the trick. I'll have them and the breastplate ready for you by Nones."

"When is that?"

"A few hours."

Reluctantly, I took off the pretty armor, chiding myself for that emotion, since I hadn't wanted to be a warrior in the first place.

"And I have no intention of actually fighting," I argued with myself after bidding Antoinette and Marigold farewell. "Maybe if I suggest word games instead of physical combat. Or perhaps I can beguile whoever I'm supposed to fight with daring tales of mystical alchemy."

The problem there was that I knew no daring tales of mystical alchemy. As a whole, alchemists were studious introverts not much given to any acts of daring, let alone those that would entertain someone enough to distract him or her from the thought of fighting.

"I'm doomed," I said with a sigh, and started off for Ethan's camp.

ELEVEN

"Lady Gwen! Lady Gwen!" I stopped, watching with growing misgivings as a squire ran up and immediately began tugging my arm. "You're late! Master Hamo will be most upset."

"Late for what? No, wait, it doesn't matter. I've done the armor fitting, so now I get to go see my mothers."

"Late for training! Master Hamo trains all the new warriors, and his lordship said you are to attend because you have no experience fighting."

"His lordship who? Or whom. No, I think it's who."

The teen didn't even look at me, just kept tugging me onward until we were clear of the tents. "His lordship. The man in charge of all of us."

"Yes, but what's his name?"

"I can't tell you, for I do not know."

"Oh, him. Well, you can tell Doug that I've done what he asked, and now it's my time."

"There ye be," a deep, bell-like voice bellowed as the squire, who was now behind me shoving me forward with both hands on my back, pushed me into a roughly circular patch of dirt. A massive man stood there, barechested, with metal bands about his wrists. He had no neck, was bald, and stood with easy grace for someone who apparently had muscles on his muscles. He hefted a great sword that was taller than me, and nodded. "Ye look like ye have the makings of a fighter. Lad, her sword."

The squire behind me stopped shoving me and darted to the side, returning with my borrowed Nightingale sword.

"Look, I really don't have time for this—*aieee!*" I hadn't even finished speaking before the massive man, who I assumed was Master Hamo, swung his equally massive sword at me. It was parry or die, and parry I did, all the while feeling sure that just that defensive act alone would result in my losing an arm.

"OK, so I was wrong," I panted, blocking another thrust, the Nightingale singing as I swung her through the air. "That doesn't mean I want to waste an hour fencing with you. Hey!"

Master Hamo had evidently just been toying with me, because I suddenly found myself flat on my back, my head ringing with the impact of it upon the dirt.

"That's what ye get for not paying attention," Hamo said, looming over me so that he blotted out the red, roiling sky above. He looked like a mountain in man form. "If I had wanted to, ye'd have been dead. As it was, I hit ye with the flat of me sword."

"How about you don't hit me with anything," I snapped, woozy enough that I took the hand he offered, which hauled me abruptly to my feet.

"I won't if ye learn what I'm about to teach ye."

The events of the next hour are painful to recount, so I shall draw a veil over them. Suffice it to say that I ended up in the dirt pretty regularly every couple of minutes, but by the time the hour was up, I was dodging, spinning, and parrying almost all of Hamo's blows.

"That be enough for today. Tomorrow we'll work on yer attack skills. Give yer sword to the lad. He'll see to its care until ye have a squire of yer own."

"Every individual atom in my body hurts," I complained as I hobbled over to the waiting squire. He looked about sixteen and wore the anxious puppy-dog look of perpetual worry and admiration that I was coming to realize indicated one who hoped to be a warrior someday. "It's not as much fun as you might think," I added.

The squire blinked at me, then bowed and trotted off clutching my sword.

"Right, now I see my moms," I croaked to myself, and limped with a bent back toward the direction of Ethan's camp. I moved with all the grace of an elderly crab, and my body screamed for a hot bath and a soft, comfortable bed, but I had to check on my mothers before I could give in and collapse into a ball of mewling, whimpering Gwen.

"Oy! You there!"

"Oh, for the love of . . . no. Not going to listen," I said loudly, one hand on my back as I continued on my way.

"You! Hold up!" another voice called.

"Not on your life."

Two men rushed up from where they were loitering on the fringe of the camp. I ignored them, brushing past them to the tree that had been felled and dragged over to make a bridge across the stream.

One large hand shot out and grabbed my arm, right where Helene had left bruises. I yelped. "Watch it! My arm was sore to begin with."

"We've got you now," the arm-holding man said. Wearily, I gave him the once-over. He was big—not muscles-upon-muscles-big like Hamo, but what I thought of as club-bouncer big—with tattoos of snakes that circled his neck, and dragons that emerged from under both sleeves of his shirt to run down the length of his arms.

"Unhand me, knave," I said in my best Renaissance Faire manner.

"What did she call me?" Arm-boy asked the second man.

He was just as big and bulky as the first guy, and like him, had copious amounts of ink, but his tattoos consisted mainly of nude women in various poses. "A navel. The daft-witted hen called you a navel."

"Like an orange?" The first man squinted at me. "Did

you call me an orange, missus? Why did you call me an orange?"

"I didn't. I called you a knave."

He shook his head in dismay. "Now I gots to rough you up a bit. I don't want to, but I gots to."

"Aye, you gots to," the second man agreed. "Can't have people calling you an orange when you're not an orange."

I suddenly wished I had my sword again. "Look, I said 'knave,' not 'navel orange,' and even if I had said 'orange'—"

"You can't rough her up too much, though, Irv," the second man added after some thought. "Boss won't like it."

Irv, who was looking sadly at me, chewed that over for a minute.

"Help!" I yelled at the top of my lungs, deciding that in this case, it was better to seek aid before the situation got out of hand. "Help! I'm being roughed up by two be-tatted hulks who don't understand medieval-speak!"

"Aye, boss won't."

"Help!" I yelled louder and tried to wrestle my wrist away from Irv.

No one in camp so much as looked my way. I wondered where Gregory was, and why he wasn't where I needed him to be: namely, conveniently located adjacent to the stream. Damn the man for going off and doing his job.

"Better you don't rough her up at all," the second man said, having evidently completed some great undertaking of thought processes.

"Aye," Irv said slowly, then nodded his head. "That way, boss can rough her up."

"No one is roughing me up!" I bellowed, and making a fist, punched Irv in the nose as hard as I could.

He caught my fist about a quarter of an inch away from his face. "Here, now!" he said, clearly offended. "There's no call for that! Frankie, did you see? Daft hen tried to smack me in the gob."

"Aye. Feisty wench, she is. Best we take her to the boss

afore she hurts herself. Boss won't like that any more than he'd like you to rough her up."

"Helleeeeeeeeeerp!" My last cry for help morphed into a startled scream when Irv bent down and hefted me onto his shoulder. "Put me down, you great lummox!"

"What's a lummox?" I heard him ask his friend as they crossed over the tree to Ethan's side of the stream.

"Don't know. Might be another fruit."

"Daft hen."

"Aye, daft hen."

"I'm not a hen, and I'm not daft. Oh, for the love of the stars and moons, would you put me down?"

"Imagine someone calling you an orange," Frankie said conversationally as the two men strode along.

"I didn't—wait a minute. Why aren't you taking me to Ethan?"

I had fully expected that the two bully boys would go straight into Ethan's camp and deliver me to their boss, but they didn't. They made a sharp right at the camp and headed for the woods that ran along the far side of the encampment.

"Who?" Irv asked.

"Ethan! The man who owns . . . runs . . . the camp just there."

"Oh, him." Irv made a gesture with his shoulder that had me sliding down his back a few inches. "What's he got to do with anything?"

"Daft hen doesn't know what she's talking about," Frankie offered.

"I'm going to be sick all over you if you don't set me down!" I warned them.

That did the trick. Irv stopped and set me onto my feet, retaining a hold on my wrist as he did so. "Don't be thinking you are going to get away," he warned. "Boss said we wasn't to let you get away."

"Aye, he said that." Frankie nodded and took my other arm in his beefy hand.

"Who, exactly, is this boss?" I twisted around to look over

my shoulder at Ethan's camp, stumbling when the men started forward. I had half hoped to see Gregory lurking about the edges, in the process of thieving, but although I could see people moving around in the camp, we were too far away for me to yell for assistance.

"Boss is boss," Irv answered in a bewildered tone, as if he couldn't understand why I hadn't figured that out.

"Yes, but what is his name?"

"Oh. Tessersnatch. Baldwin Tessersnatch."

I froze, and was promptly jerked off my feet when the two men kept walking. They paused to help right me. "Tessersnatch?" I cleared my throat when my voice came out a squeak. "The lawyer?"

"Aye, that's him." Frankie gave me a pitying look. "You've gone and made him angry, you have. I wouldn't want to be in your shoes."

"No good being in your shoes," Irv agreed, marching forward again.

My brain whirled those two words around and around. Baldwin Tessersnatch was a mortal lawyer who had ties to the Otherworld, most recently with my two moms. Desperate for funds for their school, they—foolishly, and quite illegally—had agreed to sell, through Baldwin, some incantations to another mortal man.

The dread that filled me at the name turned swiftly to hot, consuming anger. "Well, now. How about that. Baldwin Tessersnatch, the man who threw me off a cliff to my death when I told him my moms wouldn't be fulfilling the transaction. You know, I think I'd *like* to see him. I have a thing or two to say to Mr. Murderous Tessersnatch."

"Baldwin," Irv corrected me.

"Daft hen was making a funny," Frankie said. "At least I think she was. You never know with one what calls you an orange."

I shook off their respective holds on my wrists and marched forward, saying in a voice that should have dropped the birds from the trees, "Oh, I have several things to discuss with Baldwin Tessersnatch!"

"It's a good thing that we got to her before that other hen," Irv told Frankie.

"I wonder if I can remember the spell for shriveling up a man's testicles," I mused as we entered the woods. "I know it started off *Misbegotten wart on the backside of humankind*, but I can't remember if the second line is *Go and boil your bollocks in a vat of rime*, or *barrel of lime*. Hmm."

"Aye, she gave me the willies, she did."

"Maybe it's *Shrivel the stones till the end of all time*? Damn my crappy memory for spells. Wait—what other hen?" I stopped again, turning to look back at them. "A woman is looking for me? Is her name Holly?"

"Don't know her name. She never said, did she, Frankie?"

"I'm of a mind that she didn't, Irv."

"All she said was that her boss wanted to see you, and that she would see to it that we were paid twice what the boss pays us if we'd help her find you." Irv looked thoughtful again. "We were tempted, weren't we, Frankie?"

"We were," his buddy admitted. "But only until she told us who her boss was, and then we figured we'd be better off with our boss."

I was a bit confused by which boss was which, but managed to sort it out enough to ask, "Ethan, you mean?"

"Naw, he's not badass like the hen's boss."

"We like Ethan, don't we, Irv?" Frankie said, apropos of nothing in particular. "We were helping him."

"He had the wrong idea about how you wage a war," Irv confided. "He didn't once think of using a car bomb, or offing the competition's family."

Horror filled my veins. "You guys are hit men, aren't you?" Really stupid hit men, but still, obviously, professionals in the art of killing.

"Not us," Frankie said at the same time Irv answered, "Yes, but we don't always do that."

"That's right. It's only *sometimes* we take care of the boss's bigger problems." Frankie didn't even blink over his sudden change in story. "Mostly we're the boss's right-hand men."

"And enforcers."

"Sometimes we do a hit or two, just to keep our hands in."

"It doesn't pay to get rusty," Irv agreed.

"Messy." Frankie nodded sagely. "It can get messy if you don't keep your hand in."

I was tempted to run screaming away from them, but given this new and more deadly light on their characters, I felt a little subterfuge was in order. Subterfuge and distraction. "So who is this woman's boss if it's not Ethan?"

"Badass," Irv said, giving me a little shove forward. To my relief, he didn't try grabbing my arm again.

"Really badass. Badder than the boss, and he's pretty bad."

Just the thought of Baldwin had me squaring my shoulders. "Yes, well, you haven't seen my ass. It's going to whup your boss's."

They both looked at my butt. I made an annoyed sound and charged forward through the woods. I would deal with this woman once I had vented my spleen on Baldwin. "Where is your boss? I want to get him taken care of quickly so I have time to see my moms before I'm due for my shift."

"Boss is in Cardiff," Irv said.

I stopped and looked at him. "Cardiff? You mean the town? He's not here in Anwyn?"

"Naw," Frankie said. "Boss can't come into Anwyn."

"He was banned for trying to sue the boss of Anwyn. Boss said our boss can't come back. So he sent us to fetch you, said we wasn't to come back unless we had either you with us or your head in a duffel bag."

"Now that was a great movie."

I stared at them both in horror.

"What movie is that, then?" Irv asked his buddy.

"*Eight Heads in a Duffel Bag*. Don't you remember? We watched it right before the night we had to take care of those trolls what were making a stink about the boss forcing them to plague folks in Manchester."

Irv shook his head. "Six heads, that was."

"Eight. It had that American bloke in it. What's his name? Italian, he is."

"It was *six* troll heads that we collected that night in Manchester," Irv insisted. "I remember because I thought if we had one more, we could play that dice game with them."

I took a deep, deep breath, my mind spinning with all sorts of thoughts and plans. I wasn't going to end up with my head in a duffel bag, that was for sure. I had to leave, to get away . . . but I couldn't leave Anwyn—not with my mothers and Gregory still here. Plus, there was no telling if the Watch was outside just waiting for me to pop back to the mortal world. I hadn't asked Gregory about that, but I had a feeling that they might be. And yet, if I told these two that I wasn't going to leave Anwyn with them (head firmly attached to the rest of me), they'd most likely go down the duffel bag avenue.

I weighed the likelihood that I would be able to escape them once we left Anwyn, decided it had no potential for success, and pointed behind them, saying loudly, "Oh my god, look at that! It's a head in a duffel bag!"

When they turned to look, I bolted, racing through the trees and hurdling both small shrubs and large rocks, well aware that both men were only seconds behind me.

Crashing noises followed me—the sounds of two large men shoving their way through the forest, both shouting for me to come back.

I was fleeter of foot, however, and more agile, and what's more, I had motivation to give me strength. I stayed in the forest as long as I could before I broke cover and raced for the camp. If I could just get to my mothers, they could cast a spell to protect me from Irv and Frankie. . . . That thought died a cruel death when I glanced over my shoulder and saw that Frankie was about twenty yards behind me, and Irv the same distance behind him.

"Change of plan," I panted to myself as I swerved around the fringes of the camp and dashed for the downed log bridge. I had a feeling that the two men would not be welcomed in Aaron's camp if they were helping Ethan, and I pulled every last ounce of strength I had to get myself across the log and into the camp before Frankie caught me.

It was a close thing. He'd eliminated the gap between us, but as I suspected, pulled up short as soon as he crossed the log bridge. I raced down one aisle of Aaron's camp and up another, losing myself in the confusion of tents and people. It wasn't until I burst into Doug's tent and bent double, my hands braced on my knees as I tried to catch my breath, that I realized just where I was.

Doug was taking a bath in a large wooden tub. He cocked an eyebrow at me. "Changed your mind and decided to dump your thief boyfriend?"

"No," I panted, trying to straighten up. A stitch in my side had me clutching my ribs. "Sorry. Didn't mean to interrupt you. Two guys chasing me. Helping Ethan."

Doug sat up from where he had been lounging against the sloping back of the tub. "Who is helping Ethan?"

"Two men. Chasing me. Big guys. Tattoos. They want my head."

"Don't we all."

I stared at him.

He sighed. "And these men followed you here to this camp?"

I nodded, swearing to myself that I was going to start jogging again.

He stood up, water and sudsy bubbles sliding down his body.

THE ART OF STEALING TIME 233

"Eep," I said, and turned around when he yelled for his squire.

"Tell the guards to capture two of Ethan's spies who have chased Lady Gwen into our camp. They are located at—Lady Gwen?"

"The log bridge. Or they were a minute ago. You can't miss them. They're big guys. One's named Irv and the other is Frankie."

The squire nodded and trotted out. I waved a hand behind me at Doug. "Sorry about interrupting your bath. I was a bit panicked."

"I don't suppose I could entice you into the tub with me?"

"No," I told the entrance of his tent and started moving toward it. If he got too pushy with me, I'd simply run out and go to the nearest group of people.

"I thought not. You appear to be quite smitten with the thief. Of whom, it need not be said, I have no knowledge."

Smitten? Me? I thought about that while Doug made rustling noises behind me that I took to be him dressing. Was I smitten with Gregory? So much so that other people could tell?

"I don't know about smitten," I said slowly. I certainly wasn't going to go into the details of my blossoming relationship with Gregory, let alone analyze my feelings to Doug. "We get along well."

"Ah. I suppose if you are willing to settle for that, then you will be quite happy."

"I don't think I'm settling for anything," I answered, annoyed.

He strolled past me, now fully dressed, and shoved aside the tent opening. "I see it is almost vespers."

I followed him out of the tent, ignoring his change of subject. "'Settling' implies that I can't find anything better. I don't know that I want to spend the rest of my life with Gregory, but I do know that—" I stopped suddenly, realizing that I was doing exactly what I'd sworn I wasn't going to do. "Never mind. It doesn't concern you."

"You say that, and yet it was to my tent you came when you were frightened by these men, not to your lover's arms."

"That's because I don't know where Gregory is. Your deranged monk woman drove him off."

"I was naked. You did not leave my tent. You stayed there and chatted with me, pretending that you were not interested in my body, and yet even now I can see the desire in your eyes." He leaned in close to say softly, "You want me, Gwen. It is written on your face just as it is written in your heart."

I pushed him back, my lips narrowing. "And you are delusional. There's only one man in Anwyn who I want, and you are not him. So stop hitting on me, or I'll make you one sorry no-name warrior."

"You think to threaten me?" he asked, his eyebrows rising.

"Got it in one." I turned on my heel and marched away, feeling that was a suitable exit line.

TWELVE

I muttered to myself as I hurried along the aisle to my tent, where I found Marigold waiting with my shiny new armor.

"Stupid, conceited man. Oh, hi, Marigold."

"Lady Gwen. Who is stupid and conceited?"

"Doug. Er . . . whatever the name is of the guy who's in charge."

She looked startled for a moment, but evidently decided it was better to stick to business. She held up the lovely metal skirt. "Master says that if it doesn't fit, she will have to add another row of teardrops."

"Oh, that's truly beautiful." I examined the additional bit that Antoinette had to put on to fit my girth. The addition was woven seamlessly into the existing skirt. "She does lovely work."

Ten minutes later I was clad in what amounted to quilted long johns to prevent injury, a mail shirt, and the lovely floral teardrop skirt, a metal breastplate, and matching arm and shin protection.

"This is almost too pretty to wear," I told Marigold as I left my tent. "I'd hate to get it scratched or dented."

"You bear the Nightingale of Dawn," she said, handing me the now-cleaned sword. "Surely you would not wield such a sword as that if you were unable to keep others from striking you."

"Yeah," I drawled slowly, deciding it was better that I not go into the whole thing about me not being an actual warrior. "Here's hoping my tongue is faster than my sword."

She looked confused, but I just thanked her for her help and marched off to the battleground. There were no large men lurking around the edges of the camp, so I assumed that the guards had either captured them or driven them off. I encountered no one as I made my way to the slight hill that sat smack-dab under the roiling red center of the sky. A lone figure was there waiting for me.

"Hello," I called out conversationally as I approached. "My name is Gwen."

"Oooh," was the reply. I couldn't see the person's face, since a helmet obscured the sight of it, but the voice was definitely female. "You aren't supposed to tell me your name, are you?"

"I'm a substitute warrior," I said, stopping at the top of the hill to consider my opponent. She sounded reasonable enough. "So everyone knows my name. What's yours?"

"Peaseblossom." She lifted a mailed hand. "Um. I'm new, so you'll have to tell me how we start. Do I just begin hacking away, or do you get first swing since you are the senior warrior?"

I would have slumped in relief, but the gorgeous armor gave me very good posture. I did, however, relax mentally. "Oh, mercy, no. How about we chat for a bit, so we can get to know one another, and then we'll get around to the actual fighting. Peaseblossom is an interesting name. Was your mother a fan of *Midsummer Night's Dream*?"

"I don't think so," she said, pulling off her helm. Her face was red and sweaty from being confined in the helmet. "You have very pretty armor."

"Isn't it nice?" I modeled it, turning around so she could admire the intricate mail skirt. "Antoinette said it was made for the queen but she never showed up to claim it, so I get to wear it for a bit. It's a lot lighter than you'd think it would be."

Her eyes widened. "You're wearing the queen's armor? My leaves and twigs! You must be a very great warrior in-

THE ART OF STEALING TIME   237

deed. I am honored with the opportunity to meet you in battle, although I fear that my inexperience will shame me."

"Bah," I said, swaggering just a little as I strolled around
the top of the mound. I waggled my sword in what I hoped
was a casual manner. "I'm the same as anyone else. So,
whereabouts are you from?"

"Is that the Nightingale?" She pointed a shaky finger to
my sword. I thought for a moment she might hyperventilate.
"You wear the queen's armor and bear Lady Dawn's sword?
I am doomed! Doomed!"

"Not if we don't actually fight," I said in a low voice.

"We must fight! It is what we have sworn to do."

"Actually, I didn't swear to fight . . ."

"But you are a warrior of Aaron. It is your duty to protect
the name of your lord."

"About that . . . look, I'll level with you—the truth is that
I don't want to get this armor damaged. It's just too pretty,
and Antoinette had to do a rush job on the skirt and all. So
why don't we just sit and chat away our shift? That way no
one will get her armor scratched, and no one will be doomed."

"We are warriors," she said stubbornly, but with less vigor.
"We are meant to fight. It would be wrong to disregard our
duty."

"I think so long as we're up here for the full length of our
time no one is going to care. Or notice. See? Everyone in
your camp is over at the picnic tables having dinner." She
turned to look where I was pointing. "No one is so much as
glancing our way."

She bit her lower lip, considering this. "I cannot hold up
my head knowing that my sword did not even touch yours—"

"Easily enough done," I said, hefting the Nightingale.
"We can bash the swords together a few times, and then you
can say, in all honesty, that we did our warriorly thing."

After a minute's silence, she blurted out, "I will agree, but
only on one condition."

"Oh?" I was wary of what that might be. "And that is?"

"I would dearly love to fight like someone who is as great as you. Would you teach me a few things?"

It would take a better person than me not to be flattered by her admiration. The knowledge that I had less skill than she did was not, however, something I was going to admit. "Sure thing. Go ahead and hit my sword—carefully, because it's pretty, too—a couple of times, and I'll teach you a few things, and then we can have a nice chat."

Her sword, a great big beast of a weapon, had been placed in a wooden stand meant for holding spare weapons while combatants beat the crap out of each other. She struggled to lift it up and out of the stand, finally getting it free. The tip immediately dropped to the ground with a scraping sound that had me wincing on behalf of the finely honed blade edge. "It's . . . it's a bit heavy," she said, panting as she tried to heave the sword up.

I watched her for a few minutes, grunting and sweating, before I took pity. "That sword is way too big for you."

"I know, but it was all that Sir Colorado had. He said he would have a smaller one made for me, but that I could use this one today." She rubbed at her palm, making a pained face. "Now I have a blister."

"That's a sign that we should just call this good and get down to the chatting part of the battle."

"I would never be able to hold my head up if we didn't clash swords," she said in a pathetic voice.

"Yes, but you can't even lift your sword."

She stared at me in mute appeal.

I sighed.

"If anyone had ever told me that one day I'd find myself on the top of a minute battlefield in the afterlife, having to fight with swords, I'd have declared them to be certifiable." I held out the Nightingale with one hand, grunting as I heaved up her sword in the other hand, and banged their blades together a few times.

"There." I put her sword back on the rack and put mine

into the sheath that was strapped to my back. "Now we chat."

"All right, but you have to show me some of your moves later," she said, sitting cross-legged on the red dirt.

"Done. Have you seen my mothers in Ethan's camp?"

"Would that be Lady Magdalena and Lady Alice?"

"That's them. I take it they're OK?"

"Oh, yes. They are housed in Mistress Eve's tent, which is right next to Lord Ethan's, since Mistress Eve used to be his . . . er . . ." Peaseblossom blushed and leaned forward to say in a whisper, "His leman."

"His . . . oh. His girlfriend? Before Holly, I assume."

"Yes. Your mothers have been making plentiful spells, and Lord Ethan is very happy because he has witches and Lord Aaron does not."

"What kind of spells?" I asked suspiciously.

"All sorts," she answered, waving a hand. "Spells to turn baked goods into other baked goods—"

"Ah, the infamous plain doughnut to frosted chocolate doughnut spell. I know it well." I was relieved. If my moms were doing only minor magic, then they couldn't get themselves into trouble.

"Yes, those are most popular. And spells to sweeten the smell of the latrine."

"Fresh-air spells are always useful."

"Especially on days when the cooks make chili," she agreed. "And then there's the spell to increase the prowess of the manly arts."

"Just between you and me, that one owes any success to the belief in the man using it rather than any actual magic," I told her. "Even my moms are the first ones to admit that there's no way they can beef up a man's . . . er . . . bits with magic. But the silly men think they can, and that makes them feel better about themselves, and everyone's happy."

"Is the old woman who is with your mothers also a relation?"

"Mrs. Vanilla? Not really. I assume she's staying with my moms?"

"Yes. She is knitting a coat for Lord Ethan's horse."

"A horse blanket, you mean?"

"No," she said blithely. "A coat. It has lapels and pockets."

I let that go, feeling that the less comment about Mrs. Vanilla, the better. We chatted for a few more minutes, but Peaseblossom had nothing to say that gave me cause for concern. So it was that I spent the next hour and forty minutes teaching the pleasant Peaseblossom everything I'd learned a few hours before.

Master Hamo would have been proud.

"It was a pleasure meeting you," I told her, shaking her hand once our time was officially over.

"Likewise. I will see you tomorrow night. Perhaps there will be more you can teach me?" The last was said so wistfully that I knew I'd have no problem talking her out of fighting again.

"I'm sure I can. See you then."

I made my way back to the center of the camp, where Aaron's men had arranged a bunch of wooden tables around a huge bonfire. The light from the latter danced along the front of Doug's big tent, casting long shadows as my fellow warriors and all the support members of the camp ate, drank, laughed, and sang in the way that people do when they're out camping.

"Lady Gwen. I am pleased to say that we've found you a squire. Seith, come forward and meet your lady and take her sword." Doug strolled out of his tent to greet me, waving toward the bonfire and the accompanying crowd. One small, dark form scurried out.

A boy of about eleven or twelve considered me with large pale gray eyes that were startling against his swarthy skin and the shock of black hair that hung down over his forehead in spikes. He reminded me of an anime character come to life.

"Seith?" I repeated. It meant "seven" in Welsh. "Are you a seventh son?"

"Of a sixth son," he said with a nod.

"Missed being special by just one son," Doug commented in an aside to me. "Seith is actually my child. Stop staring at the lady and take her sword, lad, lest she lose her temper with you."

"Whoa now," I said when the kid hurried forward to take the Nightingale from me. "I do not lose my temper with children. And even if I did, I'm not going to hit him or anything. I don't believe in violence."

"You are a warrior of Aaron," Doug pointed out, making a gesture that had his son hurrying off with my sword.

"Aside from that, I'm just here for a week. You have six other sons?"

"Ten sons, fourteen daughters," Doug answered, taking me by the elbow and escorting me to the fire.

"You must have an amazing wife." I put a little extra emphasis on that last word to remind him that he should be ashamed of hitting on me when he had a family already.

"Wives plural. I've had eight of them. The last one divorced me two years ago. I am currently sans spouse." He looked steadily at me.

"Wow. That's a hell of a record to have going against you. Ooh, is that salmon?"

It was salmon, and I managed to get a plate of it and accompanying rice and veggies without Doug making any more overt references to something that just wasn't going to happen. I settled down at a table to enjoy my dinner.

"Ah, here comes the entertainment," Doug said from behind me.

I turned, my mouth full of delicious planked salmon, and almost choked when a troupe of about ten women in a pornographer's idea of harem outfits flitted into the camp, nipples flashing, silken scarves flying, and catcalls from my fellow warriors filling the night air.

"Holy sh— That's the entertainment?" I had to grab my plate to save it when one of the nearly naked women leaped onto the table and began to undulate her way down it, much to the pleasure of the men around me.

Doug reached out and caressed the woman's (mostly bare) breast. "Yes, indeed." He stopped fondling her to glance down at me with a leer. "You prefer male company instead?"

"For the last time, I am not interested in you—"

"We have dancing boys, as well as girls," Doug interrupted, waving a hand to my left, his attention elsewhere as one of the women began a move that I can only describe as using his leg as a stripper pole.

I looked away. "Wow. So you do. I don't think I've ever seen an actual dancing boy before. They really can dance, can't they?"

"I'm told their buttocks are divine," Doug said, smiling down at the woman who was twining her slightly clad self around him. "I have no interest in male buttocks, so I couldn't judge, but I trust you will come to a decision on that matter."

I considered the well-oiled specimens of male dancers' behinds, clearly visible since they wore basically G-strings and not a lot else, and decided that interesting though the subject was, I had probably better take myself off before things got too rowdy.

"Would madam care for a prostitute?" A soft voice next to me asked as I picked up my cup and plate. A small, balding man held a notebook, with pen poised over the paper. "Male or female? The rates are the same for both sexes, if that makes a difference."

"It doesn't, and, no, thank you."

"Perhaps madam would like a complimentary ten-minute preview? We allow those for very important persons. You may use your ten minutes as you like, either in flogging your prostitute, having him (or her, if madam swings that way) engage in acts of an oral nature, or even trying out a sample of the prostitute's sexual methodology—"

I escaped before the man could go any further. I felt oily just by association, and hurried back to my tent with my plate, where I found Seith sitting outside.

"Hungry?" I asked him.

He nodded. I gave him my plate.

"Doesn't your dad feed you?"

"Aye, but I'm always hungry. Dad says I'd eat his horse if he let me." The boy shrugged, then scarfed down the salmon and veggies.

"Well, enjoy. You wouldn't happen to know where I can take a bath, would you?" I rubbed my arms. Even through the mail, my skin felt dirty.

"Ladies have baths in their tents. The men use the stream." He got to his feet, cheeks stuffed, chipmunk-style, with food. Little bits of rice flew out as he said indistinctly, "I'll fetch it for you."

"That would be lovely, thank you." I entered the tent and began to unhook all the armor and mail strapped to my body, wondering where Gregory was and whether he would manage to find me before the night was over.

I certainly hoped so. I had many things to tell him . . . and more things to *do to* him.

THIRTEEN

Gregory Faa was a man annoyed. *Again.*

"Faugh," he said as he shook his cell phone, then swore under his breath. He'd never been the sort of man who said "faugh," and yet there he was, standing in the middle of the Welsh afterlife, saying not only words like "faugh," but coming perilously close to adding a *tch!*

"And I'll be damned if I turn into the sort of man who *tch*es at the drop of the hat," he growled to his phone, and shook it again as if that would make it function. "Connect, damn you!"

The notification across the screen remained NO SIGNAL for most of the time, but once in a while, CONNECTING TO NETWORK would tantalize him, only to immediately return to the previous state. Damn it, he had hoped the king had been exaggerating the isolation of Anwyn from modern computer networks. Reluctantly, he gave up the idea of trying to contact his cousin to find out what was going on in the real world.

"Peter'll have me drawn and quartered for staying here," he muttered to himself, guilt making his skin itch in an irritating manner. He emerged from the edge of a forest to consider the scene spread out in front of him. To the left, across the stream, lay Aaron's encampment. Even now Gwen was probably busily being kitted out to do her warrior thing.

He smiled at the thought of her reluctance to fight anyone, then became distracted—and aroused—at the idea of stripping armor off her one piece at a time. When he was down to nothing but her bikini underwear, he shook himself, told his erection to relax and hold on until that evening when he could allow it free rein with Gwen's lady parts, and tried to make a plan of action.

He sat down with his back against a tree while he planned, and woke up some time later to find the sun slanting across the sky at an angle that indicated early-evening hours.

"That's what I get for staying awake the night before watching over Gwen," he told himself sternly, and deciding that he'd wasted enough time, he marched into the camp of Aaron's enemy.

"I'm looking for Amaethon," he said, stopping the first person he saw.

"Lord Ethan always swims before supper," the young woman told him, nodding to his right. Through the tents, he could see a glimmer of water, probably a pond.

He thought of Gwen in the lake and had to once again mentally chastise his penis. That done, he made his way through the dogs, people, and tents to what was indeed a smallish pond. It was lined with irises and daffodils, and Gregory thought to himself how much Gwen would enjoy the location. Two women walked along one edge of the shoreline, while about fifteen feet out, water splashed in a rhythm that indicated a swimmer.

"—care what he says, I can't possibly have that volume done before Samhain. I've yet to tackle my angsty teenage years, and volume twelve follows that. Make a note that I still need a title for that," the swimmer called out, pausing to add, "Here, who's that next to you?"

"My name is Gregory Faa. I take it you're Ethan?"

"Faa? Faa? Do I know a Faa, Pervanche?"

"No, m'lord," one of the two women answered, barely giving Gregory a glance. "You know a Fern, though."

Ethan began to emerge from the water. He was nude, and Gregory noted that the water must be very cold indeed.

"What title would you give a book about your angsty teenage years?" Ethan asked him, accepting a towel from the woman named Pervanche.

"I don't believe those years were particularly angst-riddled. At least, not in my case."

"Bah. That's not going to help me. I need something emotional. Portentous. Meaningful." He dried his hair brusquely with a second towel, and with the first one wrapped around his waist, started toward the tents. "What are you doing here if you're not going to help me with titles?"

Gregory decided that the direct approach was the best. "I'm here to collect the king's dog, roebuck, and lapwing."

To his utter and complete surprise, Ethan made a rude gesture. Before Gregory could react, Ethan grabbed the hand that was flipping Gregory off and held on to the wrist, saying as he did so, "You're welcome to 'em, the whole lot if you can find them. The dog's dead, but you can have one of her approximately eight hundred descendants. They're all over the camp. Had to make a rule that everyone owned one, just so the bulk of them would have care."

Gregory eyed him. Ethan appeared to be fighting with his own arm. "And the roebuck and lapwing? Where are they?"

"No idea. Pervanche, strap. Diego is being obstinate again. Consuela!"

They stopped as Pervanche slipped a black leather strap over his shoulder, angling it across his chest like a sling. Gregory watched in silence as, with a slight battle, Pervanche and Ethan managed to get his wrist bound, effectively strapping his arm to his torso.

"Er . . . Diego?"

"My hand. It's always stroppy in the afternoon. It gets that way until it's had a little nap. Ah, there you are."

A lovely woman with long golden hair popped up beside them. "Yes, my lord?"

"Bring supper to my tent. I have to prepare for the photographer. I need several new author photos."

"As you will, my lord."

Gregory, feeling a bit bemused, was convinced that despite appearances, Ethan had more information than what he was telling. He followed as Ethan went straight to the largest tent. The inside looked like something out of the Arabian Nights, what with the silken hangings, scattered pillows, and low beds (three) that dotted the massive interior. There were also a handful of desks, one of which Ethan sat down at, flipping open the lid to a laptop. He looked up when Gregory stopped beside him. "You still here?"

"I am."

"Speak quietly, then. Diego is sleeping, and I don't want him woken up early. He's hell the rest of the night if he doesn't get his proper nap."

Gregory glanced at the arm. "I hesitate to ask . . ."

"Then don't."

Gregory thought about that a minute and decided that the advice was sound. Who was he to point out just how odd it was to treat one's own arm as if it was a cranky toddler? "I was sent to find the lapwing and roebuck. I'd appreciate help in finding them."

Ethan sighed, and leaned sidewise to peer around Gregory. "Consuela!"

The woman entered the tent, followed by three men bearing platters of food and drink. "You bellowed, my lord?"

"Where's the deer?"

She gestured for the men to set down their trays, waiting until they'd done so and left before asking, "What deer would that be?"

"This man"—Ethan gestured at Gregory—"keeps going on about a deer. You must know where I put it."

"Would that be Lord Aaron's deer, the one you stole from him almost a millennium ago?" Consuela asked, giving Gregory a look that didn't contain so much as one iota of curiosity.

"That would be the one," Gregory answered.

She pursed her lips and thought. "I'm not sure. I haven't seen it since . . . I would say approximately the year 1415. I can have one of the boys look for it, if it's important."

"It's very important," Gregory said before Ethan could say otherwise. He needn't have worried. Ethan was pecking away at the laptop's keyboard with one finger. "And the lapwing?"

"What's that?" Consuela asked.

"A bird."

"Ah. My lord?"

"Eh?"

"This gentleman wishes to know where is the bird that you stole along with Lord Aaron's dog and roebuck."

"Gone," Ethan said without looking up from the screen.

"Dead?" Gregory asked, his spirits sinking. Perhaps, like the dogs, there was a descendant that he could bring Aaron.

"No. Just gone. Flew the coop, so to speak. Ha! Pun. What do you know about angsty teen poetry? It shouldn't be too difficult to write, should it? I mean, it's mostly just all dreck, isn't it? Lots of bad imagery, and depressing self-examination, and a morbid fascination with death and destruction, yes?"

"Unfortunately, I'm unfamiliar with angsty poetry, teen or otherwise. You have no idea where the bird escaped to? Did it have any distinguishing marks?"

"Would 'My soul was like a one-legged eagle, brought to the harsh, dying earth by the willful, unending ignorance of those around me' be a metaphor or a simile?"

"It's a simile. A bad one. Do you even remember the bird?"

Ethan looked up, obviously catching the harsh edge in Gregory's voice. "Of course I remember her. Aaron let her have free run of the castle. I remember that most distinctly, because he doted on the little thing, ignoring important visitors in order to feed her succulent bits of food when he should have been offering them to me."

"You were at Aaron's castle?"

Ethan looked down his nose at him. "Who are you that you are so ignorant of my past? I am the slayer of many beasts! The ruler of all of Wales! I am the bringer of war to Anwyn! I lead an army that my brother raised from the trees and shrubs and plants across the breadth of my realm! Can you doubt that when I entered Anwyn, Aaron groveled at my feet in an attempt to placate me?"

Given his (admittedly slight) knowledge of Aaron, Gregory did actually doubt that, but he knew better than to express that thought. "I don't believe I ever learned why you did steal the dog, deer, and bird from Aaron."

"Oh, that." Ethan sniffed, and focused his attention on his laptop screen again. "I fancied the bird, and Aaron wouldn't let me have her. So I stole her, and the dog followed me."

"And the deer?"

"My brother liked deer." He made an odd sort of face. "A little too well, if you know what I mean."

Gregory decided that he preferred ignorance on that subject. "There's nothing you can tell me to help me find the bird and roebuck? Nothing at all?"

"The deer's around here somewhere. Bound to be. Gideon never could throw anything away. The bird, as I've said, has long since left. Does a sonnet have fourteen or sixteen lines?"

Gregory murmured the answer and left the tent before he was caught in any more of Ethan's self-absorption. He almost bumped into the woman Consuela as he exited, apologizing when she jumped back.

"I have a record here that shows a listing for 'roebuck, one, large marble' in the last inventory, made sometime around the turn of the twentieth century." She held the paper out to him. "It appears to have been relegated to Lady Dawn's herb garden. You will find that to the northwest, just beyond the apothecary's tent."

"Thank you," he said, bowing slightly to the woman. He couldn't help but indulge in a bit of curiosity. "Is it true that everyone here—Ethan and his family excepted—are plants?"

She gazed at him steadily, but once again, without any sign of emotion about the oddness of his question. "The warriors are all trees and shrubs, turned to human form by Lord Gideon. I am not of their ilk, however, if that was going to be your next question."

He smiled his most charming smile, the one that his cousin's wife said could drop a nun at fifty paces. Consuela didn't so much as bat an eyelash. A sudden longing for Gwen swept over him. Gwen would love his most charming smile. She would swoon, and leap on him, and touch him in places that made other places hard and demanding. She would never stand and stare at him as if he were no more interesting than a plate of boiled eggs. "I see. Thank you for the help. If you hear anything about the lapwing, I'd be grateful for news of that, too."

She inclined her head and then entered the tent.

"Odd woman," he murmured to himself, then studied the paper she'd given him. "Marble? It's a statue?"

He went off to see if, in fact, the roebuck was an actual statue, and not a depiction of the infamous animal in marble, and after an hour's search through a weed-choked wilderness that had obviously once been a garden, he uncovered a stained, broken statue of a stag.

"It's a statue. How . . . odd." He picked it up, staggered a little at the weight, then retrieved the leg and one set of antlers that promptly fell off, and with them under his arm, headed for the camp across the stream.

He wanted to see Gwen. He wanted to tell her about Ethan's plant warriors, and the odd woman who didn't seem to have any emotions, and how his very best smile had failed so miserably. He wanted Gwen to reassure him that she thought he was still sexy, and charming, and desirable. He wanted to make love to her, rest for a reasonable amount of time, then make love to her again.

He just wanted her.

"Here, don't I know you?"

He stopped at the edge of Aaron's camp and turned to see who had spoken. A woman picked her way across the fallen tree trunk that served as a bridge over the stream. She paused at the end of it, her expression turning black. "Oh, it's you! The one who stole my time! Well, I have a thing or two to say to you!"

Dammit, it was Death's reclamation agent. Since he hadn't seen any sign of her or the two neckless wonders, he'd assumed they had given up on finding Gwen and had left Anwyn.

"Why are you here? Anwyn is outside of your master's domain." He wasn't exactly sure that was true, but he assumed that if the Watch had no power here, then neither would any entity other than the ruler.

"Just because I can't take that which rightfully belongs to me doesn't mean I can't persuade the subject to leave this place." The woman stepped off the log and looked around her with obvious distaste, moving toward him as if she were walking in a minefield. "Ugh. Is that a cat? What is it with these people and cats? They were everywhere at the king's palace, and now there's more here. Not to mention the dogs in the other camp. It's enough to make a person deranged."

Being a Traveller meant that Gregory had grown up believing that animals were unclean and not to be associated with. He didn't hold any personal animosity toward pets, but he didn't see a need to fill his life with them, either. And yet despite that fact, he was irritated by this woman's blatant hostility toward the cats that roamed Aaron's encampment. It was almost as if he felt the need to defend them. "They're just cats. They aren't doing anything to you. If they bother you so much, you'd do best to leave."

"Ha! You'd like that, wouldn't you?" She stopped in front of him and transferred her glare from the nearest cat to him. "You owe me for my time, Traveller."

He hesitated, surprised that she had been aware that it was her time he had taken for Gwen. Most people weren't aware when their time was being used elsewhere. He wished he could bluff his way out of the situation, but now that he was with the Watch, he couldn't lie to save himself grief.

Sometimes he had to wonder if the job was worth all the sacrifice.

"You were paid for your time."

"Bah. A few silver coins."

"Those coins were worth a small fortune. I paid you well, reclaimer."

"I shall lodge a complaint with the shuvani in charge of overseeing your usage of time." Her mouth was held in a prim line. Gregory wondered how his Gwen could be so warm and inviting, while this woman was as sour as a pickle.

"If the shuvani had an issue with me using your time, then I would have already paid that price." He wondered for a moment if he hadn't been punished for the act after all; the situation he found himself in with Gwen's mother and the Watch certainly could be described as hellish in nature.

"It's not right that you can just take something that is mine!" the woman stormed.

"You are immortal. I took a minuscule amount of your time—for which you were more than amply compensated—time that you won't even notice missing. If you know anything about Travellers, you will be aware that the penalties for our actions are reduced when it concerns your kind."

"But it is still illegal," she insisted.

He waved that fact away. "Barely so."

"The fact remains that what you did was wrong, morally and legally, and I shall be sure to inform the Watch of that fact. Oh, yes, I know who you are." She had obviously noticed his reaction to her threat. "I had some people look you up once it became clear to me that you had stolen my time. You're only a probationary member of the Watch, and it shouldn't be difficult to have them kick you out for your illegal actions toward me. Not to mention interfering with me in the course of my duty."

"I did nothing to stop you."

"You brought my client back to life by resetting the time!"

"The outcome of which was that Gwen didn't die, and thus your duty to collect her soul was abolished. Therefore, I couldn't stop you from doing a job you didn't have."

She narrowed her eyes at him. "Don't think you can get around me with your time doublespeak. There's causality for actions by people who affect time. I looked it up; there are laws that you are obligated to follow, so don't think you can pull that wool over my eyes. I can see right through it."

Gregory didn't think she could, not really. Travellers had more than a millennium to perfect their circular thoughts on time, especially those concerning paradoxes, but he didn't feel that she would benefit from knowing this. "You were paid for your time. I admit that the Watch will have something to say to me about the act"—that was an understatement—"but given the circumstances of saving a woman's life, I am confident that their chastisement will not be too egregious."

"We'll see about that." She scowled at the nearest cat. "What are you doing here in Anwyn?"

He thought of telling her that it was none of her business, but since he wanted to deflect her attention from this camp, he engaged what Peter's wife called his charm mode. "The king sent me out to recover some items stolen from him. What are you doing here?"

"Items? Oh, the things that started the war? I'm here to reclaim my client's soul, as you must know. Two mortals at the other camp told me that she had been taken to the king's castle, but there was no sign of her, nor any sign that she had been there." The reclaimer looked extremely annoyed. Gregory was frankly surprised that no one had told her that they'd been there, but that confusion was cleared up with her next words. "How those people live with all those cats—it's unhealthy! There was cat hair everywhere. I couldn't stop sneezing, and the second I set foot in the castle my eyes started streaming so badly that the officious little twit of a tour guide asked me if I was crying."

Gregory made sympathetic noises. "So you didn't speak to Aaron himself?"

"No, he was off doing something with an elephant, or so his wife gave me to understand. I spoke to her—or I attempted to."

He froze. Constance had wanted them executed; it wasn't likely that she would keep mum about their presence in the castle. "Did you indeed?"

"I don't know about Aaron, but she is clearly dotty." The reclaimer pulled an embroidered handkerchief from a pocket and dabbed at her nose while sending another potent glare at the cats nearest them. "Obsessed, obviously. And rude! She was downright obnoxious when I insisted that the cats be removed from the room. She said that allergies were all in one's mind. Have you ever heard anything so ridiculous?"

"Never," he said, breathing again. Thank the deities for Constance's feline obsession.

"So I came back here to find those two mortal ignoramuses who were after my client and give them a piece of my mind. Only they aren't at that other camp. The people there said they'd been brought over here." She eyed him with a speculative glint in her eyes. "I don't suppose you know where they are?"

"Two large men with no necks?"

She nodded.

"I have no idea where they are. For that matter, I don't know who they are, other than that they are, as you say, mortal."

"They work for some sort of crime lord, from what I understand. I spoke with them briefly when I got here, but they knew little other than that their boss wanted my client for refusing to deliver something she'd sold him. It matters little—my claim takes precedence." She eyed him with growing suspicion. "You know her name. And yet my sources couldn't find any proof that you were acquainted with her. Is that why you are here? To find her?"

"No," he said in all honesty. He knew exactly where she was. Well, not the specific tent, but he knew she was in the camp. "I was captured by Aaron's men and agreed to find three items that were stolen from him in order to secure my release."

"Oh." She looked away, clearly losing interest in him. "Then you are of no use to me. I must find the human idiots and roast their balls until they tell me where my client is."

"There are a lot more cats in the camp than you see here," Gregory said quickly, wanting to keep her from snooping around.

She had moved off a few feet, giving the nearest cat a wide berth, but stopped at his warning.

"Perhaps we could come to a deal," he said slowly as he strolled toward her, his mind busily sorting through ideas.

"What sort of a deal?" she asked, suspicion back in her face.

He spread his hands to show his good intentions. "Let's say that I search the camp for the two men—I've seen them from a distance, so I should be able to recognize them—and in return for my doing so, you drop the charges you'll place against me with the Watch."

She clicked her tongue against her teeth and appeared to be about to refuse his suggestion, but after a cat started toward them to investigate the new people, she agreed. "Very well," she said, dabbing at her nose while backing away from the oncoming cat. "But you should know that this is very irregular, and if you ever again think of taking so much as a second from me—"

He spread his hands wider and turned up the wattage of his charm. "I can swear to you on the grave of my beloved mother that I would not do so."

"I will be over in Ethan's camp." She hurried toward the downed tree to cross the stream. "I will expect you to report to me as soon as you find them."

He bowed, waited until she had disappeared into Ethan's encampment, and turned to examine the cat who sat next to him licking her paw. "Well done. Your timing was perfect. You may now remove yourself and attend to your other duties."

The cat decided that more intimate ablutions were in order, and Gregory, feeling that was his cue, moved off to find Gwen. He would have to warn her about the reclamation agent. Perhaps Gwen would agree to lie low until he could persuade Death's minion that she had left Anwyn?

These thoughts swirled through his mind as he searched the outer fringes of the camp.

"Would you mind telling me"—he stopped a pair of twin boys who were lugging wooden buckets lined with leather and filled with steaming water—"where I can find the tent that belongs to a warrior named Gwenhwyfar?"

"Just ahead, on the left," one of the twins said, sucking noisily on a peppermint, if his breath was anything to go by. "It's the one with Seith outside it."

"Seith?"

"His lordship's son," the other twin said, nodding toward the biggest tent, the one that Gregory recalled belonged to Doug. "What for are you a-carrying that deer?"

"I like it. I thought it would look good in Gwen's tent," he improvised.

"You wouldn't be the thief what Brother Helene said was sniffing around the camp, would you?" Twin One asked, his eyes round with wonder. "Because if you are the thief, we're supposed to call the guards, who will torture you most heinously."

"Do I look like a thief?"

"You've got a deer," Twin Two pointed out.

"Perhaps it's mine. Perhaps I want to move it to a new spot where it can be enjoyed by all. Perhaps someone gave it to me to repair. Perhaps I'm a magician, and this is a magical being bound by a curse into marble form, and I'm going to release him."

"Coo," they both said in unison. "Are you?"

He smiled, and waggled the disattached stone leg at them. "That would be telling. This way?"

"Aye, to the left."

Gregory strolled off with apparent nonchalance, but in reality he was careful to avoid meeting people. He wasn't afraid of being caught, but he didn't need the complication that extricating himself—and possibly Gwen—from another sticky situation would involve. Luckily, the sun had long since gone down, and now the night air was soft with insect noise and the distant sound of people singing severely out of tune. No doubt there was a camp sing-along or some such thing. He just hoped that Gwen hadn't felt the need to join in.

"And you would be Seith, I assume." Gregory examined the boy who sat with his back against one of the tent poles. He was wrapped in a blanket and looked very sleepy. "Why aren't you in bed?"

"I'm a squire. Dad said that I was to attend to Lady Gwen's every need, and that if I didn't, he'd send me back to my mum."

"Is that bad?"

The lad sighed a heartfelt sigh that seemed to come from the depths of his soul. "Aye. She's wed again, and my new father doesn't like me. My real father doesn't like me much, either. No one does."

Gregory tried not to let his amusement show at the expression that the boy now adopted: part martyr, part drama queen, he was the picture of noble misery. "Just out of curiosity, how old are you?"

"Thirteen. Dad says I'm runty for my age." If possible, he looked even more miserable.

Gregory nodded toward Ethan's camp. "If you're up for some angsty poetry, I know someone who'd buy it off you. Take yourself off and get some sleep."

"I can't," the boy said, yawning. "I have to guard Lady Gwen."

"I'll guard her for the night. You won't be of any service to her tomorrow if you are too tired to stay awake. Go find your bed."

The boy got slowly to his feet, hope visible in his tired face. "You'll stay here all night? You swear?"

"I swear. She won't suffer any harm while I'm around."

"Thank you," Seith said, and made him an awkward bow. Gregory donned a charming smile for a third time that day and entered Gwen's tent. He would dazzle her with the smile first, then show her the deer statue and recount how far he'd gotten with Aaron's tasks, finally giving in to the lustful thoughts that had tormented him all day and sex her up like she'd never been sexed up before.

She was naked.

He stopped dead, the broken leg and antler falling to the soft carpets that lay underfoot. He barely managed to hold on to the deer itself as Gwen, her hair caught up in a ribbon and tied at the top of her head, sat in a metal bathtub draped with a white linen cloth. She turned to look at him, her face damp and rosy, her flesh slick with the bathwater.

The scent of flowers hit him then, of sun-warmed flowers, and warmer woman. His woman. The one who set his blood alight with want and need and a desire so great, he knew he was going to have trouble walking the few steps it took to get to her side.

"Oh, it's you," she said, relaxing after a startled moment. She gave him a slow, sultry smile that seared a path from his brain to his groin. "I wondered if you'd find me."

He shed articles of clothing with each (painful) step. By the time he reached the side of the tub, he was naked. Her eyes widened as he held out his hand for her.

"Up," was all he could manage to get out.

"I wasn't finished—"

"Up!"

She took his hand with a little frown, obviously about to tell him that she didn't appreciate being bossed around. He stepped into the tub before she could leave it, sat down, and pulled her down onto his legs.

"Oof!" she said in a delighted tone, then scrunched up her adorable nose and added. "Leg cramp!"

He scooted forward, adjusting her on his thighs so that her legs wrapped around his hips. "Better?"

"Much. Do you have a thing about making love in the water?"

"Not particularly. It just seemed like too good of an opportunity to miss. Plus, I'm covered in dog hair."

"Unfortunately, the water will be cold soon, and it has to be brought in by buckets."

"The temperature of the water matters little to me." He surveyed her as she perched on his legs, unable to decide where to start. Her glorious breasts, so temptingly close right there in front of his face? Her belly, all soft and satiny? Her hips? Her legs? The sensitive inner depths of what he was coming to think of as his own nirvana? "I will start at the top and work down," he decided.

"Chest!" she squealed, and flung herself forward on him so that she could swirl her tongue around his nipple even as he attempted to do the same thing to her. Their heads collided with an audible *clunk*.

"Ow!" they both said in unison. Gwen rubbed her forehead while Gregory, with a manly disregard of minor pain, took the opportunity to access the breasts that bobbed so enticingly in front of him.

"I love your breasts," he murmured against her, his hands wonderfully full of them. They were warm and slick and he couldn't resist tasting first one, then the other. They were both so perfect, so delightful, he didn't know which one he liked more. In the end he pushed them together, and buried his face in their magnificence, tasting, nibbling, and teasing them as Gwen laughed.

"I guess that proves you're a breast man."

He looked up from the wonderful land of her bosom, and

smiled. "When it concerns you I am. And a derriere man. And a leg man. I'm a Gwen man, pure and simple."

"All right, you've had enough time, Gwen man. I get my turn with your chest."

"I'm not done taking my turn yet. I have your belly and hips and legs and nirvana to explore first."

"Nirvana?" She laughed again. He applauded the effect such an act had on her breasts. "That's a new name for it. Didn't your mother ever teach you to take turns?"

"Yes. But my father taught me it was important to complete a job once it was started. Slide back a little if you will . . ."

Gwen obliged, but Gregory soon came to the conclusion that the tub was just too limiting. It didn't allow him to explore her the way he intended.

"Up," he said again.

"I wondered if you'd figure that out." She got out of the tub, grabbing a towel to briskly dry herself. "Oh, no," she said when he reached for the towel. "I get to do this. It's my turn whether you like it or not."

He stood patiently while she patted him down with the towel, gritting his teeth when her fingers trailed the rough material of the towel. He would never last if he gave in to thoughts of just what those magical fingertips were doing to him.

"Would you mind if I asked about this tattoo on your upper back? Not to be offensive, but it's not what you normally see on a man. This is all . . . well, delicate. Like one of those scientific pictures of subatomic particle tracks."

"It's called a lightning flower, and it's not a tattoo. All Travellers have one. It is a mark signifying who we are, and it is made by lightning."

She traced one of the feathery lines, making him grit his teeth with determination.

"Huh. Interesting."

He allowed her to continue while he dwelt with much detail on the effects of syphilis on the human body. When that didn't distract him from the sensation of her mouth kissing a path down his spine, he thought of radiation poisoning, the bubonic plague, and flesh-eating bacteria, in that order.

"I must not be doing something right," she said when the torment was at last over. "Because I thought by now you would be pouncing on me."

"I am a gentleman. Gentlemen let their women dry them if said women are insistent on using up their turn in such a manner. Are you quite finished?" His voice sounded strained, but Gwen didn't seem to notice.

"I guess," she said, stepping back, a slightly disappointed look on her face.

·"Towel." She handed him the towel. He whipped it around her hips, backed her up to the bed, and pushed her down on its soft depths. "Then it is my turn again. And I choose to do this."

"Merciful goddess," she gasped as he knelt between her spread knees. She clutched his hair as he paid homage to her hidden parts, the ones that made her squirm with joy when he gave them their due attention. She writhed. She twitched. She moved restlessly, making soft little moans that filled him with pride in a job well done. And when she gasped and arched upward, he thought he might just burst with the pleasure he'd given her. "Glorious stars and moons and comets and . . . and . . . I can't even think of any other astronomical things. That was amazing. Is that something your father taught you, too?"

He sent a quizzical look over her pubic mound.

"Not literally," she said, her body giving more of those wonderful little aftershocks that so delighted him. "I meant more did he teach you to do the job properly and not give up before . . . never mind. There's no way I can explain what I mean without it sounding weird. I blame the fact that my mind has shut down. Would you mind if I reciprocated?"

"Yes," he said, moving up her body, pausing to kiss her

belly, hips, rib cage, and both taut nipples before claiming her mouth. "You may reciprocate at another time. Right now, I intend to show you that my father did, indeed, teach me that a job worth doing is a job worth doing to the fullest of my abilities."

He slid into her body, making her moan with pleasure. He himself was incapable of sound, incapable of anything except the knowledge that she was made for him with exquisite fineness. And when she bit his shoulder and demanded that he stop teasing her and finish the job, her body tightening around him in a way that had him seeing sparks, he knew with a finality that shook him to his core that she was his forever.

"We're doing it again." Gwen's soft voice caressed his ear. He couldn't so much as lift his head from where it lay cradled against her neck. He felt as boneless as a jellyfish.

"I'm fine with that," he told her neck, "but you'll have to give me a little bit of time to recover. Say a week. Possibly two months."

She pinched his ass, right at the spot where her damned horse had bit him. "Not that. I don't think I could again for a while. To be honest, I didn't know I was multi-orgasmic until you proved I was. What I meant, Mr. Does the Job Right, was that we're *porraimos*ing again. Look."

"I can't look. I don't have the energy to open my eyes. You have drained me of every last ounce. Besides, I don't need to see the effect. I can feel it."

Despite his words, he rolled off her, felt immediately bereft, and pulled her over to him until she lay draped atop him.

"It's amazing that it doesn't hurt," she said, contemplating her hand, which was indeed alight with the short, snapping tendrils of electricity. "It just feels . . . tingly. Oh. It's going away already."

"It'll be back," he said drowsily, feeling extremely happy despite everything. He hadn't the slightest idea how he was going to resolve the situation between the Watch and Gwen's

THE ART OF STEALING TIME   263

mothers, or how he could protect her from the reclamation agent, but he knew without a single doubt that he would find a way.

He had to. He didn't think he could live without his Welsh temptress.

FOURTEEN

"**G**wen."

"Mmrph."

"Gwen, you must wake up."

"No." I burrowed deeper into the Gregory-scented blankets on the (surprisingly comfortable) sleeping pallet, and refused all attempts by my brain to wake me up.

"It's almost dawn, and I must leave before the guards can see me."

I stuck a hand out of the warm cocoon of blankets and waved it vaguely in the direction of his voice. "Later, tater."

Cold air brutally assaulted me when the blankets were ripped off my inert form. As if that wasn't rude enough, Gregory swatted my bare behind, not hard enough to sting but enough that I shot upward and glared at him.

He smiled, the bastard.

"You hit me!"

"I did not. I gave you a tap on your derriere."

"That, sir, is technically abusive behavior, and I will have none of it," I said huffily, pulling the blankets up around my breasts.

He cocked an eyebrow and looked down on me. In the dim gray light of the coming dawn, I couldn't help but notice that he was dressed, and wished wholeheartedly that he wasn't. "Do you seriously believe I'm the abusive type?"

"No," I admitted, trying to hold on to my huffiness but admitting to myself that he wasn't that type of man at all. "I wouldn't be with you if you were. What is so important that you had to wake me up? I'm not a morning person. I need a long time to wake up and be able to brain things."

"Brain things?"

I pointed to my head. "You know, do that thing with your brain."

"Think?"

"Yes, that. Mornings are evil." I looked longingly back at the pillow next to me. It still bore the imprint of his head. I bet it smelled like him, too.

"No," he said, snatching the pillow away as I started to dive for it. "Not until we've had a little talk."

I sighed and scooted back so that I was leaning against the canvas of the tent. "All right, but in the future, you must supply me with coffee before you expect me to either brain or comprehend things."

"Duly noted. Do you remember when I told you how I saved your life by taking the time I needed to stop that mortal from tossing you over the cliff?"

"Yes." I frowned when he sat at my feet. I'd much rather he sat next to me so I could drape myself over his chest and doze off while he talked. "Do you want me to thank you for that again? I will, but I thought I already did."

"You did, although it wasn't at all necessary." The light was too dim to make out the expression in his eyes, but his voice was filled with wariness that penetrated the dense fog of morning that always seemed to wrap itself around me. "The person who I took the time from was an immortal, of course."

"Where are you going with this?" I asked, suddenly too impatient to give him a chance to tell me properly. "Does the person want his time back?"

"No." He looked at me steadily for the count of eight. "She wants you."

I snorted. "She can't have me. We may not have a brilliant future ahead of us with you in the Watch and my moms being who they are, but I consider this a relationship until we both decide otherwise." A sudden fear shook me. "You do too, don't you?"

"Yes," he said gravely. "What we have together isn't the point. This woman is a reclamation agent. When you died, she expected to gather your soul and take it to the afterlife of your choice. Perhaps even Anwyn. But she wasn't able to do that because I manipulated time so you didn't die in the first place."

The horror grew until it crawled along my skin like ants. "My soul? This woman wanted my soul? What kind of person—merciful lord and lady! It's Death, isn't it?"

He nodded, placing his hand on my leg so that the warmth of his palm seeped through to my suddenly chilled flesh. "She works for Death, yes. Evidently she was tracking you in the mortal world. I ran into her in the park in Cardiff shortly after you ran off."

I felt sick. "I don't want her to take my soul. I like it. I think I need it, don't I?"

"Yes, you do, and I won't let her take it or you. Gwen—" He leaned forward and pulled me onto his lap, wrapping a blanket around me. "I'm not telling you this to frighten you, merely to warn you so that you'll be aware of your surroundings. I can't be with you every minute, much though I would wish otherwise. You need not be scared, just more aware of things. If you see this woman while you are away from the camp, return here immediately. She has some sort of allergic phobia to cats, and I doubt if she would try very hard to penetrate the depths of the encampment."

"She's here?" My voice rose on a squeak. "She's in Anwyn? Goddess! Is *everyone* here?"

"What do you mean, everyone?"

"There's two hit men here, too. They work for Baldwin, that lawyer who has it in for my moms and me because I wouldn't let them deliver the magic they sold him. He's the guy who threw me over the edge of the cliff."

"Two men with no necks?"

"That's them." I shuddered despite the warmth of his embrace and the blanket. "Irv and Frankie are their names. They have an obsession with heads in duffel bags. I can't tell you how that makes me feel."

"I can tell you how it makes me feel," he said grimly, his hold tightening painfully around me. "I will simply forgo my pledge to Aaron and stay with you. You must be protected."

For a moment, I wallowed in the sensation of being cherished, but I've never been a woman who shoved her responsibilities onto others. "You can't do that, although I appreciate the sentiment." I kissed him gently, then scooted off his lap, taking the blanket with me. "Aaron would be pissed if you broke your promise to him, and as for Irv and Frankie, I've already taken care of it. Doug sent out guards to nab them when they followed me to this camp."

Gregory chuckled. "The reclamation agent will have trouble gelding them as she wishes, then. I'll have to tell her that they are out of her reach."

I gathered up my clothing and began to put it on, feeling that further sleep was not going to be in the cards. "I suppose you could, although I don't see why you'd go out of your way to tell her anything."

"Er . . ." An odd expression akin to embarrassment crossed his face. "As it happens, I was supposed to report to her last night about what happened to the two men."

"Why?"

"I ran into her as she was about to enter the camp, and played upon her feline phobia in order to keep her from hunting for you." He made a face. "It seemed preferable to having to run through the camp attempting to make sure you were out of the way."

I shivered again, slipping on the long linen tunic that was among the clothing Seith had left for me the night before. "Definitely. Doug has issues where you're concerned, and he wouldn't hesitate to carry out his threats of jailing you if he sees you. Which means," I said, pulling aside the tent flap enough to peer outside, "that we should get going. It's getting lighter."

"We?"

I pulled on the pair of leggings and my tennis shoes. My sword had been cleaned and set just inside the tent. I hesitated a second, then strapped it around my waist, feeling that it was better to have it with me than not. "I don't have to be on duty until late this afternoon, and besides, I've always wanted to see what a thief does. I can shadow you."

He stood up and pulled me against him, his lips curling when I melted into his chest. "Not while I report to the reclamation agent."

"What *is* her name?" I asked, giggling when his hands went exploring down my back to my butt.

"I haven't a clue, and I don't particularly care. You can help me find the bird if you like."

I wiggled against him, wondering if there was time for a quickie before too many people were awake. "Did you find the dog and the deer?"

"No and yes. The dog is long since deceased, although I suspect a puppy from one of its descendants will stand in for it. The deer I left outside your tent."

"You did? Did you feed it? What are people going to say when they see it?"

He kissed me quickly, then took my hand and led me toward the tent opening. "That you have exceptionally bad taste. Behold, the famed roebuck of Aaron."

I gazed upon a stained, broken marble statue that was propped up against a tent pole. "That's his valuable deer?"

"According to Ethan it is, and I don't think he was lying about it. He seemed much too preoccupied with himself to care what happened to the spoils of war, so to speak."

"Hmm. It's kind of a letdown, to be honest. I was hoping for a magnificent, randy buck."

"And you have one, my vixen," he said against the nape of my neck, pulling me against him.

I thought seriously of pushing him back into the tent and having my womanly way with him, but voices from the tent beyond had me quelling that idea. "Come on, let's get out of here before someone sees you. You can tell me about the bird on the way over to Ethan's camp."

We managed to make it to the stream without being seen, and while we crossed it and skirted the edges of Ethan's camp, Gregory told me about his meeting with Ethan.

"I didn't realize he named his hand. To be honest, I didn't think Alien Hand Syndrome was real until Colorado said that's what the problem was with Ethan."

Gregory looked askance while I explained my experience with Ethan. "He is an odd man."

"Yes, but he does seem to be kind of helpful. At least you got the deer, and he said you could get one of the dogs. Oh! I think that's the tent where my moms are. Peaseblossom said it was next to Ethan's."

Gregory looked toward where I was pointing, to a purple and white tent. "Why don't you visit them while I hunt out the reclamation agent? I don't want you wandering around the camp until I know where she is."

"You're cute when you're overprotective," I said, giving his hand a squeeze.

"One moment." He moved ahead of me, checking down first one aisle, then the next before beckoning me forward. "Stay at your mothers' tent. I'll find you once I've spoken to Death's minion."

A chill went down my spine at his words. I didn't want to lose my soul any more than I wanted my head in Irv's favorite duffel bag. "All right, but if you're not back in a couple of hours, I'll have to risk leaving on my own. I want to check with Doug that those two hit men are safely confined and not likely to get out. I don't need them telling this woman that I'm just a stone's throw away."

He glanced around quickly, then pulled me into a kiss so hot it left a little shimmer of electricity snapping and crackling along our skin.

"Show-off," I whispered against his lips as the charge faded away.

"You bring it out in me. Stay safe, sweet Gwen."

I watched him walk away because . . . well, because he looked really good from the rear and I enjoyed the view. That thought had me pondering, on the way to my moms' tent, just how I was going to fix things so that we could have a future together.

"There's got to be a way," I muttered to myself, my gaze skittering from person to person in search of the woman Gregory had described. "I won't ask him to leave the Watch for me—not that I know if he would . . . no, he would . . . maybe—but there has to be something we can do to get the Watch to ignore Mom and Mom Two. Hmm."

No solution had struck me by the time I entered my mothers' tent, but I had resolved two points: I was going to warn them about the woman who wanted my soul, and I wasn't going to tell them about Gregory and me. Over the course of my life they had both, singly and jointly, gone into periodic matchmaking modes, trying to hook me up with men and women . . . and one or two androgynous individuals about whom I was never really certain.

Usually I resisted their efforts, but sometimes, when I was feeling particularly lonely, I'd go out on a blind date or two just in case they were right and they really had found me the perfect person.

They never did. Trust the one organization that made my life a hell to bring my attention to a man who actually might well be the person with whom I wouldn't mind spending the next few hundred years. Regardless of whether he was or was not a life mate, I wasn't going to inform my moms about him. They would be merciless in their attempts to find out information about Gregory and would probably demand that he do something silly like marry me. They were very big on binding ceremonies.

"I'll just keep mum about him, and focus their attention on ways to deal with the Death woman," I told myself, slapping on a carefree smile when I entered their tent. "Mom! Mom Two!"

"Hello, Gwenny, dear," Mom said, not glancing up from a large mixing bowl where she was vigorously beating a viscous pink liquid. "Eighty-eight, eighty-nine, ninety. There, that's the sleeping draught finished, Alice."

"Did you make it into a batter so we can bake little Eat Me cakes?" Mom Two asked. She had her back to me and was busily measuring various powders and liquids and placing them in little stoppered vials. "Gwen, you're just in time. The alchemist has a tiny supply of fey motes in, and I told him you'd like to buy it from him. I know how hard it is for you to find them."

"Yes, absolutely." The only other person in the tent was the tiny form of Mrs. Vanilla, curled up in a voluminous armchair. Her hands flitted about in quick little movements, knitting small octagons one after another in a giant object so massive that it spilled out over her lap and onto the floor. I relaxed, the sight and scents of my mothers busily creating potions and physical manifestations of spells making me think of home. How many years had I perched on my favorite three-legged stool and watched as they practiced the physical side of their craft? I dipped a finger in the pink batter and touched it to my tongue. It tasted of peppermint. "How much does the apothecary want for them?"

"Now, Gwenny, that's not for you. Lady Holly asked us to make something that would cause all of those nasty soldiers to the north to fall asleep so she can capture them all and force the evil king into subservience. You don't want to be falling—" My mom looked up in midsentence, and froze, her eyes growing huge. "Alice!" she shrieked, making me spin around in fear that something horrible had crept in behind me.

There was nothing, just the tip of the tent flap—pulled aside to let air and light into the interior—gently moving in the breeze. Behind it, a couple of dogs rolled on the ground outside, and a weary-looking old man wandered around with a bucket and a metal scoop, the latter obviously used to keep the grounds poop-free.

"What is it—" Mom Two started to say, but then she, too, stopped and stared at me. Mrs. Vanilla glanced at me, made a few squeaking sounds, and returned to her knitting.

Mom pointed a shaking finger at me. "She's found him!"

"Or her," Mom Two said sagely. "Is it a her, Gwen?"

"She's found a man!" Mom said, still pointing.

I gawked. "How the hell can you tell that just by looking at me?"

Mom dropped her finger, and Mom Two strode over to give me a hug. "Oh, Gwenny, dear, you should know better than to ask that."

"We're your mothers," Mom Two said, as if that explained it.

"We can tell these things," Mom added, wiping her hands on a cloth before coming around the table to give me a hug as well. I hugged them both back, giving them each a kiss on their respective cheeks before shaking my head.

Mrs. Vanilla got creakily to her feet and shuffled over to us. I hugged her as well, and even gave her wrinkled cheek a little peck. She made happy noises and returned to her chair.

"It's like it's witchcraft," I said with a smile. "It is a him and not a her, Mom Two. I'm sorry."

"Eh." She patted my cheek and returned to her worktable. "I had hopes that someday you'd find the right woman, but so long as this man makes you happy, I can live with him being male."

"Who is he? Where is he? Is he here with you in Anwyn?"

"He must be here, Mags. We'd have known if she'd met him before."

"You tell us all about him, dear," Mom said, leading me

over to a small love seat in the corner of the tent. The interior was quite large, consisting of the main work area and what looked to be a smaller sleeping quarter that was hidden by long silken draperies. "Although you're going to have to be quick, because Lady Holly likes to see us directly after breakfast, and it's almost that time now."

"As a matter of fact, I did meet him before we entered Anwyn, although I hadn't realized that he was—" I bit off the word "good" and tried to think of a way to explain about Gregory without mentioning the fact that he worked for the Watch. I had a feeling they would plan copious ways to take advantage of him if they knew who his employer was. "I hadn't realized he was quite so wonderful at that time."

"What's his name?" Mom Two asked, packing a bunch of bottles into a wicker basket.

"Gregory Faa. He's a Traveller."

"Faa?" She draped a linen cloth over the top of the basket, her brows pulled together. "Mags, do you remember that woman we met right after the war?"

"Which war?" my mother asked, giving me a pat on the hand before she set about filling muffin cups with her pink sleeping batter.

"The one with the nuclear bombs."

"World War Two?" I asked.

"That's it. We met a woman Traveller whose husband had been killed. She was very distraught, and one of her daughters-in-law had come to us seeking something to ease her pain. There was nothing we could do, of course, because there is no magic but love to heal a broken heart, but her name was Faa. I wonder if she could be related."

"I have no idea. While we're on the subject of Gregory—"

"Oh, mercy, look at the time, Alice!" Mom said, hurrying over to a line of baskets that had already been packed. She shoved two of them at me, picked up three herself, and nudged me toward the door. "Mrs. Vanilla, you stay here where you're comfy. We won't be long, and then we'll get you a nice cup of tea and take you for your walk, all right? Gwen, dear, take this. We're going to be late, and Lady Holly is most acerbic when that happens. You can tell us about your young man once we've given her the day's potions."

"Er . . ." I held back when they bustled out of the tent, not wanting to risk seeing Holly in case she had heard that I was working for Aaron. There was also a chance that Death's minion might be lurking about. I peeked out of the tent, but didn't see anyone aside from the usual collection of dogs wandering around, begging for food, playing, sleeping, and generally just lounging and watching all the people moving to and fro. No one resembled the woman Gregory had described.

"Don't dawdle, Gwen!" Mom Two called before disappearing into the large tent next door.

I swore under my breath, sent a little prayer to the lord and lady that I wasn't about to step into a trap, and followed them into the big tent.

"You remember our daughter, Gwenhwyfar, don't you?" Mom was saying to the gaunt, leather-wearing Holly. She shot a quick disinterested look my way, then continued pulling out items from one of the baskets. She raised her voice to say, "Lord Ethan, have you met our daughter, Gwen?"

Mom sidled over to me and whispered, "He's a bit odd, dear. He has an illegal alien hand."

A man walked toward us from the far end of the massive tent, which, like my mothers' accommodations, had floor-to-ceiling silk hangings that blocked out sections requiring privacy. He wore an odd leather harness that strapped his alien hand to his belly, the hand encased in a red glove.

"We've met," I said, politely smiling at him. "Good morning. How's Diego?"

Ethan glanced at his hand, frowning when the fingers twitched. "No, you may not fondle her breast. Stop it. No, stop that, too. It's rude, and there are ladies present."

No one said anything. My mothers both attended to unpacking the baskets. Holly rolled her eyes and picked up a potion, unstoppering it to take a sniff. Ethan waited until his hand stopped making obscene gestures, then addressed me. "He is a bit angry this morning. He did not have a solid night's sleep because some idiot woman kept charging into my tent and demanding to know where two mortals were. I know you."

"We met a few days ago," I said, wanting to change the subject quickly. I needed time to warn my moms about the two hit men and Death's agent. "You loaned me your mother's sword."

Holly glanced up at that, skewering him with a look. "You what?"

"Ah, yes, that's right. The Nightingale. You're one of my soldiers. Holly, which head shot do you favor? I think this one makes me look too serious, but it highlights my cheekbones superbly, don't you agree?" He held out a couple of large photographs.

"You gave this woman the Nightingale?" Holly's frown grew when she turned it on me, taking in the sword belted around my waist. She ignored the photos, gesturing toward me. "Don't you think that was a bit unwise, Ethan?"

"If I thought it was unwise, I wouldn't have given it to her," he said quite reasonably. "What do you think, warrior?"

I considered the pictures he showed me. "I like the cheekbones one."

"You have good taste." He tossed the pictures onto a massive mahogany table that sat smack-dab in the center of the tent. "Now then, who are these ladies?"

Holly, who had been watching me with suspicious, narrowed eyes, stopped that in order to give him a long-suffering look. "They are the witches I told you about two days ago, Ethan. The ones who are making magic for us to use to defeat Aaron."

"Ah, yes, that's right. I remember now. You will make an excellent addition to a future chapter," he told my moms.

They beamed at him.

"I want to get to the bottom of you giving away valuable swords—" Holly started to say, but didn't finish the sentence. At that moment there was a brief struggle at the door, and two large men entered, blocking out all of the morning light.

"There now!" the biggest of them said, catching sight of me. "I thought I might find you hereabouts."

"Hello, Irv," I said wearily, one hand easing the hilt of the sword out of its scabbard. "I thought you were being held by Aaron's guards?"

"Aye, and that we were, but Frankie here, he got an idea." He looked proudly at his friend, who responded with a deprecatory gesture and a modest expression.

"I know I shouldn't ask," I told the room in general. "And yet I'm unable to keep from doing so. What idea was that?"

"Frankie thought we ought to use some of the magic them witches give us."

"Oh, no, moms, tell me you didn't . . ."

"That's right, I did think that, and so we did, and as soon as them soldiers of that other boss got a whiff of the happy juice that we got from those two, they was laughing so hard, they couldn't stop us if they wanted to. We took care of them while they was rolling around laughing, and then ups and walked right out of the tent they was holding us in."

"You sure do know your business, all right," Irv told my mom. She looked pleased with the compliment until she caught my eye.

"Threefold law, Mom," I told her sternly.

She donned an aggrieved expression. "I don't know why you cast that at our heads, Gwenny. We are always accountable for our actions and have done no one any harm."

"Including giving potions to two hit men?" I pointed to the men with my sword. "The potion you gave these two has resulted in the deaths of who knows how many innocent guards. *That* is doing harm."

"We did not give them any potion," Mom Two said indignantly while my mother snorted to herself. "They took it while we weren't looking. Didn't you?"

"Liberated it," Frankie said, scratching his belly. "Boss likes us to call it liberating rather than stealing."

"Here, this lady's your mum?" Irv asked, nodding toward my mothers.

"They both are, yes." I turned to Ethan. "I don't suppose you'd like to lock these two men up? I can assure you that they are murderous villains and should not be allowed to remain free."

"Oy!" Frankie said, looking oddly hurt. "None of that, now."

"These men are working for me," Holly said, looking up from where she had been writing in a small notebook. She'd been so quiet that for a few minutes I'd forgotten she was in the tent with us.

"Then you share the blame for the death of Aaron's guards."

She seemed immune to my cold stare, but my mothers weren't. They moved together for solidarity, both their faces wary.

"I am responsible for many deaths. A few of that devil's men are nothing to me. Ethan, I must go have that meeting I mentioned with the guards and warriors. I've heard a foul rumor that some of them aren't fighting as they ought, and clearly I need to lesson a little motivation into them." She gave me a look that I met with one of absolute innocence. "I will meet you after lunch to discuss the new weaponry."

"Eh?" Ethan continued to poke at his laptop with one finger.

She shook her head and marched off, her long hair swinging like black and green silk daggers behind her.

"She's so intense," Mom told Mom Two.

"She'd be much better for having a cup of dandelion tea each morning," Mom Two agreed.

"Oooh, I'd kill for a cuppa right about now," Irv said.

Frankie laughed and elbowed him.

"What?" Irv asked.

"You'd kill for a cuppa."

"So? I haven't had any tea this morning."

"No, you'd *kill* for a cuppa." Frankie elbowed him again.

It took Irv a minute to see the irony of it.

"Aha ha ha. That's right, I would," he allowed with a chuckle.

"I do not think killing people is funny." I whipped the sword through the air so that it sang. Both men watched, their merriment fading. "Especially innocent people."

"What innocent people?" Irv looked at Frankie. Frankie looked at Irv.

"The guards you said you killed in order to escape. Aaron's men."

"Who says we orfed those blokes?"

"You did."

"I did?"

"Yes. You said you took care of the guards while they were incapacitated with my mothers' laughing potion."

He waggled his hand in the air while Frankie said, "There's take care of, and then there's *take care of*, if you see what I mean. Now, I'm not saying we didn't tie them up, but Irv here, he pointed out that since this is heaven and all, the folks here was already dead, so there's no use in trying to kill them when they can't die again."

"That's right," Irv agreed. "It's been our experience that once you're dead, you won't be coming back to life any time soon."

I shot a potent look at my mother when she opened her mouth to correct the two mortal men's false assumption. "I'm glad to hear you've given up your propensity to violence. There's no reason to go about killing anyone—or rather, trying to—when a simple conversation will clear things up."

"What conversation would that be?" Irv asked, looking confused.

"The one that stops you from killing innocent people in Anwyn."

"Do you know what the daft hen is talking about?" Irv asked Frankie out of the side of his mouth.

"Not a clue."

"I think we'd best wrap this up as soon as can be. I'm thinking she's not quite all there."

"I'm totally all here!" I protested, throwing grammar to the wind.

"You may be, or you may not be, but either way, we was sent to bring you back with us," Frankie reminded me. "Boss said he prefers you alive, but if we wasn't able to do that, he said we could just bring your head back with us and you could be a lesson to those what would cross him."

I was feeling a bit more confident now. Not only did I have my spiffy sword, but the two men weren't likely to hurt anyone in Anwyn due to their belief that everyone here was deceased. I saw a chance to get rid of them once and for all, and decided boldness would pay off in this case. Accordingly, I strolled around them, gesturing with my sword as I spoke. "I hate to break this to you, but you're wasting your time. I have no intention of leaving Anwyn to speak with your boss."

"You said you wanted to earlier."

"True," I told Frankie. "But I've since changed my mind. You can feel free to tell him that I'm armed and I resisted all attempts to subdue me. Thanks! Bye-bye."

I strolled over to my mothers, whistling a carefree little tune that didn't at all reflect my inner turmoil.

"Ha ha ha."

I spun around at the laughter. The two men were nudging each other and nodding toward me. "Daft hen thinks anyone would believe we couldn't subdue her," Irv said.

"That's a good one, that is," Frankie told me. "You may be daft, but you've a wicked sense of humor."

"Look," I said, my hands on my hips, my sword still

clutched firmly. "I've just about had it with you guys. I'm not leaving Anwyn, all right? So you can just buzz off before I lose my temper."

"And what'll you do then?" Irv asked, giving me an indulgent smile that just made me irritable. Dammit, it was like they didn't take me seriously as a threat to their well-being.

"You don't want to know. Now bugger off."

"Gwen!" both mothers said in unison. "Language, dear," Mom finished.

"I can't believe you kiss your mother with that sort of a mouth, I really can't," Frankie said with unbearable self-righteousness.

"It's the modern generation," Irv agreed. "They have no sense of what's right and what's not right."

"Are you totally unaware of the irony of that statement?" I asked. "You are hit men!"

"So?"

I let it go. I just didn't have the energy to point out the obvious.

"Know what I think?" Frankie asked Irv.

"She's going to run off again?"

"I'm not going to run away." My voice was sharp with irritation, but I felt it was justified. "You, however, are leaving. Ethan, you're the head honcho around here—tell these guys to leave."

"I cannot believe someone had the nerve to give my book only three stars! The last volume was all about how I dealt with having a famous mother. It was filled with celebrity insider information! Three stars? It's ten stars' worth of a book at least. Twenty stars. Three is just utterly ridiculous." He looked up. "Who is this Mr. Amazon? I wish to have a word with him about the people who leave stars on his Web site."

"You really do live in your own little world, don't you?" I couldn't help but ask. "Does nothing register with you?"

"Not really," he said, leaning back in his chair. "I'm not really cut out for all of this, you see. Oh, there was a time when I fought every battle and bested every foe, but really, what's there to look forward to once you've conquered all there is to conquer? That's when I decided to begin writing my autobiography. In seventeen volumes. Who are you?"

I was about to tell him—again—who I was when I realized he was looking at Irv and Frankie.

"They're hit men." Surely even Ethan wouldn't be uncaring if murderers were wandering around his camp.

"Enforcers," Irv corrected me.

"I'm sure that someone as erudite and learned as you must see that having such uncouth mortals around your camp is not going to reflect well on you." I pursed my lips and looked thoughtful, figuring that Ethan might be swayed by commercial concerns. "After all, people might get the wrong idea about books written by the sort of man who has hired thugs hanging around him. I certainly wouldn't want to buy the book of such a man, no matter how interesting the material was."

"Hmm." Ethan appeared to be considering the idea.

"We have no quarrel with you, mate," Irv told him and pointed to me. "It's this one who we was told to bring back. And now here she is waving that sword in our faces and telling everyone that we killed a bunch of giddy guards when we didn't. Trying to black our good name, she is."

"I'm sure that was just a misunderstanding," Mom Two said, indignation rife in her voice. "Gwen would never cast an aspersion upon someone unless she felt it was just."

"That's as may be." Irv smiled at me. I was momentarily disconcerted by the sudden gesture. And that was my undoing, because while I was trying to figure out what he had to smile about, Frankie moved as fast as a snake, grabbing Mom Two in a hold that had her yelping.

"You bastard!" I started toward him with my sword held high, but stopped at the sight of metal glinting in Frankie's hand.

"Alice!" Mom shrieked and would have lunged at Frankie if I hadn't held her back.

"Let me handle this, Mom." I took a deep breath. "Mom Two, are you all right?"

"Yes," she said, her dark eyes filled with fear. I hated Frankie at that moment, hated that he could make someone as happy and loving as my mother fearful of being harmed.

"Let her go, Frankie," someone said in a low, ugly voice that was filled with so much menace it made me shiver. I was momentarily startled to realize it came out of my mouth.

"Boss said we was to come back with you, or your head. This isn't you, but maybe he won't mind so much when we tell him that the head we have belonged to your mum."

"Gwenny." My mother plucked at my sleeve, her anguish as palpable as Mom Two's fear. I stood on the balls of my feet, my gaze locked on Frankie's knife, trying to think of how best to disarm the situation. If I rushed him, he'd likely sink his knife into her neck, and although she wouldn't keel over from a wound like mortals would, she could be killed.

"This appears to be a tricky situation," Ethan commented, and rising, he strode over to where Frankie held Mom Two. "You there, whatever your name is, release my witch. Holly has much work for her to do and would be most unhappy if you were to disarrange those plans."

"This has nothing to do with you, mate," Irv said, moving over to stand next to Frankie. "I'd advise you to stay out of it and let us handle it."

"Ethan," I said, gently pushing my mother behind me, all the while never taking my eyes off that knife. "I bet Diego would like to come out to play."

"I doubt that. He's testy today."

"Ethan." The word was ground through my teeth in an attempt to get him to understand what I was suggesting. "Let Diego out."

"Look here, you," Irv said, pointing at me. He and Frankie were close enough that if Ethan unleashed his alien hand, it might be enough of a distraction that I could rescue Mom Two. "I don't know who this Diego bloke is when he's at home, but he isn't going to help you any. Frankie's going to lose his patience in a minute if you don't agree to come with us."

"Very well, but if he misbehaves, I'm holding you responsible." Ethan unbuckled the strap holding his arm to his belly, sliding the leather slinglike structure off. Immediately his hand reached out and grabbed my left breast.

I stared down at it in mingled horror and surprise. His fingers flexed.

"I told you he was testy today. Diego! Release that woman's nipple. It isn't yours to fondle."

Frankie and Irv snickered.

"This isn't quite what I had in mind," I snapped, shoving the hand away. It reached back as if it was going to cop another grope, but I shifted, pointing the tip of the sword at it. The fingers twitched and slunk back to Ethan.

"If playtime's over, we'll be getting along now," Irv said.

Ethan frowned at him. "I do not wish for you to kill my witch. You, woman, do something to stop them."

"I'm trying," I snapped, waving my sword in the air. "But thus far I haven't had a lot of luck, and Diego was a huge letdown."

"You're an alchemist. Do something."

"Like what?" I gave him an incredulous look. "Transmute them to death? That would take centuries, not that I can do it to begin with."

"Time's up," Frankie said, clearly having reached the end of his patience. I didn't blame him. I wanted to slap Ethan for being such an idiot.

"Either you come with us now, or we'll be taking the head of your mum here back to our boss." Irv stepped forward with a nasty smile.

"How about you two return to your boss and tell him to mind his own damned business."

We all turned to look at the source of the voice, a surge of joy filling me as Gregory entered the tent. He looked relaxed and carefree, with a slight smile on his lips, but I knew without a single shred of doubt that he was furious. I could feel his tension prickle along my skin like the static electricity that we generated when things got hot and heavy between us.

"You have excellent timing," I told him.

"It goes along with the whole Traveller thing." His gaze held mine for a few seconds, and I suddenly understood why I felt the electricity in the air.

"Mom," I said softly. "The egg spell. Do you remember it?"

Mom frowned, sliding me a worried look. "Egg spell? No, I don't think I know a spell that has anything to do with eggs other than—" She stopped.

"I don't know who you are," Irv told Gregory, "but you're not wanted here, mate. Best be on your way."

"Ah, but I know well who you are, and I object to you holding Gwen's mother in that manner. Let her go, and there won't be any trouble between us."

"Ooh." Mom Two stopped being afraid for a few seconds, rolling her eyes over to examine Gregory. "Mags, this is *him*."

"Is it?" Mom stopped whispering her spell, also giving Gregory the visual once-over. "He's not what I expected. Gwen's never liked blonds before."

"Well, he is technically handsome, if you like that sort of thing," Mom Two admitted.

"But she's not been one for letting a pretty face turn her head," Mom argued. "Do you know, Alice, I think that bodes well for her future. He's totally different from all the other men she's brought to see us."

"Really?" I asked, turning to her. "Do we have to have this conversation right now?"

"*All* the other men?" Gregory asked at the same time, giving me a look that warned he had a lot to say about the subject. "Just how many other men has she brought home to meet you, madam?"

"None of your business." I spoke loudly and pointed with

the sword to Frankie. "Can we get back to what's important here, please?"

"It's not really that many," Mom Two told him. "Maybe ten?"

"Twelve, I think, dear. No, I tell a lie. It's thirteen."

"Mom!" I gave her a long-suffering look. "I have not had thirteen boyfriends. Five, maybe. Six at most."

"Thirteen," Mom said with a knowing expression on her face. "The first was that poet who wore all the lace and that smelly hair oil. He went down with the *Titanic*, didn't he? Then there was the politician who supported the suffragettes. He was quite nice, but mortal. And then you fell for your alchemy instructor, and after that was an actor. Do you remember him? He was so good at charades."

"He was a very nice boy," Mom Two agreed. "As was that young man in advertising she was with during the fifties."

I glanced at Gregory. His jaw was tight, and his eyes glittered like particularly pissed blue topazes. "Maybe we can do this another time—"

"I do remember the clown." Mom shuddered. "He was horrible."

"Then there was the dog trainer, and the accountant—"

"He made her cry a lot. I didn't like him at all."

"And the astronaut, and then those twins that she couldn't decide between, even though they were both clearly quite, quite gay—"

"Bi," I interrupted, my cheeks hot. "They were bisexual, not gay."

"And the man who created that vacuum cleaner, and finally, that rock climber. That's thirteen."

"Astronaut?" Irv asked, giving me an appraising glance.

I waved it away. "Everyone was dating test pilots and astronauts in the sixties. Besides, it's not like I was a fragile little thing living in an *egg carton*."

Mom caught the emphasis on the last words, and finished whispering her spell.

"I'm more disturbed by the thought of dating a clown," Ethan said from where he was, back at his laptop. "That's just creepy."

"Thirteen," Gregory said, his eyes glittering.

The hairs on my arm stood on end.

"It's not important!" I yelled, taking everyone by surprise. Luckily, Gregory was waiting for it, and having gathered up enough electricity, called down the lightning.

Right on top of Frankie and Irv.

FIFTEEN

Gregory did the best he could to shield Gwen's mother from the lightning that exploded around him in a brilliant blue-white ball of light, jerking her out of the hold in which one of the no-necks held her, pulling her close against his body so as to channel the charge onto himself.

She didn't even jerk as the electricity crackled and snapped around him, and glancing down, he was astonished to see a protective glow of yellow light skimming her body.

"Mom Two!" Gwen yelled and ran to them.

"I'm all right. Your mother got that protection spell off just in time," the woman said into his collarbone. He released her just as Gwen reached them. She hugged her glowing mother, ignoring the electricity as it embraced her, then turned a look on him that was so filled with admiration and gratitude, it had his chest swelling with pride.

"Thank you," she told him, gently touching his face. Her mothers embraced, their voices a low murmur that seemed to fade when he caught that sweet wildflower scent that always seemed to surround Gwen.

He didn't want her thanks. He wanted her. "My pleasure. It seemed you could use a hand. I hope you don't mind that I interfered."

"Mind?" She shook her head in confusion. "Why would I mind that you saved my mom?"

"Some women don't hesitate to make it clear that they

don't need to be rescued by a man. I had an idea that you might follow that belief."

"There's not being a victim, and then there's being stupidly stubborn and not taking help when it's offered," she said, giving him a swift hug. "My mom's life was at stake. I am more than happy to have your assistance saving her from that bastard."

"What the devil just happened here?" They both turned when Ethan marched over, scowling fiercely at Gregory. "You, sir! You stole the very lightning from the heavens and wielded it as if it was a weapon!"

"I did." Gregory considered the two men who lay twitching on the ground before them. Both their faces were blackened, their hair standing on end in unruly clumps, with the faintest hint of smoke emerging from one of them. "My apologies about the smoke stains on the carpet."

"You are *not* a thief as you said you were!" Ethan poked him in the chest. His other hand reached up and cupped his pectoral muscle in a surprisingly intimate gesture.

"Down, Diego!" Gwen said, glaring at the hand. "He's mine. That includes his fabulous chest."

"Er . . . think nothing about this." Ethan grabbed his hand and pulled it back, quickly slipping in place the leather harness that held the hand down. "My hand gets confused about genders sometimes."

"Your hand has issues," Gwen said. "And not just with genders."

"The fact remains that you lied to me," Ethan ignored Gwen to tell Gregory. "You are not a thief. Therefore, you are up to mischief. You will tell me exactly what that is, and then I will call Holly and she will know how to deal with you."

"I have not lied to you," Gregory said calmly, wrapping an arm around Gwen. One of the two men at their feet moaned. The other moved his arms and legs in a motion vaguely reminiscent of swimming. "I have been engaged by the king as a thief. It is not my normal form of employment, however."

"And what might that be?"

"I'm with the L'au-dela Watch."

"They have no jurisdiction here," Ethan told him, still suspicious. "And I have not heard that members of the Watch have lightning available at their whim."

"What is going on in here?" A slight woman with long black hair touched with dark green strode into the tent, her eyes angry and her movements sharp and fast. "There was a huge flash of light and—what happened to those two mortals? Who killed them?"

"They aren't dead," Gregory said, nudging one of them with the toe of his shoe. The man moaned and curled up into a fetal ball.

The woman swung around, her gaze pinning him. Her expression turned dark. "A Traveller! What business have you here?"

"Holly! I'm glad you're here—I was about to call for you. That man is here on the king's command," Ethan said before Gregory could answer. "He said he was here to steal that dog and deer statue, but the truth is much more frightening. He smote those two mortals with lightning! He is a lightning-wielder, a manipulator of time and weather, and I for one intend to protest this breach of protocol!"

Holly studied the two men briefly before leveling her gaze on Gregory. The look in her dark green eyes wasn't at all friendly. "Indeed. That is a clear violation of the War Agreement of 1717 and, I believe, grounds for punitive action. We shall take this up with that blasted no-name knight. Come, Ethan. You must lodge the protest."

"Wait! What?" Gwen asked, looking confused. "Why is Gregory being a Traveller a violation? He hasn't done anything wrong. Those guys had a knife on one of my moms!"

"That is of no concern to me. Ethan!"

Ethan had looked like he was about to slip away, but a sharp glance from Holly stopped him from sidling past them. "What is it, dearest?"

"You have to go tell that knight of this atrocity."

"But I was about to start a new chapter, and you know how I need to concentrate when I do that—"

Holly grabbed his arm and dragged him over to the private section of the tent. Silence fell around them, making it very easy to hear Holly chastising Ethan for lack of enthusiasm about his own martial campaign, and his feeble protestations.

"Why are they so pissed about you?" Gwen asked Gregory.

He shrugged. "To paraphrase the spiky Holly, it is of no concern to me. Do you have time to help me hunt for the missing bird, or must you report for duty soon?"

"I'm not on until the afternoon shift, but . . ." Gwen cast a worried glance toward her mothers, who were huddled together, conferring quietly.

"You'd prefer to spend the time with them?" He ignored the burn of jealousy, telling himself that he wasn't so needy that he couldn't share her with her family.

Although really, they'd had her for over a century, and he'd only known her a few days. It was only right that his claim on her time should take precedence.

"No, it's not that." His heart lightened at her words. She bit her lower lip and added in a near-whisper, "I don't like them being here where I can't easily keep an eye on them."

"They don't appear to be in any danger now." He nudged one of the two inert men, who made an involuntary rude noise. Gwen and Gregory moved away. "If it will make you feel better, I will bind them and secure them in a location away from your mothers."

"It's not just them. It's this whole setup." She rubbed her arms as if she was cold. "I don't trust Holly, for one. And Ethan isn't the most reliable person in the world, what with his self-obsession, and—" She waved her hand around in the air.

"I admit he has odd personality quirks, but I doubt if he means any harm to your mothers. He appears to be quite happy with them."

"*Now,*" she said with emphasis. "But I have all too much experience with how a happy relationship with my moms can go pear-shaped. And if that happens, I'd prefer being here to run interference."

"Are you always called upon to protect them?" He wanted badly to tell her that it wasn't her job to do so, but wasn't sure how she would respond to that. She had a strong protective streak in her, that much he knew, but was it so overpowering that it drove her to forgo her own life in order to oversee theirs?

"Goddess, no. If I had to do that, I'd never be able to leave their side and would, at this very moment, be stark, staring insane. I only intervene on the really serious stuff in an attempt to keep things from going too hideously wrong."

"If it will make you happier to have them near you, then that is what must happen," he said, relieved that he wouldn't spend the rest of his life being at his mothers-in-laws' beck and call.

Mothers-in-law. The words resonated in his head. When had he decided that Gwen was the one woman he wished to bind himself to? He studied her as she watched her mothers, noting her delicate features, the way her hair flowed back from her temples, the fine black line of her brows, the cute little nose and sensible chin. She had a light scattering of freckles across her cheeks and nose, which for some reason, made something in his belly tighten.

Oh, yes, he wanted her, all right . . . but he wanted her in more than just a sexual way. He wanted her in his life. He wanted her waking him up in the morning. He wanted to show her off to his family and watch the looks of envy pass among his cousins. He wanted to make his grandmother appreciate just how wonderful and unique she was. He wanted to see the years pass with her at his side, knowing she wanted him just as much.

He took her hand, and led her over to where her mothers stood. He bowed first to them, then to Gwen, bending over her hand and kissing it. "Gwenhwyfar Byron Owens, I ask you before your mothers to bless my life by joining it with yours. Will you be my wife?"

Gwen's eyes widened in a manner that had him suddenly worrying they might just pop right out of her head. She tried to snatch her hand back, but he tightened his hold, stroking the back of her fingers. Her mothers exclaimed, one of them clapping her hands happily. "You what?" Gwen almost shrieked.

"Will you marry me?"

"No!" Gwen succeeded in jerking her hand from his.

"Oh, Gwenny!" her mother cried.

He felt like someone had punched him in the balls. She didn't want to marry him?

"Gwen, I think that perhaps you're not giving this young man a chance," her second mother said, frowning at her. "Since you insist on being heterosexual, you might as well take the best that the males have to offer, and this one seems to be very competent and considerate."

"Thank you," he said, too despondent to give the older woman another bow.

Gwen's touch ceased the slow, icy fingers of despair that had started to creep through his heart. She laid a hand on his chest, and said, "I didn't mean no, I meant . . . I meant . . . oh, I don't know what I meant. Not no, but . . . crickets on a cracker, Gregory! Do you really think that now is the time to talk about a possible future together?"

"Is it because of what I told you about Travellers marrying their own kind? Because I can assure you that you are worth any sacrifice—not that I believe our life together will be in any way a sacrifice. My grandmother is stubborn, but I believe that she will, in time, be persuaded to see reason."

Irritation flashed across her face briefly. "Yes, well, that's a whole other subject—"

"It's quite simple," he told her. "I wish to spend the remainder of my days with you. I have been brought up to believe that if I feel that way about a woman, the honorable thing is to marry her, and thus I have asked you to marry me. Do you wish to likewise spend your life with me?"

"We've only known each other a few days," Gwen protested, shifting uncomfortably.

"It's long enough for me to know that I want you."

"Yes, but in the overall scheme of things, it's not exactly normal to tell someone you just met that you want to marry them. I'm not a mortal, Gregory. I don't believe in disposable marriages. When I marry, it will be forever."

"That is exactly how I feel," he agreed.

"I knew I liked him," Gwen's mom said.

"He will be a good son-in-law," the other agreed.

"Moms! I'm not getting married!"

"Marry? Who's getting married?" Ethan and Holly emerged from the private section of the tent. Holly had marched toward the door, and judging by the submissive way that Ethan followed her, Gregory assumed that she'd reasoned or threatened him into falling in line with her plan. Ethan paused at the door of the tent, his dark expression brightening. "I am perfectly willing to officiate at your wedding."

"Are you some sort of a religious personage who can do that?" Gwen asked, wrinkling her adorable forehead.

"Not in the least. But my mother is a demigod, you know."

"I don't see what one has to do with the other." Gwen looked even more puzzled.

Gregory smiled at her, just to let her know that he was not upset about the thirteen men with whom she had opted to share her life before they had met.

She looked startled, then pleased, then somewhat flustered. He didn't think he could adore her more. No, not adore . . . love. He loved her.

He almost took a step back at the revelation, so stunning was it. He loved Gwen. The word rolled around in his mind for a bit while he tried to get used to it.

"We will have to see how he shapes up as a husband." Gwen's second mother frowned. "We shall have to have the ceremony at home, though. I've always envisioned Gwen marrying her ideal woman at home, in a dignified, quiet ceremony."

This newfound love was a strange thing to him. Oh, he'd felt infatuation before. Lust came with the territory of being male, but love . . . He narrowed his eyes as he thought about it. Love was new. Love was different. He hadn't ever loved a woman the way he loved Gwen.

"In the bower!" the first mother said happily, clapping her hands in delight. "When the roses are in bloom!"

It was as if a warm burst of sunlight filled his chest, leaving him gently glowing with the wonder that was love for Gwen.

He looked at her again, wondering if she could see the love spilling out of him.

"Argh!" Gwen screamed, her hands making vague gestures of frustration. "No one is listening to me! Gregory, make them list—are you OK?"

He beamed at her. He'd never been one for beaming before, but all this love had to go somewhere, and although it wanted to go straight to his penis and get down to the business of lovemaking, he was a reasonable man, and he knew that Gwen would have an issue with him simply scooping her up and carting her off to the nearest bed. Therefore, the excess of emotion needed a target, and Gwen was the likeliest recipient.

She stared at him as if he was deranged.

"I'm in perfect health, thank you."

"OK." She gave him a disbelieving look. "It's just that you have this pained expression on your face. I wondered if the lightning hurt you."

"It's not pain. It's love. I love you, Gwen. Marry me so that I can take you off and make love to you for days on end without your mothers being upset that I'm male."

She froze, her eyes huge. "You . . . what?"

"I love you. With all my heart." Given the stunned look she currently wore, she needed that clarification.

"Glorious goddess!" Gwen's first mother said, clutching the second mother. "Isn't he wonderful? I'm not upset that you're male at all, young man. And neither is Alice."

"Well . . . ," the second mother started to say, but at a look from the first, she added, "Gwen has clearly made up her mind, and since you make her happy, then we shall welcome you to our family without reservation."

Gwen closed her eyes for a moment, shook her head, then opened her eyes to give him a steely look. He beamed more love at her. He couldn't stop himself; it just seemed to keep welling out of him.

"Maybe we should talk about this later," Gwen said, nodding toward the two men on the floor. "Things are a little bit hectic right now."

"Life," he said with as much sagacity as he could muster, "is never too hectic for love."

"August!" the first mother said. "We must have an August wedding. The bower will be in full bloom then."

"Consuela!" Ethan bellowed out the tent entrance. "Bring my datebook. What does my schedule look like in August? Can I get away for a wedding at a bower? No, I don't know where it is, but clearly they need me. Diego, no!"

Holly reappeared, grabbed Ethan by his alien hand, and pulled him out of the tent. The faint cries of, "Holly! You're hurting Diego! You know he's just going to want more of that later—" trailed behind them.

"Gwen?" Gregory took her hand and pulled her against his chest. The mothers were busily planning what events would take place at the wedding, while Ethan could still be heard, arguing with Holly about whether or not he could leave Anwyn. He didn't like the stressed look around Gwen's beautiful eyes, and thought seriously of kissing her silly right there. "You do want to spend your life with me, don't you?"

She wouldn't look him in the eye. She stared at his ear, and a line appeared between her brows. The faintest shadow of doubt pricked his skin. What if she truly did not want to wed him? What if she couldn't learn to love him as he loved her? What if he was just a number on a long list of men with whom she spent time?

Fear gripped him hard in the pit of his belly at her words. "I'm not sure what I want. Everything's so confused right now, what with those men trying to hurt my moms, and Death chasing me down, and we have to find that bird or else Aaron won't let us go, and . . . and . . . I just don't know."

She didn't want him. He released her, wanting to stagger over to the nearest chair and weep as he'd never wept before.

She truly did not want him. How could that be? How could he love her so fully and deeply and irrevocably as he did—he ignored the fact that just a few minutes before he hadn't the slightest inkling that such an emotion existed—and she not reciprocate those feelings?

He wanted to cry. He wanted to yell. He wanted to beg her to love him, even just the tiniest little bit. He'd be happy with just a tiny little morsel of love.

"That's a lie," he said aloud, despair swamping him. "I wouldn't be happy with a morsel. I want it all. I need it all. If I can't have it, then . . ." The sentence trailed off, unfinished.

He truly did want to cry.

"I'm sorry, Gregory. I just don't know what I want—" Gwen's gaze met his, and in her eyes he saw the only hope he had of happiness. And as her pupils flared with awareness of him, of what he hoped they had between them, she gave a little hiccuping sob and threw herself into his arms, kissing his jaw and chin and nose and finally his mouth, and with that touch, the love within him threatened to burst forth in a blaze of . . . well, love. He couldn't think of an appropriate metaphor, not with Gwen kissing him like she'd been without his lips for a lifetime, and it would have been rude of him not to give that kiss all his due consideration.

"Of course I want to spend my life with you," she said a few minutes later when he was forced to stop kissing her so they could breathe. "Even though you are the enemy, I want to be with you. But what are we going to do—"

He laid a finger across her mouth, stopping her from finishing the question. She bit his finger. "We'll work something out. I don't suppose you'd like to tell me now how very much you love me? Perhaps a quick statement regarding how you can't live without me, and how life would be bleak if you were forced to do so?"

She stared at him.

"Too soon?" he asked.

"Yes." She reached behind him and pinched his ass.

He couldn't possibly love her more than he did at that exact moment.

"What are you going to do about what?" her mother asked. "Is there a problem with you marrying? He's not married already, is he?"

"No," he answered quickly. "There are just a few people that must be taken care of. These two"—he nudged the man nearest him with his shoe—"and another woman who's hanging around Ethan's camp trying to find Gwen. Not that I'll let that happen, but I'll have to deal with her once and for all."

"Not the reclaimer!" gasped the second mother. "She's here?"

Gwen stared at them both, openmouthed with surprise. "You know about her?"

The two women exchanged glances . . . *guilty* glances. "Er . . . yes. Don't you remember before we came to Anwyn how we hurried you out of that psychologist's office? That Death woman had followed you there, and we felt it wiser to have you elsewhere."

"Yes, I remember that. But what I want to know is why you are both looking so guilty *now?*" Gwen asked, her eyes narrowed in suspicion. "You didn't *do* anything to her, did you?"

The first mother made a gesture that could only be described as wringing her hands. Their faces expressing their distress, the second mother blurted out, "It's all our fault that she's chasing you, Gwen. We weren't going to tell you because you were safe here in Anwyn, but if you say she's here now . . ."

"It's not your fault in the least," Gregory told them. "If anything, the blame lies with me, since I am the one who made sure that Gwen didn't stay dead."

The mothers gawked at him. "You mean she was telling the truth when she said that she died and came back to life?"

Quickly, Gregory explained the pertinent events.

"Honestly!" Gwen slapped her hands on her thighs. "What is the world coming to when your own mothers don't believe you when you tell them you've died and been mysteriously resurrected!"

"The issue of the loss of time is why Death's minion is after Gwen," Gregory added when the two women looked doubtful.

"Er . . ." Once again the two mothers exchanged a telling look.

"Er what?" Gwen stopped looking annoyed and switched back to looking suspicious. "What aren't you telling us? Does it have something to do with the reclamation woman?"

"We might as well tell them," the second one told the first. "It's better if they know, Mags."

"Yes, but . . ." The first mother fretted with the apron she wore, giving Gwen a doubtful look. "Gwenny will be so . . ."

"Angry? Annoyed? Irritated? Because I'm quickly getting to all three," Gwen told them sternly. "Spill."

"The woman may say she's coming after you because of dear Gregory stealing the time to save your life—and really, that was terribly sweet of you, and Alice and I will always be grateful to you for it, because we just couldn't be without our darling girl—but it's not exactly the truth."

"What is the truth?" Gwen asked, taking his hand. He

twined his fingers through hers, a sudden sense of content-
ment stealing over him. Whatever the problem was, he told
himself, he and Gwen would handle it together.

"Well . . ."

"No." Gwen shook a finger on her free hand at them. "No
more of those pregnant looks you're giving each other. Just
tell us how bad it is so we can set about fixing the situation."

He was even more pleased that Gwen now included him
in the mop-up duties of whatever mess her mothers had created.

"I love you more now than I did five minutes ago, and
that's saying a lot," he told her.

She squeezed his hand. "No distractions from the peanut
gallery. Mom? Tell us."

Her mother took a deep breath, and said so quickly that
the words tumbled over each other, "Death is annoyed with
us because about three hundred years ago we sold him a love
charm that . . . er . . . went awry."

"Instead of attracting the lady he desired, the spell was
intercepted by a behemoth. One that had unconventional
tastes," the second mother confided to them.

"He enjoyed unsavory methods of sexual engagement,"
the first mother said, waving vaguely toward her derriere.
"Very unsavory when you consider just how large behemoths
are. And when Death demanded that we fix the situation—
you know full well we never offer guarantees when it comes
to love charms because they are so unreliable—we tried to
reason with the behemoth (his name was Carl), but he escaped us and locked himself in Death's bedchamber with
Death while he was sleeping in order to have his wedding
night—did we mention that Carl wanted to marry Death? I
thought that was sweet, really, although what Death said happened that night . . . Well, we won't go into details because
that sort of thing is better not mentioned in mixed company,
and really, it wasn't our fault, but Death didn't see it that way,
and he got a bit stroppy and said that he wasn't going to rest

until he made us as miserable as he was the morning after his . . . I suppose you could call it his nuptials, although he had another word for it, and we knew that he would target you once he found out you'd been born to us because you are so very dear to us both, my darling Gwen, and it was all very upsetting and we didn't want you to know because you make the biggest fusses about things that really aren't that dire, and you wanted to go back to the States so you could continue your work, so we didn't tell you."

Gwen stared at them for the count of seven before turning to look at Gregory. "I'm going to give you the chance right now to retract your offer of marriage. It's the honorable thing to do, and I just want you to know that I wouldn't blame you in the least for not wanting to be connected to my family."

He flicked his thumb over her lower lip to keep from kissing the breath right out of her. "Not even a violated Death would keep me from your side."

"OK, that's going to win you some bonus swoon points," she told him, her eyes warm with admiration. He wanted badly to get her into the nearest bed so he could show her just how much he appreciated that look. "As for you two . . . you are so grounded."

"Gwenhwyfar," the second mother said sternly, "I will not have you speaking to your mother like that. We are not children."

"You sure act as irresponsible as kids sometimes," Gwen said with a sharp edge to her voice that softened when she added, "Regardless of what you may have done—and don't think we aren't going to have a little talk later about hiding things from me—we can't lay the blame for the reclamation woman on your heads. She's here for me because she thinks I owe her my soul."

"Don't give it to her. You're not done using it," the first mother said, picking up a bottle from Ethan's desk and giving it a sniff. "You're going to have need of it when you marry dear Gregory. Alice, pink roses or yellow for the bouquet?"

Alice eyed Gwen thoughtfully. "White. With pale pink carnations. And perhaps a carpet of matching pink rose petals."

"You have such a good eye for details like that."

Gwen gave him a long-suffering look before turning back to her mothers. "That's enough premature planning. And before you blast me, yes, I will marry Gregory, but we have more important things to do now. We have to find that bird."

"What bird?" the mothers asked.

She turned to him, nodding again at the two men on the floor, both of whom were now moaning, fainting, and making jerky movements with their arms and legs. "Can you take care of them? And by 'take care,' I mean get rid of them in some nonlethal way so that they don't come back and try to hurt my moms again?"

"Yes. Because I love you."

She rolled her eyes, then leaned in and bit his lower lip. "You're adorable when you're being sexy. My moms and I will tackle the folks around the camp about the bird. Maybe one of them remembers it and knows where it flew off to. Maybe we can find a descendant of it, too."

"We don't have any time to go bird-watching," the first mother said.

"The sooner we find the bird, the sooner we fulfill Aaron's demands, and the sooner we can get out of Anwyn."

"Who's Aaron?"

As he was leaving to find a couple of strong-looking lads to help him truss up the two hit men, he heard Gwen explaining about Aaron and Ethan's war.

Everything was going to be fine. He'd have to find a way to get rid of Death's minion, but he had an inkling of how that might be accomplished, and he was never one to back down from a challenge. He'd make sure Gwen was safe from the reclamation agent, get rid of the two hit men, and then deal with the situation regarding her mothers and the Watch . . . and the vendetta that Death evidently held against them.

Yes, it was all going to work out to his satisfaction. Gwen might not want to admit yet that she loved him, but she did. She had to. He really didn't think he could bear it otherwise.

SIXTEEN

The hunt for the missing bird didn't go spectacularly well, mostly because my mothers were so excited about the thought of Gregory and me getting married, they couldn't focus for long on anything else.

Married.

That word kept chiming in my head like the deep note of a large bell. Gregory wanted to get married. He loved me. And what was more, he wanted me to love him.

"Which of our wedding dresses do you think she should wear?" Mom Two asked Mom as we headed to their tent. "Mine was pretty, but I think yours would go with her coloring better."

Men had said they loved me before, but with Gregory it was different. He wouldn't say it unless he really felt it. And I had a feeling by the somewhat shocked expression that he had worn, it wasn't something he'd felt very often.

"Yes, but yours was made of old lace, and that never goes out of style," Mom told Mom Two.

That thought pleased me. I told myself to stop being idiotic—what Gregory did or felt before I knew him was absolutely none of my business—but all the same, I couldn't help a smug little sense of pleasure that it was me he loved, rather than anybody from the great herds of women who I was sure had tramped through his life.

"It was my mother's lace, too," Mom Two agreed. "Lovely handmade stuff."

When a squire bumped into me as he tried to get around us, I realized that I was just as guilty as my mothers of wasting valuable time.

"I repeat: the sooner we find the bird, the sooner we can leave Anwyn and I can wear the lace." I grabbed a passing squire by the arm when he tried to sidle past. "Hi, there. Would you happen to know anything about a bird that Ethan stole several hundred years ago?"

"A bird?" The boy shifted the long mail coat draped over his forearms and scrunched up his nose. "What kind of a bird?"

"Lapwing."

"Never heard of it," the lad said, and wresting his arm away from me, he hurried off on his business.

I sighed. "Someone somewhere has to know something about that bird. It doesn't help that I don't know what a lapwing looks like. Do either of you know?"

The moms shook their heads. My mother took my arm and tugged me toward the tent. "But we have the books from the woman who used to live here, and they are full of all sorts of historical notes, so perhaps something is there about it."

"All right, but while I'm looking at her books, I want you two to get packed up."

Mom stopped dead. "Why should we pack? We aren't done here. We have a batch of frogspawn potion evaporating down to just the essence, and you know how long that takes."

"Eleven days exactly," Mom Two said with a nod.

"I want you both to come with me over to Aaron's camp. My tent is big enough for all of us, and I'll feel better knowing you're safe with me."

Mom Two bridled. "We're perfectly safe here! Ethan would never let anything harm us."

"Yes, indeed!" Mom gave me a stern look and proceeded to their tent. "We're very happy here, Gwenny. Very happy. Even Mrs. Vanilla—Hello, dear, did you have a nice nap in your chair? Cup of tea? With extra honey?—even dear Mrs. Vanilla here is happy. Aren't you, dear? Happy here?"

I followed my mothers inside, wearily wondering how on earth I was going to persuade them to come with me. Mrs. Vanilla, who had been dozing in her chair, suddenly perked up and squeaked at us, her hands moving in the quick little way she had when conversing. Or when she was doing what she thought of as conversing. I eyed her critically, wondering if I could use her as a way to get my mothers over to Aaron's camp, but I had to admit she did look pretty chipper.

She gratefully accepted the cup of tea, liberally laced with honey, that Mom handed her.

"Gwenny?" Mom held up the big cast-iron teakettle from the coal stove that resided in the corner.

"No, thanks. And I'm sorry, but you are not safe here, Mom Two, as that episode with Irv and Frankie demonstrated to a degree that will give me nightmares for years to come."

"Bah," Mom Two scoffed. "I wasn't harmed, and your young man said he would remove them. I have faith in him."

I stared at her in surprise. Since when did my mothers fall under the spell of a man? Even one as charming as Gregory? "I'm glad you believe he can protect you, but he can't be everywhere at the same time. And if that bastard lawyer sent two hit men after us, then he might send more. No, it's not safe for you to be here without someone to watch over you."

"We've been taking care of ourselves for centuries, Gwen," Mom Two said as she and Mom bustled about, obviously preparing to start a new potion. "No, Mags, the dried lion's ear, not the fresh."

Mom handed over a glass jar containing dried ferns. "And besides that, we're learning ever so much from the trees."

"You're what?" I backed up when Mom shooed me out of her way. She tied an apron around her waist and got to work with a couple of small vials of colored liquid.

"I'm so glad the apothecary had a fresh shaved spikenard root. I do so hate to have to make dominator oil with lesser materials. What was that, Gwenny?"

"You said something about learning from trees." I rubbed

my forehead. I could feel a headache starting, and I had a feeling it was going to grow with every second that my mothers fought my reasonable request.

"Yes, we are. We've always wanted to learn field magic, and who better to learn it from than trees and shrubs?" Mom Two answered for her.

"Yup, headache definitely getting worse." I considered just sitting down and giving up, but the thought of remaining in Anwyn forever because we couldn't find the bird gave me enough of the willies to keep me on my feet. "Are you talking about someone who's teaching you field lore, or are you going out and learning from the trees themselves? Because if it's the latter, I'd like to remind you that there are plenty of trees outside of Anwyn to learn from."

"It's both, actually," Mom answered, her finger tracing a line of text in her recipe book. "The trees here in camp have many things to teach us. Especially that spruce. What was his name, dear? Denver?"

"Colorado," Mom Two answered.

I sat down. It was a moment or two before I could speak. "Are you trying to tell me that Colorado, the warrior who looks like a young Hugh Laurie, is a tree?"

"Yes, of course he is. All of Ethan's warriors are trees. Alice, oil of hyssop or oil of angelica?"

"For dominator oil? Myrrh and sweet flag."

"Oh, that's right, how silly of me. I was thinking of the uncrossing oil. What was that, Gwenny?"

"Nothing." I stood up again, figuring if I stayed there to find out why Ethan's warriors were really trees, I'd never get anything done. "Where's this history book that has a picture of the bird?"

Mrs. Vanilla chirruped in her strange, wordless way and waggled her hands so that the massive spread of crocheted horse jacket wobbled across her lap.

"Hmm? Yes, dear, that's right, the nice book is next to

you, isn't it? It's in the chest there, Gwenny. The one to the left of Mrs. Vanilla."

I smiled at the old lady and, moving a few bound bundles of dried herbs, uncovered a small wooden chest. Inside it were three books, two of which appeared to be grimoires. The bottom one smelled of mildew and long-dead moths. Its binding was wispy, but held together enough for me to leaf through its pages. I have a profound love for old books, and was sorely tempted to sit there and read this one, but other than pausing for a few minutes on a page that had me exclaiming, "Well, I'll be damned. They *are* trees," I ignored everything until I turned another page and found myself looking at a tiny sketch of a bird. "Hmm. White and black head, white belly, and greeny-black wings. I can't say I've seen a bird like it around Anwyn, but at least now I know what to look for. Er . . . Mom, is she OK?"

Mrs. Vanilla's hands had gone into overtime while I knelt next to her, and she continued to make high-pitched squeaky noises that increased in volume until I worried that the old lady was having some sort of fit.

Mom bustled over to us. "Are you all right, dear? Need to use the loo? No? Hungry? Do you want some soup? Are you tired? Nap time?"

I put the books away and stood next to the old woman, feeling helpless. "Should I get her something? Does she take any medicine?"

"I don't think so. What is it, dear? Can we get you anything?"

The old woman's hands alternated between plucking at the blanket and making odd little fluttering motions, but after a few minutes she settled back down with her knitting.

"Mom." I pulled my mother to the other side of the tent. "When you kidnapped Mrs. Vanilla from the nursing home—"

"Rescued her. We rescued her. She begged us to do so.

She saw an ad advertising our school, and knew that we were the only people who would be able to rescue her from the mortals."

"Did she have any medicine in her room? I don't think she's . . . right. I mean, that thing with the hands, and making those noises but not actually talking. That's beyond odd."

Mom brushed off that thought. "She's just a bit eccentric, dear. You would be too if you were as old as her."

I looked across the tent. Mrs. Vanilla's crumpled little figure was almost swallowed up by the massive coat she was making. "I'm concerned that she needs medicine for a condition that we don't know about. And if she doesn't get it, she might get seriously sick. We have to take her back, Mom."

"Oh, no, dear. She's quite happy here. Happier than she would be back in the mortal world."

"She *is* mortal."

"Don't be silly. Of course she isn't. Now, you go look for your bird, and your mother and I will finish up this latest batch of potions while Mrs. Vanilla rests. Alice, dear heart, do you think we should make another potion for Death?"

"No!" I shouted, making all three women look at me with varying expressions of surprise. "No more potions for Death."

"Very well, dear."

"I'm off to look for the bird, and then I should check in with my warrior trainer before it's my shift time. He said something about me learning how to lop off heads today, and I wouldn't want to miss that, now would I?"

My voice had a tinge of hysteria to it that both my mothers failed to notice.

"When I'm done," I said loudly at the entrance to their tent, "I expect to find both of you and Mrs. Vanilla ready to move over to my tent."

I departed hastily, followed by stereo objections and exclamations that I had turned horribly bossy ever since I hit a hundred years, all of which I ignored. I had plenty of reason to worry about my mothers' well-being, and they were just going to have to accept that.

The next hour or so was spent trying to pin down anyone who'd stand still about the missing lapwing, but no one seemed to know anything about it. It wasn't until I was ready to give up and go find Master Hamo for my daily lesson that I ran across the apothecary my mothers had raved so much about. I explained that I was looking for information about the bird, fully expecting to get an answer similar to the others I'd had thus far. But I was more than a little surprised to have the middle-aged, bespectacled bald man look up from a wooden crock of dried herbs and say, "Oh, she left quite some time ago. Couldn't take the separation."

"Separation . . . from Aaron?" I guessed.

He nodded. "Very devoted pair they were. You'd never see the king without his lapwing. Went everywhere together. Until, of course, the day that she-cat got an eyeful of him."

"What she-cat?"

"The queen, naturally." The look he gave me was a mixture of slyness and amusement. "She took one look at the king and decided she fancied being the queen of the Underworld."

"Are you saying that she got rid of Aaron's beloved lapwing?"

The man winked and turned back to his task. "I'm not saying that, but I'm not not saying it, if you ken."

I mulled that over for a few seconds. The implication that Constance might well be behind Ethan's actions in stealing Aaron's beloved bird—and dog and deer—was unavoidable. I couldn't wait to talk about that theory with Gregory, but for now . . . "And you don't know what happened to the bird after she was . . . er . . . parted from Aaron?"

"Spirited away would be my guess." He peered at me over the thick lenses of his glasses for a moment. "If you were the queen and you wanted to get rid of the rival for your husband's love, what would you do?"

"Rival? We're talking about a bird, right? How can a beloved pet be a rival for the love of a woman?"

"Have you met Lord Aaron?"

"Yes, I . . . oh. Point taken." Despair filled the pit of my stomach when I considered what an enraged Constance might have done. "She would have wanted that bird to fly away. Far away from her and her cats."

"That's a safe line of reasoning."

I watched the apothecary for a few moments, feeling utterly lost. If the bird had been set free in the mortal world, she could be anywhere now . . . assuming she had survived all the centuries. "Thanks so much for your help."

He waved a gnarled hand in farewell. A glance at the red and gray sky overhead warned that I had little time to spend trying to round up my mothers, but I was loath to let them stay there unprotected. I just hoped that Gregory had managed to do something with Irv and Frankie . . . and that annoying Death's minion.

I compromised by warning my mothers to stay in their tent, and then racing across the stream just in time to meet Master Hamo, who looked pointedly at a sundial set near the practice ring.

"Sorry. Was checking on my mothers." I pulled out my sword. "I hope we're going to learn a way to take down someone quickly, because I know a couple of guys that I might have to use that on if my boyfriend doesn't take care of them."

Master Hamo raised his eyebrows, but simply said, "I don't believe you are ready for more advanced attacks, but I can show you a couple of simple yet effective moves that have served me well."

The next hour and a half was spent learning. I had to admire Master Hamo—no matter how many times I ended up in the dirt, he always helped me up and patiently explained what I'd done wrong. By the time my lesson was over, I was bruised but victorious. For the first time I had felt the power in the sword.

"I could get used to this," I told Seith, who appeared to take away my mail and sword for cleaning.

"Learning from Master Hamo?" he asked with an envious glance toward that man as another warrior entered the training ring.

"Using a sword." I handed the Nightingale to him. "This one is awesome. It's almost like it knows what to do without me directing it. I wonder if I could buy it from Ethan?"

Seith shrugged and trotted off to do his squirely duties. I limped to Ethan's camp, which was bustling as usual. I was careful to peek around corners before I hurried toward my target tent, just in case Gregory hadn't found Death's minion.

"I suppose it's a lost hope to expect that you've done as I asked and packed up?" I asked at the entrance to my mothers' tent. They were, as I had expected, busily preparing some potion or other.

Both of them looked up, surprise on their faces. "Oh, Gwenny, it's you again. Of course we're not packed. We have no need to leave, as your mother and I have both told you. And keep your voice down. Mrs. Vanilla is taking a nap. The poor dear was most distraught after you left, and it took three cups of chamomile tea to settle her down."

I took a deep breath, preparatory to explaining to my mothers yet again why I wasn't comfortable with them remaining unguarded and at large, but suddenly a horrible clashing, grinding noise rose up over the chatting, barking, and other normal sounds of camp life.

"What the hell?" I spun around to pinpoint the source of the noise. My mothers rushed out with gentler exclamations.

The camp members nearest me froze in the act of attending to their daily business, and all heads swiveled to look across the stream toward Aaron's camp. For one horrible moment I feared that some new catastrophe had struck us, but when the woman nearest me pointed and screamed, "It's a mechanical monster! Flee! Flee the monster!" I knew what had really happened.

"It's Aaron and his Velociphant. He must have gotten it working."

"A Veloci-what?" Mom asked.

"This I have to see. Stay here!" I ordered my mothers before bolting painfully for the stream and Aaron's camp.

"We aren't going to miss something exciting," Mom Two answered, and just as I knew they would, they trotted after me.

On the far side of Aaron's camp, several men struggled with large wooden poles, obviously in the process of erecting a tent suitable for a king. To the side of them, the massive iron machine was surrounded by what appeared to be everybody in the entire camp, the warriors and squires and support people all cheering and shouting excitedly.

"Glory of the good green earth, what's that?" Mom asked, pointing.

"That is Aaron's answer to the war." A thought struck me. "I guess, given the fact that Ethan's people are all really trees in human form, you could say it was a glorified lawn mower. Aaron intends to use it on Ethan's dudes."

"This Aaron either is very stupid or has been misinformed," Mom Two announced. "Lord Ethan's warriors are magical beings, summoned from the spirits of the forest and field. No mere machine could destroy them."

"I have to say that I hope so, despite wanting the war to end, because I kind of like Ethan and his wacky bunch. Except maybe that Holly . . . oh! Holly! You think she's—"

"Of course she is," Mom Two said, giving me a look that said I should have sussed out Holly's origins long ago. "Didn't you notice the green in her hair and her rather painful manner?"

"Yes, but I thought that was just her."

"Oh, Gwenny." Mom shook her head. "And we raised you to see all the possibilities . . ."

"Yes, well, I think a little slack can be granted due to the circumstances." I craned my neck over the shoulder of the knight in front of me, wanting to get a better look at whether or not Constance had accompanied Aaron. If she had, I wanted badly to have a few words with her.

The crowd rippled, and several people gasped, sweeping us backward and to the side in a wave of bodies.

"What's going on?" Mom said, hopping up and down in order to see over the wall of warriors in front of us. "Gwen, what do you see?"

"Nothing but helms and heads. Stick with me." I grabbed my mother's arm, and muttering apologies, pushed my way through the various bodies, finally emerging into the open.

"—and Lord Ethan wants to lodge a formal complaint about it," Holly was saying to Aaron, who stood in front of the mechanical maw of his beast. "You sent a Traveller to attack us, and that is in clear violation of the agreement of 1717."

"I did nothing of the kind. I hired a thief to take back what is mine, nothing more." Aaron, a screwdriver in hand, was fussing with something on the foot of the giant mechanical beast.

Holly didn't like being more or less ignored; she marched forward and grabbed Aaron by the arm, spinning him around so she could poke him in the chest. "Your so-called thief smote two of our men with lightning. That is against the terms of our agreement, and thus you have forfeited this war and must hand over control of Anwyn to me. Er . . . to Ethan."

Aaron said a word that had my mothers gasping. I wanted to give him a thumb's-up, but the sight of Constance strolling into the mix, followed by her cavalcade of white cats, drove that thought from my mind.

"What is going on here? Are we entertaining, husband?" Constance called out.

"Stop calling me that! We are not married. We have not been married since I found out what a devil you really are. The fact you should keep uppermost in your mind at all times is that I divorced you four hundred years ago, and you are only in Anwyn because your blasted herd of felines keeps the rodents under control."

"Stay here out of trouble's way," I warned my mothers. "I want to have a word with the queen."

"Oh, is that who that cat is?" Mom Two asked, looking with interest as Constance approached.

"Cat lady, you mean? Yes, that's her." I took a step forward to intercept Constance, but was suddenly yanked to the side. A short, dark-haired woman in a red wool power suit faced me with flaring nostrils and an extremely irritated expression.

"There you are! I knew you must be close by if that Traveller was trying so hard to get rid of me."

Oh, great. This was just what I needed. "You must be the soul reclaimer." I reached for my sword, swearing under my breath when I remembered that Seith had taken it for its cleaning. "Where's Gregory? If you've done anything to him, I will make you the sorriest excuse for a human being as has ever existed."

"Oh, Alice," Mom said to Mom Two, "did you hear how she threatened that evil soul-stealing woman? Our Gwenny is in love with that nice young man!"

I was? I hesitated a moment, stunned by the thought that my mother was right. At some point during the last few days, I had stopped being enamored of Gregory and had fallen in love with him. I shook my head at myself. The phrase "in love" seemed to be so inadequate for the emotion I felt. If I could be "in love," then I could be out of it as well, and I knew without one single shred of doubt that the love I felt for Gregory would never dim. "It's like . . . he's part of me now."

"That's exactly how I feel," a deep voice said behind me.

My heart sang with joy as I spun around. The mass of warriors parted again when Gregory walked toward me with long strides that spoke of carefully controlled strength. I hadn't realized until I saw him in the midst of the other warriors just how much an aura of power surrounded him, but as the lightning streaked across the sky above, I acknowledged that he was the sexiest man alive.

And he was mine.

"I see you found—" He hesitated, frowning at the reclaimer. "What is your name?"

She looked startled for a moment, then said, "Astrid."

"Ah." He made a slight bow. "I see you found Astrid, Gwen. And, apparently, everyone else as well. What are they fighting about?"

I glanced at Holly, in Aaron's face. He was snarling back at her, trying to grab the screwdriver that she had apparently snatched from him. Constance, her cats in tow, was staring in surprise at Ethan's rogue hand, which was on her breast. I half expected her to slap his face, but instead she covered the alien hand with her own, and smiled a slow, sensual smile.

"Holly and Ethan—although really, one gets the idea that it's all Holly—are upset because they believe that Aaron sent you over to attack them with your elite Traveller skills. Aaron appears to be annoyed to find Constance here, as well as about the fact that Holly has taken his screwdriver and won't give it back. I gather from the besotted expression on Constance's face that she and Diego are hitting it off. Ethan looks less enamored with her, but given his self-obsession, that doesn't surprise me."

"Thank you for the summation," he said politely, and pulled me into his arms despite all the people standing around watching.

Mom Two giggled.

"Do you really?"

I looked up at those beautiful eyes, the color of a flawless summer sky, and knew he'd overheard my mother. "I suppose I do. It will make everyone happy, and it's probably better that I love you if we're going to spend the rest of our lives together."

"This would be touching," a voice said just as Gregory

leaned down to kiss me, "if there was any truth to it, but alas, you will not be spending your lives together because your soul belongs to me. Or rather, to my employer."

"She has bad timing," I said against Gregory's lips.

"Extremely poor. I suppose I shall have to address this issue, however, so that I can take you to your tent and allow you to tell me, in many words and more actions, just how deep is your love for me."

"You big ham," I said, biting his lip before turning to face the annoying Astrid. "Look, I don't know you, but I've heard that you're obsessed with my soul. The fact is that I'm not dead, so you can't have it."

She picked a minute bit of fluff from her sleeve. "That's not how it works. You died. I was sent to fetch your soul and bring it before my employer, who asks you what afterlife you wish to patronize and then sends you to that place. I do not have your soul; therefore you still owe it to me."

"Yes, but I'm already in Anwyn, which is where I would have gone—" A thought struck me. "Wait a minute. When I was killed a few days ago, I woke up here, in Anwyn. How could I do that if I have to see Death in order to be sent here?"

Astrid inhaled loudly through her nose. "You violated the rules, that's how! And let me tell you, we reclamation agents take a very dim view of people who just simply up and go to whatever afterlife they like without having the common decency to let us do our job!"

"So Gwen doesn't have to see your boss before she picks an afterlife?" Gregory asked. I slid a glance his way. He had an air of being up to something. I sure hoped he was—I had no clue how I was going to get out of handing over my soul to this pushy woman, short of physical violence, and I hated to use that. She was, after all, just doing her job.

"The reclamation rules say that—"

"I'm not asking about your rules. I'm asking whether or not she has to give you her soul and see your boss."

Astrid squared her shoulders, a pugnacious expression on her face. "I would like to point out that my job is not to claim her soul for myself but to escort it to Death, at which point it is reunited with her body and both are sent on to the afterlife of her choice."

"I think that answers my question." Gregory wrapped his arm around my waist. "She doesn't have to do either. She can bypass you and your boss and go straight to the afterlife she's most comfortable with, which is, in fact, what she did almost a week ago. Therefore, you have no job to perform, and you can leave without bothering her anymore."

"She owes me her soul, and she's going to give it to me!" Astrid screamed, and for a second I thought she was going to attack me.

"Seith!" I yelled, looking around frantically. "Seith! Blast the boy, where is he?"

"Aye, my lady?" A head bobbed up at the back of a large stretch of warriors, only to disappear a moment later.

"Get me the Nightingale!" I bellowed.

SEVENTEEN

"**A**aron, might I have a word?"

I stuck like glue to Gregory's side when he, with blithe disregard of Astrid's fuming stare, walked nonchalantly over to where Aaron was now physically trying to wrest the screwdriver away from Holly. I felt somewhat naked without my sword, and I didn't trust Astrid not to pull out some trick that would enable her to run away with my soul.

"Give it . . . to . . . me . . ." Aaron panted in his struggle with the wily Holly.

"Not until you hand Anwyn over to me!"

"Never! I'm the king. You are merely a usurper. Now give me my damned screwdriver so I can tighten up the screws around the loose bolt, and then my beloved Piranha shall mow you and all your leafy friends down!"

"He really doesn't have a clue as to how a proper threat works, does he?" I whispered to Gregory.

"Not really. But he does have an ability that I believe will solve a big problem. Your Majesty, might I have a moment of your valuable time?"

"You!" Aaron said, still struggling. "You're a thief—get me back my screwdriver."

"Easy peasy," I said, and while Holly was distracted by Gregory turning to her, I slipped behind her, kicked her in the back of the leg, and snatched the screwdriver when she staggered forward. I handed it to Aaron with a flourish. "Here you go."

"Excellent work. Excellent." He beamed at the screwdriver and was about to turn back to his machine when Gregory stopped him.

"Would you mind banishing that woman from Anwyn?"

Astrid, on the receiving end of Gregory's pointed finger, gasped. "You can't do that!"

"Actually, I can. I'm the king and rightful ruler of this realm." Aaron cast a disparaging glance at Holly, who was getting to her feet with a furious look in her eye, one that was aimed at Gregory and me. "I'm not going to banish you, but I could if I so desired."

"Why not?" I asked, my sudden hopes dying a cruel death.

"Because I asked him"—he pointed at Gregory—"to do one simple thing, and he has failed to do it."

"I have the roebuck in my possession," Gregory said, a little frown pulling his brows together.

I really must be in love, I thought to myself, *because even his frown looks sexy.*

"And I can get you the descendant of the dog that was stolen from you. The dog itself has been dead for centuries, but one of her direct descendants should fulfill that requirement."

Aaron gestured with the screwdriver. "I suppose it would. She was a damned good bitch, though. But my bird, man—where's my Vanellus?"

"You call your bird Vanellus?" I couldn't help but ask.

He gave me an impatient look. "That's her name. *Vanellus vanellus,* or northern lapwing."

There was a faint murmur behind me, I half turned, catching my mother's eye as she mouthed that she'd be right back. She and Mom Two melted into the crowd, leaving me to debate whether or not I should follow them, but I assumed anyone who was a threat would be right here.

"I'm afraid I couldn't locate the bird," Gregory was saying when I turned back. "But we will make every effort to find her. I'll put the full resources of the Watch—assuming

I'm still employed by them after they find out about my time here—into finding out what happened to your bird and locating her or her descendants."

"I don't want her descendants," Aaron snarled. "I want my bird."

At his raised voice, Constance twirled around, one of her hands in the process of stroking Ethan's head. Holly hissed something quite rude and strode over to them. Constance, her gaze locked on Aaron's, asked shrilly, "Did you say something about a bird? What bird?"

"My bird, my beloved Vanellus who you drove away, you she-devil!" Aaron stabbed the screwdriver into the air at her and she recoiled and backed up a step, bumping into Holly, who promptly shoved her forward. Ethan bore the look of a man being harangued by a sharp, pointy bit of foliage in human form.

"Aha!" Aaron continued, narrowing his eyes as Constance and her cats tripped lightly forward. "You didn't know I knew the truth about that, did you? Why do you think I divorced you all those hundreds of years ago?"

Constance's long, gorgeous hair moved in the breeze, making her appear larger than she was. "We are still married—" she started to say through clenched teeth, but she was interrupted by Aaron shouting at the top of his lungs. "Get out of my sight before I banish you and all of your kinsmen once and for all! I have important work to do, and no one is going to stop me! The Piranha must be fed!"

Several pennies dropped at that moment, enough that it had me staring in stupefaction at Constance, who was hissing and shying away to the side. "She's a cat?"

Gregory looked nonplussed. "Evidently so. It would explain her perpetual guard of honor."

"And a lot of other things." Quickly, in a low voice, I told him about my discussion with the apothecary.

"So Constance got rid of the bird before she was queen,"

Gregory said in a thoughtful tone. "Interesting. Do you know, I have an idea about that—"

"Hello, all," said a voice with a heavy Australian accent. "Am I late for the party? Astrid, luv, mind fetching me a cocktail? I'm as parched as a skin flake in the middle of the Great Victoria Desert. Aaron, you bastard, long time no see. Constance, you're looking rather rumpled, but still beautiful. Ethan, you great bushranger! How is Diego doing? I can't say how much I've enjoyed your recent Facebook posts about your upcoming book. I do hope you've worked out your problem with the angsty teen poetry."

We all turned to look in surprise at the man who had emerged from the mass of soldiers. He was a bit taller than Gregory, had lovely chocolate brown hair that curled back from his brow and swooped down to his collar and a pair of the blackest eyes I've ever seen. He smiled engagingly at me and Gregory.

"Sir!" Astrid bustled toward him, shooting me a smug glance as she passed us. "I'm so glad you got my message. I'm having a bit of difficulty with that job I mentioned, and I thought that you might wish to take charge of the situation yourself."

"Oh, great," I said sotto voce. "Death is here. Just what was needed to add one last touch of surreal to what is an already Salvador Dalí sort of day."

"It's De Ath, actually," Death said, taking my hand and brushing his lips across my knuckles.

Beside me Gregory stiffened.

"I find it's less intimidating that way. Crikey, that's a look. This sheila yours, then?" Death—or rather, De Ath—asked Gregory.

The latter took my hand and rubbed his thumb over the spot that had been kissed. "Yes."

"All right, all right, no need to spit the dummy, mate."

De Ath turned when Aaron, done tightening his screws,

noticed him. He didn't look happy with what he saw. "What are you doing here? Didn't I banish you?"

"One hundred and fourteen years ago, to be exact, right after I took over the job from the last bloke," De Ath said with a sunny smile. "I was summoned back by one of my secretaries."

"Reclamation agent!" Astrid said furiously, smacking him on the arm. "I told you that we are now called reclamation agents!"

"How come he can enter Anwyn if he's been banished?" I asked Gregory in a whisper. "And why is Death so charming and handsome and nice?"

"I'm not sure, but I suspect that we'll find out, and do you really think he is handsome?"

"Yes, in a Hugh Jackman sort of way. I think it's mostly the accent. And the hair. And he has nice—" I stopped when Gregory shot me a mean look, giggling quietly to myself.

"My lady! I have the Nightingale for you." Seith pushed his way through the crowd, aided, no doubt, by the sword, despite its being sheathed.

"What?" Holly, who was evidently still engaged in chewing out Ethan for something or other, spun around so fast her hair smacked him in the face. He took the opportunity of her being distracted to move quickly over to where De Ath stood, the two men instantly falling into conversation. "You still have that sword? Give it back. You shouldn't have been given it in the first place."

I grabbed the sword that Seith held out before she could stomp over to take it. "Ethan said I could use it, so I don't see that it has anything to do with you."

"Ethan!" She wasn't happy to see that he'd moved, her eyes narrowing as she marched over to him. "Tell that woman to give back your mother's sword."

"Sir," Astrid said at the same time, plucking at De Ath's sleeve. "That's the woman there, the one who's been giving me so much trouble. You should take care of her first before you enjoy a reunion with Lord Ethan."

"I'm busy," Ethan told Holly in a lofty tone that had her face turning dark red with fury. "Bother me not."

"That Astrid is nothing but a troublemaker," I muttered under my breath. "Gregory, what are we going to do about this? The best I can think of is to fight our way out, and I hate to do that with my mothers around. They tend to get into trouble, and as you heard, Death already has it in for them."

"I believe that was his predecessor, but I agree that I would hesitate to have to fight our way out." He looked thoughtful for a minute. "I think my original plan is still the best: we will have to convince Aaron to banish Astrid."

I eyed the chatting De Ath, now giving his minion a look that had her apologizing. "It doesn't seem to have stopped him from being here."

"No, but just as the Watch has no power here, I suspect that neither does anyone who has been banished."

"Assuming that's so, what good will it do us? I'd be trapped here, never able to leave lest she be waiting for me to set foot in the real world, where she does have power over me."

"I'd rather have you safe than soulless."

He had a point, although I hated the thought of being trapped here.

"The first step is to find out if our supposition is correct. Shall we?" Gregory pulled me with him and walked over to Aaron, who was now in consultation with his engineer. "My lord, a question, if you will. The man who has taken on Death's role over there—am I correct in assuming that his banishment merely limits his powers in Anwyn, and not his physical presence?"

"I don't know why you care, but that is correct," Aaron said, peering at something the engineer was pointing out. "No, no, it's been oiled well enough. It's the tension in the nether spring that's too tight. Loosen that up, and the jaws should move again."

"We would very much appreciate it if you would banish

the reclamation agent known as Astrid. She has threatened one of your warriors, the lady Gwen, who has fought valiantly in your honor."

Aaron stopped fiddling with his machine to glance at me. His gaze fell on the sheathed sword in my hands, causing him to step forward to give it a longer look. "Indeed, she appears to bear the sword of my enemy's mother." His lips pursed as he thought for a few minutes. "No," he finally said, shaking his head. "I can't do that. You promised to restore my bird, and you shall have no more boons until the time that she is at my side again."

Despair was once again my companion. I looked mutely at Gregory, wanting him to come up with a brilliant solution to the problem, but knowing it was an unfair expectation. I'd never been one to shirk responsibility, and this problem was as much mine as his.

"We're just going to have to find that bird, or her descendants," I told Gregory.

He pressed my hand to his mouth, his lips sending little streaks of electricity jolting down my arm, straight to my belly. "I'm afraid that's so."

I ignored my body's demand that I should wrestle Gregory to the ground and do a little lightning-calling of my own. I hefted my sword. "I guess we're going to have to take care of this the hard way. What did you do with Irv and Frankie, by the way?"

"Had two of Ethan's guards haul them to the entrance and toss them through the portal into the mortal world."

"Think we could do that with Astrid?"

He glanced upward as red and gray clouds gathered overhead, and flexed his fingers. Lightning streaked in a brilliant arc across the roiling sky. "We could try, although she's not mortal as they were."

"This ends now!"

"Oooh." We both watched as Holly, with a firm grip on Diego, hauled Ethan over to us. "Someone has a mad."

"I'll deal with you later," she snapped, piercing me with a look that had me gripping the hilt of my sword tighter. She turned back to Aaron. "You have violated the terms of our agreement. Either hand Anwyn over to Ethan, or prepare for battle. This war will end today, one way or another!"

Aaron stood silent for a moment, his expression grave, but not overly concerned. I figured he'd just tell Holly to get stuffed, or banish her, or whatever a king did when someone lipped off to him, but he did none of those things.

"Very well." He wiped his hands on a filthy oil rag. "Since you have called for a challenge of the body, you shall have it."

"Wait!" Ethan almost shrieked, jerking Diego away from Holly in order to clutch his arm tight to his body. "I'm a lover, not a fighter. Well, I *was* a fighter, but that was centuries ago, before Diego took over. I refuse to fight."

"You do not," Holly snapped. "You'll fight and like it! Because if you don't, I'll see to it that you will never be able to be called a lover again."

We all raised our respective eyebrows at her tone. Ethan had evidently had enough of her bossing him around, not to mention obviously threatening him with gelding, because he straightened up and looked down his nose when he said, "You go too far, woman."

"Strewth, your sheila's mad as a cut snake," De Ath said, strolling over to us. "Stop her earbashing, and let's go have a butcher."

"Oooh. Australian accents are just so . . ." I stopped when I felt Gregory glare at me. ". . . not nearly as sexy as slightly middle-European ones."

"Nice save," he murmured in my ear. "But you will pay for that later."

"Promises, promises."

"I know my rights," Ethan continued, scowling at Holly. "And they say that I am entitled to elect two champions to fight on my behalf. I shall do so. De Ath?"

"Happy to oblige, mate."

"Champions, eh?" Aaron's gaze wandered along the semi-circle of warriors who suddenly stood at attention. Doug, who had been on the far side of the Velociphant, moved forward into a flanking position. "As you like. I name the thief and the lady with the sword."

I turned what I feared were bulging eyes on him. "Gregory and me?" I squeaked just as Doug came forward and said, "My lord, I fear that would be unwise. Lady Gwen has little battle experience, and the thief has none that I'm aware of."

"No takebacks!" Ethan said quickly. His alien arm reached out and visibly pinched Holly on the ass. She jumped and slapped it until Ethan, murmuring softly to his arm, regained control over it.

"I shall be Ethan's second champion," she said through gritted teeth, sharing an angry look with all of us before spinning around on her heels and marching over to a laden squire.

I looked at Gregory. "How do you feel about running away while screaming at the top of our lungs?"

"It sounds like an excellent plan, but unfortunately I don't think we can do it."

"Why? Doug would happily take our places, and he could probably whup Holly's butt."

Gregory leaned over to Aaron. "If we do this, you will banish the reclaimer."

"Not unless you bring back my bird."

Gregory looked at him silently for a moment, then to my horror, nodded his head. "Very well. But you will owe us a further boon."

"What sort of boon?" I asked.

Aaron gave a half shrug. "If you return my bird to me, you shall have anything you want."

Ten minutes later, the six of us stood on the mounded battleground, the clouds overhead thundering with ominous warning. Ethan stood on one side behind Holly and De Ath, who had been given a sword and was busily flirting with a woman in the crowd. Gregory had likewise been offered a sword, but had opted, upon seeing Holly with her daggers, to go with a wicked-looking shiv. Around us, in a circle, were the inhabitants of both camps. I saw several familiar faces—Master Hamo, Seith, Buttercup, Antoinette, the apothecary—they were all there. All except my mothers. I had mixed feelings about that; part of me wanted them to see me in my pretty armor, wielding my impressive sword, but the other part, the part that knew just how little skill I had with both, was happy they wouldn't see me wiped into the red dirt.

"Stop it. You're not going to fail," a soft voice said in my ear.

I stared at Gregory. "Are you reading minds now?"

He laughed. "I didn't have to. Your expression made your thoughts quite clear."

I took a deep breath. "I think the odds are pretty good that we aren't going to be asking Aaron for that boon anytime soon. I've only had a couple of battle lessons, and I doubt if you've ever been in a knife fight in your life."

"You also bear what is more or less a magic sword, and I have something very valuable at stake—our future happiness. Have faith, my sweet. I am confident we will prevail."

"But I have to fight Death, Gregory. Death!"

"Who has no power here because he has been banished, and stripped of his abilities in Anwyn."

"There is that, at least. You're sure you're OK with fighting a woman?" I asked, nodding at Holly, who was running a whetstone over her daggers.

He pulled me to him in a kiss that had me sweating under my armor. "Yes," he said a minute later when he allowed me to catch my breath. "I'm quite sure."

I slid a glance down at his chest. "No *porraimos* lightning?"

He just smiled and released me.

"This battle shall commence along these terms," Aaron

said, speaking in a voice that resonated with grandeur. He was so down-to-earth that it was easy to forget he actually ruled this realm. "The two champions shall fight until only one remains standing. The losers will unequivocally yield to the winner, with no objections to any ransom sought. Are the terms agreeable?"

"They are," Ethan said. Two women were in the process of helping him into his arm harness. "Let the battle commence."

"I say that!" Aaron said with a frown. He took a deep breath, eyed Gregory and me, and then said in a peeved tone, "Let the battle commence!"

Holly was on Gregory before he could so much as blink, the two of them rolling down the mound in a cloud of red dust, but I couldn't do anything to help him because De Ath bowed to me and said, "I believe the technical term here is *en garde*."

I lifted my sword in an answering salute, and tried frantically to remember everything that Master Hamo had showed me earlier in the afternoon.

The Nightingale sang as I swung the sword to parry, my armor feeling heavy and clunky despite fitting me perfectly before. I stumbled backward, just barely blocking the attacking thrusts that De Ath made with apparent ease. He wore armor on his chest, but no helm, which meant his faint smile that never seemed to waver was right there, mocking my belief that I could survive this experience.

"You're not very good at this, are you?" he asked, swinging his sword in a move that would have decapitated me had I not managed to heft the Nightingale just in time.

"No, but I don't have to be. I just have to give Gregory time to disable that annoying Holly," I ground out through my teeth.

His smile grew broader, and the crowd gasped as he suddenly jumped forward, forcing me back several steps, the Nightingale singing furiously as, miraculously, it managed to parry a flurry of strikes that moved so fast they were a blur. The Nightingale kept up with it, although how, I had no idea. It had to be the magic inherent in the sword, because I certainly didn't have the skill to do it myself. I tried to make one attack, but he easily spun away, sending me stumbling forward onto my knees. I was up on my feet before he could attack again, but unfortunately I fell backward onto my ass when I tripped over a large rock, the impact knocking the Nightingale out of my hand.

A cry of horror went up from Aaron's people. De Ath strolled toward me as if he hadn't a care in the world. Behind him, I heard Gregory snarl. He emerged from the cloud of red dust, one of his arms hanging limply, dripping blood into the ground as he staggered forward. Holly screamed and leaped onto his back, her dagger dark with blood as she tried to sever his jugular.

The crowd roared when I jumped to my feet and snatched up the Nightingale, but instead of attacking a surprised De Ath, I lunged at Holly, smashing the hilt down on her head just as her knife blade pierced Gregory's throat. She clung on, although her knife tip dropped.

De Ath yelled something. Time seemed to slow down at that moment, seconds crawling by like minutes. I felt the rush of air behind me heralding the oncoming blow from a massive sword. At the same moment, Gregory turned his head in slow motion, his pupils dilating as they focused beyond me, his expression changing from one of mingled anger and pain to one of fear.

I knew, I just knew that we were both about to be killed. Holly's hand was even then moving back to Gregory's throat, but there wasn't enough time for me to hit her again before De Ath's blow would strike me. I wanted to tell Gregory just how deeply I loved him, but the words were stuck in my mouth. It was the end, and we both knew it.

Blue light flashed in front of my eyes, a brilliant white-blue that sizzled along my skin and exploded outward in a booming flash that seemed to consume the world and leave it silent and empty.

"Gwen?"

I opened one eye. My vision was blurry, but the voice was as familiar as my own. "Are we dead?"

"Not quite. Although we are in Anwyn."

I opened the other eye and concentrated on focusing my vision until the vision of multiple Gregories merged into one. "You are the best Traveller ever," I told him.

He smiled, kissed me gently, then touched a tender spot on my forehead. "You hit your head on your own sword."

"It was worth it to see an enraged Traveller do what he does best." I let him help me up to my feet. It looked like a bomb had been dropped around us; the ground was scorched black, while the several hundred warriors and attendants had been felled just as though they were trees in the middle of a nuclear explosion. I was relieved to see that they weren't dead, since they were slowly moving and sitting up. Ethan was on his knees, shaking his head. Aaron staggered as I watched, said something about his beloved Piranha, and stumbled off toward the giant machine. Holly lay still in a sort of a crater. De Ath was sitting with his hands dangling between his knees, his face black and his hair smoking.

"Crikey," he said in a rusty-sounding voice, then promptly fell over.

"We won," I told Gregory, and flung myself on him. He flinched, and I suddenly remembered his arm. "Goddess! She cut you!"

"It's nothing that won't heal, although I believe she managed to dislocate my shoulder," he said, a patient look on his face when I ripped off his sleeve to examine the damage. His arm was sliced in several spots, but the flow of blood was already beginning to thicken.

"My moms can probably fix the dislocation," I said.

A look of embarrassment crossed his face. "Would you hold it against me if I said I would prefer to have a proper healer look at it? It's not that I don't like and respect your mothers, but they do have a tendency to . . . to . . ."

"Mess things up?" I bound up the worst of the slashes, then cuddled into his good side, kissing the edges of his lips. "I wouldn't mind in the least. Gregory—"

"No thanks to the thief's light show, the Piranha is unharmed," Aaron announced, coming back to where we stood. He surveyed the people who were in various stages of recovering and getting back to their feet. "Although I regret that Constance left before she could be blasted. I would have paid good money to see that."

"I take back any objection I had to the thief," Doug said from behind us. Aaron went to help him onto his feet.

"I'm just glad my moms aren't here—oh, hell, there they are. They must have heard the lightning explosion. They're going to want to fix you, Gregory. I'll go tell them to go back to Ethan's camp until Aaron's healer can see to you."

Gregory grabbed the back of my mail shirt as I started off, pulling me back. "You don't want to do that, Gwen."

"Why don't I?"

"Because they have something we badly need."

"They really aren't that great at healing, although they do try their best—"

"No," he interrupted. "Not that. See?"

I looked at where he nodded. My mothers were picking their way through the half-sensible people, the slight form of Mrs. Vanilla in their grasp. "See what? All I see are my moms and Mrs. Vanilla."

"Yes." He looked expectantly at me.

I shook my head. "What is it that you see that I don't?"

"It's not see so much as hear. What's the name of the bird that Aaron is looking for?"

"Vanellus."

"Right. And what does that sound like?"

"Vanessa?"

He looked at me.

I pointed to my forehead. "I have a head injury. Stop giving me the look that says I'm missing something . . . Oh. Vanilla." Enlightenment dawned with a prickle of electricity along my arms and legs. I turned to look back at my mothers. Gregory very gently placed a finger beneath my chin and pushed it upward until my mouth stopped hanging open in surprise. "You are kidding me!"

"I think, unless we are very mistaken, that we are about to make Aaron extremely happy."

"Goodness!" Mom said as she and Mom Two lifted Mrs. Vanilla over the moaning, recumbent form of De Ath. "What did we miss?"

"Nothing other than Gregory being awesome and stopping Death and Holly in one lightning-bedazzling blow." Gregory smiled at the pride that I couldn't keep out of my voice.

"Death?" My moms stopped and looked worried.

"He's a new guy, evidently." I waved toward De Ath, who once again was sitting up. "Not the same one you had the run-in with."

"G'day," he said, lifting a shaky hand to my moms.

"Oh, thank the goddess for that. Gwenny, dear, I believe Mrs. Vanilla is needed here."

"I do believe she is." I watched as my moms stopped in front of me, gently setting Mrs. Vanilla onto the ground. She was just as crumpled as ever, a wrinkled old woman with hair that stood up in the back, and weathered skin that hinted at more years than most mortals saw.

But she wasn't mortal. At least, I didn't think she was.

"Do you want to do the honors?" Gregory asked me.

"No. You figured it out. You can be the one to tell him."

"I love you, Gwenhwyfar Byron Owens."

"Almost as much as I love you, Gregory . . . er . . . what's your middle name?"

"I was born Rehor Ilie Nicolae Faa, which is Anglicized to Gregory Elijah Nicolas Faa."

"Rehor? Really?"

"Really."

I licked the corner of his mouth. "Almost as much as I love you, Gregory Elijah Nicolas Faa."

"Do that again, and I won't wait for a healer before I take you to bed," he growled.

I smiled, enjoying the way my heart sang when he turned and called for Aaron.

"What is it? I'm busy right n—" Aaron, who was assisting the warriors nearest him, froze in mid-word, his expression blank as he stared past us.

"I have goose bumps," I whispered as Mrs. Vanilla, who had been making her usual unintelligible squeaks, stopped. She took one tottering step forward out of my mothers' grips.

Gregory said nothing, just held me with his good arm, his breath ruffling my hair in a way that was both sensual and comforting. We were meant to be together, meant to be at that place at that time, watching as a frail old lady moved past us, every step she took transforming her. Her back straightened, her skin smoothed, her hair darkened and lengthened until it flowed down her back in ebony waves. Her bathrobe lengthened as well, becoming a long dark green velvet gown that hugged blossoming curves.

"Vanellus," Aaron breathed, his voice filled with awe at the vision of young womanhood that stopped before him.

"Aaron," she responded, her voice as light and high as . . . well, as a bird's.

I sniffled happily as they stared at each other for another minute, and then she was in his arms and the air was full of birdsong.

"OK, that's seriously romantic," I said, blinking back a few happy tears.

"It truly is," Mom said, handing me a tissue before using another to dab at her own eyes. "And aren't you glad that your mother and I liberated her when we did? Just look at how happy they are."

I turned to look up at Gregory and basked in the love evident in his beautiful eyes. "They can't possibly be happier than we are."

"Not in a hundred lifetimes," Gregory agreed, and took my breath away with a kiss that sent lightning shimmering about us both.

EPILOGUE

"Right, so I get the bit about that Death guy not having powers in Anwyn and calling off Astrid after you beat him, and I understand that Aaron was so grateful that you found his bird that he is letting you guys have visitation privileges as well as allowing Gwen's moms to stay there where they won't get into any trouble, and I even understand that Ethan's tree dudes refused to go back to being plants once he was defeated, and they were assimilated into Aaron's folk, but I do not get the whole thing about Mrs. Vanilla. Why did everyone call her a bird if she was really a woman? And why didn't she do something to find Aaron when she was back in Anwyn?"

Gregory greatly enjoyed the warmth of Gwen, pressed close to him, seated on a couch in the sunny Paris apartment that belonged to his cousin Peter.

The cousin in question, sitting across from them, patted his wife's leg. "I think, my love, you need to let Gregory and Gwen finish explaining what happened."

"I know, but I'm just so impatient to hear it all." Kiya gave them both a smile that was just as sunny as the living room. Gwen, who had her lap occupied by three squirming pug puppies, was too busy murmuring to them to notice. "Go ahead, Gregory."

"You cannot take them home," he told Gwen quietly.

"Sure I can. There are no quarantine laws in the States."

"You said you wanted to live in Wales, in order to take

care of your mothers' house. You said you loved that house. You said I would love it as well, and we'd both be happy there and make love in the bower, and I could open up an antiques shop in order to fund a lifestyle that you warned me will need ample resources."

"That doesn't mean we can't have dogs. Kiya said we could have a puppy." Gwen looked up and Kiya nodded. "Besides, the UK relaxed its quarantine laws. We just have to wait three weeks now, so we can have our puppy settled by the time we go visit my moms."

"You seem like a very dog-friendly person, and I know Gregory is despite him being all Travellery and claiming they're dirty and other ridiculous things like that," Kiya told Gwen. "I would have no problem letting you have one of the puppies, but only if you finish explaining why no one realized that an old lady was really a bird."

Gregory laughed, and rejoiced in the sense of happiness that Gwen brought him. Not even the threat of a puppy keeping him up nights and, if he knew Gwen, snuggling in bed between them, could diminish his well-being. "We didn't know because we were repeatedly told she was mortal, which in hindsight, was by design. Ethan's mage brother who effected her exit from Anwyn—at Constance's behest, no doubt, although she refuses to admit anything—did so in a manner that would defy detection by anyone looking for a bird, either in her natural or her human form."

"That's why she was so helpful about getting us to Anwyn in the first place," Gwen said. "Ethan's rat bastard brother had enchanted her so that she appeared to be her actual age, which meant she was a helpless old lady stuck in care over the centuries, first by private individuals and later in nursing homes."

"But why didn't she just go find Aaron once she made it there?"

"She couldn't." Gwen glanced at him. He gave her an encouraging nod, unable to keep from trailing his fingers along the back of her neck. She shivered and sent him a steamy look that held much promise. "She wasn't physically capable of it. She hoped that we'd bring him within her scope at some point, which is why she got so agitated when I was looking at the history of the bird and Aaron."

"Such a sad story, their separation. I don't understand why Aaron hasn't kicked out that evil ex-wife of his. I wouldn't want the person who was responsible for making me so miserable around where she could cause more trouble."

"I don't think Aaron will allow her to do more than take care of the castle vermin," Gregory said, recalling just how furious Aaron had been once he knew the truth about Constance's treatment of Mrs. Vanilla.

"And that's another thing—what's with all the animals being humans?"

"And trees, and bushes and shrubs, and even some flowers," Gwen added. "You have to remember that in Anwyn, legends are more than just myths—most of them have a strong basis in fact. So if you find a handy mage to change you into human form, then whammo! You can be queen."

"Well, it's all very fantastical, but I'm glad it turned out for the best for you." Kiya looked anxious for a moment. "You're sure Death isn't going to come after you again for your moms' transgression?"

"He hasn't mentioned it."

"I don't believe he knows anything about what happened to the man who held the position before him, to be honest," Gregory said. "He seems to be a fairly reasonable fellow. He deliberately swung wide when he could have struck Gwen down, which is why I didn't blast him to kingdom come."

"Holly, however"—Gwen's voice turned cold and brittle—"is another matter."

"My arm is fine, and you have no reason to be so angry anymore," he told Gwen, bathed in the warmth of her love. Really, could she be any more adorable than she was when she was incensed about a few cuts and a dislocated shoulder?

"She's left Anwyn, and Aaron has ordered that she be barred from entering again. She poses no harm to anyone in our family."

"Speaking of family—" Kiya leaned into Peter. "We wanted to tell you—"

"She's here! Peter-ji, she is here!" A slim young man of Indian heritage burst into their room, followed by two pugs, one of which was obviously the mother of the puppies on Gwen's lap. He turned to Gregory, asking, "It is the most exciting event, is it not? The esteemed grandmother of Peter-ji and yourself has traveled all this way to see you and your popsy. I have such a happy warm feeling thinking of this, and so I will go to the kitchen and make sure that the curry is of a most magnificent form for lunch."

Sunil bounced happily out of the room before anyone could reply.

"I'll get the door," Peter said with a look at Gregory. "You stay here, love."

"I'd better put the puppies back in their room." Kiya waited until Peter left before taking the three puppies from Gwen. "Mrs. Faa has a weakness for pugs, and the minute she sees my babies, she'll want them all, and I so want you and Gregory to have at least one."

"Oooh." Gwen's face lit up. "Two pugs . . ."

He sighed, knowing full well he was doomed.

"Tell me again how that nice young man was actually a ball of light?" Gwen asked when Kiya carried the puppies out.

"It's a long story. I'll have to tell you after my grandmother meets you."

"OK, but I'm a bit nerv—"

Gwen's words stopped when the door was opened and a small, doubled-over woman hobbled into the room with a cane.

"Wow. Déjà vu there for a second," Gwen muttered. "She could be Mrs. Vanilla's twin."

"I assure you, they are not the least bit alike. Puridaj," he said, rising and bowing before holding out his hand for Gwen. "You look well. I take it your flight to Paris was without incident."

His grandmother's sharp eyes took in everything at once—the apartment, Peter, himself, and Gwen.

"Yes. This is the one?"

Gwen stiffened, her fingers tightening painfully around his.

"This is my fiancée, Gwenhwyfar Byron Owens," he said, letting a note of steel enter his voice. He'd be damned if he would let his grandmother upset Gwen. "She is an alchemist."

"It's a pleasure to meet you," Gwen lied. He knew just how worried she was about this meeting. Which was just one more adorable facet of her personality.

"Hmm." Lenore Faa considered Gwen silently. At last she turned her attention back to him. "What is this Peter says about you being kicked out of the Watch?"

"He wasn't kicked out," Gwen said before he could answer, her eyes sparkling with anger. "He was just reprimanded. The two things aren't even remotely alike, and even so, the reprimand was totally full of bunk. Gregory didn't do one thing in Anwyn that invoked his official status as a member of the Watch, and for them to get bent out of shape just because he went in there to save me is beyond wrong. But he still has his job, although he has to report directly to his cousin's boss now. Which really isn't fair to Peter, either, because all Peter did was follow protocol and not enter Anwyn. It's all ridiculous and too stupid for words, but the bottom line is that Gregory is still with the Watch. Just . . . er . . . more probationary than he was before. He'll tell you." She turned to him and waved toward his grandmother. "Go ahead. Explain it all to her."

He laughed and couldn't keep from pulling her into his arms, where it was his opinion she belonged. "I don't need to, *dulcea mea*. You just explained it all."

"I suppose I'll have to give my blessing to this marriage as I did for Piotr and his bride," his grandmother said, sitting down when Kiya came back into the room, murmuring a welcome before she leaned against Peter. "Rehor has ever been precious to me, alchemist. I would have you cherish him as I have."

Gregory fought to keep the surprise from showing on his face, feeling that a moment of great importance was upon them, and it would behoove him to refrain from pointing out that he had never felt particularly cherished.

"He's pretty precious to me, too," Gwen said with dignity. He simply could not love her more.

"And my name is Gwen. I am an alchemist, but that is *not* my name."

No, he was wrong. He loved her more now that she talked back to his grandmother. She was perfect in every way. She had a large heart, a body that made him want to move mountains to keep her in his bed, and a character that had him on his knees with gratitude every morning.

"I worship you," he told her, pulling her into a kiss that he hoped would shock the dickens out of his staid grandmother.

"As is right and proper," she told him, laughing into his mouth when he put both his hands on her delectable ass.

"The times, they are a-changing," Kiya quoted, and smiled broadly when Peter put his arm around her. "And I hope you're getting used to it, Mrs. Faa, because there is more change coming. Peter and I are going to have a baby next spring. And if the way Gregory and Gwen are going at it is anything to judge by, you may well have another great-grandbaby soon as well."

Gwen pulled back from his mouth, a startled look in her lovely eyes that slowly faded to speculation.

"You can have two puppies," he told her. "I'm just selfish enough to want you all to myself for a while before we start thinking of expanding the family."

"Deal," she said with a grin, and pinched him on his butt

before turning to join his grandmother in congratulations on the newest Traveller-to-be.

"Rehor, Piotr, your cousin Sayer wished to me to pass along a message to you both. Against my wishes, and those of his father, he desires to join you in the Watch." Lenore Faa closed her mouth tightly for a moment before continuing. "I do not agree with our people leaving the family and joining outsiders as you both have done. You know this, and I will not repeat my arguments. He threatens to leave our family despite this, so with many reservations, I have decided that if you give me your promises that you will guard your cousin against harmful influences, then I will allow him to join you."

Gregory met his cousin's eyes across the women, and saw in them the same sense of wonder, pride, and satisfaction that he knew was in his. They had done something that no Traveller had done before—they had brought change to a people who had kept to themselves for centuries. And the warm, wonderful woman who pressed against his side was the result of that action.

He grinned at his cousin. Life promised to be very, very good . . . for all of them.

GLOSSARY

Akashic League: The L'au-dela organization responsible for all things related to death, spirits, and connected beings.

Alien Hand Syndrome: A condition wherein a person feels a lack of control over a hand or arm (i.e., that the limb has a life of its own).

Amaethon ab Don: The traditional name of Ethan, a formerly mortal warrior who went to battle with Arawyn, king of the Underworld.

Anwyn: The Welsh version of the afterlife, ruled by Aaron (Arawn).

Arawn: The Welsh name for the king of the Underworld. He prefers Aaron, the modern version of the name.

Death (person): The title given to the current being in charge of handling the movement of souls after an individual (mortal or immortal) dies. The current holder of the title goes by the name De Ath.

Ethan: The contemporary name of Amaethon ab Don. Ethan was once a warrior, and is now an author who suffers from Alien Hand Syndrome.

L'au-dela: The formal name for the Otherworld, the society of people who live beyond mortal laws.

L'au-dela Watch: The police force of the Otherworld, the Watch is responsible for keeping the peace amongst mortals and immortal beings, as well as protecting the mortal world from abuses by members of the Otherworld.

lich: A person who was resurrected from the dead, a lich looks like a normal person, other than black irises. Most liches are bound to the individual who holds their soul.

Lichtenberg figure: The pattern made by an electrical discharge through a soft medium.

Lightning flower: The name for a Lichtenberg figure as made on a human being. The resulting pattern is of a delicate feathery nature, and thus often referred to as a lightning flower or tree. The pattern is most likely due to capillaries rupturing as the current passes through. Although lightning flowers are temporary effects on mortals, they are a permanent brand on Travellers.

mahrime: A Traveller (and Romany) word for those who are deemed unclean. For Travellers, this can mean one who has impure blood (i.e., one non-Traveller parent), or someone who has no Traveller blood whatsoever.

Piranha: A giant mechanical war machine known also as a Velociphant, created by the king of the Underworld.

porrav: A Traveller word with Indo-Aryan roots, it literally means "to open up" or "blossom." In Traveller culture, it refers to the joining of a man and woman, and their shared abilities mingling to form something greater than the parts.

puridaj: A respectful way to refer to a Traveller grand-mother.

Reclamation agent: One of the people who work for Death, fetching and escorting the souls of the recently departed to their next destination. Some of them can be quite tenacious in the pursuit of their duties.

Rehor: An Eastern European version of the name Gregory.

Rom, Roma, Romany: A word describing an ethnic group most commonly referred to as Gypsies. Travellers and the Roma may share a common ancestor since they share a few traits and words. Like the Travellers, the Romany were fre-quently persecuted for being outsiders.

shuvani: Spirits who hold Travellers accountable for their actions. There are four flavors of shuvani: Shuvanies talk with spirits: earth, water, air, and field. A shuvani can be friendly or unkind, depending on his or her nature, but all are charged with punishing Travellers who abuse their abilities.

Travellers: A group of immortal people who can steal time and have an affinity with lightning.

Vanellus vanellus: The northern lapwing, also known as a peewit or green plover.